A WESTERN LI

The Cobbler
of Ridingham

JEFFREY E. BARLOUGH

GRESHAM & DOYLE

A Western Lights Book™

This is a work of fiction. Names, characters, places, and incidents
are the products of the author's imagination or are used fictitiously.
Any similarity to actual persons, living or dead, or to actual firms,
events, or locales is purely coincidental.

THE COBBLER OF RIDINGHAM
First Edition / November 2014

Published by Gresham & Doyle
Los Angeles, California

Cover: *Whose Traces in the Snow?* by Carl Kronberger (1841-1921)
Josef Mensing Gallery, Hamm-Rhynern, Germany / The Bridgeman Art Library

To learn more about the Western Lights series visit
www.westernlightsbooks.com

Library of Congress Control Number: 2014938636

ISBN: 978-0-9787634-4-2

Text set in Garamond Antiqua
Printed in the United States of America
on acid-free paper

The Cobbler *of* Ridingham

To my brother Gary

CONTENTS

PART FOUR

Happy the change that alters for the best.

Arden of Faversham, xiii

PART ONE

❧

THE FIRST CHAPTER

Something in the Trees

"HALLO! — hallo! — is someone there? Hallo!"
The stranger's voice is a bit excited as he drums knuckles on the tiny latticed window beside the gate. Anxiously he glances over his shoulder — it is not the first time — at the fast-darkening wilderness of marsh beyond the causeway. Meanwhile the wind blows piercing cold, showering him with snowflakes like a particulate rain. His coat-collar is turned up against the chill, and his old wide-awake is screwed down about his ears, to keep it from flying off his head. Beside him his mare paws the ground and with delicate nostrils is sniffing at the blustery weather that has arisen.

The stranger, shivering, knocks once again at the window beside the gate. That gate — of a sturdy, wrought-iron construction — is attached to a gatehouse, of which the window is a part. A couple of iron bars screen its latticed panes, on which he is about to knock a third time, when the sound of footsteps is heard within.

He looks off again towards the marshes, at a squatty clump of Scotch firs whose tops are being shaken by the wind. He will not have an easy moment, he knows, until he has gained the concealing safety of the house to which his journey has brought him. Even the feel of a good traveling-cutlass at his hip is insufficient to allay his concern.

Abruptly a latch is drawn and the window is opened a crack, to reveal a woman's face, her eyes alert and charged with expression, peering expectantly out. Ere the stranger can venture a word she calls to him through the bars —

"You're early tonight, dear. I haven't yet prepared the lamp. And why have you come to the gate — oh, my God!" she exclaims, starting back in surprise.

She is a small slip of a woman, whose chin barely rises to the level of the sill. Two crisp black eyes stare roundly at the newcomer. For an instant a hint of panic shows in their deep pools; then, comprehending her

I

error, she checks herself, and inquires in a more proper tone what might the gentleman's business be at the Hall?

She is not the sort of gatekeeper he had anticipated, nothing like the crusty old specimen he had imagined would be keeping watch and ward at the portal of the great house; not this tidy, small woman, middle-aged, curly-haired, who is regarding him from the lattice.

The stranger gives an apologetic tug at his hat-brim. "Sorry to have disappointed you. My name is Hathaway — Richard Hathaway. I have traveled many miles from Market Snailsby, clear the other side of Marley Wood. This is Haigh Hall, is it not? I am to stop here for a week or two at the invitation of Lady Martindale. Please, might you open the gate?"

His glance strays past her to the wood-fire that is burning in the chimney, and to the small table before it, pleasantly lighted and decored, with its white cloth and snug furnishings for supper. She had been in the act of dressing the table when he had interrupted her. He sees that a tray of food has been assembled and is warming at the hearth, and that there are settings for two on the white cloth. It would seem she had not been expecting someone called Hathaway, but a different gentleman entirely.

She nods in answer, as the blustery wind scatters another rain of flakes over the impatient traveler.

"Oh — Mr. Hathaway — of course — remember it now — but you're late, sir," she remarks. Plainly his name had registered, but it temporarily had slipped her mind in her attention to other business. "I shall summon a boy at once to collect your horse," and as she draws on a cord a bell can be heard sounding at the rear of the gatehouse. To the traveler's relief she then steps forth to unlock the gate — the portcullis of the place — and as it swings wide, creaking as it goes, he leads his mare through the passage into the sanctuary of the courtyard. There the gatekeeper instructs him to follow along the drive to the entrance-door of the Hall.

"Well, I shall bid you a good evening, then — and thank you," he says, with a parting touch of his hat.

But the woman seems scarcely to notice him, as she closes the gate and shoots home the bolts — safety at last! — only to stand awhile at the portal, gazing through its bars at the marshy dusk and the haze of snowflakes swirling about, off in the direction of the Scotch firs, in an attitude of expectancy. Then, without glancing again at Richard Hathaway, she retires indoors.

In the waning light the traveler approaches the Hall, but it is some moments ere his knock at its ponderous oak door is answered.

On the threshold stands a chubby youth, in a loud plaid vest and trouserings of the sort favored by college men. He had been gnawing on a cold chop but had left it off, the chop gripped cudgel-like in his hand. Facing him on the step is a dark-haired gentleman in a caped overcoat and wide-awake hat, the greater part of him littered with snowflakes.

"Yes? And who might you be, then?" says the youth, eyeing him suspiciously.

The stranger proceeds to introduce himself. Directly the youth's guard is relaxed, as if a weight has been removed from his shoulders. "Suit yourself," he says with a smile and a throw of his tousled head, and resumes his work on the chop.

At that moment a stable-boy — well, scarcely a boy as such, for he is a full-grown man — comes swaggering along the drive to take the gentleman's horse. He is a hardy-looking sort, with the weathered features of one who has lived much out of doors. His cheek is blazoned with an ugly scar, and his prominent ears — huge, flapping things — stick out from the sides of his head like the handles of a slop-jug. The gentleman informs him that the mare is to be returned to the inn known as the Goose and Gander, in Ridingham, at the earliest opportunity.

Meanwhile the wind has risen again with a dismal howl, its rough gusts stirring the trees in the courtyard and scattering the flakes of snow about.

"It promises to be a wicked night," the gentleman observes.

"Sink me, that's plain enough," nods the groom, taking the mare in hand. "We're in for a blusterous time, by the look of it. This be a shiversome wind."

"I fear so. We shall have a decent fall of snow by morning, if this is any judge."

"Aye, 'twill be bitter cold. Mean you to bunk here long, sir?"

"Er — about a week at least. Perhaps a fortnight."

"Beautiful. Ah, fine girl, sir."

"Eh?"

"Mare, sir," nods the groom, stroking the horse's shoulder.

"Ah, I see. Yes, indeed she is."

"Fine place — glorious pile," he adds, indicating the Hall, whose looming presence crowds the darkening sky above their heads.

"It is my first visit to the Hall."

"Is it, just? Confidentially, sir," the groom remarks, dropping his voice a note and sidling closer, the better to gain the other's ear, "the joint is skint — not so free with the brass — lubberly outfit — won't do. By the

by, sir," he adds, in a still lower tone, "being the gentleman you are, might
you see fit to spare a poor jack a couple o' quid?"

"Really — cheeky fellow — off with you!" protests the gentleman, in
some surprise.

The groom, nothing daunted, shrugs his indifference. Leading the mare
by the reins he ambles round a corner and is gone.

Well, I'm jiggered thinks Richard Hathaway. He hardly can believe that
so mannerless a rogue should be employed at Haigh Hall. He is about to
remark upon it to the lad in the doorway, when he notices that the young
man, like the groom, has vanished.

The foyer being entirely void of company, he is obliged himself to shut
the door behind him. Not only has the youth and his chop evaporated, but
no servant had appeared to relieve him of his bag, coat, and hat. He understood that Haigh Hall no longer was as prosperous as it had been in earlier
times, in the days of the late baronet. Still it remained by far the grandest
house in the district, and Lady Martindale — or more properly, Dowager
Lady Martindale, widow of the baronet — a figure of consequence in north
of Fenshire society.

Glancing round him there in the foyer, two objects immediately claim
his attention. The first is as fine an example of a Welsh harp as any he has
ever seen — an ancient instrument, with horsehair strings and an abundance of decoration curiously and richly carved, that stands against a wall.
He recollects that the tinkle of a harp has been sacred to Welshmen since
the time of the Druids, and that the bards of old had enjoyed great privilege. Above the harp hangs a portrait of the late baronet himself, Sir Pedr
Rhys Martindale, who had been of Welsh stock. He wonders whether it
is Sir Pedr's own harp that is displayed there, for he recalls that the baronet had been something of an authority on the instrument.

"It belonged to my uncle, if you're interested," says the chubby youth,
who has reappeared munching on a biscuit. "He was quite the performer.
He was a Bard of the Gorsedd, as it's termed in Welsh circles. That's his
picter there. It's a decent enough likeness, though in point of fact I don't
remember him much. He was rather older than my aunt."

Seconds later the servant makes his belated entrance. A tall stately specimen of the butler's race, he glides swiftly across the floor, a stream of apol-
ogies tumbling from his lips.

"Mr. Hathaway, I ask your pardon, sir, for the delay. On behalf of her
ladyship I bid you welcome to the Hall. My name is Treadwell. I see you
already have made the acquaintance of Mr. Edgar, her ladyship's nephew."

"Yes. Edgar Harbottle, isn't it? He was good enough to show me in."

"Her ladyship begs leave to say she cannot attend at present. She is suffering from a slight indisposition, and has retired for the evening. She asks, however, that you make yourself comfortable, and assures you that she has every intention of joining you for breakfast in the morning-room."

"I do hope it is nothing serious."

"Her ladyship occasionally is subject to these little headaches, whenever the MacWallop business grows tiresome."

"The MacWallop business?"

"A trifling difference with a neighbor. It is nothing of any moment, but these little disputes often are disagreeable to her. It should in no way hinder your examination of the Crust letters."

"Yes, I am looking forward to seeing them."

"Her ladyship has instructed me to render you every assistance in your researches. Might I offer you something at present, sir? A glass of sherry, perhaps? And a light meal before retiring?"

"That's a capital idea. Some sherry sounds wonderful, and a little supper as well. Thank you, Treadwell."

"Not at all, sir. Perhaps you would care to refresh yourself in the interval? I'll conduct you to the chambers her ladyship has prepared for you. You shall find some hot water there, and if there is aught else you require you need only ring for it." He takes the gentleman's effects in hand and leads the way upstairs. The nephew, with little else to occupy him evidently, trots behind them champing on his biscuit.

"'Pon my word, sir, I really beg your ten thousand pardons. I altogether took you for a dun," he explains to Richard.

"There's no harm in it. So you are Edgar Harbottle? We've never met, but your aunt has written to us about you — to my sister Jemma and myself, at Mead Cottage in Market Snailsby. Our late parents were acquainted with the Ganders before your aunt was Lady Martindale."

The youth immediately goes on the alert. "Oh, yes?" he says, pausing in his biscuit as they reach the landing at the head of the stairs. "And what has the money — er, my aunt that is — had to say about me? Anything to the good?"

"Certainly nothing to the bad. She has written of you with naught but pride and affection. You're a second-year man, aren't you, at Salthead University?"

"Er, yes — that is, I'll be second-year next term."

"That's capital. Your aunt is altogether pleased."

"I didn't know you'd come to see the money — er, the auntie — er, my aunt, that is. Aunt Lizzie — she's got a heart as big as a barrel. So you're having a bit o' grub directly? I think I'll join you if I might. We'll see what we can scrape up in the buttery."

The thought of supper brings to Richard's mind the tidy small woman at the gatehouse, who had seemed preoccupied and eager for him to be on his way, in her anticipation of her gentleman caller.

Young Edgar, scratching his head, is a little puzzled on hearing of it.

"Mrs. Aberdovey? She's a widow, like my aunt. And now she's gone and lost her son. Owen Aberdovey — delightful feller, and a trump, in his country sort of way. Can't think who would be calling on his mother, and on a night like this."

They had gone no more than a few steps in the passage when a weird, unearthly cry, a sound like none ever made by human throat, breaks upon their ears. From the reedy fens and lonesome marshes it comes sweeping through the Hall, filling its every nook and cranny with a palpable menace. It is not the wind — would to heaven it were only the wind — but the deep-voiced howl of a marsh devil, that particularly savage breed of saber-cat which is indigenous to the fen country. The sound of it, carried on the wintry night air, is enough to chill the blood of the hardiest Fenshireman, and send a quiver through the hearts of those in the passage.

The initial cry is followed by a second — an answering roar. It is well known that marsh devils, like saber-cats throughout the realm, commonly hunt in pairs. In the gathering dark outside, beyond the sturdy defenses of the Hall — where, not many minutes before, Richard Hathaway had been traversing the road from town — the giant devil-cats of the marshes are on the prowl.

In the passage Richard and his companions have halted in their tracks, and for a long moment they remain thus, exchanging uneasy glances.

"Jiminy," breathes the nephew, rubbing his chins — both of them — uncomfortably.

"The creatures are not far off," Richard observes — "likely just beyond the curtain-wall."

"I detest that noise," Edgar says with a shudder. "You managed to make it home and dry, sir, and none too soon, either. It's the dusk that brings 'em out."

"Seldom a night passes that we don't have intruders of one kind or an-other in the home fields, either from the marshes, or from Marley Wood — devils mostly," Treadwell explains.

"There is something out there tonight other than marsh devils," Richard says.

"Sir?"

"Perhaps you'll think me a crank, but I could have sworn I saw something lurking in the tops of those old Scotch firs which stand about a bow-shot from the gatehouse."

"I know the group you mean, not far off the causeway. What did you see?" Edgar asks.

"It was like a great lump of shadow — a heavy, dark mass, a trifle angular round the edges, couched amongst the topmost branches of the firs as they leaned eastward from the wind."

He had strained his vision to make the thing out, as he was riding past, but had been able to distinguish little beyond its general shape and dimensions. But it had been there, of that he is certain. It had been no illusion, no trick of the eye, as Edgar ventures to suggest.

"Might it have been a teratorn, sir? For although not common round these parts, they are not unknown," Treadwell offers, alluding to the giant, vulture-like birds of prey that haunt the skies of the sundered realm.

"It was too large for a teratorn, I believe, and not at all the right shape. Whatever it was, my mare really pounded along for all she was worth on that final stretch of road. She put on her best speed, as if the very deuce himself were at her heels."

"Perhaps it was a kind of devil she sensed — the marsh-devil kind," says Edgar, "for by the sound of those cries, they likely were within a smell's reach of you there on the causeway."

A chill breath of horror steals from Richard's brain to his heel. It is just such a night as this, he reflects, that oft gives the freest rein to man's imagination. But the heavy, dark mass — the great lump of shadow — had been only too real, of this he is convinced.

"But might it not have been one of the devils? Or both of 'em?" Edgar persists.

Richard considers further before answering — no, he decides, the dark mass had been too large even for a saber-cat, a species known to scale trees on occasion.

"Dashed odd thing. What do you reckon it can have been? I haven't an inkling. A spotted lion, perhaps? They're by far the larger."

"Never known a spotted lion to roost in a tree," Edgar muses, fingering his chins. "We're not all that far from town here, but the causeway can be dangerous at times. There's no knowing what the monsters may try next."

"Perhaps they've picked up a new wrinkle."

"There's a grim thought. Spotted lions hiding in Scotch firs would be a nasty bad thing. I wouldn't give tuppence for a feller's chances."

"Whatever it was, likely it will discourage your town tradesmen from calling too often."

"I suppose a gent ought to be thankful for small favors," remarks the youth, with a nervous chuckle.

Bump in the Night

S UCH had been the reception accorded my brother Richard at Haigh Hall, some few years back, while making one of his periodic journeys to our county town of Newmarsh.

For some time he had been visiting the Municipal Library at Newmarsh in pursuance of his studies concerning a fellow countryman, the late Sir Pharnaby Crust. A composer of no mean attainment, and the only one ever to have sprung from Fenshire, Sir Pharnaby remains but little known outside the borders of his home county. Now city wags might argue that this is only to be expected, that having come from so obscure a backwater as Fenshire assured a man a like reputation in the wider world. In an effort to put right the world's view of him, my brother had begun work on a treatise covering Sir Pharnaby and his music. In this endeavor he is eminently qualified, having received his degrees in musicology from Bearsnose College, Salthead. Furthermore as his sister I can attest to his talent as a musician respecting the violin, on which instrument he oft has joined in recitals with me on the pianoforte.

As everyone did who had business in the north, my brother had the lengthy drive around Marley Wood with which to contend. An immense and seemingly impenetrable fortress of evergreens and oaks, Marley Wood stretches from east to west like a great, bosky belt across the whole of middle Fenshire. As I recollect this journey of my brother's took place in the year before Mrs. Chugwell and her team of shovel-tuskers began pushing their new road through the wood. That road, when finished, was to link those of us in the south with communities northwards of Marley Wood by allowing swift travel directly through its shadowy forest aisles.[1] At the time of my story, however, the wood still served as a noteworthy impediment, by isolating the south of Fenshire and the boggy wastes of Slopshire from the more prosperous towns in the north.

---

[1] See *Bertram of Butter Cross* (2007) for further particulars. — *Ed.*

On this occasion my brother had chosen a mastodon train, in place of the western coach, for the drive round the wood — a journey of some ninety miles altogether. The Dragonthorpe Road skirts the wood along its western face, and although the busier route it can be the more troublesome as well. Already there had been an early fall of snow, incursions of the marshland, and a general miring of the roadway, so that the coaches had encountered delays along the route. But snow and bad roads will not stop a thunder-beast, to say nothing of an entire train of them. Even so, a train may encounter difficulties of its own, as chanced at Locksley some miles to the westwards. The harness securing the passenger cab on one of the animals had failed, and required some hours to mend, so that Richard had been late in his arrival at Ridingham.

For Newmarsh was not my brother's immediate destination in this instance, but Ridingham, amongst the marshes north of the wood. Nor even was the quaint old town itself his objective *per se,* but venerable Haigh Hall, the home of Lady Martindale, along the causeway to the southwards of the town proper.

As I've mentioned, Lady Martindale had been an acquaintance of our late parents. In those good old days of our childhood she wasn't Lady Martindale yet, but pert little Lizzie Gander of Ridingham. She and her father Samuel had kept the Goose and Gander, one of the chief posting-inns of the town, and as fine a house as was to be found in the district. Although but an innkeeper's daughter, nonetheless she had succeeded in attracting the eye of Sir Pedr Rhys Martindale, the local grandee and master of Haigh Hall, and a bachelor. Her father now had long since retired, but the inn remained in his hands and those of his daughter; hence the ease with which Richard had hired a post-horse from its stables.

Well as I've said the train was overdue, and the feeble gray light of the marshes was fast fading when at last the thunder-beasts rumbled to a stand before the inn. The presiding landlord, a man named Cuffley, in the Martindale employ, had suggested that Richard put up at the inn for the night, and strike out for the Hall in the morning. There had been marsh devils abroad of late, and — worse yet — a spotted lion had been seen along the marshways by the coracle men. These latter, fen-slodgers mostly, who gained their living fishing the marshland streams, had spied the beast while paddling their coracles, or basket boats, near the old road to the Hall.

It was getting on towards night, but owing to the delay at Locksley and the general fatigues of travel, my brother had been keen to push on to his destination. It was a risky enterprise, the which in hindsight he since has acknowledged; but he had been steadfast in his desire to reach the Hall. So from the landlord he had secured a speedy mare, that he might cover the ground as rapidly as possible. A saddle-horse was considered safer, being a deal swifter than rattling along in a fly; as well my brother carried a traveling-cutlass at his belt. Indeed it was only a short dash to the Hall — it had seemed a good idea at the time — and he had not cared to waste any more precious hours.

The road to the Hall follows an ancient timber causeway bridging the marshes that stretch southwards from Ridingham to the eaves of Marley Wood — those same marshes wherein the coracle men did ply their basket boats with their nets slung across the water. All round it is a sparsely-peopled country, and the farther from town my brother rode the wilder and more sequestered it became. Presently he came in sight of the Hall in its lonely station on the flats. Amidst the gathering gloom he could discern its outlines — the long sweep of battlements crowning its central structure, flanked by squat towers of an octagonal design, the whole of it enclosed by a high curtain-wall. It stood in a sedgy tract of ground amongst the water-side fields, within view of Marley Wood.

It was then, as he was passing a clump of Scotch firs away to his right, he had glimpsed the dark mass couched in their upper tiers. His mare too had responded to something she had sensed, but whether it had been the thing in the trees or the marsh devils was impossible to say. Sufficient that she had accelerated her pace as a result, and ere he knew it he had reined up with a splatter of mud and gravel before the gatehouse.

Haigh Hall is an ancient fabric, on the castellated model. Yet it is not a castle as such, but a fortified manor-house some three stories in height — fortified against those nightly intruders from marsh and wood of which Treadwell had spoken. Embedded in the curtain-wall at one point is an ornamental gatehouse, in the old, half-timbered style, with a single dormer, and a chimney-stack capping a high-pitched roof. Its upper stories jut out slightly over its ground floor, above the gated passage that led to the courtyard. Its range of upright timbers set close together create a barred effect, mimicking the appearance of the gate, eased by plaster of a mellow amber tint.

Apart from this small flourish of a gatehouse, Haigh Hall, owing to its age and history, exhibits but scant evidence of that fanciful style of architecture which distinguishes our marshland homes — the curious, hat-shaped peaks, bell-shaped gables, and flaring eaves for which they are justly celebrated, and which render their appearance so pleasing to the eye.

Repeatedly, as he rode, my brother had glanced over his shoulder at the Scotch firs, in whose upper boughs he had seen or sensed a dark presence. There was something very wrong there, and in the actions of his horse he recognized that she had scented danger of some kind. At one point he believed he had heard a low growling on the wind, as if something were dogging them there on the causeway. Was it related to the lump of shadow in the trees, or was it something else entirely?

A sound skin is better than a slashed one is a saying we have in Fenshire, concerning the need never to relax one's vigilance while on the road. As a consequence my brother's every sense remained on the alert for the unseen peril, whatever it was. Already his mare had doubled her speed, for she had been hired from the inn and doubtless knew the causeway and its hazards well.

And so, having made himself known at the gatehouse, with its flush of firelight showing in the lattice, my brother had received the welcome you have heard described. Exhausted from his travels, he found himself at last in the apartment that had been made ready for him. The room, darkly furnished, was at the top of the Hall in a wing across from the gatehouse, of which he had a slender view, barely visible in the twilight — or rather the no-light — that had set in.

Having washed his face and hands and treated himself to a change of clothes, he folded back the covers of his bed and smoothed the pillow, in anticipation of a welcome night's rest. Glancing at the clock, he wound his watch and adjusted the time accordingly. Then he put out his candle and was about to shut the door behind him, to descend the stairs for his sherry and supper, when he heard, or thought he heard, something like a thump resonate upon the timbers of the ceiling, and felt the walls shake a little.

"That's odd," he murmured, and being at a loss to explain it he paused awhile to listen. Silence reigned. Again he was on the point of leaving — the sherry and supper beckoned — when there came a dull thud as of feet striking the roof, followed by a creaking of the timbers directly over his head, as if something were treading on the leads.

He was a little startled by it, and wondered what its cause could be. Yielding to curiosity more so than to wisdom, he approached the diamonded casement and, opening it, craned out for a look. Standing on tiptoe he contrived to peer upwards as best he could. As I've mentioned however the no-light had set in; of the line of battlements — alternating merlons and embrasures — edging the roof he had but a faint impression. Nor did the snowflakes being hurled in his eyes by the wind aid matters much.

What can the noise have signified? A teratorn alighting on the roof? Can it really have been teratorns crouching in the Scotch firs?

This odd occurrence in his apartment he described for the others shortly afterwards in the dining-room.

"What do you suppose it can have been, Treadwell?" he asked.

"I'm sure I don't know, sir. Perhaps it was the timbers settling? For there's many an odd crack and groan in these ancient walls. Curious the sounds an old house will make of an evening."

Nor had Edgar any light to shed on the matter, save to note that "if it's teratorns on the roof, there's liable to be a massacre in the A.M. You'll alert the others to the possibility, won't you, Treadwell?"

It had left Richard shaking his head. The meal done, the cloth had been removed and a nightcap placed before him, which he was sipping with a meditative air. Considering all that he had experienced in the few short hours since he had departed the inn, he found himself regarding with some slight unease what the morning might bring.

A massacre? He sincerely hoped not. A day spent in calm perusal of the Crust letters was more in his line.

Only time, as the saying is — in Fenshire as elsewhere — would tell.

THE THIRD CHAPTER

Obstinate, Ungrateful, and a Wretch

B REAKFAST commenced promptly at nine o'clock. In the morning-room, which looked upon the courtyard, the long table had been laid for five. On a sideboard, under covers, were dishes of bacon and eggs, and griddle-cakes, and some little fishes in a row, some toasted cheese, and oatmeal porridge. While not a lavish affair, the meal of a certain was not shabby — hardly evidence of a skint outfit, Richard reflected. As well there were pots of tea and steaming hot coffee to hand, racks of buttered toast, and marshberry preserves.

In the big bay window there hung a writhesome fog which in the night had settled over the Hall and yard like a ghostly effluvium. In that yard a clumber pine — what could be seen of it — was flaunting its livery of new snow that had spilled out of heaven. No breath of wind stirred its limbs now; all was silent and still. The gravel court, the long walk leading to the stables, the yew hedge — all were whitened over. And the soaring curtain-wall of stone that ringed the Hall? Swallowed up by the fog.

For the dreary seasons of the year creep like a snail through Fenshire, while the brief summer flits like a mayfly. But we marshers are accustomed to it.

The morning-room was a cheerier place for all that, with its rich wainscot and panels of cedar, pleasant fire blazing in the hearth, and roster of dishes on the sideboard. The furnishings, like those in Richard's apartment, were quaint and old-fashioned, and from the clumber cones decorating the table a tangy scent of pine filled the air.

Thankfully Edgar's worries had been unfounded, for with the coming of dawn no massacre ensued. No terators had swooped upon them from the battlements to assail the Hall's early risers in the yard. Dan Hedges, her ladyship's chief outside man, had uncovered no answer to the mystery, however — nothing that might explain the sounds my brother had heard in the night.

Lady Martindale herself was expected presently, having left word with

Treadwell not to wait breakfast. She was enjoying a bit of a lie-in after her headache, he said, and would join them in due course.

Already seated and well into his feeding was Edgar, his youthful appetite on show as he put away rasher after peppered rasher. Opposite him sat a spare, slight-made little old man, with bushy eyebrows and a shiny head, who had been noisily slurping his porridge in blithe disregard of the others at table. Although the old man was greatly changed, he remained distinguishable to Richard. How the years had altered him — how differently Richard's childhood eyes had viewed him! For in the wizened figure, thickly grizzled of cheek and chin, Richard recognized Mine Host of the Goose and Gander from those childhood days of long ago.

"Excuse me, sir, but I'm sure I know you," he said kindly. "You're Mr. Samuel Gander, are you not? My name is Richard Hathaway. But likely you'll not remember me."

"Should I?" snapped the erstwhile publican, fixing him with two crinkly eyes like slits in a carrot.

"In times past we often lodged at the Goose and Gander — my parents, my sister, and I — when visiting friends in Ridingham."

"Whoopee," exclaimed the old man, who seemed to possess but one or two functioning ivories.

"My parents — Robert and Alice Hathaway?" Richard suggested hopefully.

"Never 'eard of 'em."

"That is how we came to be acquainted with your daughter, Miss Lizzie — that is, she is Lady Martindale now."

"A pinch for stale news," scoffed the proprietor.

"Since our parents died, my sister and I have kept up a correspondence with her ladyship, who had befriended us in those days when we were children."

"Children, yer say? Not overfond of 'em meself. Good eating, though," cackled Mr. Gander, with a cheerful smacking of his lips.

"I'm afraid you'll not get much out of him so early in the A.M.," Edgar advised my brother. "He can be a positive fright before he's had his gruel."

"He was quite the convivial chap in those years," Richard recalled, "always bustling about, always rushing up and down stairs showing guests to their rooms, and superintending the servants, and entertaining customers with no end of ribald tales."

"Oh, not to worry — he can be as lively as a cricket when it suits him. Drives the doc to distraction that way. Why, already he's made his morning's circuit of the wall-walk — more of a fog-walk this A.M. — along the battlements. More than once, some days, you'll see him pacing the wall or the roof-tops, his cutlass at his shoulder, like a sentry walking his dreary round. He says it sharpens the eye and keeps him in trim, against the day the marsh devils storm the Hall."

"He looks a frugal eater. Will he have nothing more than his gru — er, his porridge — and a cup of thin tea?"

"He'll follow it with bogberry juice, I dare say. That's the stuff there — that inky syrup in the jug."

"Matter of fact! Bogberries are all very well for making wine — our vicar in Market Snailsby is rather fond of it — but they're dashed distasteful to be drinking the juice of."

"They're awful, but that don't bother him. He's used to it."

"He'll have no bacon and eggs? No griddle-cakes?"

"Can't eat that muck," spoke up Sam, and fixing the two with his slit-eyes he cackled — "Ooh! Didn't know I was listening, did yer? Well, what d'yer think o' that, eh? Hee, hee!"

There was another guest seated at the breakfast-table — a big solid man, large-boned, with faded hair — who in his externals and demeanor was as altogether an opposite to Mr. Samuel Gander as could be imagined. His features, like himself, were largely shaped, his brow tall, his eyes wide, blue, and shining, his countenance frank and open. His name was Gecks, and he was Lady Martindale's solicitor, and had been her husband the baronet's as well. Like Richard and myself, he had known Lady Martindale in the early days, when she had been pert little Lizzie Gander drawing beer from the engine in the tap-room of the inn.

Mr. Everson Gecks was not only a shrewd country practitioner, but a friend of long standing. A frequent guest on matters of business, he had overnighted at the Hall, having already retired when Richard had pulled up before the gatehouse.

The attorney now joined in the conversation. His rich, baritone voice resounded with the fenny accents of the marshes, for Mr. Gecks was very much a marsh man, through and through.

"It was hardly the way in olden times, eh, Sam? In the whole catalogue of cookery was there a concoction that sprightly Sam Gander would not have tasted, in days gone by? And now you abstain from the mildest of gastronomic vices. Why, what has happened to you, Sam?" he chided the old man, in mock reproof.

"I've reformed meself," the proprietor explained. "For in olden times, yer see, I weren't so pertickler. Never gave a thought to me breakfast, nor to me luncheon, nor to me supper neither. But me youthful follies I've put behind me. Bacon? Awful. Eggs? 'Orrible. Toasted cheese? Might as well be eating lard as that swill. Shoo!"

"Now it's all marsh tea, bogberry juice, milk, and gruel," said Edgar.

"And the wall-walk," added Sam. "Don't yer forget the wall-walk, neffy."

"He is excited by the exercise, and the bracing effects of the chilly air," Mr. Gecks explained to Richard.

"I see nothing wrong with exercise, for it keeps a man in trim, as Mr. Gander has observed," my brother remarked.

"You should hear the doc on that score," Edgar chuckled, with a roll of his eyes, "for he's of quite another opinion."

"Does Mr. Gander not take a little wine? A little sherry before dinner? A little brandy afterwards?"

"He seldom drinks — alcoholic, that is. *Aqua vitae* ain't for him. He has a mania for juices. Bogberry juice. Marshberry juice. Juice of the kine."

As if suiting the action to the word, the old man poured out a measure of his inky syrup and downed it at a swallow. Richard, knowing the tartness of the juice, could but watch in horror. Fortunately his attention then was drawn to the room-door, for through it had stepped Lady Martindale, attended by her maid.

Scarcely five feet in height, the dowager was the very spit and image of her father, on the distaff side. Her shrewd, inquisitive glance surveyed her guests at table, all of whom rose save for Mr. Gander, who had noisily resumed his porridge. Like her father, her ladyship had the same high, thin nose, over which her eyes had a way of peering like those of a spy over a wall. Her face was pale but intensely alert, and Richard, knowing her as he did of old, little doubted but that she was aware of most every thought that passed in the room.

The girl in attendance on her was Gwenda, her personal maid and confidante. She was a pretty little thing, slighter even than her mistress, with curls of a brilliant, golden tint, and eyes as bright as dew-drops on a May morning. (Or so my brother described her, for I never saw her. But gentlemen, I have found, are prone to exaggeration on the topic.)

It turned out that Lady Martindale was vastly better. Her headache had vanished with the night, and after her lie-in she was feeling much refreshed and ready to meet the day. The usual complimentary greetings having been exchanged, she took her place at the top of the table, between her father and Edgar. Chuckling the old man poured himself another bogberry and quaffed it off, while his daughter addressed herself to Richard.

"It has been some time, young man, since I have seen you. And how is your dear sister? As delightful as ever? For she wrote to me not above a month ago, after your visit to examine the letters had been arranged."

"Jemma is very well, thank you, Lady Martindale, and sends you her best. I'm very much in your debt, you know, for your invitation. The Hall looks a capital place. I hope my presence is not an inconvenience."

"Not at all — put it out of your mind. We have known one another for more years than I for one should care to admit. Besides, the baronet would have been pleased to know that some correspondence he had received from his old friend Sir Pharnaby might find their way into your scholarly hands. For my husband himself was something of a scholar, on a number of his Welsh topics."

"As I understand it, the letters from Sir Pharnaby were only recently discovered?"

"Indeed. They were found, amongst some other correspondence, in an old dispatch-box that my husband had put away in a trunk. My Gwenda happened on them whilst at her duties, and referred them to me."

"And by sheer luck my sister round that time had written to you in passing of my interest in Sir Pharnaby and his music."

"Just so. A happy coincidence all round," said her ladyship.

"Sir Pharnaby Crust? That old buzzard?" cackled her father, who had left off his porridge and was adjusting his tea.

"Did you know him, Mr. Gander?" Richard asked. "For I should like it very much if you might grant me an interview — your recollections of the man — "

"My father did not know Sir Pharnaby," her ladyship explained, breaking in, "although of course my husband did. My father is speaking in reference to a portrait of Sir Pharnaby he saw once. Hence the allusion."

"Ooh — his face was 'orrible," recollected Sam with a grimace.

"He's spot-on there," Edgar nodded soberly, for he too had viewed the portrait.

"Yes, well, I dare say Sir Pharnaby Crust was not the handsomest of men," Richard allowed, "but a musician and a composer *extraordinaire* he surely was, the most talented to have arisen in our own Fenshire marshes. And that is the object of my treatise. It is only fitting that his work should be brought to the attention of a wider public.

"I am myself a keen amateur musician, and have known of Sir Pharna-

by and his music since childhood. To my surprise, I discovered while in
college that his name was but scarcely recognized by the music tutors. So
I resolved to compose a treatise describing his life and works. Fortunately,
some additional records and correspondence have come to light in the Municipal Library at Newmarsh. I have been making a study of them and will
be continuing my researches there following my visit, to fill out the picture
of Sir Pharnaby and his contributions to the musical life of the county."

"And who is the publisher you have in view for your treatise? His firm
is in Ridingham, I believe you said?" her ladyship asked.

"His name is Mr. Charles Van Ness, of Van Ness and Sons, in Scriveners' Lane. I've arranged an interview in his offices later in the week. I do
hope he will agree to take the manuscript once it is finished. If he declines,
I mean to show it to my old music tutor at Salthead, on the off chance the
University press should have an interest in it. But there is much work yet
to be done before it is in shape for the printers."

"Dogged and steady does it," nodded Mr. Gecks. "We wish you every
success in your enterprise."

"Mr. Hathaway is a graduate of Salthead University, Edgar," Lady Martindale informed her nephew.

The youth shifted uneasily in his chair. He raised his head and left off
his feeding long enough to ask — "Oh, really? And which college was that,
sir?"

"Bearsnose," Richard said.

"Oh, that's — that's quite a good college."

Bearsnose College — otherwise B.N.C. — indeed is one of the better
foundations amongst the seven that comprise the great University of Salthead. The huge stone bears carved on its portals, and the plated bear's-head
knocker adorning its chief entrance, are amongst the most recognizable of
University landmarks.

"Yes, I read music there. And yours is Queen's?"

"Er, yes — right," Edgar answered, after a moment's hesitation.

"Well, that's by far the best. Magdalen, the queen of the colleges."

"Right — that's the ticket — "

The youth seemed less than thrilled to speak of his undergraduate pursuits, and when an opportunity to change the subject arose he quickly leaped at it.

"Might I trouble you to pass the marshberry preserves?" he said to Mr.
Gecks, and spent the next few minutes scrupulously dressing his toast.

It was later that Lady Martindale confided to Richard that her nephew had been rusticated from his college — that is, temporarily sent down — owing to some "little difficulties" he had encountered there. Having been entered as a gentleman commoner at Magdalen College, familiarly known as Queen's, he had accepted the rustication like the gentleman he professed to be. But she expected him to make a triumphant return in the new year.

Richard, recalling Edgar's uneasiness on the threshold the night before, wondered whether tailors and duns might not have been as responsible for his "little difficulties" as had been the dons. Well did my brother remember the experience of his own college years, the long hours of study and reflection, the lectures, construes, chapels, the dreaded examination papers. He too at times had found himself "hard up for ready dibs", as the saying is. He too had been fond of the loud plaid vest and trousers Edgar affected, and the shaggy coats, which passed for fashion amongst college men. But really, was such dress any more ridiculous than the academicals all collegians were obliged to wear — the mortar-board or "square" and the preposterous gown and streamers?

At a point in the course of the breakfast the talk turned to Mrs. Aberdovey, Lady Martindale's lodgekeeper-woman, as she was called, who occupied the gatehouse. Her late husband Morgan, early in his life, had gone to sea — "to have had the adventure of it," as he often said — before returning in time to the marshes. More recently her son Owen had followed in his footsteps, and had been serving aboard a merchant vessel when he had gone missing in a storm. The sad news had been slow to arrive; only in the past couple of weeks had they learned of his fate. It had come as a mighty shock to everyone, for Owen Aberdovey had been much admired at the Hall. Everybody liked him; no one had a wrong word to say about him; he had been "as good a man as ever rowed a boat." Modest, unassuming, and a hard worker, he had sought to emulate his late father by signing aboard ship, that he might experience the joy of straining sails and humming cordage, of trim decks and wide ocean, and the piping song of the wind in the rigging. Needless to relate his mother had been firmly opposed to his choice, and now had suffered a tragedy.

"Our rector, Mr. Cassock, spoke most movingly of him at the service," Lady Martindale recalled. "He was an excellent young man. We deplore his loss."

"He was a regular feller — a trump," Edgar nodded soberly.

"And so my lodgekeeper-woman has no one now. Both husband and son are gone."

Richard hesitated a moment before speaking. "By your leave, Lady Martindale," he informed her, "but there is someone — a gentleman caller. He came last evening."

"Impossible! Who would be calling on my lodgekeeper-woman?"

Richard observed that the pretty eyes of Gwenda, the dowager's maid, had stirred faintly at the mention of a visitor. Concurrently it had brought to his mind an image of Mrs. Aberdovey, as she had stood looking out at the gate as if in anticipation of her caller.

No one had any idea who it was the woman had invited to supper. She had no gentleman friends that anybody knew of, for like Lady Martindale she was devoted to the memory of her husband.

"Perhaps someone to commiserate with her over her loss?" Richard suggested.

Perhaps. If so, then one of the outside men might be privy to it — Dan Hedges, for instance, or one of the stable-hands, perhaps the weather-beaten groom with the sticky-out ears who had come in answer to the gatehouse bell.

"He seems a likely choice. Certainly the fellow is cheeky enough to have ferreted it out."

Lady Martindale was unacquainted with the man, who had been hired only recently, Treadwell reported, to muck out the stables. But as there was nothing further to be gleaned from idle speculation, the subject was dropped.

Now that breakfast had been concluded, with but the tea and coffee — and bogberry juice — still on the table, a discussion was commenced of the MacWallop business, as it was known, that tiresome matter for which Mr. Gecks had come to the Hall.

"I see my neighbor has been at his tricks again," her ladyship remarked with a sniff. She made no allusion to the headache that had sent her to her bed, but the purport of the sniff was clear.

"You know how the matter rests," said Mr. Gecks.

"I wish that it would let *me* rest."

"He'll not be moved, chief."

"The man seems to think there are no rights of property. And no one but a hare-brain would establish a right of way so near to Eel Island."

"Beg pardon, Lady Martindale," said Richard, "but who is this fellow MacWallop — if you'll not mind my asking?"

"In this part of the globe, young man, Mr. Phergus MacWallop thinks himself a king, when he is in fact a joker," the dowager snipped.

"Mr. MacWallop," explained Mr. Gecks in his rich Fenshire brogue, "is a landowner whose property adjoins that of her ladyship, to the south-wards and westwards of Haigh Hall. It is, in the main, deemed poorer land than that of the Hall, having rather more of marsh and bog about it than of gravel and alluvium. Moreover the Hall is nearer to town, and its paths and byways, although not of the finest, are much superior. As a result Mr. MacWallop has for some years looked upon Hall lands with a jealous eye. The man is of a hasty temper and is forever in broils, if not with her ladyship then with one or another of his neighbors. His affairs are considerably involved; his chief occupation appears to be the bringing of turbulent suits in law."

"Well, the man has no other business to fill in his time," Lady Martindale huffed.

"Lately he has declared a right of way across Martindale land — in Hatter's Close, hard by Eel Island — slap across it, in fact, a couple of furlongs distant from her ladyship's own gatehouse door."

"For what purpose?" Richard asked.

"I'll tell you for what purpose," said her ladyship. "Spite, young man — spite, pure and simple — and an effort to drive me from my land. The wretch knows perfectly well how these matters irritate and annoy me. It's pests like him who are giving our country squires a bad name."

"For the purpose," resumed Mr. Gecks, who was used to his client's frequent interpolations, "of providing for himself a better and shorter road to town; or so he claims. He means to circumvent his long way round by cutting directly through Martindale land, without so much as a 'by your leave'."

"Why then should he be thought a hare-brain, as Lady Martindale put it?" Richard asked.

"Because that entire area round Hatter's Close and the Island is subject to periodic flooding. Oh, it's no secret — been that way for centuries. That is why the Martindales have never established their own path there. It regularly washes out."

"Then this right of way of his must indeed be the result of malice."

"For past perceived slights Mr. MacWallop has suffered at the hands of her ladyship. Or so he views them."

"If the area round the Island is not useful, why then not simply ignore him?" Richard asked.

"Because, young man," said her ladyship, fixing him with a gimlet eye, "I am being accused of trespass — trespass on my own property!"

"Good gracious, can this be true?"

"I regret to say that it is," nodded Mr. Gecks.

"And how is that?"

"Because I built a fence across his path, upon my own land, to bar his way," Lady Martindale explained, "but the silly fool chopped it down and burned it. And so I built a second fence — ditto result. Now a third fence he has chopped to pieces and burned as well, and has vowed to bring an action against *me* for trespass."

"Is it possible? Can you in law bring suit against a person for trespass on her own ground?"

The attorney shrugged, and spoke at some length about certain quirks of the law that Mr. MacWallop was using to his advantage, precedents that had been established, and statutes from long years agone, which, after a due consideration of the facts, might render the point equivocal in the eyes of the Justices.

"Those are the Justices at the approaching Petty Sessions, before whom the matter is to be laid, as we are informed by Mr. Wormwrath."

"Wormwrath?"

"He is the neighbor's solicitor."

Lady Martindale screwed up her eyes and snorted. "Neighbor? The man is obstinate, ungrateful, and a wretch. Well, fair is fair. Let him bring on his Petty Sessions. I'll shut up his path, I think — the dirty skunk!"

"Now, now, chief," cautioned Mr. Gecks, shaking his head and smiling. "Temper, Lizzie, temper."

"Ooh, mix it up, mix it up!" her father encouraged her, with a gay revolving of his fists. "I like a bit o' fun, same as the rest. A pox on the skunk, and a figo for his Petty Sessions."

"Brayvo, Auntie!" applauded Edgar. "She's a regular female bull, she is," he confided to Richard.

In an instant the dowager of Haigh Hall had been transformed into the pert little Lizzie Gander of our childhood, she who had reigned supreme over the beer-engine at the Goose and Gander, and who had captured the heart of a baronet of the sundered realm. And none doubted but that her father's injunction to *mix it up* would have been obeyed to the letter, had the offending neighbor and aforesaid dirty skunk that minute shown himself in the morning-room.

"The imbecile thinks to take advantage because I am a woman, and to win judgments against me by playing fast and loose with the law," she continued, her eyes flashing. "He never would have dared stoop to such chicanery in my husband's time. In the flood years the baronet often did give aid and assistance to the silly fool, whose roads were forever washing out. You see the thanks it got him."

"You're right there, chief," nodded the attorney, folding his big hands on the table. "I sympathize with you."

"This is not your first brush with Mr. MacWallop, I take it?" Richard said.

"Oh, heavens, no. We are old foes, Mr. Hathaway, in Petty Sessions. Every season comes some new scheme to extract either coin or concession from her ladyship."

"Obstinate, ungrateful — *and* a wretch," reiterated the dowager. "Why, the fool insists I still owe him tuppence for a pint of spruce he had from me once at the Gander. And for this he brings action upon action against me. Powers above, I shall need a cold compress if I hear any more about this or that statute or the vagaries of the Bench. Ungrateful wretch — ungrateful piker! Thank heavens he isn't English."

"His heritage is Scotch," the attorney informed my brother.

"Well, there you are — tighter than a short shoe. Doubtless it serves as his favorite tipple as well," remarked her ladyship.

It happened that Mr. Gecks that morning was to present the wretch with a letter, in advance of the Petty Sessions, giving notice that should he (the wretch) persist in his unwarranted assaults on her ladyship's property, meaning the fence, upon her own ground, that a corresponding action for trespass, naming Mr. MacWallop, would be brought before the Justices.

"I can't see how to shift him otherwise. We have given him fair warning," said Mr. Gecks.

"You are forever presenting him with these little notices of yours, and the imbecile is forever tearing them up and laughing."

"We can but try, chief. This should take some of the snap out of him. Now, if you'd care to run your eye over it . . ." and he handed the letter across. She scanned it with shrewd appraisal. It did not take long.

"Do you approve?"

"I suppose," she returned, hardly mollified. "What that skunk needs is a good poke in the face."

"Well, well, we shan't dispute over our methods. Dogged and steady we must be. We must explore every avenue." Mr. Gecks patted his lips with a napkin and returned the missive to his blue bag, which he then buckled down and locked. "Is there anything more, chief?"

There was nothing more. The attorney rose, just as a maid entered to announce Dan Hedges.

A cheerful young man, sturdily built and full of energy, appeared at the door. He was clothed in a blue jersey and muffler, ditto cords, and leather leggings. At his feet danced a wire-haired terrier, a game little lad, sporting a sleek white coat with brindle markings round the face and tail. The lad's name was Toddy, and he was the outside man's trusted assistant, a plucky little fellow with a gift for nosing in the earth. Directly he commenced a noisy lapping at the water-bowl that stood in the corner — not unlike Mr. Gander at his porridge — while master Dan proceeded to state their business to her ladyship.

"It's just as you suspected, m'lady. There be tracks of a spotted lion in the snow just outside the walls, leading to and from the causeway. So it weren't only devils that were heard singing in the night."

Lady Martindale turned to her guest from the south of Fenshire.

"See there, Mr. Hathaway. Perhaps you ought to have heeded our Mr. Cuffley's advice and overnighted at the Gander. It would appear you have had a fortuitous escape."

Richard, in view of this new evidence, could hardly gainsay her. But he was reminded now of the thing in the trees, and so he asked Dan Hedges if he knew of an instance wherein a spotted lion had climbed a Scotch fir, or any other species of tree in the neighborhood.

The outside man pushed a hand through his thick black hair. A reflective light shone in his eyes as he mulled over the question.

"No, sir," he replied at length, "don't reckon as ever I've heard of any such thing. A marsh devil maybe, but a spotted lion? I shouldn't think it likely, sir — any more than that a stallion should scale a clumber pine."

One of the responsibilities of Dan Hedges was to see that all was secure in and around the Hall, and in the home fields outside its gates. Now that the reports of the coracle men had been confirmed — that at least one spotted lion, the mightiest and most feared of marshland predators, was at large in the area — henceforth all would need to maintain the highest alert when venturing beyond the curtain-wall.

It was at this juncture that Mr. Gander, who had been quietly nursing his tea, sat up and, leaning forward in his chair, turned his crinkly eyes on Richard.

"What's this about devils in trees? What's the score, young feller?" he demanded.

Richard repeated for his and the others' benefit what he had seen — or thought he had seen — in the Scotch firs along the causeway, and what he had heard — or thought he had heard — on the leads above his room.

The old man glanced round him with an air of vindication. "Well, what d'yer think o' that, now? It's somebody other has seen it too!" he exclaimed, nodding excitedly.

Richard's interest quickened. "Seen what, Mr. Gander? Something outside the beaten track, is it?"

"Outside the beaten track, says yer? That's grand! Why, the mere sight of it would blow a hole in yer wide-awake."

"He's got an imagination, he has," Edgar confided to my brother. "He sees things from the wall-walk. And once he gets his tooth into a thing he's a regular bulldog over it."

"What's that? Imagination? Regular bulldog? There's none o' yer as believes it — not a one o' yer in this house. Well, let it be yer own lookout," scoffed Sam.

"Sadly, Mr. Hathaway, my father is not a well man," Lady Martindale explained, to which the alleged sufferer retorted — "Gammon!"

"Naturally Dr. Bussey takes a different view. The doctor speaks very despondingly of his state."

"Bother yer doctor," said Sam.

"It's a wonder my father has any life left in him at all. He eats so very poorly, and all the wrong things, so the doctor tells us."

"A figo for yer doctor!"

Undaunted, Richard asked him again — "What have you seen, Mr. Gander? Something on the roof-top of the Hall, perhaps?"

"Aye, so yer've seen it yerself then, young feller?"

"I have heard it. A thump on the roof above my room, and a noise as of something treading on the leads."

The old man rubbed his hands energetically. "Better and better!" he exclaimed. But his elation was short-lived, being swiftly checked by the disapproving glance of his daughter, reminding him that he was not a well man, and that he cannot have seen anything from the wall-walk because there was nothing there to be seen.

It did the trick. Sam, taking his daughter's hint, withdrew into himself and subsided. He dropped his chin on his hand, his eyes tracing the residue of porridge he was stirring idly round in his plate. He did not look again at Richard, but could be heard voicing unintelligible mutterings under his breath.

"It puts him off his gruel whenever Auntie gets her Irish up," Edgar informed my brother, who had been left pondering the old man's words. "I say — there's a lark. Of course she hasn't got any Irish."

His aunt meanwhile had risen from her seat.

"Come along then, Gwenda," she said, addressing her maid, and with a brisk nod to the others she took her leave of them.

Of an Eclectic Nature

R ICHARD set to work in the library at about half past ten. He was glad of the chance at last to begin his examination of the Crust letters. It was a fine room, this library of Sir Pedr Martindale's, with its dignified shelving and its abundance of Welsh relics on display. There was a good fire in the grate, handsome carpets on the hardwood, and the curtains had been thrown back to admit what light might be afforded by the misty day. Some candles were burning on a table in brass sticks, to augment the light, and the table itself was a spacious one, with plenty of room for Richard to lay his materials out before him. He had just removed his paper and blotting-book from his valise when Treadwell appeared.

"The glass has gone down this morning," Richard told him. The servant had paused a moment to inspect the barometer that stood inside the door. "Ah — I took the liberty of reading it before breakfast, and again a minute ago. The snow is not finished with us, I dare say."

"And how the days are drawing in," Treadwell nodded. "I'm afraid we shall have no autumn this year. I should not be surprised, sir, if we are not snowbound directly." He then inquired whether all was in order for Richard to commence his researches. It was.

"In his lordship's time, sir, this room was much in demand. Indeed it is one of the most splendid in the Hall."

"Yes, it's capital," Richard agreed. "I could spend hours in here."

"As did his lordship."

"And as doubtless I shall do myself, in view of the work that lies before me."

Treadwell was justly proud of the library, almost as if it were his very own. His entire attitude emitted a steady and unwavering confidence. The reason for this was not far to seek. He had served at the Hall since he had been a boy; he had lived there all his life; he had known nothing else. His parents too had been in service there. Thus he could speak with authority of bygone days, and his knowledge of Haigh Hall and its history, truth be told, in many ways surpassed that even of her ladyship.

The Martindales were an old and respected family in Ridingham. They came of an ancient race, one with many Welsh connections, and were held in high esteem by most all the provincial gentry. Sir Pedr himself had been well-schooled in Welsh lore, and had spoken the language like a native — of which natives, of course, there no longer were any, nor had there been any since the time of the sundering. Regardless, his devotion to the lonely, misty, marshy realm of his birth had been complete.

"I never saw a Fenshireman who did not swear by his county, and the baronet was foremost amongst them," noted Treadwell, who himself was as proud of his native soil as he was of his lordship's library.

"Well, we are so removed from the world here — even more so in Market Snailsby — that we Fenshiremen all must stick together," Richard said brightly.

From Treadwell he learned that Sir Pedr Rhys Martindale had claimed descent from the famed Prince Madoc, or more correctly Madog ap Owen Gwynnedd, the Welsh chief of eminence who, in the twelfth century, had set forth in ten ships in search of new lands. He and his followers had departed their native Cambria — Wales — the Principality — their dreaming homeland of mountain and moor, mist-haunted castles, and bardic Druidry — in the historic migration out of Old Britain, which had been prompted by the gradual icing-up of their ancestral territories, and with the vaunted courage of Welshmen had crossed a mighty ocean to establish new homes in a new world.

His lordship and his lordship's grandfather had been Bards of the Gorsedd, members of an ancient order of poets and harpists that traced its origin to the Druids. It had been said in Wales, and was current amongst the Welsh-descended in the sundered realm, that any man may be a poet; but not every poet was elected a Bard of the Gorsedd, which further distinguished the Martindales of Haigh Hall. The Welsh — the ancient Cymry — had been a fierce and barbarous people, so the histories tell us. Welsh princes like Madoc had dwelt in ceaseless conflict with their warlike neighbors, the Lords Marchers of England. And yet had not such Englishmen as the Earl of Richmond, formerly Henry Tudor, and Oliver Cromwell, Lord Protector of England, themselves been of Welsh descent?

Here in Fenshire — so far removed from the world — that fire of the hot-blooded Welsh over time had been reduced to a nostalgic longing, a romantic love of bygone things. It was a love shared by Treadwell, too, although his claim to Welsh heritage was slim, through a widowed aunt in Drizzlehurst. Still he was rightly proud of it, no less from his association with Sir Pedr. And had not a famed Welsh seer, or *dryw*, in Ridingham foretold that he should one day assist a gentleman in a literary endeavor of considerable moment?

Treadwell now placed before my brother the Crust letters — a sizable sheaf of papers, done up in a blue wrapper. Richard undid the packet and spread the first of the letters flat on the table. It consisted of three closely-written sheets of yellowed foolscap, covered in Sir Pharnaby's distinctive, spidery hand.

"Do you know the *Fenshire Suite*, Treadwell?" Richard asked, making a preliminary inspection of the document.

The *Suite* is Sir Pharnaby's most celebrated and popular work, and indeed Treadwell knew of it.

"Some of its tunes strike very pleasantly on the ear, sir."

"Yes, there is much of folk song in it. Certain of the strains are directly quoted, while others are derivative — pentatonic themes which have the air of folk songs but are original compositions."

As he ran his eye over the pages, Richard mentioned a few other of Sir Pharnaby's better-known works — the *Culliford Symphony, Peascod Variations,* and the *Four Fenshire Dances* — with which only the dances was the butler familiar.

"Do you know the *Farewell to Bogminster?*"

"Bogminster? Do you mean the county town of Slopshire, sir?" Treadwell asked, looking puzzled.

"Indeed."

"But is Bogminster not *in* Slopshire, sir?"

"Yes, but not to worry. The piece reflects Sir Pharnaby's yearning for his home fields, following a lengthy stay in Slopshire — or so has been the common report. I hope to unearth something more definitive in his correspondence. Altogether the *Farewell* is a delightful work, very dry and witty, reflecting the taste and style of a thorough Fenshireman."

"One is grateful for that, sir. But why is Sir Pharnaby's music so little heard?"

"Another matter I hope to resolve with these documents and those in Newmarsh. It seems Sir Pharnaby did not value fame a rush, and made no effort to promote his works. So they were not much remarked upon, or talked about, or written up, and in time became neglected. He did not cultivate the limelight, you see. For he had so many other interests, so many other pursuits to occupy him. His composition and his playing were of scant importance by comparison."

"Ah, so that was it. Well, well. It seems an unfortunate circumstance, sir."

"It is. And it is precisely that circumstance I mean to remedy with my treatise," Richard assured him. And having arranged his quire of ruled paper and his blotting-book, a freshly-cut pen, and a glass inkpot before him, he fell to his work with relish.

Treadwell meantime prepared to resume his duties. "But if there is anything you should be wanting, sir, do not hesitate to ring for me. I shall not be far from the library."

"Thank you, Treadwell. I am much indebted to her ladyship for her generosity."

So saying, Richard filled his pipe — my brother is ever a great one for a pipe, as it aids his concentration, so he informs me, and helps to keep the chill off — and with a few whiffs and a brisk rub of his hands he applied himself to his task. The first letter he intended to copy was a note to Sir Pedr, dated some five-and-twenty years before, that made reference to a late work of the composer's, the *Picton Idyll*. It contained much material of interest, so he straightened his note paper before him and dipping his pen began to write.

Having done with the first, he turned to the next several in order. He quickly fell to examining one in particular, which made mention of one of Sir Pharnaby's chamber compositions, his quintet for oboe and string quartet in three movements, a delightful piece redolent of his sedgy home fields. In it, the oboe's plaintive singing seemed to capture the very essence of the bleak but alluring landscape of the marshes. One of the composer's most poignant and evocative works, Richard knew it well, having played second violin in a recital in Market Snailsby a couple of months earlier. He still could hear its atmospheric *lento espressivo*, by turns sweet and sad, sprightly and tearful, running through his mind.

In another letter he found a brief allusion to a cello concerto — one of the abiding mysteries of Sir Pharnaby's *œuvre*. The concerto had been finished, evidently, but never performed, and had gone missing in the fire that had destroyed many of the composer's writings. Unfortunately, the letter offered no clue as to the fate of any manuscript copy of the score. It was entirely possible it had been destroyed by Sir Pharnaby's own hand, as he himself had been his own harshest critic of his musical endeavors.

Absorbed in his studies, time for Richard passed swiftly. A short while later a visitor appeared at the door — a maidservant bearing the tea-things, at the behest, she said, of Mr. Treadwell. Having accomplished her errand, she dropped a curtsey and stood dimpling and blushing — a pretty, little, red-cheeked milkmaid of a housemaid.

"Excuse, please, sir. Elzie Peek, sir. Mr. Treadwell, he's gone a-doing, sir, and asked I should inquire if you'll be needful of anything more, sir?"

Richard, glad for the brief respite from his copying, eased himself back in his chair.

"Well, Elzie Peek, I thank you for inquiring. But I've no need of anything at present, as I've just now made a capital discovery. Have you heard of a man called John Deal?"

"Never have, sir," the maid told him.

"Well, there is a composition of Sir Pharnaby's — *Elegy for John Deal,* it's called — whose origin has been rather a puzzle, because for the longest time no one has been able to identify Mr. Deal. But I have just found in a letter here, written to Sir Pedr Martindale some years ago, that Mr. Deal had been Sir Pharnaby's tobacconist."

The milkmaid, unsure whether to be impressed by this revelation or no, blushed and dimpled her indecision.

"Yes, sir. Should you be needful of anything more, sir?"

"No — no, nothing at all. Thank you, Elzie Peek."

"Very good, sir."

And so saying she dropped another curtsey and was gone.

She must think me a crank. But directly it left his mind as he became absorbed in the next letter. It contained nothing of interest, however, and so he put it aside, reckoning it need not be copied.

Already he had made much progress in his studies, but there remained yet many pages of correspondence to be gone through. Feeling more at his ease, he sipped his tea and settled back again in his chair. His eyes glided about the room, taking in the long rows of shelves filled with volumes of Welsh history and lore, and the wealth of artifacts that adorned the walls and furniture. Intrigued, he got to his feet and took a stroll round to have a look at the different items.

There was a Welsh *rote,* or small lute, resting on a cabinet beside the shelves. He plucked its strings a few times and marveled at its crisp, bright tone. Above it hung a massive longbow of yew wood, doubtless one of Sir Pedr's choicest possessions. The Welsh, Richard recollected, had been excellent bowmen. Other relics on display testified forcefully to the medieval Welshmen's skill at arms — bills and halberds, the wicked-looking axes called Welsh hooks, a goatskin buckler, Welsh knives and glaives, and a more recent cutlass or two. On one wall, above the wainscot, was spread a banner depicting a red dragon — heraldic symbol of Wales — rampant against a sunburst, on a blue field, with Cymric inscriptions.

Near the banner, resting on a shelf, was a Viking sunstone, and beside it lay another stone — a smooth, creamy object whose flattened surface was marked by a series of linear veins, green, blue, and crimson, in a grid-like pattern. My brother knows something of sunstones and their properties, but the other was a blank to him; he had never seen its like.

Less mysterious, perhaps, was the tall, black "stovepipe" hat — the sort that had been favored by Welsh ladies of old — with a lace kerchief affixed, crowning the alabaster bust of a grim-faced gentleman in a bag-wig.

"It is Mr. Edgar's doing," Treadwell had explained, meaning the hat.

An inscription on the pedestal established the identity of the gentleman as Sir Padrig Martindale. Some curious things had been told of him, Richard seemed to recall. He knew that Sir Padrig Martindale had been a judge, at one time or other, but the finer details eluded him at present.

It was while he was musing on this and other subjects that his eye — a corner of it, actually — thought it detected something in motion there in the room. A shadow, it seemed, had fallen across a wall. An instant later the stovepipe on the head of Sir Padrig dropped to the ground, as if the shadow, in passing by, had brushed against the hat and toppled it.

Richard drew a startled breath. His scalp tingled; an icy chill tickled his spine.

"Yes? Hallo? Is — someone there?" he heard himself call out.

No one was. No one but Sir Padrig, uncovered now save for his bag-wig.

Definitely there had been movement of some kind, but apart from the flicker in the grate nothing was stirring. Perhaps the shadow had been an illusion of the firelight? But if so, how had it caused the hat to drop?

Perhaps someone in the yard had stepped by the window? But how much of a shadow would be cast, he wondered, given the gloom that was filtering through the lattice? Moreover he had been looking in the direction of the window at the time and had seen no one.

He shrugged his shoulders, as though trying to rid himself of a disagreeable sensation.

"Dashed odd," he murmured, as he stooped to recover the hat and restored it to its place on the head of Sir Padrig. He thought of resuming his copying, but noted that he had accomplished a fair bit of work already in the short time he had been at it. By the clock the morning was far advanced, and so he decided that an adjournment was in order, to clear his brain of Sir Pharnaby and of stovepipes that toppled over for no reason.

He went up to his room to put on his boots, took up his coat and hat, and repaired to the yard for a breath of air. For a while he crunched along through the snow, smoking his pipe and musing on the fog that had not lightened an iota since breakfast, and which seemed to follow him wherever he went. Lost in reflection, after a time he began to wonder whether it was the fog, or the shadow from the library, that was dogging his steps. All in a moment the curtain-wall loomed up before him. It was reassuring to know it still was there, for in the fog one scarcely could tell.

He glanced back at the Hall, its flanking towers and serrated sweep of battlements rising ghost-like in the mist. He half expected to see the figure of old Sam Gander, cutlass at the ready, stalking the parapets; but nothing and nobody was there. Nothing there was either to explain the bump in the night. For although he could discern — just barely — the window of his apartment on the topmost floor, he saw nothing in the least remarkable about it to distinguish it from the rest.

He was making his way towards the stables when he observed a woman crossing from the Hall to the gatehouse. She was striding along slowly, her head bent in thought — preoccupied, it seemed, as she had been when answering his knock at her lattice — and was not at first conscious of his approach.

"Hallo, Mrs. Aberdovey."

She halted and looked at him blankly for a moment, as though not recognizing him. Presently it dawned upon her.

"Oh, my — it's Mr. Hathaway — "

Her glance gave no hint what was passing behind her eyes.

"Everyone appears to be waiting for this fog to clear off," he said. "It would seem to be the common lot this morning."

"We have hopes in that direction, sir."

"And how are you today, Mrs. Aberdovey? I was sorry to hear of your loss. I was wholly without any inkling of it when I met you last evening."

An odd expression came into her face, and when she did not answer he explained that he had learned of it only at breakfast, about her son Owen, her hope and pride, having met with shipwreck.

"Oh — oh, no, sir — not so — not shipwreck. It was my son, sir, who was laboring to save those from a packet-boat as had been holed on the reef. It was in the channel, sir — Nantle — the islands — "

Then her voice trailed off in an abstracted sort of way, and she said no more. Richard was glad that she had not abandoned herself to despair, and marveled at her strength in this regard. Doubtless she drew great comfort from her friends at the Hall.

"Lady Martindale spoke very highly of your son," he told her.

"Did she? Ah, that was good of her — "

She thanked him then for his kindness, and sought to go her way when Richard, on an impulse, detained her by inquiring —

"Did you have an enjoyable supper? You and your caller?"

Again a strange look crossed her face. She seemed taken aback by his question, and for a moment she hesitated.

"Caller, sir?"

"Last evening. When I glanced in at the window, I could not help but observe that — "

"I am accustomed to go early to my bed, sir. No late callers, sir. For we haven't many visitors at the Hall at such an hour — saving yourself, sir — on account of the cats — "

Then she stopped short and with a mumbled word of apology hurried off towards the gatehouse.

Hathaway, you are an insensitive clod. Can't you see the woman still is burdened by her loss?

Nevertheless a feeling had crept upon him that something was amiss here, although he was hard put to explain just what it was. It needed some thinking out, he decided, an exercise that would require, oh, several fresh pipes at least.

Abandoning his plan for a tour of the stables, he swung about and returned to the Hall for a bit of lunch and his afternoon's go at Sir Pharnaby.

THE FIFTH CHAPTER

The Doctor Advises

"**D**ELIGHTED to have you take luncheon with us."
The rhinoceros-like gentleman of a smiling aspect who welcomed my brother thus, was neither lord of the manor, nor was he a tenant there, but was, like Richard himself, a visitor. However his long association with the household, and his familiarity with the Hall and its environs, had engendered in him a certain pride of ownership which he inhabited like a comfortable suit.

It was Lady Martindale who introduced him.

"This is Dr. Bussey. He is my father's physician."

The doctor gave my brother's hand a vigorous squeeze, as if it were a clyster-bag.

"Ooh, that's nice! Dr. Bossy, more like," Sam Gander could be heard muttering. They were assembled in the rustic drawing-room of the Hall, the four of them — and Edgar, too — to await luncheon, which was to be laid on presently.

The doctor had arrived that hour in a covered sleigh. Owing to the incursion of the marsh devils and spotted lion, he had overnighted in Mac-Wallop land — the popular term for the manor occupied by her ladyship's odious wretch of a neighbor. The physician had been sent for yesterday by the neighbor — cram full of gout he was, the doctor reported — and after medicining him had left his patient this morning in tolerable comfort.

"Not in *too* much comfort, I trust," her ladyship remarked.

The two houses happened to share the same distinguished physician, and whereas the doctor had noted some improvement in the health of Mr. MacWallop, in the case of Mr. Samuel Gander he had made but little progress. Well, no progress — not to put too fine a point on it. In brief, the old man was incorrigible. All of the doctor's decrees had gone unheeded, all of his learned directives had been ignored.

"What right has yer to come round here a-tellin' folks what to do?" demanded Sam.

"My dear chap, I am your medical adviser," said the doctor.

"On the sniff again for yer fee, no doubt. Yer hard up for a guinea or somethin'?"

"Pay no attention to my father," Lady Martindale said calmly.

"In pursuance of my habit, your ladyship, I rarely do," the doctor smiled.

The doctor seemed always to be smiling, and had a kind of jolly swagger in his air; indeed at times his friendliness could be so overbearing one scarce could tolerate it. But unlike many of his brethren he was generally harmless, and so good-natured one found it hard to dislike him. He was remarkable in several other particulars as well: in the flowery red jungle of beard and whisker that dressed his countenance, in his crisp, blue gaze, and in the huge mustaches that he brushed upwards on either side like the tusks of a boar. Rhinoceros-like, however, was how my brother described him — which is to say, there was rather a lot of him. The doctor had that flushed, bloated, overfed look, which, combined with his poise of manner and easy self-confidence, is the hallmark of assured position.

"So how are you today?" the doctor inquired of his patient. "Have you sampled that bottle of fine rum I recommended to you?"

"It's a rum go finding *yer* here — don't like strangers about the place," retorted Sam.

"That is a rare attitude for a publican to take."

"I ain't a publican no longer. I've reformed meself. It's Lizzie looks after old Cuffley and the Gander now."

"My father is not a well man, Mr. Hathaway, as you know," her ladyship explained, "and Dr. Bussey has been attempting to rehabilitate him."

From his waistcoat the doctor plucked a shiny gold snuff-box and proffered it to my brother. "I see you've just done with your pipe. Might I offer you a pinch, sir?"

Richard, not a devotee, politely declined. After helping himself copiously, the physician turned again to Lady Martindale.

"We can't have your father not smoking. Has he not taken up his old churchwarden of late?" he inquired, with a grave brushing of his beard.

"He has shown not an atom of interest in it. He listens to none of your concerns, doctor."

"That fact lies at the bottom of all the trouble. At present your father's health is my chief concern, for a man who will take neither a dram nor a smoke is, I fear, already on a downward track. Like a flash flickering slowly away in the pan."

The doctor stood on the hearthrug, his elbow on the mantel and one easy boot on the fender, and pondered the enigma that was his patient. His lectures by now had a familiar ring to them, for they were the same he delivered regularly from one end of the year to the other. But the erstwhile publican had reformed himself.

"And here am I myself in such fine trim," the doctor mused, giving a brisk slap to his paunch. "There. Just look at that, sir. What do you think of it?"

"It's immense," Sam Gander observed.

"My dear fellow, you too might be a rosy picture of health, if only you would heed your physician's advice."

"Advice? Gammon, more like."

"Whisht, man. As one with considerable experience in such matters, I don't care a fleam for your 'gammon'. Stoutness is a sign of robust health — note the condition of your grandnephew Mr. Edgar there — and leanness of its opposite — of ill health, the mark of the consumptive. It follows therefore that anything tending to stoutness tends to good health. Thus the stouter the better."

"Humbug!" snorted Sam.

"My dear chap, if only you would regulate yourself properly. Your diet — absurd — your marching round the battlements — nonsensical — your eschewing tobacco — ludicrous — "

"Eh? What's that? Never chewed tobaccy in me life. 'Ere, what d'yer want to come sticking yer nose round here again for, eh?"

"My father has slackened his exercising not a jot," her ladyship reported. "Is there nothing we can do about it, doctor? I fear we shall discover him one morning face-down in the yard with a cracked head, after his fall from the wall-walk."

"My dear Gander, if you will persist in this athletic scheme of yours — a risky undertaking, in my opinion — can you not satisfy it simply by a march round the yard? Why must you be patrolling the battlements?" the doctor inquired.

"Can't see cats from the yard," said Sam.

"But it is so entirely unnecessary. As human beings we have no further need of exercise once we have achieved adulthood. The muscles, by then having attained their mature proportions, no longer require the spur of activity for their development. Rather, it becomes harmful to them. This is no matter for scholarly dispute. This is a fact, sir."

"A figo for yer facts! 'Ere, then — what d'yer think o' *this?*" rejoined

Sam, thrusting an exaggerated grimace into the face of the doctor and cackling.

"I am telling you the truth, man. In this enlightened age we must keep abreast of new learning. Indeed today one must learn or perish. Those who trade on ignorant superstition no longer have the whip hand of us — have no doubt of that. For doubt itself is a seed from which evil trees do grow. Doubt is foreign to my nature, and I should be wanting in my duty as your medical adviser should I — "

"What Dr. Bussey means is that you must mend your ways, Father," her ladyship said gently.

"My dear chap," the doctor continued, "to exert yourself further is to do yourself harm. You will exercise yourself into oblivion if you persist in these unhealthful activities. In my view you are within a stone's cast of it already. Anyone with a grain of understanding — "

"A fig for yer 'blivion. 'Ere, d'yer know how old I am? I'm seventy-seven, come St. Odo's Day," gloated Sam, with a lively show of his teeth — both of them.

"Seventy-seven? Nearer ninety, I should have thought," was the doctor's cheerful riposte.

"As you know, doctor, my father is something of a character. He is full of antics, and nonsensical notions of every sort. And he has become rather venturesome in his guarding of the wall-walk and battlements. But I have every confidence we shall persuade him to a safer course, in time. He shall not go wrong again," Lady Martindale assured him.

"I sincerely hope not. The time to forestall him is now, your ladyship, before he ruins his health — or his head."

"Bother yer head," retorted Sam.

"Now I look at him, he appears a touch more withered since last I saw him," the doctor noted, regarding his patient with a thoughtful scrutiny.

"But doctor — that was only three days ago," Lady Martindale pointed out.

The doctor clucked his tongue. "That long? Well, the days do pass very swiftly this time of year. My valued and respected friend," he intoned, addressing her father again, "what you need is rest. Utter — complete — rest. When I contemplate — "

"Go contemplate yerself," returned Sam. "I've reformed meself, yer see, and that's flat. Not a dram. Not a smoke. Not a pinch. And none o' yer mumbo-jumbo neither."

"Pa!" protested her ladyship.

"My dear chap, where is the fault in these? Not take a healthful dram? Not smoke? Not take snuff? Not enjoy these wholesome, harmless pleasures of life? Would you eschew buttered scones — clotted cream — a prime sirloin?" was the doctor's jollying reply.

"The old feller prefers his gruel," noted Edgar.

"Thin gruel may suffice now and again, but as a steady diet? It's an old and well-authenticated tradition that stronger measures — namely the good things of larder and cellar, and their thriving, healthful influences — are essential to support the vital forces; otherwise a man should be no more than a shapeless jelly. Why, I'd sooner live in hell as eat porridge every day of my life."

"Suit yerself — I ain't stoppin' yer," shrugged Sam.

His adviser fetched a long sigh. *This is the product of a confused brain,* he reflected. His blue eyes narrowed in contemplation of his patient, whose rejection of physicianly authority was as unnatural as it was unwise.

"But Mr. Gander — bogberry juice? Vegetable marrows? Pumpkin seed? Eel oil? This is not sustenance for civilized men. What did such a diet avail our primitive forebears? Nothing. It wasn't till the ancients of Egypt undertook the brewing of beer that civilization began its rapid advance. Oh, it's common knowledge. And what of our own ancestors in Old Britain? What of mead? What of ale? For they are as indispensable for the smooth operation of the sinews and the digestive organs, and flow of the lifeblood, as is oil to a rusty lock. And there are the medicinal benefits to consider, the value of ardent spirits, for example, in remedying *tremor cordis* and fits of the spleen. A fat lot of use bog onions and calvesfoot jelly are in such circumstances." Abruptly the doctor paused in his speech and stroked his beard. "Now it occurs to me, I rather think I'd like a brandy-and-water. For I'm as dry as an autumn leaf . . ."

The esteemed physician was the only one of the company so afflicted, and when his tumbler was brought to him he raised it in pledge to his patient.

"I drink your health sir," he smiled, taking a long pull.

"'Ere, whose house is this, yers or mine?" demanded Sam, irritably.

"Tosh, man, it's neither. Haigh Hall is the property of her ladyship — your daughter," the doctor chuckled.

The old man looked first at his physician, and then at Lady Martindale, and rubbed a grizzled cheek.

"That's grand," he muttered, "when a feller ain't the master in his own daughter's house."

"I see you don't like the idea. My dear chap," said Dr. Bussey, "you fascinate me no end. If you are so set in your course, then believe what you choose. If you wish to be a daft dog, by all means be one. I am only your medical adviser; I can only urge; I can't force my prescriptions on you. But I hold to my view. All this codswallop about fen lentils and eel oil — "

"Please, doctor — I'll not have that name spoken in my presence," Lady Martindale objected.

"That's codswallop, Auntie, not MacWallop," Edgar explained. "Codswallop is bunk."

"Is there a difference?" his aunt returned.

"You haven't a pint of Willoughby gray to hand, have you?" the doctor inquired. He had finished his brandy-and-water and was casting about for added relief from his dry state. It still wanted some minutes before lunch.

"In town, at the Goose and Gander, I believe, doctor. Treadwell, have we any gray ale in the house?" said Lady Martindale.

"We have not, your ladyship," the servant reported, "but I shall see that we are amply provisioned — within means."

Gray ales — of which Willoughby gray is a type specimen — are a speciality of the north of Fenshire. On occasion our Mr. Joliffe, the proprietor of the Mudlark, in Market Snailsby, has been known to stock a cask in his cellar. Fenshire grays are something of an acquired taste, and not so much in demand southwards of the wood, where our own nappy browns are the more favored.

"Jiminy! The doc'll be pickled before the bell sounds, the way he's guzzling it," Edgar whispered to my brother.

"I expect he enjoys his 'good things of larder and cellar'."

"Don't he! Well, having a bit o' grub ain't a partickler fault. But the doc does have a great idea of his own importance."

On a sudden the physician screwed up his nose and sniffed the air. "Is that custard I smell?" he asked. It was custard, as they soon discovered, for just then the bell sounded and they all went in to luncheon.

Afterwards Richard excused himself and returned to his work in the library. There he unearthed some further particulars concerning another of Sir Pharnaby's compositions, the glorious *Lingonshire Pastorale*. Other missives disclosed some items of interest regarding the composer's private life. Late in the afternoon, his day's researches done, he went upstairs to dress for dinner. Glancing out of the lattice, with the interminable fog still thick in the courtyard air, he fell to wondering once more about the bump in the night.

He opened the window and had another peer upwards at the ghostly line of battlements, and for the first time noticed something curious — that a patch of snow had become dislodged from the roof-edge. Had there been someone mucking about up there? Sam Gander on his sentry's walk, perhaps? Or had the snow been trampled on during the night, and only later, in the daytime, had it fallen loose? Had it been by the foot of man, or had it been the grip of a teratorn's claws that had disturbed it?

It had been no illusion, no phantom of his imagination. Something had indeed trodden on the leads above his room, but its identity remained a mystery.

That night after dinner he stayed up late, listening for another thump. It was after eleven when sleep finally overcame him, and he retired to his bed, having heard nothing out of the usual.

Gecks and Gander

A s soon as daylight came, Richard hurried downstairs to the yard to have a look at the roof-edge and battlements above his window. The air was cloaked in the same chilly mist, through which a few flakes now were descending, slowly and steadily, over the whitened way. From all that he could discern, given these conditions, it appeared that the snow had filled in along the roof-edge in the night, for no longer was there any gap to be seen there.

He stood under the clumber pine, its long limbs reaching into the fog, and thought awhile. What had he expected to see? Likely just what he had seen — nothing. It had been an impulse, a sudden flash upon awakening, but it had yielded no result. Perhaps it was better that it had not done. Yet still there was no solution to the bump in the night.

Moments later Dan Hedges appeared with Toddy at his heels, tramping along in the direction of the stables. Richard smiled at them, and the game little terrier, his beard flecked with snow, offered a rousing yelp as he trotted past.

Tea had been laid in the library when Richard arrived to take up his copying. Meanwhile, in another part of the Hall, in Lady Martindale's sewing-room, mistress and maid were sitting down to her ladyship's working table, to measure a length of worsted for a new hearthrug. Sewing was one of her ladyship's favorite activities, young Gwenda acting as her assistant and companion. As they are employed there, a conversation is struck up between them, in which the subject of the late, lamented mariner, Owen Aberdovey, figures prominently. Despite the worsted the discussion soon has their entire attention, and as it progresses it becomes clear that Gwenda Goodwick had been rather sweet on the lodgekeeper-woman's son.

And how did my brother in the library learn of this conversation, you ask? That you shall discover presently. Suffice it for the moment that the discussion had some bearing on the mysteries that were starting to accrue.

"Come closer — my sight is so short these days," her ladyship invites her maid, then adjusts her spectacles as she surveys the work before them. But other topics intervene to delay the enterprise.

"Do you know how pretty you are, child?" her ladyship asks, smiling on the girl with a motherly eye.

"No, milady," answers the maid, after a pause, and a blush.

"Such pretty golden hair, and such pretty curls. It is a pleasure to have you near me."

"Oh, milady — "

The girl turns dewy eyes — my brother's words — upon her mistress, with a steady and submissive attention.

"Tell me, dear — I shall be brief — was there not talk of an engagement — at the very least of an attachment — between yourself and that excellent young man?" says her ladyship.

Another pause, another blush. The maid glances demurely aside. "I — I expect so, milady."

"Young Owen went off to mix with the world, when he should never have stirred from home. But he wished to be like his father, you see — he yearned for the adventure of it. I can't say that I blame him all that much. I knew his father well. Years ago Morgan Aberdovey was a coracle man for my late husband, but he found the marshways too confining. Even then he was dreaming of the sea; even then he was yearning for that adventure he sought. It was the baronet who arranged it for him, that he might learn the ways of the deep. It was through an acquaintance of my husband's, a ship's master called Clipperton. Did you know that?"

"I didn't know, milady."

"Lot you don't know, dear. Then, after a number of years aboard ship, Morgan Aberdovey returned home to the marshes. He had had enough of adventuring, he said, and was content to spend his last days — they were too few, as it turned out — at the Hall as our lodgekeeper. I believe it was his death that awoke in Owen a desire some day to emulate his father's experiences in foreign parts. And so he too went down to the sea."

"Owen in foreign parts? But it was only Nantle, milady. It wasn't foreign."

"It was not Fenshire, and anything not Fenshire is foreign," returns her ladyship, stiffly.

"Yes, milady. But it was his destiny, milady. He was forever speaking of his destiny."

"And now we all of us wish it had not been so, for destiny, child, often is a cruel mistress. But we must console ourselves with our knowledge of

the high regard and affection in which the young man was held by everyone concerned."

Her maid's pretty face looks brightly up. "God bless you for your kind
opinion of him, milady."

They then talked awhile of former times, and former joys.

"Poor child, I wish you to be happy," says her ladyship, with a sympathetic eye.

"But I am happy, milady."

"A period of mourning is only proper. It shows a most generous devotion, and does you credit, my dear. My faithful little friend! As dink as a
daisy, and as green as a leek. But time passes, and someone must put your
case for you, Gwenda Goodwick. Now, then," says her ladyship, coshering
her up in her best motherly fashion, "I am very much deceived if our own
Dan Hedges does not himself cherish hopes in your direction. Such an amiable young man! Confide in me, my dear — what are your feelings for Dan
Hedges?"

The maid returns her a startled look. "Dan Hedges? Oh, milady — "

"When all is reckoned up, it must count as a worthy match. Don't you
agree?"

"I think he likes me a little. But there are Ridingham girls aplenty on
the catch for him, I'm sure, milady — "

"I promised your aunt I should look out for you, and look out for you
I shall. I feel there is a keen bond of sympathy between us, is there not,
dear?"

"Oh, yes, milady — "

"To a very remarkable degree. So much so, in fact, that even now I can
guess what you are thinking."

"Can you, milady?" says Gwenda, softly.

"You are young and true, and I believe you are attached to me. And I
am much attached to you."

"Yes, milady."

"And so the happy thought occurred to me, that an attachment of another sort might be just the thing to take your mind from its late distress,
and so that these sad musings over Owen might not weigh upon you so
heavily."

"But they do not weigh, milady," Gwenda tells her.

A faint cloud settles over her ladyship's brow.

"Oh? Do not weigh? My word, I had not expected this. Explain to me
what you mean, dear."

But an answer seems to have eluded her maid, who shrugs up her little shoulders in proof of it. Her ladyship is disappointed to learn that such is the case.

"Might I inquire then, child, have you already formed a fresh attachment — and so soon? For I promised your aunt — "

"Oh, no, milady — upon my word not — " protests Gwenda, her eyes straying to the worsted, to the floor, to the window — anywhere, indeed, but to her ladyship.

"I see."

Then a ray of understanding shines through the fog — it is a metaphorical fog, not that smothering the window — and Lady Martindale rises a little in her chair, as if buoyed up by the revelation.

"Indeed I *do* see," she says, nodding her head slowly.

"You do, milady?" returns Gwenda, with some apprehension.

"Naturally. For the very same was I, after the baronet's passing. Oh, I know your mind as well as I know my own. In this we are as alike as two pins, you and I."

"Milady?"

"The future looms dull and gray without him. And so did it for me, as regards my late husband. Do you know, many were the evenings he would tell me all the little events of his day . . ." recalls her ladyship, a sudden smile breaking through her reflections. Her eyes are grown wistful and she sits silent and still for a time, absorbed in her memories of Sir Pedr. "But then, after awhile — after the dread event, when he ceases to figure in your daily affairs — when your thoughts of him become lost in the hum and press of life — only then does it dawn that truly he has left you forever. Grieving is only natural, dear — *but one must not succumb to grief*. Do you perceive the distinction? Of course you do. You'll not have these sad musings over Owen weigh upon you — of course you shan't. Not a whimper, my brave-hearted little one! It shows your strength of character. In life we must bear our sorrows as best we can, each in his own way, and soldier on with fortitude and grace. We must never forget them — *never* — but in so doing we must not forget ourselves. For the alternative is insupportable."

While speaking Lady Martindale has fallen into a kind of brown study, leaving Gwenda at rather a loss; although truth to tell she does grasp her ladyship's meaning. At the same time it has reminded her of another matter, one that has puzzled her for some time, concerning the late baronet; and so, unable to help herself, she leans over the worsted and in a hushed tone inquires —

"What then of the family story, milady?"

Her ladyship's brow wrinkles again, and she casts a dubious eye at her minion. "Family story? Don't be silly, child. There is no family story."

"The legend of the Hall, milady. The curse. For Mrs. Deadhouse, the undertaker's wife, told me once there had been a spell cast, centuries ago, and Madge Mattock too, and that it was regards a judge named Martindale, and all the Martindales who were to come, and that Sir Pedr and then Mr. Edgar would be — "

Directly her mistress checks her with a gesture, although not in anger. The brown study has vanished and her ladyship is herself once more.

"Nonsense! We'll have no talk of family stories. There is no possibility of a curse, as you call it, affecting my nephew. And despite what you may have heard it has no bearing on my husband's death. In former times evil auguries did hang about the Hall, as they will do about most any old country house. Silly child — all sorts of rumors will prevail in a town like Ridingham, for foolish folk always will be talking. All you need in proof is to hear Mr. Gecks on the subject."

"And what of Mr. Gecks, milady?" inquires Gwenda, with a sudden lift of her brows, her large, light eyes filled with a musing interest.

It is her ladyship's turn to present a startled face.

"My lawyer? Whatever do you mean, child? Pray explain yourself," she commands.

"I'm sure I don't know, milady," answers the maid, blushing into the very whites of her eyes.

"I see how it is," returns her mistress, with a knowing nod. "More talk. Who is it this time? Mrs. Deadhouse? Madge Mattock? Mrs. Flitch?"

Gwenda, smothering a chuckle, informs her — "Pretty much everyone, milady."

"Sauce!" rejoins her mistress.

Again her ladyship rises a little in her seat, as though the cushion were inflating, and stares at her maid. In truth it was common knowledge at the Hall, and in Ridingham generally, that for years Mr. Gecks had harbored an unwavering affection for Lady Martindale, ever since she had been pert little Lizzie Gander, the innkeeper's daughter. For in those distant, long-ago days young Mr. Everson Gecks had been a suitor — not in the legal sense, but rather a suitor for her hand. And, in common with many another aspirant, he had lost out to Sir Pedr, the local grandee. Indeed how could a poor country lawyer have hoped to triumph over a Martindale of the Hall?

Since then Mr. Gecks, unmarried, had pined in silence and alone for his imagined Gecks and Gander, the union of souls that was never to be. And though his unchanging regard for her had endured, her ladyship — his little Lizzie of the Gander — would have none of it, having pledged her life to the memory of her husband. For she never would forget.

There was no doubt but that Mr. Gecks was an excellent man, a worthy man — descriptions that had fallen from her ladyship's own lips. And he still admired her, occasionally forgetting himself and calling her Lizzie, as he had done so yesterday at breakfast.

"There is hardly a point of similarity between them. He is not so handsome as was the baronet, of course, and never will be. But his temperament is genial, and nothing of an unsavory character ever has attached to him. And these are not inconsequential in a country lawyer. But his regard is a matter of perfect indifference to me." Such was the claim of her ladyship.

Thus Mr. Gecks — a solid, steady man, who must content himself with serving as her ladyship's legal and professional adviser, and trusty friend of long standing.

"Fortune has dealt us each a bitter blow," her ladyship continues, taking Gwenda's hand in hers. "But we live and learn. Such is the fruit of experience. And now my poor father, broken in health — "

Her maid is mystified. "Broken? Mr. Gander? But he's so full of spirits, milady, so lively and spry, and marches with such energy upon the wallwalk — "

"I fear there is but scant hope for him, dear. You'll remember what the doctor said. A man who neither smokes nor drinks, who eats porridge and drinks bogberry juice, and will insist upon exercising himself into oblivion, cannot be long for this world."

"Oh, no, milady!"

Her mistress, nodding her head, sighs deeply. "I fear some melancholy influence has come over me today. But what is done is done, and can't be undone."

Her ladyship does not seem disposed to further conversation and is silent for a time, her fingers playing absently with the worsted. Then on a sudden she rises and goes to the window. "It was not so dismal-looking yesterday, I don't believe . . ." But as is usual for her, the cloud soon passes. All in a moment she is recalled from her reverie and, drawing herself up, smiles upon Gwenda with motherly affection.

"We must trim you up a new bonnet, child — once we have done with the worsted."

"Yes, milady."

Then she sits down again to her work, chatting the while upon indifferent subjects and taking comfort in the attentions of her maid.

Presently a knock is heard at the door. It is the housemaid, Elzie Peek, neatly attired in her white cap and apron, come to stir up the fire a little. As well it is eavesdropper Elzie — she who for the past quarter of an hour has been standing outside the door, giving secret ear to the conversation. For Elzie — dimpled, curtseying little Elzie — is one of those foolish gossips to whom Lady Martindale had made special reference.

So there you have it. My brother had gotten up to fill his pipe, and had just resumed his seat when Elzie arrived to freshen the tea-things. In the course of her duties she shared with him certain of the particulars she had gleaned — like Gwenda, she scarce could help herself — and was surprised to discover that Richard knew nothing of Mr. Gecks's long and faithful regard for her ladyship.

But my brother had been much struck with another subject the housemaid had touched upon — that of the family story, or the legend, or curse, or whatever the dash it was, that involved a Martindale who had been a judge, and of "evil auguries" that had hung about the Hall, and the notion that something sinister might have transpired in connection with Sir Pedr's death.

He heard the maid's revelations with attention and surprise, even while struggling with himself whether it were gentlemanly or no to have listened. Plainly the subject was a close secret, one which Lady Martindale was hesitant to speak of it. In fact she did not care to have anyone speak of it, so it seemed.

And what had the matter to do with Edgar?

After the maid had withdrawn, Richard spent some minutes sipping his tea and arranging his materials before him — a delaying tactic. At intervals throughout the afternoon, while at his work, he found himself pausing now and again as his thoughts strayed from his own subject, that of Sir Pharnaby and his music, to that of Sir Pedr Martindale and the family legend that was not to be spoken of. At one point he rose and started pacing the library floor, his brow furrowed and his thumbs hooked in the armholes of his waistcoat.

How much store to set by the maid's account, he asked himself? And more importantly perhaps, what concern was it of his?

What then of the bump in the night — the footsteps on the leads — the snow at the roof-edge over his casement-window — the shadow in the library — the Welsh stovepipe hat that had tumbled from the head of Sir Padrig, he who had been a judge? What of the lurking thing couched in the Scotch firs?

Perhaps the matter was of more interest to him than he knew.

Getting the Boot

"T RADESMEN in the back-parlor to see you, sir."

The announcement cast a little shadow of anxiety over Edgar's face.

"Bother the luck! Of what sort are they today, Treadwell?" he asked.

"Woolsack — tailor, sir. Pinchbeck — bootmaker, sir. Derby — hatter. Sweeting — confectioner. Dousterweed — tobacconist. Casken — vintner, sir."

"Is that the lot?"

"Six *in toto,* driven out in a sleigh, yes, sir. To see you 'on a matter of particular urgency', as I have been informed."

"Oh, dear."

Pained surprise showed in Edgar's eyes, and he fingered his collar uneasily. He saw the turn which matters had taken, and he did not like it. He had been anticipating it for some while, however, and could no more postpone it now than he could adjourn an eclipse.

"Oh, dear," he said again. "Leagued together and come from town in full force, have they? And with cats about! They must be desperate parties to be kicking up a stink over trifles with cats about."

"Grim and ferocious in the extreme, I should think, sir," Treadwell reported.

"Yes, these shopkeepers usually are. And I haven't so much as tuppence for 'em. Where is my aunt? Have you seen her this A.M.? Do you think she'll advance me tuppence?"

"Her ladyship is having another lie-in this morning, as you know, sir. So far as the tradesmen are concerned, I should think they'll be looking for more than tuppence. Particularly as they were refused admittance the last time."

The youth's face fell. "Jiminy! I expect you're right there. I'd forgotten about that," he said, dabbing at his brow with a handkerchief.

"But her ladyship is inclined so to do — to advance you tuppence — as I have observed," Treadwell added.

"Yes, she is rather fond of me, ain't she? Good old Auntie — she dotes on me, I think. Can't imagine why. Perhaps for no other end but that I'm her nephew. Still, one shouldn't — "

"What's this about tradesmen, Edgar?" Richard asked.

He and the youth had lingered awhile over their breakfast. It had been a quiet affair, the two of them being the only diners this morning. Lady Martindale was indisposed; meanwhile her father, an early riser, had taken his oatmeal and bogberry juice in the kitchen, long before the dawn had shown in the east, then had sallied forth to patrol the wall-walk.

With a feeble grin Edgar offered some slight excuse that made his predicament only too clear to Richard, for he too had been an undergraduate once. Card-parties, wines, suppers, idle riots of every kind — it was an old story. In short, Edgar had been spending rather more money than his aunt had allowed him, not only in college but there too at the Hall. His aunt who doted on him, she was his entire bread and butter, as it turned out. In college his duns already had found him out; now it was the shopkeepers of Ridingham who were baying at his heels.

"Why can't they let a sleeping dog be?" he protested. "Habitual grumblers these tradesmen are, the lot of 'em. At times a feller is rather hard up for ready dibs, and then here's another batch of their confounded reminders turns up at his door. Sport your oak — mantle the casements — it's all the same; their wretched little bills *will* find their way to a man's rooms. And now in Ridingham, too! I tell you, sir, there's no help for it."

"Life is not all pudding and pie," Richard reminded him gently.

"What good is rustication if a gent will be hounded by creditors in the very halls of his ancestral seat?"

"It's dashed inconvenient, I expect."

"Well, I like that. One hasn't a bolt-hole even down here in the provinces. It's abominable that a chap should be expected to pay these little accounts before he's taken his degree. It's — it's a gross breach of form, it is. But you know what these shopkeepers are, always aiming to bully it over a poor, struggling trog like Edgar Harbottle."

"This may pertain to Salthead tradesmen and their credit system, where often a fellow may cash up only after he's graduated. But why should the tradesmen of Ridingham be so bound?" Richard asked, reasonably enough.

"That's their lookout, if they haven't the goodness to observe a proper interval. It's every gent for himself, and deuce take the hindmost! These fellers in the back-parlor are bent on mischief, I dare say; well, I ain't a stranger to mischief myself," Edgar hinted.

"You'd better be careful what you tell them. Likely they know every dodge in the book."

As Richard discovered, however, tradesmen and duns were not the only specters haunting the dreams of Edgar. There were other terrors as well — the feared Proctor and his bulldogs, and the Vice-Chancellor, and last, but hardly least, the Master of his college, the tall, stern-faced don who had imposed the rustication.

In point of fact Edgar's temporary exile from Saltonia had little relation to his studies, and more to do with some candle-smoke cartoons that had appeared on the walls of his college staircase, in which had been depicted a rogues' gallery of irascible old dons and other unpopular characters, in unflattering poses, and spouting a host of libelous sayings.

"Come out of there!" the Proctor had thundered, when chancing upon the renegade artist at his work upon the stairs.

As a result Edgar had been forced to apologize to the unpopular characters, before taking the rustication for a twelvemonth. His ears still rang with the sound of that voice: the voice of the dreaded Proctor, the chief disciplinary officer in college and terror of University evildoers. Indeed just the thought of the Proctor and his bulldogs was enough to drain the marrow from the bones of many a stalwart undergraduate, both trog and hoplite.

"You don't know these bullers of today, sir. And the Proctor was most insistent, as were the V.C., and Dr. Creake, our Master. It may have been otherwise in your time, sir, ages agone," Edgar continued, "but they're the most awful old birds nowadays, these dons and their henchmen. They're the teratorns of academical life. 'Pon my word, sir, a regular gent hasn't a chance."

"'My time' wasn't all *that* long ago," Richard informed him mildly, "although we called them bulldogs — the Proctor's 'henchmen', as you say — and together they were a formidable lot, to be sure. But what of your tutors? Did they not take your part?"

"Those musty old things? Nary a word. I don't think they much fancied their portraits on the wall."

"Ah."

"I tell you, sir, what a feller is obliged to endure for the sake of a B.A.! Getting up his Greek particles — construing hundreds of lines of Euripides, Livy, Homer — turning a column of newspaper into Latin, and vice versa.

And then too I'll be going up for smalls next term — that is, once I'm resident again," Edgar complained, shaking his head in anticipation of the trials that awaited him.

In college, getting up one's Greek or Latin was difficult enough; for Edgar just getting up — at six o'clock in the A.M., a most unholy hour — had been a trial too. And to cap it all he was in a fright about his smalls — his responsions, or the "little-go" examination, which all second-year men are required to pass before they may continue. As Richard remembered it, a month or two of reading in the classics and a little algebra was all he had needed for his smalls. For Edgar the prospect evidently was more daunting. Richard did what he could to reassure him, but from the youth's perspective he was staring into the face of certain ruin. For once the term of his rustication had been served, a term of the scholarly kind awaited, if only for the brief interval ere he should be upended by the little-go.

"Every man should try to do honor to his college," Richard reminded him, "and in the case of the little-go and your reading, I know you won't disappoint your aunt."

"Jiminy, there's the heart of it, sir," Edgar lamented. "She's a regular trump, is Auntie, and I don't mean to disappoint her. I'll be reading like a house afire, of that you can be sure. And now these debts! Whenever I'm hard up for a little cash, I give her a gentlemanly hint of it and she tips me. But these bills of mine have grown out of all proportion. 'Pon my word, some frightful specter must be following at my side, for never a gent had such ill-timed luck. I've no governor to see to them, only my aunt — and I her heir!"

"Goodness, is that a fact?"

"At least I believe I'm her heir. Gecks is the only other besides Auntie who knows for certain, and neither of them ever has said. She and my uncle had no children, so as her nephew I'm her nearest relation; but strictly speaking I ain't a Martindale myself. However I expect the Hall must pass to me. Well," he sighed — having done some thinking as regards the tradesmen and how best to jockey them, but with little result — "I expect there's nothing else for it, now that the Assyrians are bearing down," and with a sort of groan he heaved himself to his feet. "'Be courageous, and be fortunate.' It's the Martindale motto, as inscribed on the family arms — in Latin, naturally. No such good fortune today."

"Would you care for a second to attend you?" Richard offered.

With a half-hearted smile the youth thanked him but declined. His face had gone a sickly gray, as he reached into his store of learning and plucked forth this morsel of inspiration — "'They whom the gods love die young.' Anaximander."

Richard shook his head gently. "Menander," he corrected.

"Anaximander, ain't it?"

"Anaximander was a medieval chronicler of the weird and the occult."

"Are you certain of that?"

"Absolutely."

"Jiminy," muttered the youth. Then screwing his courage up he commenced his lonely trek to the back-parlor, his heels beating their drum of doom upon the hardwood boards.

Richard, despite Edgar's refusal of aid, trailed after the lad at a discreet distance. He was curious to know how he meant to shift the tradesmen, and thought it wise to be on hand should matters go awry. They had taken no more than a dozen steps, however, when Edgar suddenly halted, lifted up his head, and snapped his fingers.

"Eureka!" Richard heard him exclaim. (Here was sure evidence of a classical education.)

The youth sprang into instant action. In the library he reached down a well-thumbed Bible from a shelf. He then proceeded to the scullery and, sticking his head under the pump, gave his hair a generous soaking. Next he took a dishcloth and flung it round his neck, stowed his Bible piously under his arm, and with a cautious step approached the parlor-door. Softly he opened it a crack, and peeped inside. There he saw the tradesmen stalking restlessly to and fro, to and fro, all too keen apparently to be about the business that had brought them to the Hall. Edgar shrank back unperceived; then, after a final mustering of his nerve, he pushed open the door and in solemn state glided into the room.

His placid gaze swept the visitors. A fine lot, these Assyrians — stern countenances, nearly every one, and all tremendously interested to learn if their little bills were to be settled today.

"Might we have the favor of a moment's interview? We ask your indulgence for the intrusion, but this matter has been brought to a crisis," they burst out in an eager clamor.

But it availed them not. Edgar, pointing to his ears and his soggy head, explained —

"Sorry, gents, but my hearing's a trifle thick this A.M.. I've just this instant left my shower-bath, and the old auricles are stoppered like a couple o' bung-holes. You simply must excuse me. I was on my way to the library for my morning's meditations — I'm going in for the Church, you know.

So you'll need to speak up, gents, as I can't hear a deuced thing you're saying."

The Assyrians, who hardly had expected this, cleared their voices and paused awhile to debate the matter amongst themselves, in a grumbling undertone, before stepping forward to advance their claims.

Edgar listened attentively, his face expressionless, until the last man — it happened to be Dousterweed, the tobacconist — had had his say; then, smiling apologetically, he pointed again to his ears to indicate that he had not understood.

"You must speak a little louder, please."

The shopkeepers emitted involuntary noises of pain; indignant utterances streamed from their lips.

"All — we — want — is — the — money — owed — us," enunciated the tailor, Woolsack, in a heightened key.

"Eh?" returned Edgar, shaking his head.

"Our bills are months overdue!" spluttered Derby, the hatter, through his wiry brush of a black mustache.

"No, no, you musn't disturb my aunt," Edgar cautioned him. "It's really much too early in the A.M."

"We wouldn't think of disturbing her ladyship!" cried Dousterweed, a short, broadish man, whose chin ran down thickly into his neck.

"If only you could pay *something* on account, sir," entreated Casken, the vintner, "for we have supplied you with good store!"

"Eh? Well, you must take it into account then, just as you say. My aunt can't possibly see you now."

"But Mr. Harbottle — " spoke up Pinchbeck the bootmaker, a little old man with pensive eyes and a kindly, cultured face.

"It's a hateful business, sir!" declared Sweeting, the confectioner.

"Say, what is this? If you've come to cadge . . ." Edgar warned them, with a conspicuous show of his Bible.

More protestations, more indignant fumings.

"This situation is quite beyond my experience," said Edgar. "While I've a nodding acquaintance with these little bills of my aunt's, I think, so far as memory serves — "

Straightway their gabbling ceased and the tradesmen stared at him with incredulous eyes.

"Your aunt's bills?" they exclaimed in surprise. "But these are *your* bills, sir."

One of them produced a sheaf of accounts and thrust them under Edgar's nose. "Are these not your signatures, sir," he demanded, a note of ir-ritation in his voice — "for my clerk reports that they are."

Edgar scrutinized the papers a moment. As recognition dawned a smile slowly overspread his lips.

"'Pon my word — remember now. Well, naturally I was signing for my aunt."

"For men's garters, sir?" queried the tailor, whose papers they were.

Red-faced, the youth retired a step. His jowls sagged. Bathed in a cold moisture — one that owed little to his ducking under the scullery-pump — he plowed his hair back with spread fingers. "There's a good joke," he mut-tered. He swallowed uncomfortably. "Ah — right — well — "

The tradesmen awaited his response with a lively interest.

"Jiminy," he breathed, casting round him for an avenue of escape.

"And what of these cigars? Some of the finest in my stock!" the tobac-conist inquired, shoving the bills at him.

"And these gentlemen's hats? Felt and beaver of the smartest fashion?" dittoed Derby.

"And these case-bottles of porter?" chimed in the vintner.

"And these trouserings, sir, of a violent plaid — all the rage among the young college men — and these neckties of Salthead blue? By your own ad-mission your aunt has purchased above a dozen articles for which she has no conceivable use. You must pay us, sir," the tailor demanded ominously, "or we shall be forced to take steps."

"Aye. Cough up," warned Dousterweed, "or we'll set the law on you."

"Gifts," Edgar blurted out — "gifts for members of the family. My aunt as you know has a most generous disposition. Always doing for others, she is. Sorry — here, would you be so kind?" The tailor, Woolsack, frowned as the Bible was thrust upon him, while the young divinity student went through an elaborate show of opening his two ears which were *not* plug-ged, for the benefit of his inquisitors. "There — that's better. I'll thank you now to return the book, for I've still my meditations this morning — a lit-tle Greek Testament, and a sprinkling of Psalms and Leviticus." His head was high, and regarding his adversaries with some dignity he continued — "My aunt is always thinking of others, as I've said, and as she don't get to town much she has me look out these little presents for her now and again. But I should hate to disturb her over trifles; I haven't the heart for it. She ain't had a wink o' sleep these two nights — the MacWallop business, you know. Do you gents know MacWallop?"

Aye, the shopkeepers nodded, they knew Mr. MacWallop, and only too well; it was a subject upon which town and Hall were in complete accord. And so they paused awhile to consider, stroking their chins and murmuring to one another in sober convocation. Edgar held his breath, making no outward show of his unease but projecting an air of confidence as best he was able. If by some miracle of chance the Assyrians should believe his story . . .

Be courageous, and be fortunate.

"We take your point, sir," the tailor announced at length, "and as we've said, we've no wish to disturb her ladyship this morning — the MacWallop business — "

"Dear me, no," Edgar cheerfully agreed. "Now I must see if something can't be arranged, once my aunt is in a favorable humor. The doc was with her the entire evening. These demands of yours, it seems to me, are just, and I'm sure she'll do the necessary to satisfy 'em."

"This puts the thing in a different light," said Woolsack — mollified, if only for a time.

"Naturally it does."

"Her ladyship has a name for honesty and fair dealing, as did his lordship. We will call again this day week — "

"Do — there's a good chap," Edgar nodded, in a tone of friendly commiseration, "and I'll relay the whole of the business to my aunt. There — there's my hand on't."

"We'll be expecting more than your hand, sir, this day week," said the vintner, Casken, a big, burly man of some fifty odd.

"Never word escaped the lips of Edgar Harbottle that his hand was not prepared to guarantee. In the meantime I wish you a good day. There, you have received your *nunc dimittis* — your leave to depart."

The tradesmen were seen scratching their heads over the Latin, but having chosen to shoulder their complaints for the time being — a week's time to be exact — they went their way.

Much relieved, Edgar laid by his dishcloth and his Bible and sank into a chair. Exhausted, but blessed with the mental elasticity of youth, he appeared little concerned what might transpire that day week when the shopkeepers returned.

It was then he noticed Richard standing in the passage.

"What a bit of luck. I dare say I humbugged 'em rather well. The mercantile parties were most agreeable — deuce take 'em!" he rejoiced, albeit wearily.

"To a point. But won't your aunt be cross with you?" Richard asked.

"I'll square it with her — another gentlemanly hint. She dotes on me, you know."

"Or used to," was my brother's thought.

"And then next week they can talk to the money, and I'll be home and dry."

In the afternoon it started snowing again. The fall had just commenced when Mr. Gecks arrived, to give an account of his interview with Mr. Mac-Wallop. He was shown to the drawing-room, where he found Richard and Edgar warming themselves at the fire. Presently Lady Martindale appeared, and after a little deliberation the attorney undertook his narrative — with some hesitation, Richard thought.

It was in reply to the letter he had delivered, that was supposed to have taken the snap out of her ladyship's ill-humored neighbor. But he seemed reluctant to begin, as if he had not the stomach to impart to her ladyship the full enormity of the wretch's response.

"Well? Do you have an answer from that termite?" she demanded.

"I've got it, chief," he nodded glumly.

Meanwhile Toddy had trotted in with an old boot in his jaws, and having settled down at the fire had been gnawing at it contentedly. The others paid him little notice, assuming the object to be one of the terrier's old chewing-shoes.

Dan Hedges then was announced (Mr. Gecks seemed glad of the interruption), and reported to her ladyship there had been no fresh traces of the cats today, either marsh devils or spotted lion. The news was welcome, and received with considerable joy. Less happily, he went on, Toddy somehow had found his way outside the curtain-wall, unaccompanied, and Dan, anticipating the worst, had gone in search of him. When discovered the terrier had been high-stepping it through the drifts with a moldy boot in his teeth.

"I've no notion where he can have found it, m'lady."

Seeing his trusty attendant on the hearthrug Dan went immediately to him, and as he knelt beside him his curiosity became aroused.

"Here, Toddy — what's that you have there?"

It is none of your concern answered the terrier, by his expression if not in so many words. For no longer was he chewing on the moldy boot, but on the knuckle of bone that had spilled out of it.

Calmly Dan removed the boot from him. Toddy, absorbed in his recreation, followed the actions of his master from the corners of his bright eyes.

Upon a nearer inspection of the boot, Dan, rising, caught his breath in surprise.

"Lord bless me," he exclaimed, falling back a pace.

"What is that delightful odor, Hedges?" inquired her ladyship, with an offended sniff.

"It's a man's boot, m'lady."

"And why should you be staring at it in that way? Is there something we should know?"

"There seems to be a foot in it," Dan reported.

PART TWO

❧

THE FIRST CHAPTER
A Grave Development

"SAY — what is this?" Edgar protested.

For the space of a few seconds nobody moved. Then Mr. Gecks gave a low whistle, as a murmur of amazement ran round the room.

Lady Martindale's expression showed surprise and her lips parted in a momentary gasp, faintly audible to the others.

"Well, I'm jiggered," Richard said, gazing into the boot.

The object in Dan's hand had been tilted forward into the light, so that its interior might be better observed.

"This is evidence, to be sure," said Mr. Gecks.

"Ain't it!" Edgar yelped, the color draining from his face.

They stared as if spellbound, so grim, so ghastly the object of their concerted vision was. For the contents of the boot proved to be just as Dan had described.

"Bones, m'lady," he said.

"Of a certainty, chief," nodded Mr. Gecks — "for it reeks of mold and the grave."

Edgar, filled with horror at the sight, loosened his collar and swallowed hard. "Jiminy," he breathed.

At length his aunt, having collected herself, proclaimed it "An ignorant, silly joke. What else can it be? People are forever playing tricks and getting into mischief. Pig's knuckles, surely."

Her nephew, unable to take his eyes from the awful thing Toddy was massaging in his jaws, stuttered out —

"Are they a — a man's b-bones?"

"Who but a man would be wearing a boot?" said Mr. Gecks.

"Well, of course, there's that — oh, dear . . ."

"Like as not some silly fool placed them in the shoe," Lady Martindale suggested.

"I hardly think so, chief. However we shall need to put it to the proof.

We must consult Dr. Bussey," the attorney recommended. "He can testify whether these are human remains or no. But by the look of 'em — "

"Looks may deceive, Mr. Gecks," her ladyship reminded him.

"Granted. But in this instance . . ."

Her ladyship notwithstanding, they were something ill at ease as a result of the find. Dan Hedges meanwhile had been examining the boot with a cautious scrutiny.

"Half a moment, if you please, Dan," said Mr. Gecks, and together they fell to studying the object in the light of the window. Time and damp had corroded the boot, or more accurately the half-boot, which was of leather, and of a design and stitching long out of fashion. As for the store of grimy bones and brown earth it contained, and the single loose knuckle that had found its way into Toddy's jaws . . .

It was hard to imagine what other conclusion might be drawn, save for the obvious one.

"My ignorance of certain subjects is positively staggering," remarked Mr. Gecks, "but in this case I can find no other explanation. It seems as plain as a pack-saddle. Here is a man's boot, and here is a man's foot in it, as we all can see."

Edgar had been dabbing at his brow with his handkerchief, to stem the tide of moisture that had risen upon it. "Jiminy," he quavered — "where's the rest of him?"

They were unsure at first what to make of the discovery. The boot and bones certainly were evidence of a kind, as Mr. Gecks had stated. But evidence of what?

There existed no graveyard in the vicinity of the Hall, none that anybody knew of at any rate. As for the Martindales, for generations they had maintained a vault in the ancient parish church of St. Mary-in-the-Mews, in Ridingham. To whom then had this boot belonged, and this foot, and how had they come to be there? That is, in the place where Toddy had unearthed them — wherever that was?

Mr. Gecks regarded the terrier thoughtfully. The plucky fellow was a wonder at the fine arts of smelling and tracking, so had Dan often boasted. Could the dog lead them to the place, or had the falling snow spoiled it for the present by obliterating all trace of the site? If the latter, it well might be spring or summer ere it could be found where Toddy had done his digging. All that might be stated at present was that it lay beyond the curtain-wall.

But Mr. Gecks's lawyerly mind could not keep from fidgeting. Were the bones evidence of some forgotten burial from ages past, he wondered, or of one more recent? And if recent . . .

The attorney's voice held a note of concern. "I believe it is our duty to inform the constable. It is possible that a crime has been perpetrated."

"A crime? Ridiculous!" her ladyship said tartly.

"But chief — "

"I'll not hear of it. A crime on my own property, on the baronet's ancestral estates? Impossible. Put it out of your head, Mr. Gecks."

"Nevertheless, chief, we must exercise caution. Bear with me. I advise you — I urge you, most strongly — to send someone into Ridingham to apprize Dr. Bussey of this discovery, and to inform the constable. That is, of course, when the weather is a bit more accommodating. Now, is there anyone who has gone missing in the neighborhood of late? Anyone who might have worn a boot such as this?"

"No one wears such boots anymore," scoffed her ladyship, "indeed not for a century at least."

"Of my own knowledge only young Mr. Aberdovey of the Hall is missing, but he was lost at sea in the channel, off the coast at Nantle, which is many leagues distant."

"Owen never wore a thing like that," Edgar told him.

"There was the slodger, sir — Matthew Brimble by name — as was taken by the cats," spoke up Dan. "But this bean't a coracle man's boot. And then there was Gaffer Crankshaw, last year, as was thought drowned in the storms."

"And you don't believe this to be his foot?" the attorney asked.

"Not likely, sir. The gaffer were a biggish sort o' man."

"And there is no one else? Someone who went missing and never was found?"

But there was nobody that anyone could recall. The attorney scratched the back of his head and confessed that he too was at a loss.

"Still it would be wise to have Constable Pettiplace examine the boot. He may have knowledge of a disappearance of which we ourselves are ignorant."

"I beg your pardon? 'Timbers' Pettiplace, that great long noodle of a string bean? Knowledge? I very much doubt that," snorted her ladyship.

"Now, now, Lizzie. Of course we can't do anything just yet, given the state of the weather. Dan, you had best remove that object from Toddy. Then as soon as is practicable you and some of the men have a scout round the home fields and along the causeway. See if you can hunt up the spot where Toddy did his excavating. And see that you have your cutlasses to hand at all times."

Reassuring the terrier with low, crooning conversation, Dan gently eased the bone from his jaws. He dried it, then ran a finger over it curiously, feeling its shape, its ridges and hollows, and weighing it a little in his hand; that is until her ladyship, watching in abhorrence, ordered that the hateful thing be removed. Dan promptly obliged — out of sight, out of mind — and left the room with Toddy at his heels.

Some moments elapsed, until Lady Martindale, feeling that all by now should have recovered from the trauma of their discovery, invited Mr. Gecks to continue with his report concerning Mr. MacWallop.

"For we have no secrets at the Hall. Tell us what the dirty skunk said."

The attorney did not answer at first, still hesitating, it seemed, to relay the message.

"He did not look upon the interview with favor, chief," he explained.

Her ladyship's small black eyes challenged him.

"I should think he would not. But I expected no honey-talk. What did he say, Mr. Gecks?"

He looked at her for some seconds before responding.

"Well, here it is, chief. In his reply Mr. MacWallop, in his broad Scots, as near as I can render it, begs leave to inform you that — 'I'll no hae ma ain right o' way, nor ma gude name neither, trodden on by that fiddle-faced auld baggage as keepit the Hall'."

Her ladyship, following her adviser's example, regarded Mr. Gecks for some seconds before speaking.

"And he's another," she retorted with a sniff.

"Well, there you have the long and the short of it, chief."

"I scarcely can understand a word that man says. He might as well have dropped from another planet. Is he from another planet, I wonder?"

"Hardly. His ancestors came from John o' Groats, long before the sundering, and settled at Hooting Lazars."

"Hooting Lazars very well could be another planet. That man has said some very unjust things about me, Mr. Gecks."

"I agree his attitude is somewhat acrid. I sympathize with you, chief."

"Now I fear I shall need another cold compress on my head. Where is Gwenda?"

"And I'm afraid it means another appearance before the Justices. It was worth the effort, I believe, but MacWallop and his man are immovable."

"Was Wormwrath there?"

"Wormwrath was there, chief."

"And the piece of ground in dispute?"

"The right of way in Hatter's Close, by Eel Island. Mr. MacWallop has cleared it again of your fence, to establish a path into Ridingham for his wagons."

"Has he, just? Next he'll have me abandoning all right and claim to the property. Well, I don't give a whoop. Do you hear me, Mr. Gecks? *Not a whoop.* Powers above, I'll cut off his right of way — see if I don't. I shall have the law on him for slander," her ladyship vowed.

The attorney's face showed surprise. "Slander? That is a serious affair. In what way has he slandered you? What has he said now?"

"It is not what he has said, Mr. Gecks; it is what he is going to say after I've sorted him out."

"And what are *you* going to say? For as it is my duty to attend to your interests, I should advise against it — that is, whatever it is you are going to say."

"I shall tell him what I think of him — ungrateful wretch — I shall tell all of Ridingham what I think of him — if it does not know already — and how he has perjured himself times innumerable before the Bench in these repeated actions of his — the slippery little toad!"

The attorney, smiling, shook his head gently. "Then it is you who shall be brought up for slander, chief."

Her ladyship's response was a laugh — short and sarcastic, directed not at her lawyer but at the object of their mutual contempt.

Mr. Gecks lifted his chin in thought. "Still, we may win through in the end. For all of Ridingham knows MacWallop, and all of Ridingham knows your ladyship and the family. Our friend is at some disadvantage there."

"That's his hard luck."

"And deservedly so, I might add. And it is your own ground. Popular sentiment may be such as to sway the Court's view in our favor . . ."

"I am no fragile mite of a creature, Mr. Gecks. I was the wife of a baronet of the sundered realm, and in my youth did quell more rows in a taproom than many a doughty landlord. I dare say I can match our Mr. Phergus MacWallop point for point." With her lips set in a firm line she stared into space, as though gazing upon the courtroom on the Sessions day and envisioning her triumph before the Bench. Then, satisfied, she screwed her oculars up and snorted — "He'll look a right fool after I've done with him. It's over my spit he'll go! Have no doubt of that, Mr. Gecks."

"Oh, I don't doubt it, chief, not for a moment," he assured her.

Inwardly, however, Mr. Gecks was not so confident. A lawyer's anxiety over the fate of his cause seldom has spoiled either his sleep or his digestion; but in the case of Mr. Gecks and his longed-for Gecks and Gander, matters were not so straightforward.

"Do then let's hear an end of it, Mr. Gecks, so that I may resume my sewing. Now where is Gwenda? For I must have my compress — "

And so resolving she turned on her heel and with an air of perfect self-confidence stalked from the room.

"Oh, dear," Edgar murmured.

"My thought exactly," Mr. Gecks nodded soberly.

A sudden frown creased the brow of the chubby youth. "Say, what was that my aunt mentioned? About no secrets at the Hall?"

"In what connection?"

"Well, what of Crispin Nightshade — and the creeping shadow? That old fairy tale?"

"Mr. Edgar, you know we're not to speak of it," the attorney reminded him.

"Not in my aunt's presence, no . . ."

But it was too late, for already Richard's ears had pricked up. "What's this about a shadow?" he asked. "And who is Crispin Nightshade?"

Here was the spice of mystery. The stovepipe of Sir Padrig Martindale who had been a judge — toppled by a shadow that crept!

"Some pretty rum goings-on, to hear Mr. Gecks tell it. Have you seen it then? The shadow?" Edgar remarked casually.

"I well may have. The day before last, in the library. It quite confounded me."

The youth turned to him with a startled face. "The deuce you say, sir!"

"Pray don't be joking about such matters, Mr. Hathaway," the attorney warned, "for her ladyship is most sensitive on the topic."

"And I have never been more serious, Mr. Gecks," Richard said.

They were seated together there, the three of them, in their chairs before the fire in the rustic drawing-room. It was a very cozy picture, with the snow falling softly against the window, and the flicker of the firelight playing over the ancient paneled walls and wainscot.

Both Edgar and Richard waited for Mr. Gecks, who for several seconds sat in frowning thought. The tips of his fingers drummed noiselessly on the arm of his chair. Then he got up and started pacing. After a few minutes of this, having come to a decision, he strode with quick, light steps to the door and, looking out into the passage, spoke to someone there.

"Er, Treadwell — might I have a word?"

"Certainly, sir."

"Would you see that we are not interrupted?"

"As you wish, sir."

"No intrusions on any account."

"Perish the thought, sir. I shall be vigilant."

"I am much obliged to you, Treadwell."

"Not at all, sir."

Then he shut the door and resumed his seat.

"All's clear," he murmured, half to himself. "Lizzie — er, the chief, that is — will never forgive me. She'll think me one of her gossips, and she has scant liking for gossips."

"I'll fix it for you," Edgar assured him. "She dotes on me, you know."

"Yes . . ." The attorney rubbed his forehead — a trifle worriedly, Richard thought.

"Besides, Mr. Hathaway knows nothing of our little legend of the Hall, and is very keen on hearing it. Aren't you, sir?"

"I'm dashed curious about it," Richard said.

"Are you?" returned Mr. Gecks, half-nodding, half-smiling. "Pity. Well, see that you breathe not a word of it to Lizzie — er, that is — not a word to her ladyship."

"You have my pledge of honor, Mr. Gecks."

"I shall hold you to it, sir."

And speaking in a low voice resonant with his rich, fenny brogue, the attorney commenced his tale.

A Legend and a Light

"   I   T began in Ridingham, in Leather Alley, in that timeless world of once-upon-a-time — that is to say, some several centuries before our own. In the Alley there dwelt an elderly shoemaker — a liveryman of the Cordwainers' Company — who had plied his gentle trade for many a year, and had enjoyed much success. His shop, of which he was as proud as a dog in a doublet, still stands in the Alley; it is that occupied by Miss Ginch's Tea-rooms today.

"One day our prosperous shoemaker took into his employ a journeyman cobbler, an enterprising young chap, who was keen to make his way in the world. The fellow's object was to become a gentleman shoemaker, as it's termed, like his employer, and not remain a mere mender of shoes. He had been bound a prentice to the gentle craft, and had set his sights on Ridingham, the nearest and most bustling town in the district, resolved to achieve his purpose whatever the cost.

"After some months in his position this young journeyman — we'll call him Crispin Nightshade, for that is the *sobriquet* by which he is known to us, his name having been lost to history — grew envious of the old shoemaker for whom he toiled in the Alley. Time was passing too slowly for him, and he was keen to be about the glorious future he had chalked out for himself. His employer, a man known for hard dealing, was of a cruel, grasping nature, and rewarded his youthful worker with but a pittance for his labors.

"Now the shoemaker in his prosperity had acquired a fancy little wife, very slim and pretty — it is an old story. Needless to relate, young Nightshade became infatuated with the wife, and *vice versa*. And so he schemed to remove his employer from the picture, so that he might have possession of the man's shop and tools, and the wife as well. The deed was effected by mingling poison with the old man's broth; hence the nickname that has been applied to the journeyman cobbler, for shoemakers by tradition are disciples of St. Crispin, and *Atropa belladonna* is thought to have been the toxicant of choice. At the time however no suspicion alighted on him. His employer had been elderly — above fifty years old — and a physician concerned in the case had attributed death to the 'visitation of God'; and such was to be the finding of the coroner's jury.

"One night, not long after young Nightshade had taken to wife the widow and assumed her husband's livery, he was summoned to an inn — tradition holds it was the Goose and Gander — at the command of a surly, dark stranger who was stopping there. A veritable giant of a man, he had broken the heel of his boot and required that it be mended. Curiously, the stranger insisted that the work be performed *without taking the shoe from his foot.*

"It was in the course of their interview that young Nightshade obtained a glimpse of the stranger's throat, while the fellow was adjusting his neck-cloth. His keen eye had observed certain marks there, and a livid bruising, such as are found on the neck of a hanged man after he has been removed from the gallows. Marks of the hempen halter they looked to be — it was most illuminating.

"Now there is a legend amongst practitioners of the gentle craft, as I am told, of a so-called 'haunted leather', which, when fashioned into shoes and placed on the feet of a corpse, will cause the deceased to rise and live again, so long as the shoes remain on the feet. It seems young Nightshade had rightly judged who and what the stranger was — an executed criminal who had been revived. Newly come into his old master's wealth, he saw here another opportunity for himself, could he but gain possession of the haunted leather. For already his facile mind had devised a scheme wherein he could profit by it.

"After examining the boot, he informed the stranger that he could better effect the repair at his shop-board, having all the tools of his trade to hand there. At once the surly temperament of the giant came to the fore — a thoroughly unpleasant character he must have been, as befitted one of his ilk — and he demanded that he be served where he was. In the end, however, he was persuaded to stump round to the Alley, which is but a minute's walk from the inn, and be attended there."

By now Mr. Gecks had begun warming to his theme. He no longer appeared uneasy or nervous, no longer was glancing round him as if the chief somehow might be listening through the paneled walls. Richard himself was entirely absorbed in the story, as indeed was Edgar, who already had heard it numerous times before; such was the power of the attorney's rich baritone with its musical accents of the marshes.

"Once in his shop young Nightshade procured a sleeping draft, blended it with some grog, and offered it to the stranger. While he labored over the broken heel the man began to nod off, dropped his chin on his chest, and eventually fell into a deep slumber from which there would be no awakening.

"Young Nightshade had been correct in his assumption, for no sooner had he removed the boots from the giant's feet than the man crumbled to bone-dust in his chair. In a matter of seconds he'd been reduced to a kind of ash, as is found in those rare instances that have been recorded of the so-called 'spontaneous combustion'. But in this case there had been no flame, and no combustion — simply the magic of the haunted leather, or more accurately perhaps, its absence. The ash then was gathered into a bucket and thrown on a dust-heap, and the surly giant no more was seen in the town.

"Eventually the innkeeper came round when his guest failed to appear, for the man's bill was owing. He was informed that the stranger had departed the shop a satisfied customer, and that nothing more was known of him. The innkeeper in his turn left a disappointed man, never to collect the reckoning.

"Soon thereafter young Nightshade began to fashion the haunted leather into new shoes. He was able to produce several pairs from the two large boots of the giant, and for awhile his last and lingel found busy employment at his shop-board.

"Then, unexpectedly, a poor relation of his, a cousin on his mother's side, took ill and died there on the premises. This woman he had employed as a sort of menial, to sweep the floors and tidy the rooms, to do the cooking and the washing, and to fetch whatever was needed for the shop. In brief, he had cast upon her all the drudgery of his household, treating her more as a servant than as a member of his family. And for the privilege of it he had paid her nothing. It seemed that her death now had presented him with a difficulty. It was most inconvenient no longer to have his cousin and drudge around, for he could not have his fancy little wife performing such tasks (the which, by the by, she flatly refused to do), nor would he shell out the coin for a proper domestic. Hurriedly then he fashioned a pair of slippers from the haunted leather that remained, and placed them on the corpse's feet where it lay, stiff and still, in an upstairs apartment of the shop.

"No sooner had he accomplished it than his cousin stirred, drew a sudden breath, and jerked upright in her coffin. Round swung her head, from which two glassy eyes as shiny and dark as the wainscot regarded him with a soulless stare. Indeed so chilling was this look that it sent a visible shudder through his mortal frame. Then up got the corpse, down dropped its feet to the floor — the feet cased in haunted leather — and without a word it shuffled from the room.

"So she had not died after all, folks remarked, when the drudge was noticed to be about her duties again in the shop, performing all the usual tasks which fell to her lot. The physician who had announced her demise was widely panned as a quack. He was the same practitioner who had judged the shoemaker's death an act of God. He scarcely conceived that the return of the cousin had been an act of the devil.

"Ominously, in the days that followed, a marked change was observed in the woman's temperament. She rarely if ever spoke, and her disposition had turned sullen and lowering, as that of the giant's had been. The cobbler remarked that his cousin was becoming insubordinate, and no longer seemed to be herself. Her formerly placid nature had undergone a violent alteration. A calculating malevolence smoldered behind her glassy stare, so that Nightshade began to fear her. One evening she took an awl from his shop-board and threatened him with it, for having dared to reprimand her. It was after this incident that he formulated a plot to rid himself of his evil slave, by removing her slippers in the night. But she was too wily for him, too vigilant, and kept her door fastened against his approach. One morning, after discovering that he had mixed something with her gruel in an attempt to poison her, she fled the shop, never to return.

"Through it all the enterprising young liveryman had put in motion his ambitious design, to fatten his coffers by raising the dead with his shoes of haunted leather. In this effort a very select clientele was needed — wealthy folk, whose child or other relation recently had died — and for this a fair-sized town such as Ridingham was just the ticket.

"Still, he took care always to forewarn his clients of possible ill effects, such as he himself had experienced with his cousin. 'I cannot guarantee a serviceable result', he would tell them, 'so long as the possibility of an evil outcome exists. In such an event it may become necessary to remove the shoes'. But in the extremity of their grief people will resort to all manner of desperate measures to have a loved one restored to them. This young Nightshade understood well, and aimed to profit by it.

"It happened that in every case, once the change in temperament had become manifest, the clients found they had no alternative but to remove the shoes. It oft required elaborate scheming in the accomplishment of it; then the shoes would be returned to the shop, having become objects of loathing in the interval. In each instance the transaction was carried out with the utmost discretion and secrecy, the cobbler having agreed to refund a portion of his fee should his clients be unsatisfied, so long as he received the shoes in return. As a result he was able to make use of the leather again and again, and thereby realize even greater profits with little added effort or expenditure.

"In time young Nightshade became much sought after amongst people of means in the district, and waxed fat on the 'rental' of his shoes — for invariably they were returned to him, and no one the wiser, his clients hardly caring to advertise the delicate business in which they had been engaged.

"But all was not well in the workshop of the young liveryman. Gradually, by slow degrees, a change in temperament began to be noticed in the young man himself. His disposition became sinister and threatening, like that of the surly giant and of his cousin had been. He was prone to savage outbursts, and regularly punished his wife, who came to despise him. He was no better now, she reflected, than had been her first husband, the grasping old shoemaker. In the midst of these evil days, remarkably, a child had been born to the couple, for whose welfare the wife now became concerned owing to the erratic conduct of the father.

"One day it was announced that there was to be a hanging in the town — a woman was to be executed for murder. The case had been a sensation, and at the appointed hour everyone turned out to watch her swing. They were a lively lot then, our good citizens of Ridingham, the hanging being an occasion for festivity — a regular spectacle — as such affairs often were. Nightshade himself was in attendance, and was rather startled to find that the condemned was his own cousin, who in the time since she had fled his shop had grown wholly and perfectly evil. Minutes before the shroud was applied, her soulless stare settled upon him there at the foot of the scaffold, where he stood awaiting her launch into eternity. It was to him that she addressed her last words.

"In the full sight and sound of all, she cursed him to the moon, the sun, and stars, for making her the creature she had become. It were far better she had been left dead in her coffin, in the room over the shop, than that she had been made to live again. Naturally the crowd, thinking her mad, egged her on. As if this were not enough, she proceeded next to lay a curse upon the master of Haigh Hall, Sir Padrig Martindale, the Justice so high and mighty who had pronounced sentence at her trial, and upon all the male successors of his lineage to come; and then in a final, savage exultation she prepared to meet her doom.

"With a stream of vile oaths pouring from her lips, the shroud was drawn over her head, and the hempen halter stretched. When it was done, Nightshade as next of kin was presented with her effects, of which only the slippers of haunted leather held any importance for him; for they were a means of furthering his ends.

"From the moment of his cousin's death, however, the young man's days and nights were troubled. A shadow — a creeping shadow — began to haunt his waking hours. In daylight or by firelight, as often as it pleased, the shadow would steal upon him — a hunched figure crawling along a wall, or a stealthy patch of darkness in a doorway, that peeped in at him and then drew back. This hated familiar dogged him wherever he went. Haunted and pursued by this demon, the irritation of its unpleasant and undesired attentions gradually became intolerable. Whenever his tormentor appeared he would strike out, often at his wife, upon whom he laid the blame for his suffering; for it was she who had refused to do the work of the drudge. But the phantom presence had no relation to the wife, but was a product of the curse that had been laid upon him from the scaffold."

The roving wind slung a fresh gust of snow against the lattice, swirling flakes that rippled and danced. Odd flickerings of the fire threw eerie shadows on the walls and wainscot that seemed to mock and warn.

"And there are queer stories about this house as well, in the same connection, and about the Martindales who have lived in it. But in such a vast compass of time there are bound to be stories concerning so venerable and ancient a family."

On the topic of Haigh Hall Mr. Gecks chose his words with care, like the lawyer that he was. "It's funny how odd things may happen in odd places, at odd times. One morning young Nightshade arrived at the Hall with a pair of Sir Padrig's riding boots, which had required mending in his shop. While in the kitchen enjoying a cup of the Justice's best home-brewed, however, he took ill and fell to the floor, stone-dead. It happened in the chimney-corner, so tradition relates. It was said he had been frightened by a shadow he saw on a wall.

"Not long after this, the lord of the manor himself was killed in a fall from his bedroom window. It was rumored he had been surprised by a shadow that had stolen upon him there in his chamber. He toppled backwards through the casement and broke his skull on the paving. And so was born the legend of the creeping shadow of Haigh Hall."

"Gracious, what a story," Richard said.

The attorney's narrative had held his whole attention, and Edgar's too. The history presented to them had been weird and mysterious in the extreme, and Richard wondered how much truth, if any, might be contained in it.

"And what of the Martindale male line? How have the descendants of Sir Padrig fared?" he asked.

"Well, some have not been treated so kindly, a few having suffered violent or mysterious deaths. There was Sir Price Martindale for instance, who was thrown from his horse at a bullfinch and cracked his head on the stile. It was said a black shadow had risen up from the ground and frightened his hunter. And there was Sir John Llewellyn Martindale, the antiquarian of the family, who tumbled from a ladder in the library while reaching down a book from a shelf. And more recently there was Sir Dafydd Martindale, his lordship's grandfather."

"What happened to him?"

"One evening the dreaded shadow appeared at his chamber-door, so it is said, and beckoned to him to follow. Startled half out of his wits, he fled through the gatehouse and, the night being pitch-dark, he fell into a stream beside the causeway and was drowned."

"Has anyone presently living at the Hall ever seen this shadow?"

"Haven't you forgotten about my uncle?" spoke up Edgar. "For some parties now and again have let it slip that — "

The lawyer raised a hand to check him, and seemed about to say something, only to hesitate, as if he had thought better of it. It put Richard in mind of a certain conversation between her ladyship and Gwenda, as it had been relayed to him by Elzie Peek. Might it be that the shadow had indeed been concerned in the death of Sir Pedr Martindale?

"Well, I'll tell you what *I* saw — in the library — the morning before last," Richard volunteered, "and I dare say you'll have hard work to explain it."

And so he proceeded to describe for them the shadow and its perceived effect on the stovepipe hat of Sir Padrig.

"Oh, dear," worried Edgar, passing a handkerchief over his face — "oh, dear."

"It's dashed odd, certainly. But Mr. Gecks, surely there can be no such thing as this haunted leather? It *is* only a story?"

"On the face of it there is no absolute proof of its existence — nothing evidential that might be introduced in a court of law," the attorney replied.

"However in this world of ours there exists the reality of coincidence. Sir Padrig, Sir Price, Sir John Llewellyn, Sir Dafydd — who is to say their unfortunate ends were not coincidence? Are there not a hundred families in these marshes with unfortunate ends in their histories? For a tragedy befalls someone somewhere every day in the week."

"And what of Sir Pedr? Did he see the shadow as well?"

"That," Mr. Gecks replied, calmly folding his big hands across his knee, "is a matter known only to the chief, if to anyone, and I for one am not about to examine her on the topic."

"Auntie always pooh-poohs the story, and never wants to speak of it," Edgar related, "but I dare say there must be a grain of truth in it. Else why should she be so touchy on the issue? 'Foolish folk always will be talking' says she, and 'if shadow it be, it would hardly dare show itself in my presence'. You get the picture."

"Reckon I do," Richard said.

"It is a tale well-garnished by the years," resumed Mr. Gecks. "Who can say what portion of it is authentic, and what is embellishment? There may be as much of trick as of supernatural agency in the business. And how are we to cast fresh light on the events of an age so remote from our own? But it's a good story, at any rate. As well there is a persistent legend, still current in these parts, that haunted leather may have been placed on the feet of the cobbler after his decease, and that somewhere, perhaps in Ridingham itself, Crispin Nightshade walks yet amongst the living."

A picture of the grisly relic which Dan Hedges had taken away flashed into Richard's mind. An old leather boot — not *haunted* leather, surely?

It seemed that Mr. Gecks had gotten this same idea, but had conceived of it an instant before Richard had done.

"I have just had a thought. We must have the evidence of the boot examined not only by Dr. Bussey and the constable, but by Hiram Pinchbeck as well. He is a bootmaker in Ridingham — Sir Pedr often called on him — and is just the man for the task. Possibly he can trace the shoe by means of its design and stitching."

At the name *Pinchbeck* Richard looked at Edgar — for of course the bootmaker was one of those whom the youth had jockeyed in the backparlor — but received no answering glance. Likely he already had forgotten about the shopkeepers and their impending return a week hence.

And so there it was, the long and the short of it, so said the attorney in concluding his tale. Then he strode to the door and gave word to Treadwell that he might relax his vigil in the passage.

That night it stopped snowing at last. Away off in the eastern sky a few stars of a quivering brightness had begun to show. Welcome as they were, they were not the only lights my brother observed as he glanced out of his casement before retiring. For across the yard, in the dark mass that was the gatehouse, a light had appeared in a window of its upper floor. This window looked out over the curtain-wall, but was angled such as to be partly visible to Richard. The source of the light was a lamp that was being held against the glass. As Richard watched, the lamp first was raised and lowered, then moved slowly from side to side. Once, twice, three times this exercise was gone through. The individual manipulating the light could be seen only vaguely, but he assumed it to be Mrs. Aberdovey, her ladyship's lodgekeeper-woman.

Richard stared in some surprise, for the motion of the lamp in the window had every appearance of a signal-light.

His mind was filled with a rush of wild imaginings. A signal to whom? To someone out upon the snowy marshes on a bitter-cold night? Who would be waiting for such a signal on such a night, and for what purpose? Her mysterious caller, perhaps?

No sooner had he begun to revolve these thoughts than the light was extinguished. He counted the leaden minutes passing, but nothing else of interest occurred. The stars still glittered but there was no repeat of the signal, and so with a yawn and a stretch he retired to his pillow.

A short while later, as he was dozing off, a vague suggestion of a sound reached his ears. What was it? Another bump in the night? Another striking of feet on the roof, another creep of footsteps on the leads?

In some alarm he rose and went to the window, but as before there was nothing to be seen there. Next he peeped out into the corridor — he had no idea why, the thought simply had occurred to him — and found nothing there either. There was not a creeping shadow in sight. He wondered about the stovepipe hat and the bust of Sir Padrig in the library, and decided he must rise early and see about them. For the present he returned to his bed and disposed himself to sleep.

THE THIRD CHAPTER

In Terra Pox

DAWN was flowing across the marshes when Richard arose — a sprightly dawn, with snow on the ground but none in the air — to find a little knot of persons gathered in the courtyard below, almost directly under his window. He had been alerted to their presence by the murmur of interested talk that was filtering in through the casement. At so early an hour it could be only the outside men and their like, and chief amongst them he recognized the voice of Dan Hedges.

Curious, he dressed quickly and went downstairs to investigate.

"It's impossible" — "Who can it have been?" — "What can it mean?" — were some of the remarks that reached his ears as he crunched his way towards the group.

"What's it all about, Dan?" he asked as he came up.

"Lookee there, sir," the outside man replied, motioning with his hand. "It's a puzzle, it is."

His colleagues nodded and murmured their agreement.

What Richard observed were two sets of footprints in the snow, running parallel and close beside one another, but in opposite directions. From their size and appearance it was clear they had been laid down by a man's shoe — a round-toed boot. The prints leading away from the Hall terminated in the slush and mire of the gatehouse lane, the spot where the opposing set looked to have originated.

"Someone has walked from the gatehouse to the Hall, and back again," Richard concluded, "or — or perhaps from the Hall to the gatehouse, and then back to the Hall. Sometime in the night, I dare say. Is it important?"

The outside man shook his head skeptically. "Begging your leave, sir, but it won't work. That's the puzzle of it."

"What do you mean it won't work?"

"Lookee here, sir," Dan invited, sinking into a crouch. Richard followed his example. "See this trail of marks here. They run straight along to the steps before the servants' door. But the snow on the steps be fresh and not disturbed. The fellow, whoever he was, halted before the steps and stood there."

"Ah, yes — I see what you mean. He must have walked along from the gatehouse, paused near the foot of the steps — likely he spoke to someone who had opened the door — and then returned to the gatehouse. What is the difficulty?"

Again the outside man shook his head.

"Begging pardon, sir, but that won't work either. Nobody opened the servants' door, for an instance — it were locked tight, as it always is, till Mr. Treadwell undoes it round seven with his key. And for another, Mrs. Aberdovey, ever an early riser, knows nowt of any man in the night going from the gatehouse to the Hall and back again. And o' course the tracks bean't Mrs. Aberdovey's herself, as any eye can see."

"Indeed? Then he must have gone from the Hall over to the gatehouse, and back to the Hall."

"No, no, sir, he can't have. See the snow on the steps, sir — no foot-marks. If this fellow walked across from the Hall, sir, how did he go down the steps without leaving a trace?"

"Well, he can't have — not even by leaping. The distance is too great."

"Yes, sir. See how the marks leading to the gatehouse begin just here — near three yards from the servants' door — as if the fellow had stepped out of empty air. As if he had stepped out of nowhere."

Richard got to his feet and studied it all again. Slowly his eyes opened wide. He pushed his hat to the back of his head and scratched his brow.

"Yes, I do see what you mean now. It's rather a puzzle, isn't it? Dashed curious thing . . . the two trails are so near together, and each of the same pattern . . . it can only have been the same fellow, marching first the one way and then the other."

"Yes, sir."

"But who was he? And where did he come from?"

"We've no notion, sir. It weren't any of the outside men, that's sure."

"And it weren't Mr. Treadwell — *that's* sure," nodded one of the stable-hands, a rough-hewn sort with prominent ears. It was the cheeky groom who had taken Richard's mare that first night at the Hall. He and his companions rubbed their chins darkly, and exchanged some further words of low-voiced conversation. They appeared a trifle uneasy with the notion of *empty air* and *nowhere*.

"And who discovered the enigma?" Richard asked.

In answer Dan pointed to the top of the curtain-wall, where a jaunty figure, leaning on the cross-guards of his sword and grinning, stood silhouetted against the light.

"Well, what d'yer think of 'em? A puzzle, ain't it?" Sam Gander called to them from his post on high; then he smacked his lips and flourishing his cutlass celebrated with a little jig of triumph on the wall-walk.

Mr. Gander it was indeed, buttoned up to the throat in an old watch-coat, and it was a good job his daughter and his doctor could not see him now. Having concluded his revel, he sheathed his sword and folding his arms stood smiling on his subjects with a satisfied air.

"He's got a teratorn's keen eye, and a spyglass to boot," Dan explained. "He spotted the marks at daybreak while pacing the wall, and suspected it were an intruder as had come stealing in after midnight."

"Was the gate secure this morning?" Richard asked.

"Fastened tight, sir, like the servants' door. And Mrs. Aberdovey admitted no one."

A third time Richard surveyed the evidence before him. His eyes, gray and thoughtful, studied the marks carefully. Here was another thing rather out of the ordinary — another puzzle to be added to the rest. Mystified, he attempted to work out in his mind how the tracks had been created, for in their particulars they were quite remarkable. In the one direction, some-one had walked from the gatehouse lane to near the foot of the servants' steps, two floors beneath Richard's casement-window, and stood there; in the other, in the trail running close beside the first, the marks commenced near the steps and proceeded in the opposite direction to the gatehouse.

Where had the man come from, and where had he gone? And who was he? Mrs. Aberdovey claimed to have no knowledge of any visitor. And yet had there not been a suggestion of a gentleman caller at the gatehouse the night Richard arrived at the Hall, a caller whose existence the lodgekeeper-woman had denied? Nor could Richard disregard the recent evidence of his eyes — the signal-light in the gatehouse window.

"We may take it as certain that the tracks were laid down in the night, or very early this morning, after the snow had fallen," he said.

"No question of that, sir," Dan affirmed.

"And yet there is no one present, evidently, who can have made them."

"None abroad at such an hour, no, sir."

"Then I dare say we must conclude, as Mr. Gander has done, that we have had an intruder in the night — a man who either is in hiding here, or has escaped beyond the curtain-wall."

"And where might he have gone to hide himself, sir? But for these few traces there be no sign of him. No other footmarks leading off."

"Aye, that's plain enough," nodded the cheeky groom. "Over the wall he's gone, split me if he han't."

"And I for one am wholly without an inkling how he accomplished it. The gate there was not opened; the postern-gate back of the stables was not opened. How then did he enter? How did he leave? Did he vault over the wall? And what was his business here? This certainly needs thinking out," said Richard, yearning for his pipe.

He ran his eye along the battlements atop the curtain-wall, in search of any clue that might present itself there. Perhaps the intruder had scaled the wall by means of a rope secured to one of the merlons? Perhaps the rope still clung to the merlon, one near the gatehouse lane, for he would have had to descend again on the outside. But there was no rope; there was only Sam Gander, his hands cupped to his ears that he might follow the discussion below.

"I had reckoned this to be a fair morning to scour the home fields for Toddy's grubbing-place, as Mr. Gecks did suggest," said Dan Hedges. "Mayhap we'll have a scout round as well for this fellow's trail?"

"Or those of his horse, if he had one. Surely he must have had a horse? For it only stands to reason. Capital notion, Dan," Richard nodded.

Having tired a little of Sir Pharnaby, my brother inquired if he might join the expedition, and was enthusiastically accepted. He returned to his chamber to complete his toilet and to fetch his hat and cutlass. All thought of breakfast and of the Crust letters fled his mind in the excitement of the moment. Yesterday he had made an important discovery concerning the *Locksley Fantasia,* one of Sir Pharnaby's most heartfelt works; but the information was safely lodged amongst his notes, and would not suffer by his absence for a few hours. Besides, he had not ridden once since his arrival at the Hall, and was longing for a morning's brisk gallop in the new snow.

Their first task was to make a complete circuit of the wall, their progress followed by Mr. Gander as he nipped along the walk above them. The results were a surprise. No evidence was discovered of any footmarks, human or animal, in the snow immediately surrounding the curtain-wall. No one had approached the Hall during the night by way of the gatehouse, the postern-gate, or from any other direction.

And that, as Dan said, was the puzzle of it.

Richard confessed he was at a loss for an explanation. How the deuce had the fellow gotten in, and how had he gotten out again? For there seemed scant likelihood, given the evidence of the tracks, that he had hidden himself somewhere on the premises.

Having no answer for it, the riders proceeded with their chief objective, which was to find the place where Toddy had unearthed the boot with the bones in it. *Where's the rest of him?* had been Edgar's query, one which they meant to answer today, if possible. It was for this reason they had brought Toddy with them, Dan having placed him on the scent of the boot before departing.

They pricked forward on their mounts, to reconnoiter the expanse of ground that lay before them — the home fields of the Martindales beneath its coverlet of new snow. Over all, the brooding silence of the marshes cast its spell. Not a breath of wind was stirring amidst the vast loneliness that surrounded them on every side. In the snow near the curtain-wall they had discovered nothing to suggest that Toddy had dug there, nor had the terrier seemed at all interested in the area. Out here, although the snowfall would have since obscured it, there might yet exist some irregularity of the terrain that would mark the spot. But thus far they and the game little lad had found nothing.

They were following an old cart-track, the horses' hooves busily churning up the fresh powder that overlay it. Not many yards distant the causeway could be seen running on its path to Ridingham. It was the causeway that Richard had traversed on horseback that first night. Meanwhile he and the others were keeping an alert watch for cats — marsh devil and spotted lion — their eyes scanning the snowy drifts, their swords prepared to leap into their hands at the first alarm. Fortunately it now was rather late in the morning, and not the savage man-eaters' favored time for hunting.

Dan Hedges cast a weather eye about him. His glance swept the distant line of trees that cloaked the horizon to southwards — the eaves of Marley Wood. In the opposite direction lay Ridingham, of which only the spires of its parish churches, rising from the wintry haze like so many Cleopatra's needles, were visible from this perspective.

Off in the nearer distance, meanwhile, across the causeway, a clump of Scotch firs had drawn the attention of Richard. They were the same firs in whose upper branches he had seen, or thought he had seen, the dark mass lurking. In the light of day they seemed inoffensive enough, and no hint of any lurking thing could he discern. Perhaps indeed it had been his imagination playing tricks, occasioned by his long day of travel and the blustery conditions that had assailed him in the road.

Minutes later a handsome sleigh, neatly striped and finished, drawn by a pair of prancers bearing tartan trappings and clear-sounding bells, appeared from round a screen of trees. It carried three men, two on the cushion, and a third, clad in gillie's tweeds, driving the horses. They were no chance travelers in the road, as Richard was informed by Dan, for the sleigh was the property of Mr. Phergus MacWallop, her ladyship's ungrateful wretch of a neighbor on the marshes.

"What a bit of luck — Lord bless me," Dan noted wryly.

"Which is MacWallop?" Richard asked.

"That be he — the Laird — the little rusty screw of a dry old hunks with the hang-dog mustaches."

The individual so described was one of those on the cushion. He was a smallish man, wrapped in an Inverness cape, with a great long muffler for his chin and throat. He wore a heavy fur hat that nestled well down on his head, but which was so thickly bulked and padded as to resemble a second head atop his own.

"And who is the other?"

"The lawyer — Wormwrath."

"I see. Rather a hard-looking chap."

"Hard-dealing too, sir."

"Well, I suppose we're stuck with them now."

It was true. At a word from his master the gillie holding the ribands called his team to a stand, and there they remained, facing the horsemen and Toddy in the road.

"What is that on the dash-rail?" Richard asked.

"His foot, sir — the MacWallop's foot — for the old hunks does suffer much from the gout."

"Ah, yes, I remember. He is a patient of Dr. Bussey's."

It was indeed a foot, bound up with bandages to several times its normal size, and propped on the dash-rail of the sleigh. In his hand the hunks held a weighted cosh like a walking-stick — or was it a thrashing-stick? Indignantly he stared the riders up and down, his lips twisted into a scowl that might have soured cream. The lines of his face were grim as he scrutinized the opposing party.

"Wha's yon?" he demanded. "Aha — is't yersell, Hedges? Hedges o' the Hall? An' whaur wad ye an' yer braw young lads o' muckle might be gaun this bonny morn?"

The outside man informed him — truthfully enough — that they were making for nowhere in particular, but were having a scout round the home fields after the recent snowfall.

"An' whaur be the auld corbie the noo? She as draps lumber across ma bit path i'the Close, an' speaks sic daffin' in her letters tae the MacWallop as wad mak' a cat laugh? Rides she no wi' ye, the auld fiddle-face?"

"I've no notion what you may mean, sir, in the way of corbies and fiddle-faces," said Dan, "but these fields and this track be Martindale land, as attaches to Haigh Hall."

"Heigh-*ho*," returned the Laird, with an exaggerated yawn.

"MacWallop land it bean't."

"And is that what ye be thinkin', Mr. Hedges? For if it is, ye be maist grievously mistaken, an' maun be muckle disappointed come Sessions day. Not MacWallop land? Get hame wi' ye!" scoffed the wretch, with a slighting motion of his stick.

"A-a-r-r-g-h-h," rumbled Toddy, his whiskers bristling and his keen eyes on the cosh.

"Opinions in law may differ, sir, as I'm told," noted Dan.

"And is't that cockle-brain of a law-writer Gecks as told ye that? Aweel I'm no surprised. But a's grippie for grippie i'the een o' the Justices. Dinna fash yersell o'er it, for a' will be clear come Sessions day."

"I'm sure it will, sir. Her ladyship will be present at Sessions, have no fear."

"Aye, that she will," said MacWallop, screwing up his eyes and smiling in anticipation of the great event. "She's a warrior, that one — I'll gie her that. But she an' the fule body Gecks maun hae no a pund o' sense atween 'em tae be tusslin' wi' the MacWallop, an' tisna crackin' crouse I am. What say ye, Mr. Law-writer?"

This last was addressed to his leading counsel Wormwrath, with whom he shared the cushion. The attorney gave every appearance of being a formidable customer, as Richard had noted, with his long, sarcastic face, cruel gash of a mouth, and steely eyes that glinted cold and unblinking like the eyes of a snake. Not only his externals but his very manner and temperament cast a palpable chill, sufficient, so it was rumored, to freeze his own shadow.

"Speaking in my capacity as Mr. MacWallop's professional adviser," the lawyer announced in a manly voice of good compass, "I believe he has every chance of success in his cause."

"Certain sure he does," Dan observed.

The attorney's lips crooked faintly into a smile, and his eyes glistened. "Is it a particle of doubt that I detect in your voice, Hedges?"

"None at all, sir."

"With reference to the matter of trespass — for that is the substance of the cause that is to be brought before the Bench — any and all who dare make an encroachment on my client's rights shall feel the sting of the law. Mr. MacWallop has every right to free passage through the Close without stay or hindrance from anyone, whether titled lady or no."

Eyeing each other with the wary watchfulness of cats — lawyer, client, and gillie on the one side, the riders from the Hall and Toddy on the other — for some moments the parties kept their own counsel. Here was further evidence, if any were needed, that Mr. Gecks's "little notice" had led to nothing, as her ladyship had prophesied. It occurred to Richard that only more of the same could come of the present meeting — nothing — and so he urged Dan to yield the day.

Instead the outside man's resolve hardened. At a sign from him the stable-hands, their cutlasses showing conspicuously at their hips, ranged their mounts one beside the other across the cart-track, facing the sleigh, and effectively barring its way forward.

"My client and I have been called to town on business of importance," said Mr. Wormwrath, "and I should advise you, Hedges, and your minions to stand clear."

Dan, his arms folded on his chest, was silent and immovable.

The lawyer answered by uncoiling his lean length from the cushion. "It is necessary, Hedges, that you withdraw. My client and I are neglecting important business which awaits. Any other response on your part is impertinent."

"Her ladyship too has her business, and her rights," Dan noted calmly, "and as this be her ladyship's land, it be an encroachment of her ladyship's rights to be granting liberty of passage without her ladyship's leave."

"The doited fule!" exploded Mr. MacWallop, shaking his stick at Dan, and then at Toddy, who had lunged at it with his teeth.

"Will you stand clear, sir?" the lawyer demanded harshly.

In reply Dan undertook to inform him that the path he and his client were traversing — meaning the cart-track — had existed in that place from time immemorial, that it was situated upon her ladyship's own ground, and that he defied them to prosecute him and the lads for trespass.

"For the law be the law, sir, as the constable says."

"This is wild talk," disdained the attorney.

"But be it wrong talk?" said Dan. "For this be Martindale land, sir — private property — and nowt to do with the cause in Petty Sessions, as I understand it. Or mayhap you have lost your way, sir, and have mistaken it for Hatter's Close, hard by Eel Island?"

At this mention of the terrible ground in dispute, Mr. MacWallop flailed about on the cushion.

"Fie an' shame on ye! By ma certie, 'tis sinful shame tae treat a neighbor sae wanton. Na mair, sir, na mair — I winna hear it. Leave us pass the noo, an' we'll no be ca'in' oot the constable frae Ridingham tae collect the scaff an' raff o' ye."

"Do you mean to trample about her ladyship's entire estates, sir?"

The wretch of a neighbor raised a caustic eyebrow. "An' wha' else wad I be meanin'?" he answered, with the coolest possible effrontery. "For isna the chief of it MacWallop land indeedy, as was ta'en frae ma gudesires lang years syne by Martindale bodies o' yore? There, sir, there be sinful shame! D'ye tak' the MacWallop for a beggar body wi' but a guinea in's breeks? Fie, sir!"

Richard, something puzzled, turned to Dan. "Can this be true? Did the Martindales of old seize these acres from his ancestors?"

Dan shook his head. "It's a ruse, sir — a forgery of an old tapestry map as gave the boundaries of the home fields. Every Petty Sessions he makes threat to have it proved. Which it never can be proved, sir, the official records having been lost in the great fire. But there's nowt but expense and lawyers' costs as faces her ladyship on that head, so that in exchange for her ladyship's giving ground on this or that matter — which be by far the cheaper course — he puts by his threat for another season."

Richard was aghast. Now he comprehended something of Mr. Gecks's equivocation as regards the cause for trespass, those quirks and quibbles of the law he had mentioned that might prove a hindrance to a successful outcome.

"And is it true that his lordship, Sir Pedr, gave assistance to his neighbor in the flood years?" Richard asked.

Dan replied that it was most definitely so, that indeed his own father had been one of the laborers dispatched by Sir Pedr to MacWallop land to assist in mending his neighbor's roadways.

Ungrateful wretch was the term that flashed into my brother's head, as his glance returned to the neighbor on the cushion, but *dirty skunk* was not far behind it. Eel Island sounded just the place for so slippery and underhand a character.

"However Sir Pedr himself had no trouble with the man?"

"None, sir. Petty Sessions be a thing as commenced with her ladyship after his lordship's death."

"This really is absurd," said Richard, his gaze shifting from the skunk to the skunk's legal adviser, "although I know so little of lawyers and their methods."

"Very fortunate for you, sir," Dan commented wryly.

The attorney's face was set and stern.

"You smile, Hedges," he said grimly — "but I assure you, before the Justices we mean to teach her ladyship that law is law, as you yourself have spoken. My client will brook no interference in his lawful concerns."

"Aye, I'll hae a judgment out o' somebody!" snapped the client, pouncing on his statement.

Dan was halfway minded to respond in kind, but instead nodded to the lads, who straightened themselves in their saddles, weapons at the ready.

"Let him walk across," Dan invited, meaning the MacWallop.

"A-a-r-r-g-g-h-h," bristled Toddy, with a warning glance at the stick.

Back of his mustaches his lips curled themselves in scorn, and glowering at Dan the Laird retorted fiercely —

"D'ye tell me that? D'ye tell me sae, Hedges o' the Hall? Are ye daft? Wha's a' this jookery-paukery the noo?"

"I do tell you. This be Martindale land, sir. You have liberty to pass — *on foot.*"

The gouty little screw clamped a hand to his hat, as though to keep the rising steam of his indignation from blowing it off his head.

"The — deil — ye — say!" he spluttered.

He would have added more, but his anger choked him.

The grin of his attorney was slow, deliberate, and sarcastic. "You know full well, Hedges, that we must pass this way to gain the high road. However, as you are embarked upon this mad piece of craziness — "

"The law be the law, sir," answered Dan, dropping a hand to his sword — "begging pardon for making so free."

"In these peaceful and enlightened times of ours, Hedges, gentlemen but rarely need resort to force of arms."

"I bean't a gentleman, sir," Dan said simply.

The attorney regarded him with shrewd appraisal. His eyes, lidless and unblinking, studied him for a time, and the party of horsemen barring the way, as he thought over the matter. "No," said at length — "no, I don't expect you are . . ." Following another pause of some seconds he turned to his client and informed him that — "None of us is above the law, sir.

I do not know what we can do at present. It is not the Close. They are within their rights and will not stand clear."

"There be a lawyer speaking truth for once," noted Dan with a silent chuckle.

It needed every ounce of the attorney's resources of persuasion to quell his client's wrath. Even the driver was enlisted in his effort to convince the Laird that they must turn back and follow the old, oft-trodden road to Ridingham, if they were to be delayed no longer in their important business there.

Dan for his part did not hesitate to remind them that their oft-trodden road was one of those which his lordship, Sir Pedr Martindale, in the spirit of neighborly good will, and without thought of remuneration, had helped to restore in the flood years. The result was predictable. Mr. MacWallop, with a great gnashing of his teeth, let it be known that he was "dooms disappointed" in his legal adviser, whom hitherto he had deemed "baith canny an' fendy" in the ways of the law, and who had refused even to consider "a bribe o' siller to the fashious caterans o' the Hall" to permit the sleigh to pass.

Meanwhile Dan seemed to be taking a rare pleasure in the discomfiture of her ladyship's adversaries.

"Lash, drive on this instant — by the old road to Ridingham," Lawyer Wormwrath instructed the gillie. Consulting his watch, he frowned and began to wind it. Dan, observing this, noted — "Her ladyship and Mr. Gecks will wind his watch for him, I'll be bound, at Petty Sessions."

Grudgingly the driver reined about his team, and off they trotted back the way they had come, towards MacWallop land and the longer and less satisfactory road to town, which his master had intended to forgo by his intrusion on her ladyship's ground. The short cut by way of Hatter's Close would not avail them today.

"Your servant, sirs," Dan called after them with a nod and a smile. "Safe journey!"

No servant of mine would be so impertinent, Richard fancied must have passed through the Laird's brain, if his ear had caught Dan's parting salute.

"There's a cool fellow," he remarked.

"And a tetchy one," noted Dan.

"*Tetched* might be nearer the truth."

"I reckon the old hunks has got calluses from the pennies he's pinched. A more haggis-witted fool I never saw."

"Such dirty underfoot methods!"

"Every man to his taste, sir, and a pox on *that* one," said Dan.

Measures then were taken to discourage the villains from simply reversing course again, by posting two guards in the cart-track to prevent another incursion. Meantime the rest of the men pursued their errand for the hours of daylight that remained.

The marshes where the coracle men dipped their paddles in the stream, the causeway, the home fields — all were explored, but without result. The fresh fall of snow made it all but impossible to discern any clue left by the intruder, or for Toddy to nose out the spot where he had found the boot. At one point an eerie, blood-curdling howl from a forest creature reached their ears, its unwholesome echoes drifting wraith-like over marsh and mist from the distant line of trees that was Marley Wood. Beyond this, nothing intervened to disturb the quiet of the lonely country by which they were surrounded.

So the afternoon wore away but nothing was found, and the party returned to the Hall without further adventure.

A winter-white night was showing in the casement when Richard snuffed his candle and retired to his bed. Some hours later, groggy with sleep, he awoke, or thought he awoke, to find his eyes drawn to the wall opposite the window. There, in a flood of moonlight, a dark figure — the shadow of a manlike creature, like some distorted apparition in a dream — was climbing stealthily upwards, making no sound, and appearing not the least sensible of his presence. He watched it for a time in fascination — horror — dread — uncertain whether it were reality or a nightmare. Then, having conquered the wall, the figure disappeared into the ceiling.

The Constable Recommends

THE first to be consulted respecting Toddy's find was Dr. Bussey, who dropped by in the morning on his regular visit to the Hall.

"What's all this nonsense then, Mr. Gander? Have you been at your exercises again — and dancing a jig on the wall-walk? For so I have been informed by her ladyship," the doctor said sternly. "My, you are a stubborn fellow."

"And ye're another," snapped Sam.

"Well, well. And how are you feeling today?"

"Never better, till yer darkened me door. 'Ere, why not trouble yerself over some other poor clot? Meself, I ha'n't any use for yer gammon."

"You have no need of me, eh?"

"None," his patient declared.

"Excuse my presumption, but are you a qualified physician?" the doctor asked him.

"I told yer, I ain't a physician no longer. I'm retired. It's Lizzie looks after Cuffley and the Gander now."

The doctor's lips formed a smile that mirrored his upturned mustaches. "I think you mean publican. Well, you appear steady enough, but I'll not vouch for your soundness — of mind, that is. However you spoke now of your daughter. My dear chap, have you no consideration for her feelings?"

"Go consider yerself."

"That is a poor attitude to take. Will you never learn? I hear her ladyship nearly fainted yesterday after hearing of your antics. Frankly, I'm appalled."

"Yer look it. What's that? Me Lizzie a-goin' off? Shoo! Me Lizzie o' the Gander's dropped bigger bucks than yer in her time. Ooh, she had a right pretty smasher for a fist had me Lizzie, one as could loosen yer head-rails and raise a tidy mouse on yer ogle."

"Bigger bucks, but were they healthier? Look here, sir," said the doctor, making a show of his paunch, "is this not health for you? Compare it to your own withered self. You'll not find *me* reduced to a scarecrow, surviving on pig-nuts and bogberry juice. I'm trying to help you, man."

"Eavesdroppers and talebearers! Who was it snitched to me Lizzie o' me capering on the walk?" his patient demanded.

And so it went, until Dan Hedges appeared and asked if he might show the doctor the boot, as it were.

"Come cast your eye over it if you would, please, doctor," he invited, after first recounting for him the circumstances of its discovery.

"Me Lizzie, she don't know what to make of it, eh? Well, that's grand," nodded Sam, rubbing his palms and crinkling.

The doctor drew his snuff-box from his waistcoat, tapped the lid, opened it, then halted with a pinch between his finger and thumb as his gaze lighted on the old mired boot with the bones in it, which Dan had placed before him. He applied the pinch, shut the box with a snap, took up the boot and proceeded to scrutinize it with a doctorly eye.

"Well, well, what have we here? It's a musty old fossil, isn't it," he remarked.

"'Ere, yer expectin' a guinea to be tellin' us that?" said Sam.

The doctor ignored him. "It's an ancient artifact, in my view."

"And the bones, doctor," said Dan — "be they human?"

"Unquestionably," the doctor replied, with a learned hitch of his head. "Doubtless some anonymous peasant — some passing rustic, a coracle man or fen-slodger perhaps, whose mortal remains have long since crumbled to dust — aside from his foot, of course. Nobody gone missing of late? Well, I shouldn't think so. This is a relic of long years agone — long, long years — an idle curiosity — and there's an end of it, I dare say. Nothing to worry your minds over."

"Thankee much, doctor."

"Delighted to have been of service. Now, have you something to hand to settle the gastric juices? A little brandy-and-water would do nicely. For it's these long hours seeing patients that can derange the digestive organs, and clog up the well-springs of life . . ."

Meanwhile a couple of men had been dispatched to Ridingham to fetch Constable Pettiplace. In due course the officer arrived at the gatehouse, in the company of Mr. Pinchbeck, the bootmaker.

To Richard the constable looked a steady-going specimen. He was unusually tall and thin, with a long face surmounted by a brow of ponderous gravity showing from beneath his cap of office, and framed by a wealth of whisker of a rich, harvest hue. By comparison the slight figure of the boot-maker looked a dwarf beside his tall steeple of a companion. A disciple of St. Crispin and an acknowledged authority on the subject of boots, and be-ing as well chair of the local historical society, Mr. Pinchbeck had been in-vited to accompany the officer and give his opinion on the boot, its age and possible origin.

The constable having communicated their readiness to enter on the task at hand, they were shown to the farm office, a snug little chamber round the side of the stables, near the cart-shed.

The chamber was fitted up in part like an office, in part like the rustic drawing-room of the Hall, and smelled of old leather, tobacco smoke, and stable-litter. It was lighted on two sides by casements, and walled round in black oak, against which were hung a few engravings in gilt frames, some hunting prints, and portraits *statant* of noble prancers and brawny beeves of yore. A pair of elk's antlers, a fox's mask staring vacantly from between two brushes, and a line of fishing-rods completed the garnish. A mirror hung over the mantelpiece, and comfortable, leather-backed chairs stood round the hearth.

Dan first poked up the fire a little, then brought out the boot from the closet where it was stored. He placed it on a piece of sacking spread out flat on the office table, between his ledgers and some back numbers of the *Countryman's Journal.*

"I'll have to take the particulars, if you please. Now then, if you would oblige me with a short summary of the events, Mr. Hedges, nice and order-ly," said the constable, as he and the others gathered round. His voice was level, his features placid and imperturbable. The constable was in a charge of great trust in his station, with a name for honesty in the town, and was supremely conscious of the eminence of his office. From his tunic he had drawn a small notebook, and as Dan related the story his pencil traveled evenly over its pages.

"We are in hopes you may cast some light on the puzzle," Richard said. "At all events it quite confounds us."

The constable nodded benevolently. "I dare say, Mr. Hathaway, I dare say. Show it here, if you please."

He took the boot in hand and turned it round, this way and that, in-specting it closely from toe to heel, and the grisly remains lodged within it.

"Yes, very curious. It's queer, right enough," he murmured thoughtful-ly.

For some minutes he pondered the mystery before him — a mystery of nameless life and death on the marshes — before pushing back his cap and returning the boot to the table. He jotted down some few more particulars and, having finished, spoke to his audience of his conclusions.

Briefly, he was in accord with Dr. Bussey's view that the remains were ancient and immaterial; that the wearer of the boot, whoever he was, was unlikely to have been the victim of a recent crime; and that further steps in an official way would be unprofitable.

There was some added talk of moldy bones, and the flight of time, and how much water slides past the mill that the miller never wots of; that indeed there might be a body lying grim and grotesque under the sod, somewhere in the vicinity of the Hall; but in the officer's considered opinion — "I see no need to disturb Dr. Grubble, the coroner, over so trifling an issue. In this case, I think we may safely let sleeping *soles* lie. Heh, heh."

It had not been so trifling to the wearer of the boot, poor chap Richard reflected.

He glanced at Mr. Pinchbeck's attentive features. Now it was the bootmaker's turn. A slight, modest, elderly little man, with scanty hair and an antique appearance, he settled his spectacles and commenced his examination. It was with some reluctance that he glanced inside the boot, shivering at what he saw there.

"This is a horror it turns a man white to look on," he said softly.

But his face showed keen interest when he turned his attention to the boot itself, studying it carefully with an earnest and unsparing eye of minute observation, the product of long years' experience in his craft.

"Hmmm . . . half-boot, country-made . . . no maker's mark . . . Fenshire old style . . . Ridingham likely . . ." he could be heard murmuring to himself as he went along. "Looks to be tanned calf . . . hmmm . . . fancy stitched vamp . . . full double sole . . ."

Presently, when he had done, he laid the object by and peered over his spectacles at the others, who were awaiting his verdict.

"Without question this is an ancient boot — I judge some two or three hundred years at least. By cut, stitch, and seam, and style of heel, I deem it to have been a local product, but time and deterioration have removed all evidence of a maker's mark. The fine vamp suggests the style was fashionable in its day — a gentleman's boot, certainly, made for walking. I see no resemblance in workmanship to that of any brother of our trade practicing in Ridingham today. The style itself, once popular, is outmoded, having long since passed out of fashion. One sees nothing like it now."

"Well, that's something," Richard said. "It confirms Dr. Bussey's view and that of the constable."

The officer nodded importantly. "I dare say that about winds it up, sir. Although the case is unusual, Mr. Hedges, I see no reason to be referring the matter to the authorities. Please to apprize her ladyship of same."

"Still, we remain in the dark as to the identity of the wearer," Richard noted.

"And so we shall, Mr. Hathaway — so we shall. Pending the discovery of fresh evidence, any other course would be a guess in the dark. But it's no person from Ridingham, that's certain — not out here, and not with a shoe like that. It was Toddy here as grubbed it up, you said, Mr. Hedges?"

"It was," said Dan, stroking the terrier's head, "but we've failed to discover the spot."

"Then likely we must wait till the spring, or even the summer, to find it."

"Who was he, I wonder?" spoke up Mr. Pinchbeck, in a voice of quiet reflection. "How came he to this place, and what tales might he have told us? And what brought him to his life's end here on the marshes? May God rest him . . ."

Dan invited his guests to come sit by the fire, that they might talk over the matter a little more, with the aid of some hot coffee from Mrs. Flitch's kitchen.

"What a good idea," smiled the bootmaker, emerging from his reverie.

"We were afraid you would tell us it was Crispin Nightshade's foot in the boot," Richard remarked, once they had settled themselves comfortably and the coffee had been passed around.

"You are familiar then with the legend, Mr. Hathaway? The legend of the haunted leather that can cause the dead to walk?" said Mr. Pinchbeck.

"Only so much as has been told to me by Mr. Gecks. I know no more than that. It sounds quite a story."

He was careful to avoid any mention of Edgar, from whom as well he had acquired a certain amount of information. The youth was conspicuous by his absence, having been forced to cry off on account of the bootmaker. It would have been embarrassing to have met his creditor again so soon after their recent interview.

"The haunted leather — it is one 'Flammarion Diomedes', as he styled himself, a brother of our trade in a very remote epoch, who has the credit of its discovery. The origins of its alleged power are obscure, but black and secret arts surely lie at the bottom of it. This Diomedes was hanged for his trouble, but after his death someone placed shoes of haunted leather on his feet, and his corpse was no more seen."

"It might be so, Mr. Pinchbeck, it might be so," the constable nodded indulgently, "but legends ain't truth, I dare say. Legends may be humbug, arter all."

"Those risen dead who wear the leather," the bootmaker continued undaunted, "inevitably are changed from their former selves. Over time their memories dwindle and gradually fade away, having been replaced by those of another, a being of a dark and loathsome character — someone who in life was not very nice. The leather, you see, is believed to serve as a vessel for this sinister personality, permitting him to live again in another's flesh. Moreover it's said that the cobbler, Crispin Nightshade, had himself undergone a change, in all likelihood from his many hours of working with the leather. The evil, it would appear, had seeped into him too."

Constable Pettiplace, regarding the speaker with a benign expression, chuckled quietly. As an officer of the law he had slight use for any claim, civil or criminal, that could not be substantiated by facts.

"But Mr. Pinchbeck, is the legend true? Is there any such stuff as this haunted leather? Have you ever seen it?" Richard asked.

"Fortunately none ever has come to my notice," the bootmaker replied, "and for that I am grateful. Those in our trade are familiar with certain — er — peculiarities of this leather, the knowledge of which has come down to us. I regret to say that I cannot detail them for you; it is prohibited. But be assured, the ordinary, tanned calf of your half-boot there shows not a trace of haunted leather."

"Lord bless us for that," said a relieved Dan. He glanced at Toddy. The little terrier lay curled up at his feet, watching with one eye open and the other snatching a moment's sleep now and then.

"But be assured as well, Mr. Hedges, that this haunted leather, legend though it may be, is as real as your mysterious boot there."

"You seem very keen on the subject, Mr. Pinchbeck," Richard noted.

"It is a topic of the deepest interest to me."

"I expect it is your work that has directed your curiosity in this direction."

The bootmaker hesitated a few moments, as if weighing in his mind the relative merits of his answering. At length he continued —

"My love of history and dear old things has much to do with it, but there is another cause as well. There is a tradition in my family, that in some manner we are related to, or descended from, this cobbler Nightshade of Ridingham. Of course 'Nightshade' was not his name, and tracing one's lineage through an anonymous person is difficult if not impossible. Nonetheless the tradition exists. And curiously, we never have been troubled by the creeping shadow. You are familiar with the story of the shadow, Mr. Hathaway?"

Richard admitted that he was, uncomfortably so, but did not elaborate. No need to be bringing up the matter of the stovepipe hat and Sir Padrig, or that of the shadowy figure that had scurried up the wall of his room in the moonlight.

"We are unsure how this can be, if we are descended from Nightshade, for the shadow was the curse of the man's poor relation on the scaffold. And have no doubt, the curse is as real as the leather. Moreover, I am in possession of a relic which bears directly on the issue."

From a pocket he drew a small silver object resembling a watch-case, and thumbed it open. Nestled inside was an ornamental wristband of pale blue, much faded, in a delicate lace pattern, upon which was embroidered, in tiny, woven letters, the name *Lise*. From its appearance and dimensions the band can only have been meant for a child, likely an infant.

"It was in the keeping of my mother, and in that of her mother before her, and so forth. I carry it with me always. We are uncertain of its exact significance, but tradition holds it has some relation to the cobbler Nightshade. It is our sole proof of our family's connection to the man."

Here then was the source of his interest in the boot and in the tale of the haunted leather. Was it possible, Richard wondered, that this kindly, cultured, self-effacing little man, could be a descendant of his brother craftsman, he who had murdered his master and married his widow? Or was the lot of it — as the constable undoubtedly believed — only so much humbug?

"Ah, but the world is not always as we would like it — far from it. And here am I nattering away," smiled the bootmaker, and with a sigh he returned the relic to its keeping-place.

"That's quite all right, sir," said Constable Pettiplace, in his easy way, "for if the world were always as we would like it, then where would the Justices and the constables of that world be?"

The interview having reached an end, it was time for the officer and his companion to take their leave. Richard and Dan thanked them both for their speedy determination of the state of the case.

"Once the snows have gone, I expect it will be possible to find where Toddy unearthed the boot," Richard said. "And who can tell? Though the leather is only calfskin, perhaps these are the remains of the man known as Crispin Nightshade. It would be a capital find. For he died here at the Hall, did he not? And I'm told it's a mystery where they buried him."

"Better not to know, sir, I've a notion," suggested Dan.

The boot itself the constable regarded with a frowning air.

"I should very much like to relieve you of the encumbrance of the evidence," he said, hitching up his belt, "but we can't have such disagreeable objects in the station. As I attach no importance to it — as there ain't a dram of proof a crime was committed, nothing grievous bodily on a living being within my purview — it ain't really evidence, arter all. A grisly business, I dare say, but no business for the law. One wishes to serve the ends o' justice, but in this case" — he shrugged, and made a spreading gesture with his palms — "who is there who can identify the deceased, or the cause of death, and so bring an action?" Smiling, he swept them all with his benevolent glance. "And there it rests, gentlemen. You may keep the object if you like; it ain't the turning of a penny-piece to me, or to the Justices, as has enough on their plate. I should caution you, however, that your best course lies in keeping the affair to yourselves. One never knows when persons bent on mischief might take advantage."

The constable, always so neat and precise, concluded his oration by returning his notebook to his tunic, symbolic perhaps of his closing of the case. Dan meanwhile pledged to follow his advice to the letter, despite the fact that the officer's examination and that of Mr. Pinchbeck had produced no solution to the mystery.

As they were leaving, word was brought to the constable by a domestic that Mrs. Flitch was desirous to speak with him in the kitchen. Upon his inquiring, it was discovered that of late certain small items of fish and fowl had gone missing from the larder, and from the kitchen generally; that it was odds and ends, mostly, and only at night; which had given Mrs. Flitch cause to ask whether it were possible the officer might see his way clear to sniff out the thief?

"Very curious, Mrs. Flitch. Very curious. A dish of anchovies the one night, some turkey chicken the next, a slice of goose-pie the night succeeding. Is that about the pattern of it?" said the constable, opening his notebook again.

"It is. Some spitchcock and stewed eel upon another night, and grilled mackerel before that, and a capon leg before *that*. Not so much as would make an ordinary body notice, but *I* noticed, for it's I as keeps an account, as her ladyship has directed me to do, of all edibles as passes through this kitchen. For her ladyship expects us to practice strict economies in these times of ours."

"Odds and ends, mostly, you say then, Mrs. Flitch?"

"Odds and ends — as if a body in haste had helped himself to whatever might be to hand."

"And never anyone seen?"

"Never."

"And have you apprized Lady Martindale of these particulars?" the constable asked.

"I have told it all to Gwenda, her ladyship's maid, and Gwenda has told it all to her ladyship, but nowt has come of it. I'm thinkin' belike her ladyship don't care to have the thief brought to account."

"If thief there be," the officer remarked, smiling at her and twinkling.

"What do you mean, Timbers Pettiplace, by those silly eyes of yours?" the cook demanded.

"I mean, Mrs. Flitch, that I should be looking for a wee small cat of the domestic sort as might have raided your kitchen, before I should be accusing persons in the business. Arter all, it's fish and fowl as are their favorite grub, and night their thieving-time, and as we all know the cat always will find its way to the cream-pot."

"It bean't cream as be missing, George," returned the cook, a fleshy woman of middle age, who putting hands to substantial hips fixed him with a gimlet eye. "And there be no such cat thieves in my kitchen!"

"Be brisk — there's a good girl," the constable chuckled, jollying her along. "It'll all be cleared up satisfactory, I've no doubt. And if ever you should be missing a fried *sole*, Mrs. Flitch, I should be consulting our Mr. Pinchbeck here — for it's his speciality. Heh, heh."

And with a genial touch of his cap he took his leave, strutting importantly into the yard with the bootmaker at his heels.

Something Wrong Somewhere

T HE quaint old town of Ridingham in Fenshire is antiquely picturesque, and one of the loveliest of any category in the whole of the sundered realm. Of all the towns in Fenshire, it is perhaps the most *Fenshirely*. By this I mean that so little changed is it in character from its youthful self, that to look upon Ridingham now is to look upon Ridingham as it was then. To look upon Ridingham now is to look back into another age, as if through a lens, and the years intervening are as naught, so negligible are the differences. It really is the quaintest and most quintessentially charming of quaint old towns in the marshes.

Some may prefer Newmarsh, our county town, to Ridingham, but I am not one of them. For Newmarsh suffers by comparison, I think, from that creeping affliction: modernity. Of course it isn't the fault of its citizens — not entirely at any rate — but a result of the disastrous flooding that occurred towards the end of the last century, when the River Swale overran its banks and inundated the town. Ridingham by comparison sits upon the high alluvial ground, and having no river, and an unbroken medieval town wall, has suffered no serious damage, unlike the marshways around it, and so no modernity. Ridingham has no barge traffic; its communication with the wider world is limited to the few trains and coaches plying the Newmarsh Road to eastwards, and the Dragonthorpe Road to the west. And so while Newmarsh was drowned in part, was revived, and has refashioned itself, Ridingham has blissfully slumbered.

The "magpie" façades of Ridingham — walls of clean white plaster striped with black oak timbers — the steep-pitched roofs of tile or reed-thatched, the high, bell-shaped gables in the old Dutch manner, the curious, hat-shaped peaks, sugar-loaves, the flaring eaves snugly shrouding latticed casements, the doors deep-set like monks peeping from beneath their cowls — such are the hallmarks of that famed architecture of our marshland homes which lends so much character and fancy to their appearance. My brother may speak in fond recollection of the "dreaming spires" of his *alma mater,* Salthead University, but in Ridingham they speak of dreams.

One morning — it was the day succeeding the events of the previous chapter — two riders on horseback were observed coming up the causeway from the marshes south of town. They had pursued their course steadily over the flat, sedgy meadowland dozing under its blanket of snow, its surface riddled and crossed by the marshways and their lazy windings through the freshly-fallen drifts. Houses along the causeway there were but few, and those at scattered intervals, and past them the horsemen had trotted at a rapid clip.

Caped and scarved, with cutlasses at their belts, the riders drew near the old pack-horse bridge over the stream that runs alongside the town gates. The two were jogging along more easily now, having relaxed their precautions as they came within sight of the bridge. Silhouetted against a field of mist the quaint old town loomed up before them, rimed and glaciered, as if overgrown with a white moss. Behind its walls blue curls of smoke could be seen rising from a hundred chimneys, above a hundred ancient checkerboard houses, their numbers punctuated by the spires and crosses of the several churches that dotted the scene.

No small wonder that Ridingham is considered the most beautiful town in the marshes. In the face of accelerating modernity, how might Sam Gander of the Hall have expressed it? *A figo for your modernity!*

For the horsemen themselves were of the Hall — Edgar and Richard — and were mounted upon two of the finest steeds in the Martindale string, Ramble and Gray Gilbert. For this was the day appointed for Richard's interview with his prospective publisher, Mr. Van Ness, of Scriveners' Lane. As for Edgar, he had needed a change of air, he explained, and as he had not been to town of late, had offered to accompany Richard on his errand. My brother for his part hoped the youth was not intending to incur any further obligations with the merchant fraternity of Ridingham. For the lad seemed to have forgotten that his hour of reckoning was approaching — that but four days remained ere the tradesmen were to resume their lively discussion with him.

A parade of shop signs, some boldly sculptured in high relief, others brilliantly painted and gilt, swung and grated in the breeze, sprinkling off little hazy showers of snowflakes as the riders passed by. After turning out of a lane the pair minutes later came in view of an ancient inn, one of the chief posting-houses of the town, and a landmark familiar to them both — it was the Goose and Gander. Its signboard, depicting in homely profile a goose couple, the one in boots and the other in a mob-cap, hung creaking from a bracket above the door. Underneath the two figures ran an inscription —

Whither dost thou wander, O traveler?
Wander here, and be refreshed.

The commercial establishment of Lady Martindale and her father was a three-storied affair, galleried and gabled, with an irregular courtyard that opened onto a range of timber stabling. In a field over the way, three towering mastodons — shaggy red thunder-beasts — were being put to harness by the mastodon men, and their passenger cabs and freight platforms applied, in readiness for the day's early train to Newmarsh. Amidst the cheerful bustle of the inn Richard and Edgar halted a moment to exchange a few words with old Cuffley, the Martindale landlord. A man of easy and garrulous benevolence, it was he who had hired out the mare to Richard on the night of his arrival.

As they continued on, Edgar, feeling the bite of hunger, drew a poniard from his belt, thrust it into his saddle-bag and speared an apple which he seized in his teeth. Another he extended to my brother on the point of his blade.

"Fancy a pippin?"

Richard smiled politely and shook his head, it being too near the time of his interview. Edgar shrugged and proceeded to devour the second apple, then a third.

By narrow courts and winding lanes they made their way to the house of Van Ness and Sons, Publishers, on an avenue in the eastern quarter of the town. On one side of the publishers' establishment stood a cigar-shop, on the other a chop-house, and a wine-vaults over the way.

"'Pon my word, how convenient for Mr. Van Ness," Edgar observed as they dismounted — "or is it Sons?"

Occupying the floor above the publishers and shops was a gloomy row of legal chambers. Its dark lattices frowned upon the busy thoroughfare below. As befitted an abode of attorneys, the corner-posts that supported it were decorated with boldly-carved wolves' heads and paws.

The visitors halted before a tall, beige-painted, brass-headed-nailed door, and were admitted into a quaint-looking apartment of tolerable size, wainscoted in clumberwood. At the far end of it, lounging behind a heavy oak desk, next to a ditto door, was a self-important-looking young gentleman in a starched collar, who raised bloodshot eyes to them as they approached. "Yes?" he inquired, squinting through his horn spectacles as if through a fog.

"Are you Mr. Charles Van Ness?" Richard asked.

"I should say not. My name is Bodfish. I am Mr. Van Ness's clerk and chief reader. You are here to see Mr. Van Ness?"

"Yes, I'm Richard Hathaway, and this is my friend Mr. Harbottle."

"Ah," said the young man, perusing with indifference a register that lay open in front of him, beside a pile of manuscripts, "you are the Mr. Hathaway of the Crust treatise, who is to see Mr. Van Ness?"

"I am."

"Well, if you'll be seated, I'll ascertain whether Mr. Van Ness can speak to you now."

The visitors did as they were bidden. The clerk rose with a yawn and rapped with bored knuckles on the oak door. It being ascertained that Mr. Van Ness *would* see his visitor, Richard was conducted into the inner sanctum of the publisher. Edgar, munching on a pippin, remained in the antechamber to wait out the interview. Meanwhile Mr. Bodfish, oblivious of the youth's existence, resumed his seat, yawned, stretched, then put by the manuscripts and, leaning back in his chair, folded his arms and composed himself for a nap.

Mr. Charles Van Ness was a big, solidly-built man with white hair and a rosy complexion. He extended a cordial hand to his visitor, and for some twenty minutes he and my brother met in secret council. At the finish of it Richard was returned to the antechamber, which in the interval had seen the loss of its clerk and reader, Mr. Van Ness's industrious employee in a fit of ambition having departed for the wine-vaults over the way.

"Well? What's the good news?" Edgar asked as he and my brother were unhitching their mounts from the rail.

"Difficult to say, really. He seemed a decent sort for a publisher."

"There's a bit o' luck."

"And all he said had the ring of truth to it . . ."

"And?"

"However, he said very little — a bit of this and a dash of that. Mostly he listened, and I'm not at all certain he was so keen on what he heard."

"These big wigs all are like that, sir. They ain't about to commit themselves right off. They know which side of the bread has the butter."

"For instance, I haven't a clue whether he understood the nature of my work. I don't believe it wholly fired his imagination. At all events something was not quite right. And speaking of bread, it seems Mr. Van Ness had mistaken 'Pharnaby Crust' for a baked-goods manufactory."

"The deuce you say."

"He asked to see some sample pages of the manuscript, and when I informed him that I haven't any as yet, he appeared to lose much of his enthusiasm."

"Well, I like that."

"He then remarked that 'there's a kind of author afflicted with an itch to put absolutely everything, down to the very last atom, on paper. You're not *that* kind of author, are you, Mr. Hathaway?' says he."

"Oh, dear."

"'Leave off your footnotes, your endnotes, asterisks, and etceteras. Too dodgy for our compositor and they give my reader a positive headache'. I took the hint — no exhaustive tomes need be submitted. I believe I shall have hard work to reclaim his interest."

"But a man of your mark, sir! Well, at least he called you an author; he might have called you worse. But you haven't actually written anything yet, have you?"

"No, I am still engaged in my researches."

"Well, there you are."

"And he did not rule out the subject of Sir Pharnaby entirely, once it was explained to him."

On this note, however equivocal, the two mounted to the stirrups. It being now the luncheon hour, and as Edgar was feeling a trifle less pinched on account of the apples, he suggested that they dine at a bun-house he knew of — to 'recuperate their vital forces'. The youth explained that he preferred the bun-house to the commercial room of the Goose and Gander owing to the superior quality of its cream teas, which were a speciality of the place.

A bell jingled musically as they entered — "Bo-peep's" was the name of the house — and a few minutes later a neatly-dressed attendant shepherded them to a comfortable table beside a lattice facing the avenue. A goodish crowd was present, all of them exchanging the news of the day with much liveliness and volubility and trading pleasant and jocular remarks.

Directly one of several waitresses approached the table. Like the rest she was a young lady of no more than eighteen or nineteen, attired all in rustic lilac and lace, with a charming smile and a lovely figure. She inquired of the gentlemen what their pleasure was.

"I should like something hot to keep the cold off," Richard said.

"Our cream teas are our special refreshment, sir," the waitress informed him.

"Capital. Well, it shall be cream tea then."

Turning to Edgar, the young lady dimpled, placing the prettiest taper finger to her lip in bashful play. She inquired what *he* would have, sir, the lad with a twinkle answering the same as Richard. So it was to be cream tea for both, and a tray of currant buns, buttered scones, saffron cake, and marshberry jam.

"Bewitching creature," Edgar sighed, after the waitress had brought the tea-things and gone away again.

"The two of you appear to be acquainted," Richard observed.

"Only just."

"She blushed when she handed you your tea, and she addressed you by name."

"Really? I hadn't noticed," said the youth in a careless tone. He chewed his bun thoughtfully. "Delightful spot, ain't it? The shepherd-girls in lilac and ringlets, and every one of 'em a peach — not an owl in the lot. I tell you, sir, a gent could do worse."

With a smile Richard noted it may have been superior quality that had drawn the lad to Bo-peep's, but not necessarily of its cream teas.

"I dare say rustication has its benefits, all things considered," he remarked.

"Better to go down into the country for a twelvemonth," said Edgar, "than to be sitting in concrete for hours at a stretch, giving ear to a lot of musty lectures, or lingering by one's lamp over some wretched construe from chapel-time till the gray dawn."

"Hasn't it occurred to you, Edgar, that you must inevitably resume the scholar's life once you return to your college?"

"Certainly it has, sir. But that don't mean a feller can't enjoy his holiday."

Both of them the whiles had been observing the busy life of the town through the lattice, with its view upon the avenue — the comers and goers and chance droppers-in, the sellers and buyers all hurrying to and fro, the carriages, horsemen, and merchants' carts passing by. At one point a cab lumbered up, bearing a fat woman overflowing onto two skinny men, and discharged the men — to their immense relief. On the footway a laundress with a tub under her arm paused before the window to study her appearance in the glass, heedless of the eyes looking out. Nearby a muffin-seller with his bell and tray was hawking his wares beneath a lamp-post, when a bent little man came hobbling along, put a ladder against the post, climbed up to clean the lamp, got down, and hobbled away again.

"And what do you intend to do with your life, Edgar, once you have obtained your B.A.? Have you a profession in view?" Richard asked, filling his pipe and settling back in his chair.

The youth shrugged. "I'll be going up for my smalls at Michaelmas. A chap first must get through his little-go before he can give consideration to his degree — or to his life, come to that." He touched a hand to his brow and sighed. It was a long road which lay before him, he knew, one with many turnings; but as much as he hated to be sitting in concrete or lingering over his lamp, he hated it more to be disappointing his aunt.

Richard cupped the warm bowl of the pipe in his fingers and asked — "Have you thought of going in for the law? I believe your aunt is favorably disposed in that direction."

"That dry study? Dry-as-dust, I call it. I dare say it's a no-go. However Auntie's biased, and justly so — and fortunately so, because she has her Mr. Gecks. He's a trump — one in a thousand for a lawyer party — who lost his heart to her ages ago. 'Be courageous, and be *fortunate.*' The Martindale family motto, you'll recollect, sir."

"Yes, indeed."

"Perhaps I'll read dog Latin in the new year — it's a lawyer's game, you know. For every gent should be master of something, and one thing's as good as another. Already I've gotten the hang of it, thanks to Smugley — chap's an all-rounder on my stair at Queen's — a regular hoplite, and very keen on the law. He can spout his dog Latin the way Toddy sheds fleas. *'Harbottle et Hathaway ad sum jam forti.'* There — nothing to it! 'Harbottle and Hathaway had some jam for tea.' The B.A.'s as good as got."

"Latin? So you're going in for the Church after all?" Richard responded with mock surprise.

"Jiminy! There's a grim prospect. From dry-as-dust to dust-to-dust. Oh, dear, no."

"Nor going in for marriage either? Lilac and ringlets?"

The youth started. "Joined in holy padlock? Edgar Harbottle? There's a good joke," he returned with a shiver. "That positively *ain't* the ticket."

In like vein they chatted awhile over their tea and sundries, pleasantly and agreeably, and without reference to candle-smoke cartoons, dons and duns, or shopkeepers and their wretched accounts. At one point the topic of Edgar's inheritance arose, and something like a cloud settled over the youth's features.

"Is there anything the matter?" Richard asked.

Edgar nodded. "It occurred to me t'other day — thinking of your experience in the library, sir — the creeping shadow — Sir Padrig and the stovepipe — the Martindale heirs — "

"You're curious perhaps whether you're not in line to become an object of attention for this — this shadow, or whatever it is?"

"That's right — bother the luck!"

"To be frank with you, Edgar, the idea had occurred to me as well."

The youth sat with his tea-cup halfway to his lips and stared, the revelation having drained some of the color from his face.

"Had you never before considered the possibility?" Richard asked.

"Never — 'pon my word."

"A possibility, I reckon — but then how can it follow? True, you are the Martindale heir — so you are led to believe — but you're not a Martindale yourself. You're a Harbottle — nothing to do with Sir Padrig and the cobbler's poor relation and the suspect curse that your aunt never speaks of."

"Spot-on, sir! Why the deuce bother a poor struggling trog who's minding his own affairs?" Edgar wondered, patting his brow with his handkerchief.

"However there is no longer a direct line, no other male kin descending from Sir Padrig. So that any collateral descendant of the family who should happen to inherit . . ."

Richard, his eyes full of thought, was studying the smoke which eddied upwards from the pipe in his hand. It occurred to him then to ask Edgar what had befallen Sir Pedr Martindale, for it seemed that there must have been something odd about his lordship's death. But the look in Edgar's face quashed the impulse. Now was not the time to be broaching the subject, for certainly the idea of the shadow had given the lad the jitters.

And what of Richard himself? He was no Martindale — no relation, collateral or otherwise. And yet had he not been visited by this same shadow, once in the library, and again in his room, when it had scurried up the moonlit wall into the ceiling?

There was an interval of silence, uncomfortable for both, each of them absorbed in his own thoughts. Edgar had become decidedly uneasy with the notion of his inheritance. Why had the danger of his position not trickled through to him earlier? Certainly the curse had been intended for the male heirs succeeding to the Martindale estates — whether their name be Martindale, Harbottle, or Whoever . . .

Ah, the blissful ignorance of youth!

All in a moment Edgar scraped back his chair. Richard quickly followed his example, and paid the reckoning.

"That's very handsome of you, sir," Edgar acknowledged.

Richard smiled kindly, for he knew the lad hadn't tuppence. Considerably refreshed, they departed the bun-house. No sooner had they gone out, however, than Edgar ducked back in, averting his face, as a thickset gentleman in black wearing a shovel hat stepped past them on the footway. He remained in hiding until the gentleman was well out of sight, before showing himself.

"Phew! That was old Cassock, our rector of St. Mary-in-the-Mews," he explained.

"Goodness, you're not averse to the company of clergymen, are you? Particularly as you're going in for the Church?" Richard asked.

"Not at all. But the reverend gent loaned me a guinea some weeks back, and I dare say he expects me to cash up."

"And . . . ?"

Edgar's face was sheepish. "Haven't tuppence," he said.

The danger having passed, they leaped astride their mounts and started for the Hall. As they were near the eastern limits of Ridingham, Edgar suggested that for a change of scene they should take the wood road, which followed the contours of Marley Wood some little distance to the southwards. My brother, not sure such an idea was entirely wise, nevertheless yielded to the lad's desire for variety in their surroundings.

Presently, having left the quaint old town behind them, and after proceeding for perhaps a mile, they stopped to rest beneath a finger-post where several roads met.

"That way lies Drizzlehurst," Edgar explained. "Treadwell's got an aunt who lives there. And that way lies Madland. And there — that's the wood road — by way of Northeave, and so round again to the Hall. Northeave's quite a tiny place, but there's a big old manse or two — hunting lodges for town swells of ages past. All deserted now. No one with any sense hunts in the wood nowadays."

"A ghost village?"

"Just the ticket, eh? But really, sir, you shouldn't leave us without having had the tour. It's a local curiosity."

"I dare say."

So they pricked their horses into the road on the right, that leading to Northeave. It was a way but little taken, evidently, for they encountered no one along the route. Meantime the tall curtain of trees that was Marley Wood was growing steadily upon their sight. Higher and higher climbed the snow-filled cedars, pines, and Scotch firs, their lofty tops swaying in the breeze like so many footmen nodding their powdered heads. In the dreary light the deeper forest aisles were a black obscurity of tangled growth, sinister and secret.

"Pleasant place," Edgar remarked. "A gent could get lost in there."

"Or worse," Richard observed.

No sound broke the deathly silence of the wood. With each turn in the road the trees drew nearer, and mounted taller. Marley Wood, as everyone knows, is a mystery, and a menace, abounding with dangers of every kind. The road had been skirting the verge of its ample domain in an idle, wandering sort of zigzag, until at last road and shadowy aisles joined together. Thenceforth the way proceeded for the most part in the gloom of arching boughs through the eaves of the wood. Many, many miles away, Richard reflected, on the far side of the wood, on its southern border, lay Market Snailsby, and Mead Cottage, the home of our late parents which he and I had shared since their passing. There would come a time when Mrs. Chugwell's plank road through the forest would bridge the many miles, to link the north of Fenshire with the remoter south; but that day still was some years off.

For the most part the riders pursued their journey in silence, conversing only at intervals. In time they arrived at Northeave, a lonely and unfrequented spot — deserted, Edgar had said — with a reputation, as it turned out, as a haunted place. Only a few houses huddled there in the loom of the great trees, all within easy hail of each other, and all equally dilapidated. The town families to whom they had belonged had long since surrendered them to the keeping of the wood.

There was one manse in particular that Edgar knew something of — a woeful ruin of stone and brick and half-timbering, the whole of it gloomed over with a sadness, in its framework of sheltering trees thick with snow. Like the other houses it too had been a forest lodge, in those gloried days of yore when Fenshiremen — our long-ago forefathers — had thought nothing of spearing venison and flat-head boar in Marley Wood. But in these modern times of ours no one hunted in the wood any more.

"It was a family called Mackery lived here once. Respectable parties — Ridingham merchant class — *nouveau riche*. None left now. Treadwell told me of 'em. His aunt in Drizzlehurst is something of an authority," Edgar related. "The place itself is called Mackery End."

A down-thrusting, stoop-shouldered, drooping old relic, in which certain Jacobean features had been blended with the quaint old Fenshire style, it had lain uninhabited and neglected for more than a century. Its front behind a substantial wall was hidden by thick masses of shrubbery groaning under their burden of snow. Here the shutters of the house were closed, there they had been thrust aside, in a riot of inconsistency. Most of the lead-lattice glazing, where visible, was cracked or broken. A small wicket clenched with many an iron nail opened before the entrance-door, which hung slightly ajar.

The riders ambled round the lodge a time or two, surveying it with appraising eyes, before dismounting in the yard which lay between the house and the brick-walled stables and outbuildings. There they climbed the backstairs for a look inside, which as Edgar explained was a component of any tour of the local curiosity.

From the state of the rooms it was evident that many years had elapsed since anyone had lived there. Richard felt a moldy chill suffuse his bones as he and Edgar passed from one empty apartment to the next, their eyes absorbing the dreary bareness of the place, where little or nothing remained in the way of furnishings to hint at the departed glories of Mackery End.

At one point during the tour my brother halted and, turning to Edgar, asked him in a low voice —

"Did you hear anything?"

The youth shook his head. "All manner of goblin noises in a house like this."

"It was no goblin noise. Did you see a shadow cross that window from right to left?"

"A shadow?" echoed Edgar. "That's a good one, sir. How can there be a shadow? There's no sun."

They approached the lattice in question — it was unshuttered, but like the others was fortified with rusty iron — and glanced outside. Nothing seemed to be amiss. Through a break in the trees Richard observed that the heavy overcast was beginning to erode the light. He scarce had realized how much time had passed since they had left Ridingham. Now it was getting on for dark, particularly here in the loom of the giant trees.

"I suggest we collect the horses and ride at once for the Hall," he said. Then he paused and looked out again at the window, his eyes drawn to something he saw on the ground there. "Good gracious. I — I don't like this at all . . ."

It was a trail of animal footprints of impressive dimensions, deep-sunk in the new snow alongside the house.

"I reckon we've had a visitor," he told Edgar.

The youth blanched. "Some poor tramping fellow?" he suggested hopefully.

Richard shook his head, then clamped a warning finger to his lips.

Edgar glanced at him in quick alarm, then at the lattice in the opposite wall. "I could have sworn I saw something — there, sir — through the bars — beyond the shrubbery — "

But already it was gone, a shadow where no shadow should be. And no creeping shadow had it been, but one of flesh and blood, of tawny fur, and claws and teeth, and blazing eyes. Of a sudden the very air seemed to be charged with its stealthy presence.

"Was that Gray Gilbert I heard?" Edgar whispered hoarsely.

"They're restive — they've sensed our visitor. I fear we have no alternative, Edgar. We must remove the horses to the stables. We haven't a tinker's chance now on the road."

"Couldn't we ride like the deuce?"

"And be slaughtered in the attempt? I should say not. Much the wiser to wait it out in some safety," said Richard, pivoting on his heel.

Edgar followed him to the back-stairs. Silently they opened the door and glanced about them. The horses, ears up-pricked and nostrils steaming, had thrown back their heads and were pawing at the ground with a nervous energy. There was nothing else for it now. Down the stairs crept my brother and Edgar, and taking hold of their mounts they led them hurriedly through the snow to the stables, which looked to be substantially entire, and which boasted a fortified door that they quickly latched and double-barred behind them.

No sooner had they halted to listen than Edgar toppled backwards over something in the dark and came down with a crash. Richard felt a sudden squeeze at his heart and, fearing they had run upon some intruder there, risked it and scraped a match into flame. It showed Edgar sprawled upon the ground, an old cider-cask upturned at his elbow.

The light having revealed no occupants of the stable other than those accounted for, my brother quickly snuffed it out. Hardly had he done so than the darkness of the interior seemed to darken further. It was then he discovered that the building was not without windows — there was one to be exact, a dirty, cobwebby little square of lead-latticed panes — and that it was the feeble light in that square which had dimmed.

"Good — gracious — " he murmured.

Something in his tone sent Edgar's flesh into a crawl. The youth's gaze swung to the lattice. What he saw there brought his heart into his mouth, and panic into his eyes.

"We're for it now!" he croaked, with the queer mangled thing that had been his voice.

The dimming of the light had been caused by the figure of an animal, which had come to a stealthy halt outside the window. A rich, tawny hide, sprinkled over with patches of a darker shade, cloaked its massive frame — a frame of immense proportions, rising some several hands higher than that of either Ramble or Gray Gilbert. A thick collar of fur, similar in hue to the patches, ringed the giant's head and neck. At present its eyes were turned from the lattice while scanning the yard and grounds in a scrupulous survey.

Richard felt a chill of fear steal over him. Silently he drew back from the window. Edgar, gaping in horror, followed his example.

"A m-man-eater," he stammered out.

"Matter of fact!" Richard nodded.

Had the monster caught their scent? Certainly it must have sensed that strangers were on the premises. Might the traces they had left behind in the lodge be enough to draw it away? Or was it aware they had hidden themselves in the stables?

And what of Ramble and Gray Gilbert?

For a terrifying few minutes Richard and Edgar strove to calm the both of them, to comfort them and reassure them, and prevent them from crying out and inadvertently alerting the man-eater. The horses' keen nostrils would have detected every scent borne to them on the chilly air, and clearly the animals were sensible of the presence of the spotted lion; of the utmost importance was to keep them from reacting to it.

Then, as abruptly as it had vanished, light was restored to the lattice. The creature had moved off. But where had it gone? Was it even now sniffing hungrily round the building or at the stable-door? How many minutes or hours must pass before the danger itself will have passed — if indeed it was to pass? For the stoutness of the door likely was no match for the raking claws and powerful sinews of a determined carnivore.

Presently, when it seemed that the immediate danger had subsided, Edgar righted the empty cask and, dusting it with a coat-sleeve, seated himself and with chins in hand commenced to thinking hard. For a time he and Richard, who had started pacing back and forth, cudgeled their brains for some means of resolving their dilemma — something short of an endless, long wait. But from their current lookout their prospects seemed very blue.

Then Edgar rose, as though the cask of a sudden had grown very hot, and tilted his head to one side, listening. Richard, observing this, ceased his pacing and listened too.

"Did you hear that, sir?" the youth asked.

"No. What was it?"

"I thought someone called my name. A faint voice, from a distance off. A gent's voice, it seemed — in the lodge, perhaps — you heard something there as well — the goblin noise — "

Can someone have been hiding upstairs in the woeful ruin?

"But who could be in the house who would know you, and why would he be there? And if he is there, he is in the same danger as we," Richard pointed out.

Edgar sighed and, noting the logic of the observation, sank down again onto the cask and dropped his chins into his hands. "No one, I dare say. Like as not it was the voice of some passing spirit — the ghost of my dead-and-gone father, perhaps, calling to me from across the Styx. I don't see how I could have made a finer mess of things. Sorry to have gotten you in-to this, sir — it's entirely my fault. I apologize without reserve."

"No need to be wilting like a lettuce leaf," Richard admonished him, "for we have our weapons and our good horses, and we have our lives."

Edgar shrugged, and glanced helplessly about him. "But for how much longer, sir? Were it not for me we should be home and dry at the Hall. Instead we're liable to be massacred at Mackery End. Mackery End! The name's appropriate, for here it all must end — wiped from the face of the earth — " And he threw up his hands in despair.

"All things considered, we're in a reasonably secure position," Richard told him, "and are not without resources. And the hours are on our side."

But Edgar seemed not to hear him. "I'm very sorry to have been the cause of it, sir. Wood road! Local curiosity! Would this were only a dream — a nightmare — no such luck — this really takes the prize — "

My brother, interrupting him, raised a warning hand. "There! Did you hear it?"

"Hear what?" Edgar groaned, expecting the worst.

"Your name — I heard it clearly this time — dash it all, there *is* some-one out there — calling for you — "

Like another Lazarus from the tomb Edgar rose from the cask, a glimmer of hope showing in his eyes. The next moment a cloud passed in front of them. "Don't you feel there's something rather wrong about this?" he asked.

"I do," Richard agreed, "but we'll learn nothing by remaining here. I distinctly heard a voice call your name. If there is someone in the lodge, perhaps we would be wise to join him. There is greater safety in numbers. On the other hand he may be injured and in need of our assistance. You've no inkling who it might be?"

"None. Who would be calling my name out here?"

There was nothing for it but to make a dash for the house. Cautiously they removed the bars from the door and unfastened the latch, and with their weapons drawn stole forth into the yard.

More time had passed, and the night was almost upon them. It was an impossibility now that they should return to the Hall before morning. The question that arose was whether they should pass the night in the stables, or in the lodge, in the company of Edgar's unknown friend there.

All seemed quiet in the yard. Neither sight nor sound had they of the spotted lion. Its tracks were there, but the creature itself appeared to have vanished.

"Feller must've hopped it," Edgar whispered, his confidence rising.

Richard had no comment. Glancing warily round, he signed to the lad that they should hop it now themselves — that is, make their flying dash for the back-stairs.

They had gone no more than a few paces, their boots deep-plunged in the snow, when a stealthy form seemed to detach itself from the trees, and with a quick, powerful stride came gliding into the yard. Like a mountain the giant loomed up before them, majestic and mighty. A cavernous growl could be heard rumbling in its throat. They had a glimpse of menacing jaws parted to disclose bared fangs, of two glowing, yellow-green spots of flame mesmerizing in their bestial stare. The face framed by the collared head was twisted into a hideous mask of savagery; to any person of sense it was the face of certain destruction.

Snarling, the monster crept towards them through the drifts, head flattened, tail extended, its fiery gaze bent on annihilation.

Richard and Edgar recoiled in horror. The chill of the snow seemed to pass from their boots directly into their blood, freezing them in place. Stiffened to attention, they could do little but watch. There was scant chance of their returning to the stables now, none whatever of reaching the lodge.

The carnivore shifted expectantly, drawing its hindquarters underneath it as it gathered itself for the fatal assault.

Richard's voice was grim. "That tears it," he muttered. He leveled his blade at the monster, its point tracing slow circles in the air.

There was nothing for it now but to fight.

Edgar squelched a sudden exclamation. *Where's your courage, Harbottle?* he demanded of himself. A gloved fist crept toward his mouth, pushing the knuckles against white lips. It seemed his courage, what there was of it, all had ebbed away. Facing down a handful of shopkeepers was one thing — facing down a spotted lion in an empty yard at Mackery End was quite another.

"They'll f-find n-nothing of us b-but our b-b-boots," he stammered out. "Like that — that p-poor old c-codger's b-boot o' T-T-Toddy's — massacred — "

A glance at the youth's stricken face gone white as chalk, another at the snarling countenance of the lion, told Richard all he needed. Circumstanced as they now were, escape by any means short of magic appeared remote.

Inch by inch towards them slunk their executioner, whiskers bristling, eyes shooting a livid fire.

"Dash it all!" Richard muttered, throwing out his chin. His cutlass leaped from his one hand to the other and back again. My brother is not the sort of man who abandons hope easily. This was not the first time — nor would it be the last — that he had found himself in so dire a predicament. Bolstering up his nerve he glanced again at the lodge, at its upper tier of windows, from which he believed the call to Edgar had come. It was just possible that —

In that instant something crossed the corner of his eye. He whipped his head around and, gazing upwards, saw a shadowy, dark mass emerge from the tree-tops. Then it swung out over the yard, hovering in space there like a thundercloud.

What the Trees Said

"MR. EDGAR!"

There it was again.

"Ahoy there — Mr. Edgar, sir!" the voice repeated.

The words had seemed to issue from the tree-tops high above them. Neither Edgar nor Richard could discern much in the waning light, save for the shadowy dark thing that had appeared from amidst the clumbers. Even the spotted lion had taken notice, its glance shifting from its intended prey to the unknown menace lurking overhead.

"Mr. Edgar — *grapple the ropes!*"

"'P-Pon my word, I know that voice," Edgar said.

Next instant came a whirling, rolling noise, and Richard felt something strike his shoulder and drop neatly to the snow at his feet. It was a cord-ladder, which had come tumbling down to him as though from heaven. Its uppermost end, however, was attached to no heavenly cloud, but to the curving timbers of the vessel riding in air over the yard.

"Yo-ho — Mr. Edgar!" cried the voice.

Now they spied a light glimmering, and knew it for a lantern hung out over the ship's side. For a ship indeed it was, whose bulk had grown upon their sight as it descended towards them. Its outline had assumed a spindle shape, like a ship's hull, and thrusting downward from it was a ship's keel, and high on its bow was affixed a ship's anchor. And craning out over the rail was a mariner's head, his face partly illumined by the lantern he held in his hand.

"Grapple 'er fast — and stand by to be hoist aloft," he called down to them.

His was the voice they had been hearing — the voice they first thought had come from the lodge, then from the tree-tops.

Stand by to be hoist aloft?

Both head and lantern vanished inboard, and moments later the ship paused in her descent. Richard, one eye on the vessel and his other on their savage antagonist, said in a low whisper — "Well, I'm jiggered. What is that thing up there? And who is the man?"

Edgar wrung his head. "Deuce if I know, sir — but the chap's voice is f-f-familiar — "

"He appears to know you."

"But what's this about b-being hoist aloft?"

Seconds later a shrill blast like the whistle of a bo'sun's pipe pierced the air, riveting their attention as well as the carnivore's. The beast's ears flew up, and its eyes too, as it glared in anger at the hovering menace. But the intent of the whistle was clear — to distract the creature and put off the fatal charge.

"Step to the ladder, sir — you and the other gentleman — and grapple 'er fast!" directed the voice aloft.

Richard glanced at the lion, whose attention remained divided. But his hopes quickly were dashed when the animal swung round again and fixed its gaze on himself and Edgar. Growling, with teeth bared and eyes staring fiercely, it resumed its stealthy creep towards them.

A strangled cry died in the throat of Edgar. It rushed upon my brother then that whatever the man aloft meant to do, he had better do it now, or not at all.

"There's nothing else for it," he said. "Step to the ladder, Edgar — and pray for the best."

"Ship your blades — grapple tight the ropes — I'll hoist you to safe harborage," the voice called down to them.

Edgar gasped out a faint affirmative. Having sheathed their weapons he and Richard did as they were instructed — placed their feet on rungs of the ladder and, clinging fast to it, awaited whatever the man aloft had in store for them.

It was not long in coming, nor was the spotted lion. By some savage intuition it had gleaned that something was amiss. Springing forward from its crouch, it covered the remaining distance in huge, bounding leaps, and with a horrid scream launched itself upon them.

Edgar, had he not been clinging like a tick to the ladder, might well have pitched forward in a swoon directly in the animal's path. Instead the ground fell away beneath him, as he and Richard were lifted high into the air, up and over the snowy yard and into the trees, as though by the hand of the proverbial giant of beanstalk fame.

Edgar, gaping blankly, watched in horror as the cat's claws went scraping past his boot-heels in its leap, missing them by no more than an atom.

Even in the gloom he could see the rage spilling from the creature's eyes, saw its frenzied pawing at the empty air. With savage lights ablaze it howled its disappointment to the woods and the darkening day.

As he and Richard hung in space there in the tree-tops above the yard, both realized that the mysterious vessel to which they owed their salvation had abruptly ascended, taking the cord-ladder and themselves with it — and their lives. Amidst the pine branches a lantern showed again at the ship's rail, and the same head poked out beside it.

"Come along up!" the mariner directed, extending his free hand in invitation.

They, who had only just escaped from the brink of disaster, now were to scale a cord-ladder precariously a-sway in the tree-tops a dizzying height above the ground?

Not bloody likely.

Edgar, for one, whose knees long since had turned to water, was feeling disinclined to do so. He hadn't the stomach for it — or the knees — and, frankly, neither had my brother. Beneath them, in the white patch of field that was the yard, they could see the lion aggressively pacing, could hear it roaring its rage and vows of revenge in great, echoing waves of sound. And over there, not many yards away and a little below, floated the roof of the lodge with its clutter of gables and chimney-stacks.

Richard, clinging to his perch, hallooed to the man in the ship his concerns about scaling the ladder. There ensued a pause, followed by a nod of comprehension. "Stand by," the mariner called down to him, before vanishing inboard.

"There's a good joke. What else does the f-f-feller expect us to d-d-do?" quavered Edgar.

"I believe we're moving again," said Richard, moments later.

It was true. Already they had drifted a distance across the yard towards the lodge, descending as they went. Presently a high balcony under a gable at the top of the house swung into view. Nearer and nearer it came, lurching crazily, it seemed, under their feet, as the ropes swayed and twisted in the air. Soon they were riding just above it, and were able to lower themselves from the rungs and plant their feet again on solid ground, or at least on solid balcony. Both had been praying that its fabric, after the passage of so many years, was indeed solid — the which, fortunately, it proved to be.

The ladder was withdrawn into the craft, whose buoyant mass then descended till it lay right abreast of them. Broadside on it swung in closer, until it was riding mere yards from the balcony. At last they had they a view of the man at the helm, who stood in a covered cockpit manipulating his ship's wheel and a lever at his right hand, as he guided his vessel towards them.

And how wondrous a vessel it was, that had no mast, no sails, and floated on air!

Having lashed the wheel, the pilot rose from the cockpit. He then tossed a mooring-rope outboard, securing it to a finial above the balcony. The ship now being made fast beside the lodge, he sprang to the rail and rigged a plank to bridge the dizzying gulf between bulwark and balustrade. Then he took up his lantern again and opened its slide to the full, to light his visitors aboard.

"Easy as you go, Mr. Edgar — and the gentleman too, if you please," he invited, extending his hand.

The light afforded them a better view of his sailorly self — mighty trim and lively he looked in his blue jacket, broad-belted galligaskins, and old sea-boots, with his boyish grin, and his thatch of orange hair flowing from under his mariner's bonnet.

Edgar caught his breath and retreated a step. His eyes widened in astonishment as he beheld a familiar ruddy countenance, one that he had little thought to have seen again this side of the Styx. He shoved his hat to the back of his head and stared.

"Jiminy," he gasped after a moment, once he had absorbed the shock of it, "if it ain't Owen — Owen Aberdovey! 'Pon my word — can you be alive, Owen?"

The mariner responded with an embarrassed chuckle, as if he were suddenly ashamed to be breathing. "Aye, that I can, sir — and I am."

The revelation had quite staggered Edgar, and left him in some confusion. But he brightened almost immediately, and in a jubilant voice (how different from his quavering tones of only minutes before) exclaimed —

"Brayvo, Owen! It ain't every f-feller as is planted in his g-g-grave and lives to tell of it."

"I reckon it's Davy Jones you mean," Richard suggested.

"Not Davy Jones, sir, perish the thought," said the mariner, ruefully, "but not afar off it. Please to come aboard, gentlemen. Not to worry — her deck is stout and solid footing, certain sure."

But first they had to negotiate the plank-bridge that Owen had laid for them. Edgar, heavily fleshed, expended a deal of effort in crawling over it. Fortunately it had grown so dark that the yard was all but invisible beneath him, which was of considerable aid; although my brother suspects the youth's eyes were shut for the entirety of the crossing. Directly Richard followed, and so at last both were safe aboard the mariner's craft. Stout and solid indeed was her deck's footing — wondrously so, for a ship riding on nothing but air.

"You're right welcome aboard the skimmer, gentlemen," Owen greeted them.

"Skimmer?" said Richard.

"That is her designation, sir. It was given her by the captain," the mariner explained, as he removed the plank and stowed it aboard.

"Why, are you not her captain?"

"Hardly that, sir! No, by captain, sir, I meant Captain Barnaby — master of the merchant lugger *Salty Sue*. The skimmer is a sort of jolly-boat for her. Aye, she's a duck she is, the *Sue*, and the skimmer likewise — both of 'em mighty staunch and skyworthy."

Observing his visitors' mutual puzzlement, Owen assured them there would be ample time for explanations. Meanwhile there was an introduction to be gone through.

"Hallo — happy to make your acquaintance, Owen," Richard said as the two shook hands.

"And yours, Mr. Hathaway, sir."

"Many thanks for the timely rescue. We were in — er — a spot of trouble."

"Aye, sir," the mariner nodded.

"It was entirely my fault," Edgar broke in. "I insisted on the wood road — we had been knocking about Ridingham in the A.M. — and well, deuce take me if we didn't run into that spot o' trouble — spotted's more like it, as in lion — oh, dear, what a mess — "

"No need, Mr. Edgar. I'm glad to have been of service."

"What a bit of luck it was to have blundered on you by accident — and at Mackery End!"

"Aye, sir."

Meanwhile a dozen questions were crowding the minds of Richard and Edgar, as they pondered the mystery of Owen's return.

How came the young man to be alive, when all reports had been that he had perished at sea? What strange business had brought him back, and why had his mother and the others at Haigh Hall not been made privy to the fact? And what was this wondrous ship of his, this "skimmer" as he called her, this flying miracle of wood and no canvas, and how came he to have possession of her? For the slight experience they had had of the craft had filled them with amazement and not a little awe.

It was with a note of pride that the mariner spoke of his marvelous vessel, for it was he himself who had helped fit her up. She had been a ship's cutter, he explained, when the skipper of the *Salty Sue* had acquired her for a new purpose, about which Owen pledged more later. For the air was bitter cold, and he urged them now to join him in his ship's cabin below.

Despite her smallish size she was a roomy craft, owing to the ingenious arrangement of her fixtures and furnishings, and a stout-built as well. In the cockpit, mounted vertically on a post, was her ship's wheel, which at one time had served as a fore-wheel of a carrier's van. Affixed to a bulkhead beside it was a pair of crank-handles, as might have come from a mangle, and at the helmsman's feet were a couple of pedals like those of a grand piano. All these various devices, Owen explained, were crucial for the proper piloting of the skimmer.

"But what buoys her aloft?" Richard asked.

Again the mariner promised an explanation in due course.

From the cockpit they descended a narrow companionway, short but steep-pitched, to a long, low cabin, which was illuminated by a silver lamp that hung above a table midway, and flanked on both sides by cushioned lockers that doubled as seats. A second, smaller cabin opened through the forward bulkhead, wherein were two sleeping berths or bunks, as trim and orderly as the mariner himself. Both cabins were pierced by tiny portholes, and the main by a small hatch to carry off the smoke from the lamp and from the vessel's small cook-stove. The shut door in the aft bulkhead led to a modest-sized store-room, Owen told them.

Edgar, still recovering from his experience, sank down onto a locker in a kind of soft collapse. Richard, seating himself rather than sinking, followed his example. Their host meanwhile, having shut the companion-hatch behind them, hung his lantern over the stove and proceeded to busy himself there.

"You'll take some coffee?" he asked.

"Please," said Richard. Edgar added his eager assent.

"And biscuits?"

"Delightful!" the youth exclaimed.

With a practiced hand the mariner set to work, the cook-stove serving to heat both the coffee and the cabin. He filled a pannikin with water from a keg, some of which he used to make the coffee. The rest he poured into pewters for his guests' refreshment. A tin of biscuits was supplied as well.

Edgar found himself regretting having finished off the pippins from the Hall, as he should have liked to have shared them now with his friends.

Soon the pleasant aroma of the coffee filled the air, and the coffee itself their cups, and then their inward selves, its warmth suffusing them from their insides out, much as the heat from the stove had warmed the cabin.

Richard produced his pipe. "May I?"

The mariner nodded. Richard filled the bowl, tamped it down, and puffed it into smoke. Directly Owen followed with an old black cutty. As for Edgar, he had no pipe — never had fancied one — for like most college men he was partial to cigars. But as he had none about him at the moment, he contented himself with the coffee and biscuits in repairing the late shock to his nerves.

Comfortably ensconced there in the snug cabin of the skimmer, Richard was struck by the unique character of their position. Here they were, the three of them, in a ship floating in air high above the ghost village of Northeave, at the edge of Marley Wood in the night-time — and where no spotted lion or marsh devil could trouble them! Was it not proof positive, he mused, that most any obstacle in this life might be overcome? It seemed like a waking dream, all of it due to the good offices of a dead man who had *not* died.

And so how had Owen Aberdovey come not to be dead? For every report was that he had perished in a violent storm in the channel off Nantle harbor, while engaged in a rescue operation. There even had been a memorial service for him, in which the rector, Mr. Cassock, had spoken of the deceased mariner and native son in the most glowing terms.

"Hang on — what's this? I know this grub," said Edgar, abruptly rising in his seat and staring at the biscuit in his hand. "This is one of your mother's, Owen — I know 'em well — ginger and marshberries — they're a speciality of hers — *and it's fresh . . .*"

"Do you mean these biscuits are from Mrs. Aberdovey's kitchen?" my brother asked him.

So he did mean, and if there was anyone who knew food it was Edgar Harbottle. As one he and Richard glanced at Owen for an explanation.

The mariner was silent for a time. When at length he did respond, his answer was prefaced by a deep breath and a sigh. The cloud from his pipe cloaked his words in a smoky aura; needless to say they won the entire attention of his listeners.

It turned out that in fact he had returned to the marshes some weeks ago, and that both his mother and Gwenda Goodwick knew of it, but no one else. It had been Owen's wish that his presence should be kept a secret, at least for the time being, and with their connivance it had remained so — until tonight.

"But I'm glad of your company for all that," he said heartily. "Scorch me and burn me, if it isn't joy to see you again, Mr. Edgar! However I crave your indulgence, yours and Mr. Hathaway's, to tell no one of my biding here."

"But why, Owen?" Edgar asked.

The mariner shifted uneasily in his seat, took another few whiffs, and thought over it some more.

"It has to do with the skimmer, has it not?" Richard suggested. "You're not her captain, yet you are in command of her."

"I am her guardian, Mr. Hathaway — for the present. Let me explain. The captain of the *Salty Sue,* Jack Barnaby — as fine a man and a mariner as ever sailed the long coast — is her skipper, for she is the lugger's jolly-boat. Captain Barnaby has followed the sea his entire life. In his youth he sailed with Wulf Clipperton. Do you know of Clipperton, sir?"

"I've heard the name, I believe."

"Amongst men of the sea, Mr. Hathaway, the name Wulf Clipperton is a name to be conjured with. He was a great explorer, who sought to improve our knowledge of the southern coast and its sundered seas, and who lost his life to Davy Jones in the endeavor. It is Wulf Clipperton whom men of the sea hold in the highest reverence and respect, and it is Clipperton with whom my own father sailed in his youth-time. For Sir Pedr Martindale was a friend of Clipperton's, and it was Sir Pedr who made arrangement for my father's entry into his service.

"So you see, in sailing with Captain Barnaby I have made the link with my father, for both men served under Clipperton, and now I serve under the captain. It was my destiny, I feel, to go to sea — to follow in the steps of my father, who I regret did not live long enough to see it. I tell you this because it will convey to you how fortunate am I to serve under Captain Barnaby — it was destined that I should do so — and the respect I have for the man on account of my father. Captain Barnaby, whose skimmer this is, knows naught of my present charge of his vessel, I don't believe. Like most everyone else, I'm sure, he thinks me dead — and a thief and a traitor."

"A traitor? Whatever do you mean, Owen?" said Edgar.

"Aye, a traitor, Mr. Edgar — and a thief for taking this vessel, which he must believe was lost."

"But how is it you are alive, when all thought you had perished?" Richard asked.

Again the mariner sighed, and after further recourse to his cutty launched into his tale. He had served aboard the lugger for some year and a half, he explained, when a fellow shipmate, a deck hand and new recruit called Amos Teech, had sought to befriend him. Almost from the first Owen had sensed that this Teech was a man of dubious character. Why the fellow had singled Owen out for his friendship was a mystery.

"The afternoon of the pile-up there was a heavy sea running, the wind having blown up a sudden squall from the sou'east. A frightful, shiversome wind it was, that came roaring up the channel spitting hail — an ice storm, as it turned out, one of the first of the season. In the same hour the packet-boat from Goforth, bound up-channel for Nantle, was thrown nigh on her beam-ends by the gale, which struck with little warning. Slopping a ferocious sea over her bows, and the air full of hail and whirling spindrift, the packet in minutes was as good as lost.

"Afore she could gain the shelter of Nantle harbor she was blown upon the reefs in the channel, hard by Span Rock, and piled up there. She was heavy with passengers, and without means to succor them. She lay over on her starboard beam, and in languishing thus, bilged and shattered past repair, and the sport of each incoming wave, was sure to be pounded to a litter of driftwood. One tide was certain to finish her, the rollers breaking over her in foaming thunder, her deck a mess of fallen rope and cordage, and with nor aid nor shelter for her company and passengers.

"It was the keeper of the light at Fairlight Station, over to the mainland at Paignton Swidges, who spied the wreck in his glass and sent word to the harbor-master at Nantle. But what could be done? In the narrow neck of the channel there, not another ship sailed; all boats had been near enough inshore to have gained safe harborage in the storm, but for the packet. And no harbor-master in his right senses would send men out in such a sea to aid those on the reef.

"But there was one ship, he recalled, that needed no sea to ride upon — that was Captain Barnaby's lugger, the *Salty Sue*. The harbor-master was aware she lay in port at the time, that her skipper had been enjoying a rare visit with Mrs. Barnaby at their lodgings in Jolly Jumper Yard."

"I've heard something of this wonderful flying ship," said Richard, "but I've never seen it, nor have I known anyone who has, until now. Nor, to be frank, did I altogether believe the story."

Again a note of pride filled the voice of Owen. "Sink me, but she's the primest duck of a craft as ever sailed, and a marvel to behold. Though she rides the air stream so clean and sweet, yet can she ply the ocean swells with her canvas flying as sailorly as any vessel. But in the extremity of the moment it was her sky-helm that was needful, in hasting to the assistance of those stranded on the rocks. So at word of command from the captain we hove anchor, downed our coils and, rising aloft, stood out for the reef across the tumbling spume of waters vague in the half-light.

"Beneath us was riotous sea, above a whirl of riven, low-driving clouds. At the steerage, shaping our course for the reef, was the captain himself. Said reef lies by Span Rock, at the most easterly point of Truro, one of the islands in the channel and the nearest inshore. It's there the channel cinches down, and is perilous passage for any vessel but in fine weather. The captain made for the rock and its reef straightaway, with the tempest blowing athwart our bows. But the captain held his notable good sky-boat steady beneath us, for in the wash of air she rides the gravity waves of the earth, so the captain explains it, with no rag o' sail flying with which wind might play havoc.

"Amidst the fierce clamor that had arisen, the splatter of hailstones, the roaring terror and crash of the breakers, the hazard of the errand was all too plain as we drew in over the reef. There below us lay the packet, now a shattered tangle, and amidst a flurry of hail her company and passengers huddling close at the highest point of the rocks, out of reach, for the moment, of surf and zeugs. But second by second a hungry tide was rising; worse still was sight of the zeugs watching from the shoal waters hard by."

"Zeugs?" queried Edgar.

"Aye, sir, hugeous fierce dragons of the deep. Serpent-behemoths, some call 'em — great gliding monsters — the saber-cats of the sea. More usually it is the fathomy trenches that is their habitation, but the tempest and the heavy swell had driven them nearer inshore than is customary. Close about the reef a horde of the creatures lay gathered in ambush, awaiting any poor unfortunates as might be swept away in the race of the tide. Food for zeugs all were certain to be, in time, which was plain to every eye aboard the lugger, as the captain guided her in over the wreck.

"Our company being very nimble, we made haste to deploy ladders to bring all survivors aboard. The steersman spelling the captain held his helm steady in teeth of the buffeting wind, some yards above the wreck, as the ladders were draped overside. As the storm raged about us the tide continued to rise, the zeugs snapping mighty jaws in the waters nearer and nearer. But there being some survivors too weakened to ascend the ropes, the captain ordered the skimmer outboard to collect them.

"Being one of but few aboard who could pilot her, I asked the captain if I might take her out. All unexpected, the fellow Teech did stumble over himself in his readiness to assist me. And so with thunderous spray to right and left of us, and a howling fury of wind and hailstones blowing in our faces, we put off in the skimmer.

"Scarce had I eased her into place aside the rocks than the loathly dog, Teech, did grapple me by the arms and deal me a numbing blow, with the traitorous intent of making off with the skimmer. The scurvy rogue — blast his deadlights! — had seen his chance, and had grasped it. You'll note yet the bruise upon my sconce here, Mr. Edgar, as may offer proof of the villain's treachery. For a time I remained senseless. When I awoke I discovered we had fetched about under cover of storm and spindrift and, having crossed the channel, were racing overland a distance up the coast. Through perilous haze buffeted by hooting wind we sped, the black masses of cloud scudding fast above us. The dog Teech, who had gained his skills, such as they were, by observing the helmsman of the lugger, had had no end of trouble piloting the skimmer through the gale. It was a miracle we had not gone down while I had lain insensible on the boards. For had I not revived when I had done, we surely would have plunged to earth and such would have been the end of us."

It was clear the villain Teech meant to have the skimmer for himself, and that he had been long in the planning of it. Likewise was it clear that Owen himself would be suspected in the theft, for it was he who had taken the boat out — had *volunteered*, in fact, to so do. It would have been his word against that of Teech, and Teech — scoundrel that he was — certainly would have implicated Owen as the chief machinator, should they be apprehended. Doubtless he would have made oath that the two had planned the thing together. Thenceforth he and Owen would be "as close to one another as two cloves of an orange," as he had phrased it — bound together by the theft. The man Teech was naught but a criminal, a perjurer, and — in Owen's words — a loathly dog.

"With ceaseless creak and groan of the ship's labor, the water jetting from her scuppers and with droning wind astern, we had run inland some miles when the villain ordered I take charge of the wheel, or he would cast me overside — or so he threatened. His lubberly skills had been sore tested, as he worked to hold altitude and keep our bows from coming broadside on to the wind. So I ran to the helm and had soon steadied her. But the dog did eye me closely the whiles, and kept a watch on our ship's compass to see our course did not stray far from nor'easterly.

"The afternoon was far advanced when over the horizon came rolling the boggy wastes of Slopshire, and by dusk it was Fenshire that lay beneath our flying keel, and Marley Wood stretching off into the gloom. A while later, in the last gasp of the light, I did spy Fitful Farm, along the wood's northern edge, and knew us to be near Ridingham. It was then I thought of Northeave, and of the ruined lodges here; for a derelict village might serve as a prime hiding-place for skimmer and fugitives, woefully short of provisions though we were. The dog Teech, though suspicious, and knowing us to be in range of my home fields, nonetheless joined in this opinion. So to Northeave we came, to Mackery End, there to bide awhile.

"Morning brought fog and we lay becalmed in a white mist among the clumbers and Scotch firs. The tempest had abated. In the lodge we found some few items of use and took them aboard, but of course no victuals. So it was our task next to plenish stores."

Despite the heat from the stove and the warmth of the coffee, the air in the cabin had grown decidedly chilly as Owen's tale had progressed. The mariner explained there were some boat-cloaks aboard that ought to serve our purpose.

"Reach me them from the locker yonder," he asked Edgar.

As the youth obliged he was startled by a furry black thing with two green eyes in it that sprang from the locker and, scampering up his arm, clung to him with steely claws gripping his shoulder.

THE SEVENTH CHAPTER

The Seventh Stone

E DGAR, starting in surprise at the animal that had chosen his shoulder for a perch, exclaimed —

"Here! Who's this cat, then?"

For a cat it proved to be — a very large and a very black one, with a huge head and jowls — who was sniffing curiously at his face.

"Crave pardon, Mr. Edgar," Owen broke in, "but it's only Melon-head — Captain Barnaby's cat. I've an inkling he'd been affrighted by the gale, and had sought to ride it out in a locker."

"Mewed himself up, as it were," noted Richard.

"Though it was not till peep o' day next morning that he did steal from his hidey-hole, while Teech and I sat at our breakfast. It was the aroma of the victuals that drew him out."

The tomcat, to Edgar's relief, promptly leaped from his shoulder to the deck, there to be scooped up into the arms of Owen. Sailors, as we know, are very fond of pets, and Owen Aberdovey was no exception. His voice and hands were gentle in their affection for his fellow adventurer, who settled himself comfortably in the mariner's lap, rubbing the sleep from his eyes and yawning.

Was this the behavior of a thief and traitor, Richard asked himself? Was this a man who had betrayed the trust of a captain he professed to admire, showing such kindness now to the captain's pet?

Hardly.

Melon-head, having had enough of the lap, of a sudden arched his back in a long stretch and with a throaty *meow* sprang heavily to the nearest cushion, and there commenced a vigorous cleansing of his face and paws with a pink tongue.

"Certain sure, he can be venturesome at times. I've had hard work to keep him from roaming, as he is accustomed to the habit aboard the lugger," Owen said. "The captain would scarce forgive me if he were lost now while ashore. So you see, sir, I have the cat to look after besides, and not only the vessel. But more of this later. Now it was the boat-cloaks we were speaking of . . ."

The apparel was retrieved from the locker, and while Edgar and Richard nestled into their garb, Owen, sufficiently warm in his jacket and jersey, busied himself at the stove to kick up its fire a little. Then he settled himself again on his cushion, briskly scratched the ears and jowls of Melonhead lounging beside him, and after a few draws on his cutty resumed his narrative.

In the way of provisions there had been a flask of rum in a locker, he explained, which he and Teech had found, and some ship's biscuit, and a few spice nuts, but little else, for the skimmer had been but poorly stocked at the time. The rum they had divided betwixt themselves and drunk from pewters. It was during the ensuing conversation that Owen learned what had transpired aboard the vessel while he had been unconscious, and what Teech had had in mind in absconding with the craft.

"Where was he making for?" Richard asked.

"That he never would divulge, sir. 'Won't do', says he, 'to tell you of it. No, won't do'. The dog forever is 'won't-doing' this and 'no-going' that, but is as full as an egg, sir, whenever speaking of himself, the which he did often, and in a boasting sort of way. I had guessed him to be a fishy customer from the start. In my view it was Foghampton that he was making for. For once he let drop that he had signed aboard his first venture on the quay there, and let it be assumed it was his home port. Amongst his messmates it was pretty much accepted as such."

"And his objective in taking the skimmer? For certainly he would have been found out in time. At all events one can't hide a flying ship for long, I shouldn't think."

"A form of ransom, sir. He expected to conceal it, and let it be known that he had possession of it, and to blame myself for the taking of it while at Span Rock. He would boast how he had wrested the ship from me, and then make oath to return it to the captain after payment of a sum o' silver. And no paltry sum — plague and perish him!"

The loathly dog was my brother's first thought.

"This Teech sounds a very low-lived party. How did you tolerate him? And where is he, by the by? He's not hiding in the lodge, is he?" Edgar asked.

"There is no one in the lodge. He is — not there. The dog — well, that is — he did show his heels — decamped some time ago — sheered off apace — "

"The deuce you say. He ain't here? I don't get the picture, Owen. The villain hopped it? Where has he gone?"

"And why is he not guarding the skimmer that he went to such trouble to commandeer?" Richard asked.

"Well, as to that, sir — " Owen began, then abruptly checked himself, shrugged, and looked away.

His guests regarded him with some puzzlement. For the first time they had a sense the mariner was not being honest with them. There seemed to be something he was keeping back. After further questioning he confessed to them that the loathly dog had received a scare — he remained evasive as to the cause — that had prompted the fellow to scramble overside and flee the vessel. Groggy with rum, and weaving uncertainly on his pins, the dog had last been observed making for the wood road. There had been no sign of him since.

"It's queer, right enough — his sheering off that way," the mariner remarked.

"Dashed curious," Richard nodded, eyeing him thoughtfully. "Why indeed should he have abandoned the skimmer? I reckon he must have lost his nerve."

"A wretch like that? No such luck," said Edgar. "He should be brought to book. He deserves to be put under a pump for his treatment of Owen."

"I suppose it's possible he may have had an experience similar to our own. A spotted lion or a marsh devil may have met him in the road."

"How lucky for him. Do you figure he may have kicked it?"

"It may explain why he has not returned to Northeave. Of course, his reason for departing Northeave seems a mystery as well," Richard hinted.

If his words were intended to prize an explanation from Owen, they failed signally.

"Crave pardon, sir," the mariner said instead, "but it's like as not he may be awaiting his chance to recover the skimmer. So I daren't leave the vessel for long; the dog may be watching her from the woods. I remain her guardian till she can be returned to the captain — whenever that may be . . ."

His speech trailed off into silence, his light, large eyes staring on vacancy and his forehead creased in thought. Then on a sudden he shook off his mood and, turning to his visitors, entreated them not to divulge his presence there just yet.

"Not till Captain Barnaby has rendered a judgment," he said.

"And when will that be, do you think?" Richard asked.

The mariner responded with a vague motion of his hand. What he told them next he told them slowly, and in measured tones, for the subject had become a dreadful weight on his mind.

Having no means by which to prove his innocence, he had been in an agony of despair over his future. For the present he could do nothing but wait. In the ensuing days, however, he gradually had reconciled himself to his plight — to his destiny, as he called it. His task, impossible as it now seemed, was to persuade the captain he had had no role in the theft of the skimmer. Of course the dog Teech, if alive, would be the first to call him a liar. It was Owen who had been in command of the skimmer; whatever befell on his watch was his responsibility and his alone. By law of the sea the theft of the vessel would be laid at his feet.

Why then had it been reported that he had perished in the channel? And why had there been no mention of the theft? It had been, and still remained, an entire mystery to him.

He had no choice but to consider himself a fugitive, whether the world thought him alive or dead. But he could not live a fugitive forever. If he showed himself, he would be viewed as a criminal who had eluded justice, to be prosecuted with the utmost rigor of the law. If he did *not* show himself, then he must live in seclusion, take another name, and never again be known to his friends.

And what to do with the skimmer? For the time being he could but sit vigil over her there at Northeave. The deuce of it was that there was not an ounce of proof against him; and yet his guilt was all but assured by the fact that he had been in command, and had no witness but Teech to substantiate his account of events. And what were the chances the dog would take his side?

"It's long odds against," Edgar noted glumly.

Meanwhile he had evolved a routine of hiding out at Northeave in the daylight hours, and then under cover of night bringing her in to the Hall, where his mother had been providing him with victuals — the source of the biscuits — and where Teech, if alive and in the neighborhood, would be unable to approach the craft.

Hardly anyone ever came to Northeave — Edgar and Richard notwithstanding — and during the day there Owen maintained an alert watch for his enemy, in the event he should surface and attempt to seize the skimmer. From his lookout amongst the trees he could readily observe events in the area, as when he had caught sight of Richard and Edgar and their "spot of trouble" below. After a few weeks, however, this ritual of his —

the daily watching and waiting — had grown a little tiresome; although he had a few books there in the cabin with which to occupy his mind, volumes that had been borrowed from the Hall library by Mrs. Aberdovey.

"Dashed if you're not the caller your mother was expecting the night I arrived at the Hall," Richard said, "for her table had been laid for two."

"Likely, sir. Always she has our bit o' supper in readiness when I bring the ship in. And Gwenda, too, has carried victuals from the kitchen, just some etceteras now and again, for myself and Melon-head aboard ship."

"I recollect Mrs. Flitch did complain to the constable that certain 'odds and ends' had gone missing from her larder — "

"Stay a bit, sir," spoke up the mariner, his brow clouding with concern, "but what is this about the constable? Is it George Pettiplace you mean?"

"Not to worry, Owen," Edgar said, hastening to reassure him, "for it's nothing to do with the skimmer. It's about a boot — and a foot . . ."

"Too, that is why your mother has seemed preoccupied, why she did stand for a time looking out at the gate as if she were expecting someone," Richard continued, thinking aloud. "She was watching for the skimmer! Dashed curious it seemed at the time, on so blustery a night and with flurries in the air."

"It is her usual practice to show a light in a window of the gatehouse," Owen said. "Round dusk I slip moorings and stand away for the Hall, taking the ship in as near as I dare at first, and bide awhile in the tops of some old Scotch firs. There I watch for the light. It is my mother's signal that the Hall and grounds are quiet."

"I've seen it! I did not doubt but that it was a signal of some kind. And the lump of shadow I took for an animal crouching in the firs — it was the skimmer. I thought it a teratorn, or a marsh devil, or some such thing."

"Once the light is shown I bring the vessel in over the curtain-wall and set her down amongst the peaks and chimneys of the Hall roof. It's by far the safest berth — nigh impossible to clap an eye on from the yard, and the towers are but seldom occupied. If I were to moor her at the gatehouse, inside the wall, then all might see her from their windows, while outside she should invite the notice of the wandering beasts of the marshes — and the dog Teech as well."

"Goodness — then you are the bump in the night!" Richard exclaimed.

"Sir?"

"I have heard it, on more than one occasion, on the timbers above my room . . . a gentle thump in the night . . . so it was the skimmer touching down . . . then a noise as of someone treading on the leads . . ."

"Sink me, is it your room, sir, there on the topmost floor, across from the gatehouse? I had thought it but little used."

"And the odd footprints in the snow . . . the tracks running to and fro, from near the servants' door, down beneath my casement, to the gatehouse lane . . ."

"It was Owen — descending from the roof to see his mother, and going back again?" Edgar suggested.

"And once a shadow in a flood of moonlight climbed up my wall and disappeared into the ceiling. At the time it seemed like a dream. I took it for the creeping shadow. But it was your shadow, Owen, thrown through the casement while mounting the ladder to the skimmer."

"Bleed me and burn me," the mariner exclaimed, with a woeful shake of his head, "I'd no notion I'd made so lubberly a mess of my comings and goings. But you speak of the shadow, sir. Are you familiar then with that venerable legend of the Hall? For her ladyship in days past scarce would have it talked of."

"The story of the cobbler of Ridingham, Crispin Nightshade, and the curse of the creeping shadow — yes, Edgar and I were entertained by Mr. Gecks with his rendition of the tale."

"And what was that about a boot and a foot?"

Edgar, still a trifle nervous on the subject of the shadow, glanced round uneasily. "Well, it was Toddy who found the boot — grubbed it up somewhere outside the wall — a regular antique, and had a man's foot in it."

Briefly Richard sketched out the story for the mariner. Can it possibly have been Crispin Nightshade's boot, Owen wondered — and Nightshade's foot? For tradition held that the cobbler had died at the Hall. However Mr. Pinchbeck, the Ridingham bootmaker, did not think the relic had any connection to Nightshade, and he was an expert on the topic. For he himself had cause to believe his ancestors had been related to the man.

But there was a further mystery that one *could* connect with the legend — that of the stovepipe hat and the bust of Sir Padrig. What was it that Richard had seen in the library, the shadow that in passing by had knocked the hat from Sir Padrig's head? For this baffler there looked to be no ready solution.

Nor was there any answer to the mystery of Amos Teech. What was it had frightened him off and caused him to abandon the skimmer? But on this point the mariner remained stubbornly vague.

"So what do you mean to do now, Owen?" Edgar asked him, changing the subject.

"Yes, how may we be of assistance to you?" said Richard.

From that dire moment in the cockpit when Owen's life had been ir-revocably changed, the mariner had been thrown back upon his resources. For weeks now he had been engaged in a mental struggle how to redeem himself. If he showed himself, he immediately became a wanted, hunted man; he had no cause to believe otherwise. Yet the longer he remained hid-den, with the skimmer in his keeping, the more it would seem to incrimi-nate him and persuade others of his guilt.

"Well," Richard told him, "I suppose you know, Owen, that the truth always is your best safeguard."

"Absolutely," Edgar agreed.

The mariner nodded his understanding. "Sink me, that's plain enough. But it all shall be worked out presently, once the captain arrives. He may well have my letter in hand now."

Richard drew the pipe from his lips and stared at his host. "Your letter? Goodness, you did not tell us of a letter."

"No, sir."

"This puts rather a different aspect on the thing."

"Aye, sir."

It seemed that about a week ago Owen had come to a resolution, and had sent off a letter by post to the captain's lodgings in Jolly Jumper Yard.

"I had quite a hard job of it, the writing of it I mean," said he, "and in my poor words did tell him the entire, unvarnished truth o' the matter, to the best of my knowledge and recollection. It was my mother who posted it for me. It's uncertain if the captain is away on a new venture, or how he is heading, or when he might return; I can but pray he has the letter now. His wife is something of a tartar, and it keeps him much at sea — or rather at air, as he has no need of seas any longer."

So there really was nothing for it but to wait, the which Owen had gotten rather used to doing. For how long this agony of suspense might continue was unknown, but he was in hopes it would end shortly. His dread of the answer was only too plain, and yet this ordeal of *anticipating* the answer seemed worse. Once the captain's verdict had been rendered, Owen had pledged he would make his presence known to the others at the Hall. But first he must have the captain's response to the facts as they had been laid before him, for a captain's word is law aboard his vessel.

Owen let his breathing go in another deep sigh; then abruptly he slam-med his fist down onto his palm, in mute anguish at the preposterous in-justice of fate. The loathly dog Teech, if alive, would be heaping falsehoods on the name of Owen Aberdovey, and there was nothing that Owen could do about it. It was a hard lesson to learn.

Yet for all that, the ready selflessness of Owen in the face of his personal trial had come shining through. How he had saved the lives of Richard and Edgar, and made the skimmer a haven of hospitality for them — it was the same old Owen, Edgar declared, not a whit changed by his ordeal. A trump of a feller he was — a first-rater — who had made of himself an apt representative of the sailorly race, despite having been born and bred up a marsh man. As he sat there with knotted brow, he could be heard muttering to himself, as if he had no other company but Melon-head to heed him. Then all at once he flushed a little and, recollecting his visitors, glanced at them in some embarrassment.

"Bless my guts," he said, "was I speaking aloud?"

"Not to worry," Richard told him, seconded by Edgar, "for we shan't repeat a word of it. Nor will Melon-head."

In my brother's view another change of subject was in order, and what better topic to fire the interest of Owen, he thought, than that of his beloved skimmer?

"By the by, Owen, just how does this ship function? What holds her up? And what are those thimajiggs by the compass and ship's wheel?" he asked.

The effect of his words was striking. At once the eyes of Owen kindled with enthusiasm, and throwing off his mood as if it were a boat-cloak he inquired of his guests —

"Would you have a peep at her mechanism?"

They would. Eagerly they followed him through the door in the aft bulkhead, the one he had told them led to a store-room. A kind of a store-room it was, true, but one remarkable in several particulars. Richard and Edgar quickly fell to examining it.

In the center of the compartment stood a narrow, cage-like apparatus, which extended vertically from deck to overhead. Running down through it was a turning-shaft, and threaded on the shaft was a coil-like structure, or *cage-coil,* made of a number of thin, metallic disks, stacked one above the other. The timbers at the foot of the cage had been removed, and just below deck level the threaded shaft could be seen to terminate above a large, flat stone, which was being held in place by a rigid frame of brass. Converging on the stone were four additional cage-coils, each running horizontally under the deck and at right angles, as from the four points of the compass.

"And this is the mechanism which allows the skimmer to ride the gravity waves of the earth?" Richard asked.

It was, and in the ensuing minutes Owen did his best to explain the principle of the thing, as he understood it, to his friends. To make short, the large, flat stone at the heart of the mechanism — a rich, creamy kind of stone, marked by parallel veins of blue and green, intersected by cross-striations of a reddish hue — was called a *hoverstone*, and the element within it that was acted upon by the cage-coils was known as *gravitite*. The stacked disks of the cage-coils were made of lodestone — magnetic ore — and as the various coils were revolved on their shafts, and the ore and the gravitite brought closer together, their interactions generated a repulsive force that powered the skimmer.[1]

Further the mariner explained that his ship's altitude was governed by the crank-handles in the cockpit, through chain-belts linked to the vertical cage-coil before them. Cranking the one handle turned the threaded shaft in the cage, sending its coil downward towards the hoverstone (hence the command "down coil"). As the lodestone entered the gravitite field, the repulsive energy sent the skimmer aloft. Revolving the other handle reversed the process, causing the ship to descend.

Similarly, the horizontal coils below deck — the *steering-* and *speed-coils* — governed the fore and aft motion of the craft, her direction of flight, and her velocity. The steering-coils were commanded by the ship's wheel, and the speed-coils by the foot-pedals. The action of these controls was made easy by reciprocating springs that were incorporated into each mechanism.

The visitors were deeply impressed and remarked upon it all with rapt admiration. "A cunning piece of work", "a splendid achievement", "capital" were a few of the praises sung by Richard; "jiminy", "by gad", and "never would have believed it" were the chief contributions of Edgar.

It was plain no little engineering skill had entered into the vessel's construction — or rather, its transformation into a flying ship of the air — and Owen was rightly proud of his role in fitting her up. He explained that the gravitite, the active principle in the hoverstone, had been discovered by a retired grocer, one Mr. Malachi Threadneedle. He had purchased a number of the curious white stones from a trader called Hicklebeep, intending them for doorstops in his home on the island of Truro. The stones themselves had been unearthed by no less a personage than Wulf Clipperton, on one of his voyages of exploration in far southern waters. For some years

---

[1] See *Strange Cargo* (2004), ch. 19, for a fuller discussion of the topic. — *Ed.*

they had languished in the ore office at Goforth, where he had deposited them. But the explorer having been lost at sea, the stones, deemed valueless by the office, eventually were purchased at auction by Hicklebeep, who in his turn sold them to the grocer while on a trading expedition aboard the *Salty Sue.*

Quite by accident Mr. Threadneedle, who was something of a tinkerer, had uncovered the principle of the gravitite — it was he who had named it such — and after much effort had transformed his workshop, a converted coach-house, into a flying coach-house of the air. Upon one of her flights, however, a fierce channel storm — not unlike that which had doomed the packet-boat — had blown up and sent the coach-house crashing on the island of Soar, to the southwards of Goforth. In time Mr. Threadneedle and his companions were rescued by Captain Barnaby in the lugger, which herself had sustained damages in the gale. The coach-house had been wrecked, but the grocer, thankful for having been saved, and having had enough of flying, presented the hoverstones to the captain as a gift. Six of the seven stones and their cage-coils were salvaged from the coach-house and incorporated into the *Salty Sue,* which ere then had been an altogether ordinary, seafaring three-master of a coastal lugger, to supply the power by which she now roamed the coastal skies.

It was some while later that an idea had suggested itself to the captain, to turn an old ship's cutter into the skimmer using the seventh hoverstone, which had been damaged in the wreck. It was this seventh stone that lay at the heart of the skimmer's mechanism — the creamy white object sitting at the intersection of the vertical and horizontal coils. It had been Owen's task to devise a means of using this one stone to power the separate operations of wheel, crank-handles, and pedals; indeed nearly the entire design of the skimmer had been his. In the lugger, and earlier in the coach-house, individual hoverstones were employed for the different functions. But in the skimmer, Owen's ingenuity had made it possible to combine these functions by channeling them through a single stone.

Richard peered again at the stone there in its dark pocket below decks, and scratched his chin in thought.

"Dashed if I've not seen another stone like it before," he remarked, "in the library at the Hall — on show there, beside the Viking sunstone — one of a similar appearance . . ."

Edgar nodded. "I know the one, 'pon my word. It belonged to my uncle."

"It was sent to his lordship as a curiosity, as I've heard it, by Captain

Clipperton," Owen told them. "The captain knew not what a treasure he had in the stones, nor indeed did anyone at first. He believed them to be pieces of the shooting star that some say fell to earth and caused the sundering. I know it sounds a cock-and-bull tale, but there it is."

"And here are we," Richard noted, "riding comfortably at our ease in the skimmer high above Mackery End! On the face of it, it too sounds absurd. It's almost too fantastic for belief, as though someone had written it down in a book — and yet there *it* is."

"The entire day seems a wild dream," nodded Edgar.

Fatigued by the strenuous events of that day, he and my brother thanked Owen for the tour and resumed their seats. Owen meanwhile, having closed the store-room, asked his guests if they fancied a cup of Willoughby gray? Their answers being in the affirmative, he produced a couple of bottles from a locker and invited them to partake, while he worked over the stove to fire up the heat a little more.

Somewhere an owl hooted dismally. Richard's glance strayed to the tiny port beside him, its round eye filled with the black dark of a Fenshire night. He mused to himself that most everyone in Market Snailsby would have laughed him to scorn had they heard Owen's cock-and-bull tale. Yet there could be no doubting the power of the seventh stone, for he and Edgar would have kicked it today had it not been for Owen and the skimmer.

He accepted a cup from Edgar which the lad had charged with a measure of ale. Taking a preparatory sip, he paused to weigh the strength and flavor of the liquor, when his eye was attracted to the curious vessel into which Edgar had poured his own draft.

"It was in the locker here," the youth explained.

"It" was a pewter mug, bearing the features of an impossibly wicked old lady — a toothless, grinning crone, gaunt and skeletal, with widely-staring eyes — cast in high relief on its surface, after the manner of a character jug.

"Gruesome, ain't she?" said Edgar, admiring the hag's leering countenance.

Owen, alerted by his words, swung round at the stove and flinging out a warning hand suddenly cried —

"No, Mr. Edgar — not the gammer's cup — "

But it was too late; already the youth had downed a goodly swallow of ale, and was smacking his lips in satisfaction. "Superexcellent stuff — thick and muddy — and no heel-taps!" and before anyone could prevent it the remainder had gone the way of the rest.

The ale proved a delightful tonic, and more besides: for in the next instant Edgar and my brother were shocked to find that a stranger had joined them in the cabin, a woman, to all appearances a foreigner, who promptly demanded —

"Eentroduce me, Owen!"

PART THREE

◆

THE FIRST CHAPTER
A Woman of Spirit

S AID a startled Edgar — "Yoicks! Who's she now? And where did she drop from?" — and lurched to his feet as if a wasp had stung him. He gaped in alarm at the stranger, who had appeared in their midst all unannounced.

For some moments not another word passed. The surprising nature of the woman's entrance — the sheer, stealthy quiet of it — sent eerie prickles through my brother's scalp. He fought back his surprise, and like Edgar was mystified how the newcomer had stolen upon them unawares.

His eye could not help but notice her trim figure, which was displayed to advantage in a gossamy gown of antique design. She was a comely lass, but pale as the moon, with flowing hair a shade lighter than straw, some of it in braids, the rest streaming loose about her shoulders, and cherry-lips parted to reveal flashing white teeth.

For long seconds he and Edgar regarded the woman in silence, and she them, her eyes meeting theirs with a look that was one part coquette, one part innocent. It was her eyes that held their interest most, for there was something mysterious about them — blue eyes that were one moment luminous, the next wistful and remote, yet with a trace of impudence in their depths.

Smiling, the young woman cocked her pretty head aside. In the end it was she herself who broke the spell.

"Who are these fallows, Owen?" she inquired, her arms folded and her strange eyes shining. "Eentroduce me, *s'il vous plaît.*"

The mariner, after a brief pause, obliged her.

"This — this is Mr. Edgar Harbottle, of the Hall. And this is his friend, Mr. Richard Hathaway, from Market Snailsby. Gentlemen, this is — this lady is Henriette."

The visitors nodded dumbly. *Very glad to make your acquaintance* — so spoke their minds, but their tongues refused to stir.

"Thees one I 'ave before seen. I recognize the face of him — *oui* — he

138

is *neveu* of hair ladysheep," the woman remarked, fixing Edgar with her steady gaze.

"Aye — for Mr. Edgar's aunt is Lady Martindale," said Owen.

My brother was observing the mystery-woman thoughtfully. She looked to be in her late twenties, or perhaps her early thirties. There had been no slightest hint of her presence aboard the skimmer, for Owen had guided them round every inch of his craft — and it was a snug craft besides — and there had been no one else there.

"My wits must be going. Where can she have been concealed?" he asked himself. "In a bulkhead, perhaps? For the lockers are rather cramped, and the companion-hatch is shut. *But in a bulkhead?*"

"I 'ave just arrive," the young woman informed him.

At that moment he realized he had speaking his thoughts aloud, much as Owen had done before.

"Sorry," he apologized.

Edgar, having composed himself somewhat, put the question for him. The strange eyes of Henriette dwelt for a time on both their faces, before settling on Owen's. It appeared that she, too, was interested in hearing his answer to Edgar's query.

The mariner exchanged glances with his attractive friend, who smiled sweetly while awaiting his reply. At length he cleared his voice and, drawing a deep breath, said slowly —

"From the gammer's cup, Mr. Edgar, that I had stowed in the locker. I quite forgot — I should have been more careful. When you filled it with Willoughby gray and drank of it, she was loosed from her moorings there."

Puzzled frowns greeted this announcement. Richard took his pipe from his lips in surprise and glanced at the speaker, as if with a latent suspicion that there must be a jest or hidden meaning in his words.

"Well, there's a curious notion," he remarked.

"All joking apart — 'pon my word, Owen, you're not talking sense," Edgar said.

"I am shock," exclaimed the mystery-woman, who seemed rather more amused than otherwise by the confusion she had caused. *"Hélas,* Owen, 'ow can you talk like that? You try to make fool of these fallows. Who could 'ave imagine?"

Exasperation flushed the ruddy cheeks of Owen. "Crave your pardon, Mr. Edgar," he said, wringing his brow, "but it's the very truth, what I've told you, and no cock-and-bull tale — on my oath as a seaman and a Fenshireman."

"But who is she?" Edgar asked. "How did she get aboard? And what is that peculiar way she has of speaking? For dog Latin it ain't."

"Henriette's French — or that is, she was — or is — or — "

The poor mariner seemed as confused as anyone.

"French? But how is that possible?" my brother inquired. "And where was she hiding? For we saw no one."

"She was here, sir, as I've said — as I've tried to explain — in the gammer's cup, plague and perish me," Owen insisted.

"You've told us that before, but what does it mean?"

The young woman, who was observing the mariner's distress not without a little enjoyment, Richard thought, said archly —

"Wat you theenk, Owen? Is not clever trick by Henriette?"

In answer the mariner knotted his brow and proceeded to take several turns up and down the deck, thinking hard and throwing up blue clouds of smoke from his cutty. Henriette regarded him with an indulgent smile hovering round her lips.

Edgar meanwhile remarked in a low tone to my brother — "Have you noticed her skin particularly, sir? She's a peach, to be sure, this Henrietta, a stunner even, but rather a colorless one."

"As white as her gown," Richard nodded, observing the deathly pallor of her flesh.

"Can she be ill, d'you think? And her eyes are downright peculiar. And those togs of hers — who wears clothing like that any more? It's practically Renaissance. Ain't she cold in it?"

It was the young woman's gossamy attire — her ankle-length gown, or kirtle, loosely-fitted, and belted just under her breasts, with its wide sleeves and woven bands of trimming — that had struck him as odd, like her eyes.

"Curious outfit for a woman nowadays," Richard agreed.

"Owen is a first-rater — as honest and open as the dawn. But what's his game, d'you think? It's a dead certainty she wasn't here when he took us round."

"I agree. But where was she hidden? And how did she steal upon us so quietly?"

They found their eyes drawn to the mug — the so-called gammer's cup, with its image of a toothless, grinning crone starting out of the pewter. Surely there could be no truth in what Owen had told them? And yet was it not a fact that the mystery-woman had made her startling entrance only after Edgar had filled the cup and drunk from it?

Coincidence, surely? Mr. Gecks often spoke of the importance of coincidence in legal affairs and in the gathering of evidence. What of its importance in everyday matters?

"I reckon we'll have our answer now," my brother whispered, as Owen ceased his pacing and turned to address them.

"Let me explain, gentlemen, by your leave," he began — "and then you may tell me what you make of it."

So saying, he extended a hand to Henriette and invited her to place her own in his. This she did, or attempted to do, with startling effect. Her fingers, reaching for his, instead passed directly through his hand, as a stray cloud may be said to pass through a mountain-top. This same performance was repeated once, twice, three times. Still they were unable to clasp hands; it was as if Owen were endeavoring to grasp empty air.

"*Well, I'm jiggered!*" Richard exclaimed.

He and Edgar traded disbelieving glances. The youth's face went blank and he felt a chill of horror steal over him, one that made his hair rise and that turned the blood in his veins to ice.

"Jiminy," he whispered, shrinking back, "jiminy, she's a — she's — " Further speech died on his lips.

"Aye," Owen nodded grimly, "she's a ghost, that's sure — soak me in bilge-water."

Spellbound, Edgar stared at the apparition. Her winsome smile, it seemed, was as doubtful and unreal as she; at any instant it might vanish like a soap bubble. With a shudder he dropped down onto a cushion and began planing his forehead with his handkerchief. Would the wonders of this day that had been like a dream never cease?

"It's enough to f-frighten a gent out of his b-bluchers," he protested.

It was a sight at which the mind, if not the body, must tremble. Here before them stood one who once had been a human being, and who had traveled that path which we all one day must tread, had taken those dread steps that never can be retraced . . .

Hold on — never be retraced? *Or might they be?*

For did not she who stood before them comprise the living — er, so to speak — proof of it? Proof that she who had crossed the Styx had returned to tell of it?

"I am not only ghost," she spoke up in her defense, "but am — wat you call — poor widow woman."

"Good heavens," Richard said.

"But 'ayvens not vary good for Henriette," the widow sighed.

But how had such a thing come to pass?

"She had been asleep for a spell until the loathly dog, Teech, one morning did drink from the cup, and out she popped. Bless my guts, sir, it's the very truth. I saw it with these two eyes," Owen related.

"That villain man, Teech — soche impertinent fallow — I deed not like him so moche," said Henriette.

"It scared him silly, and he sheered off. That's the thing that frightened him — Henriette appearing from out of the cup. For sailors, you know, are a superstitious lot."

Owen explained that he and Teech had found the gammer's cup in one of the lodges there at Northeave. It had lain half-buried amongst the ashes in a fireplace, where someone long ago had. discarded it. They had taken it aboard the skimmer, and only later discovered why it had been cast into the fire. Although singed and scarred, it had weathered the flames without major injury.

Having awakened her from her slumber, Owen had come to feel a certain sense of responsibility for the woman. Now he had the skimmer AND Melon-head AND Henriette to look out for, not to mention his own self and his reputation in the eyes of Captain Barnaby and the law.

"I never did b-believe in such things," Edgar said, glancing furtively at the apparition — *as white as her gown*, had been Richard's words — and despite his appreciation of her figure, "although I'm prepared to reconsider my view. But Owen, how can she be French? No one speaks French any longer. It's practically a dead language — like that old Greek and Latin the academical parties make us get up in college."

The widow's peculiar eyes flashed.

"Wat you know? Since when has mine been dead language, as you say?" she challenged him, in her rich Gallic *patois*.

Never in his life had Edgar been spoken to by a ghost, certainly not in such a manner, until tonight; for the very existence of such a being as Henriette defied all churchly doctrine. It was some seconds ere the youth found his voice again.

"Since w-when? Oh, since q-quite a — since quite a long time, actually. Since the s-sundering."

He noted the mystified look which came into her face, spectral illusion though it was.

"And wat is thees — 'ow you call it — sundering? Wat means thees, *mon cher?*" she asked Owen.

"Jiminy! She *has* been asleep for a spell," Edgar remarked in an undertone.

"Her time was long afore the sundering," Owen informed him.

"Explain to me thees sundering," Henriette said crisply.

"You've not told her of it, Owen?" Richard asked.

"Tale a me wat? Wat you mean by sundering?" the widow demanded impatiently.

The mariner confessed he had not told her. And so he proceeded to describe for Henriette the catastrophe that had engulfed the world nearly two centuries before. Some thought its cause to have been a volcanic eruption, while others, people like Wulf Clipperton, believed that a shooting star had fallen to earth. Whatever the truth, the result had been the same: a massive freezing-up of the continents, as the glaciers swept down from the north, and the extinction of all life apart from that within a narrow strip of land known as the long coast — the sundered realm. It was here that the descendants of the survivors were endeavoring to carry on as their ancestors had done before the disaster. Those like Captain Clipperton who had ventured southwards of the realm had found there only waste and devastation. To the north, the glacier-helmeted peaks, stark and brooding, reared their threatening heads. As for the old ancestral lands far beyond the long coast — Old Britain and France for instance — no one journeyed that way any more, and no one had come from there ever since.

Henriette's response on hearing the awful news was thoughtful and reflective. She bit her lip and was silent for awhile, as though endeavoring to accustom her mind to the changes that had been wrought in the world she had known. For her time, as Owen said, had been long before the sundering.

"*Quel dommage,*" she murmured, shaking her head sadly. "Wat shame. Soche *triste* affair, and Henriette know no ting of it. All is rueen, and no one tale a me."

"Sink me if anyone remained long enough to be yarning with her about it," Owen confided to his friends. "Likely the response of the dog Teech was the more usual — to trip anchor and away."

"It's difficult to believe she exists," Richard said, "and yet there she is. I never would have believed it myself. But neither would I have believed in a flying ship. So why have you yourself not tripped anchor and away?"

The mariner shrugged. "I've little choice, sir. I am guardian of the skimmer, and must bide here till the captain reclaims her. But she's not so bad a sort — Henriette, I mean — not in her new life, at any rate . . ."

His voice trailed off, and he seemed about to confide something more to them when Edgar, having bolstered up his courage, mused aloud —

"True, she ain't a bad sort for a peach."

Her trim figure, her lovely features, her dazzling smile — whether real or imagined — had made quite an impression on him, almost as much as had the shepherd-girls in lace and lilac at Bo-peep's. Save for her deathly pallor, there was nothing grim about Henriette. Not that he had entirely lost his fear of her; it was simply that an appreciation of her finer points had grown upon his mind, sufficient to outweigh his dread at what she represented. If she were a ghost, so be it; the fact that she was a pretty one only added to her charm.

"She calls herself a widow — is it true?" he asked. "For I dare say she hardly looks a spinster."

The next instant he shivered as he saw Henriette's chin come up, saw her strange eyes flash their indignation.

"I am no speenstress," she retorted, stamping a well-shod little foot. "I was married woman — poor widow woman now."

"But — "

"Hish! Be quaite, weel you, cheaile? You are fatigue Henriette wi' soche *sottise.*"

There was no disputing the crisp ring of authority in her voice, that is the privilege and hallmark of a married woman.

Incredulous, Edgar glanced from Owen to Richard, and back again.

"Did she just call me a child?" he asked.

"She calls most everyone a child, sir," the mariner explained.

"Given her age, in her eyes the three of us must seem as children," said Richard, "if indeed her time was before the sundering."

"Long, long afore it, sir. A bygone era."

"But if Henrietta's time — " Edgar began.

Again the widow cut him short.

"No, no, cheaile — is pronounce AWN-REE-ET. Cannot you say? AWN-REE-ET. Say again, if a you plaise."

"Orn-ri-et-ta."

She shook her head emphatically. "No, no! Say again."

"Hon-ri-et-te."

"No, no — AWN-REE-ET," she enunciated, more slowly this time, as one does when (dare I say it) addressing a child.

"Hen-ri-ette."

At length, after several more tries, he received the widow's approval. "You speak a so weel now, cheaile — allmost like *natif.*"

"Fancy that," Edgar smiled, glancing round. "Those old Greek and Latin birds haven't a thing on Edgar Harbottle."

Having set straight her pupil, the widow turned her attention again to Owen. Both Richard and Edgar had observed the wistful light that shone in her eyes, the warmth of affection that dwelt there, whenever she glanced Owen's way. It was an affection which seemed ill-concealed by design, like the indulgent smile that often was on her lips, and which appeared to cause the mariner some embarrassment. In death, as in life, this Henriette was a woman of considerable personal charm, from which Owen, in his present straits, doubtless had derived a sense of comfort. But it had made him uneasy as well, despite the fact that nothing of significance could come of it.

"Does she know about Gwenda, I wonder," Richard mentioned in an aside to Edgar — "and does Gwenda know about her?"

The youth shook his head, but ere he could reply the widow answered for him.

"Wat for you fallows speak a so quaite? You theenk Henriette cannot 'ear wat you say? Your talk of Owen and his leetle Geeblets? Silly, silly!"

"Who is Geeblets?" Edgar asked.

"She means Gwenda, sink me," Owen answered with a blush.

"Do you mean to say she knows Gwenda?"

"No. Well, aye. That is, Gwenda does not know *her*. But Henriette has seen Gwenda — "

"Gracious, has she visited the Hall?" Richard asked.

"Only very discreetly, sir."

"Do you mean it's possible?" said Edgar.

"Well, in a manner of speaking, sir, it is . . ."

It turned out that Henriette had it within her power to leave the skimmer at times, whether the ship was moored at the Hall or at Mackery End, for occasional "visits". Not surprisingly, those with whom she had become familiar were persons close to Owen, chiefly Geeblets — that is, Gwenda Goodwick — and Mrs. Aberdovey. None of them however had any awareness of her ghostly presence; it was Owen who had insisted upon this, and Henriette had acceded to his wish.

It was an uncomfortable notion, my brother reflected, and potentially embarrassing, that the spirit of Henriette might be present in a room with a fellow, watching and listening, and the fellow be entirely insensible of it. He glanced at Edgar, and it was evident that a similar thought had crossed his mind.

"Although she mustn't stray too far from the cup — or for too long a spell," Owen hastened to relate.

He was concerned that the villain Teech might try to steal the skimmer by day while at Northeave, more so than while it was safely moored at the Hall. Henriette had pledged to warn him if such an attempt were made, but it seemed that he did not entirely trust her. In the first place, she was French; and in the second — at which point he stopped short, and did not complete his thought. He had seemed about to say something, but having reconsidered held his tongue. Instead he took another few turns round the cabin, rubbing his chin and smoking, as if he were searching for the proper avenue by which to proceed.

Richard and Edgar were puzzled by his sudden hesitation, and by the relationship of the gammer's cup to Henriette. What had the mystic goblet to do with Owen's reluctance to trust her?

They glanced again at the horrid visage in pewter, with its staring eyes and wicked grin, and compared it to the lovely features of Henriette; but absolutely no resemblance between the two could they discern.

"What's this about Henriette's popping out of the cup, as you termed it, and that she mustn't stray too far? Of what significance is the cup to her?" Richard asked.

"As to the cup itself, sir," said the mariner, having ceased his pacing and joined them again, "well, it — it — "

"Yes?"

"Well, sir, Henriette — split me if she didn't — she did murder her husband with it."

The noise of Edgar's jaw falling was attended by a squeak, as his mouth swung open like a rusty gate.

"Oh, d-d-dear," was all he could stammer out, although much more was rushing through his head.

"Matter of fact! She confessed it to you?" Richard said.

The mariner nodded. "Indeed, sir — for it's her punishment, as she tells it. And she'll confess it to Mr. Edgar as well, for it was he who drank from the cup. She would have confessed the whole of it to Teech, but he'd sheered off from fright."

"Good heavens."

She did murder her husband with it. Again Richard's eyes strayed to the wicked old lady in pewter, and as his imagination took flight he began to wonder whether there wasn't more of a likeness between the crone and Henriette than he had hitherto suspected.

"Although she don't hardly look 'bargee' enough to have brained him with it," Edgar whispered. "However did she manage it?"

"I expect she waited until he was asleep," Richard suggested.

"Awful! It's enough to put a feller off holy padlock entirely."

"I suppose she's no longer such a peach as you did think?"

They glanced a moment at Henriette, and it was clear that she understood what was the subject of their discussion.

"Soche bad man! Cruel to me he was — vary 'orrid. And tighter than knot in shoelace," she explained, with a fervent jut of her chin. "*Hélas!* wat bad world is thees. Soche *triste* place."

"Still, there's no cause to be murdering your husband," Owen told her gently.

Again a look passed between them; then the set of Henriette's chin relaxed and she flashed him a smile so wistful and sweet, with its air of innocence, that she seemed to reserve for the mariner alone.

"*Mon cher,* you speak a so direct. 'Ere is poor Henriette forget hairself — is that not so? Wat does signify if it is good cause or no? For it was vary great *péché.*"

And having spoken she promptly subsided, leaving it to Owen to explain it was the just and proper doom that had been meted out to her, in the shape of the gammer's cup, that was responsible for her protracted stay upon the earth.

"It's her *pénitence* — her penance, as we should call it," he told them.

It was her means of atoning for the murder of her husband. It had been adjudged her fate to be bound to the gammer's cup, which she inhabited in tolerable comfort, guilt-ridden — or should so be — and where the passage of earthly time was but scarcely comprehended by her. Within limits, she was free to come and go as she pleased. But when anyone who never had done so did drink from the gammer's cup, it was her task and lot to warn that individual against the murder of a spouse, that the person should not endure the same consequences as had she. By this means was she perpetually reminded of her crime, and doomed to confess her guilt aloud — again, and again, and again.

All this Henriette heard in silence, her eyes lowered, the tips of her fingers daintily smoothing one or another imaginary wrinkle in her gossamy gown. Then, Owen having finished, she turned her attention to Edgar.

"So you weel leesten to me, cheaile," said she, with a virtuous countenance, "and so weel not run *risque* to suffer same fate as poor Henriette, by making promise not to keel a your wife. Wat shame it would be, certally. Weel you make promise not to keel a her? Weel you do thees for Henriette?"

How could Edgar have refused her plea? How indeed could any man? And so there and then, in the presence of witnesses, he pledged his solemn oath that never, under any circumstances, would he undertake the heinous business of slaughtering his wife. (That is if at some future date he should acquire a wife, for whatever reason — the very fact of his having done so, by the by, to serve as proof positive that he had lost all reason; for by his own admission Edgar Harbottle was not the gent to be succumbing to holy padlock.)

Her duty discharged, the widow's ready smile returned to her lips, and her glance to her favored object of admiration — Owen Aberdovey.

"And for how long must this go on? And for how many years now do you reckon it has been going on, this sentence of hers?" Richard asked.

"Rather say centuries, sir," Owen replied, "for by all that she has told me, it's certain sure the case. Sink me, but she's five hundred or more if she's an hour. The flight of time is as naught for one such as she."

For their mortal eyes, Owen explained, saw only that which Henriette wished them to see; saw her only as she herself wished to be seen, in the full blossom of her earthly beauty. The Henriette who stood before them was a kind of memory — an image of Henriette as she remembered herself, and as she wished to be remembered — preserved in spirit-substance for all time.

Hearing herself so spoken of, the widow sighed and shrugged her little shoulders. She had heard it all before; others had heard it; there was no great secret to be kept. Her path to a loftier state of existence had been obstructed by her own actions in this our earthly realm, to which she now was bound for an indefinite period. The terrible word *forever* crept into Richard's mind, but he did not speak it out, for he did not know that it was the case.

Observing her now in the bloom of her loveliness, insubstantial though it might be, it was difficult to imagine that she had been moldering in her grave for lo these many centuries. In the meantime her essence had existed as a being apart, remote from both this world and the next. It was no wonder that in Owen she had found someone to admire; he at least had not fled from her in terror.

However her circumstances were not so unusual, as she herself went on to explain. Indicating Melon-head where he sat on his cushion, she informed them that he himself once had been a man, whose spirit had returned and was rendering its own *pénitence* in the guise of a black cat, in expiation of his sins when last he was on earth.

"Bote he take his medicine like leetle sojer, is not so?" she smiled, gazing upon him not unkindly. "Poor Melon-head. Soche is price of folly."

"Jiminy," Edgar murmured, inching himself away from the cushion, which the cat was lazily kneading with its paws, "I altogether took him for a regular feller. And now I find he *is* a regular feller — or he was — or is — " His voice trailed off in a silence of confusion.

Henriette, answering the looks given the cat by himself and Richard, glanced at the two with an air of annoyance and demanded —

"And why the so long faces on you, like Gravy? Why so downward-in-mouth? No more would I bother my 'ead about it. Is way of the world."

Edgar frowned. "What does she mean by Gravy?"

Owen, reddening, explained that it was her nickname for Treadwell, on account of the gravity of his demeanor.

"She knows Treadwell then, eh?"

"She is aware of him."

"The deuce you say."

"There have been philosophers who believe that people may be born over again," Richard observed, "and who think that some people have been animals, and some animals people. But this is heresy, surely?"

Given her knowledge of the subject, which was extensive and had been acquired at first hand, Henriette had little patience for what she considered superstition.

"Fussbox! Soche petty detail! Wat means thees hairesy? Really, cheaile," she sighed, "you do give me conquassation. You make Henriette vary tire."

Her words proved prophetic, reminding my brother and Edgar how tired they themselves were after their long day that had seemed like a dream. Indeed it seemed ages ago now that they had been jogging their mounts along the causeway . . .

Abruptly Richard snapped his fingers. "What of the horses — Gray Gilbert and Ramble? For we left them in the stables."

"Was the door secured, sir?" Owen asked.

"As best as we could manage."

The mariner scratched his chin in thought. "We can but pray they are spared the curiosity of the lion and others of its ilk. But they ought to be safe enough till morning, when something may be done for 'em."

"My aunt can send Dan Hedges and a party of men from the Hall," Edgar suggested.

"Aye, it would seem the wisest course, sir."

This decided, it was time to prepare the skimmer for flight. The hour was rather later than usual, and so Owen's mother would be watching for him, and worrying perhaps. Wrapped in their boat-cloaks the mariner and his guests ascended to the deck. Henriette, having no need of cloaks, remained behind, or so Richard supposed; but when they arrived at the cockpit there she was, her luminous form eerily aglow, waiting for Owen.

The mariner's first action was to unlash the wheel. Next he loosed the mooring-rope and, bracing himself in the cockpit, and urging Richard and Edgar to do the same, began to revolve one of the crank-handles. Almost immediately there was a feeling of movement. The boards underfoot seemed to be pushing up against their shoes; then the dark outline of the lodge gable dropped from view, as the skimmer lifted smoothly and silently into the night.

"'Pon my word," Edgar exclaimed, holding on the more tightly as he glanced about him, "the deuced ship really flies — fancy that . . ."

"Is not clever ting?" said Henriette, gazing proudly at Owen. "I am so rejoice. Was vary great accomplishment of Owen — soche clever *marin* — to make skeemer that fly away like bird."

"She does tend to exaggerate," Owen explained.

A further turn of the handle, a slight adjustment of the wheel, and the ship veered upwards and away over the tree-tops. The shaggy dark mass of timber that was Marley Wood slid beneath her rising prow; then a second, more vigorous motion of the wheel, and a touch at one of the pedals, sent the skimmer gliding out over the marshes.

"Shouldn't you be watching your compass heading?" Richard asked, for given the black night the instrument was impossible to read.

"Not to worry," Owen assured him, "for I know the way well enough. Lookee there, sir. D'you see the scatter of fire-light away to starboard yonder? There lies Ridingham — due northwesterly. Now clap your eye below. D'you see the marshways there — the dark streams crossing the snow fields, like the veins on the back of your hand? One has but to follow the course of one stream in particular — that lying afore us there — Dud and Bodo's — and 'twill take us dead straight to the causeway, scarce a furlong from the Hall."

"Goodness me — it's not so difficult at that."

"No, sir. It's like driving a four-in-hand, or sailing a ship to windward. It's easier once you've done it a time or two."

"Who are Dud and Bodo?"

"Coracle men, sir, brothers, and old friends of my father's. I've known the pair of 'em since I was a lad. Near seventy they must be now, and still plying their boats in the stream."

"Nearer eighty, I should think," Edgar suggested.

Further pressure on the pedal sent the skimmer darting ahead. The rush of wind in their faces was exhilarating, but a trifle dangerous, the air being so cold as to freeze the skin. So wisely the visitors, who had been watching from the rail, returned to the cockpit, where Owen, with Henriette at his side, was scanning the way forward. The mariner's handling of his vessel in all respects was right sailorly; plainly he was familiar with every trick and quirk of her helm. Some further minutes passed, at which time he released the deck-pedal, causing their velocity to diminish.

"Ah, there they are, sir — right ahead of us," Owen announced.

"They" were the clump of Scotch firs in whose upper tiers Richard had had a glimpse of the skimmer during his ride to the Hall. Easing his craft down in their sheltering embrace, Owen had not long to wait, only a few moments passing before the signal-light appeared in an upper lattice of the gatehouse. With a creaking of timbers and the subtle sway of her deck underfoot, the skimmer rose from her place of concealment and flew on towards the Hall.

The familiar sweep of battlements flanked by octagonal towers stood out darkly against the night as Owen guided her in. Over the curtain-wall she floated, and across the courtyard, to settle her keel with the gentlest of thuds on the Hall roof. Then the ship was made fast, and the cord-ladder dropped to the ground some three flights below — and some few yards beyond the steps of the servants' door.

"So that is how it was done," Richard mused.

"Aye, sir," nodded Owen. "And now, Mr. Edgar — there is a small trap in the roof, over yonder — that leading from the lumber-rooms — do you recollect the one? Once I've cleared it of the snow, you and Mr. Hathaway may go in by that means. I've a notion the cord-ladder would be disagreeable. And then I'll offer my good-nights to you. I must pay my visit to my mother and afore dawn return to Northeave. I'll make check of the horses there, and be safe ensconced in the wood ere the boys come for them."

It was so agreed, when all at once Edgar, glancing round, exclaimed — "Say, what's happened? Where is she?"

Their eyes searched the deck, but the ghostly luminosity that was Henriette was nowhere in evidence.

"I reckon she's gone visiting for a spell," Owen said.

On the Watch

U NDER a still, frozen sky, a party of riders was spurring on their mounts, eastwards along the wood road, in the direction of Northeave.

With an air of steady purpose the horsemen kept watch on the tall curtain of trees passing by on their right — the eaves of Marley Wood, where it skirts the marshes — at all times alert for the slightest motion in its dim recesses, and ready to bring their cutlasses into play at the first alarm. For those who know the marshways know Marley Wood, and know that all must have their wits about them wherever marsh and wood adjoin.

Breakfast that morning had been a muddled affair. Mrs. Flitch, it seems, had sustained a shock of some sort in the night, and as a result was keeping to her bed; so that her minions had been pressed into service to dish up the eggs and rashers of bacon, griddle-cakes, and oatmeal porridge needed for the sideboard. Without their mistress to direct them, however, their efforts had produced but a pale imitation of breakfast.

Afterwards Edgar had trotted round to the farm office to confer with Dan Hedges, instructing the outside man that a party of stable-boys should be mustered to fetch Ramble and Gray Gilbert. When questioned how he and my brother had returned from Northeave without their mounts, Edgar explained that a spotted lion of uncommon size and ferocity had ambushed them at Mackery End, and that in the A.M. he and Richard, hesitant to expose their valued horses to the perils of the wood road, had obtained a lift from a passing wagon, and needed now to return with a force of men and arms to collect the horses in safety. Accordingly a band of rescuers quickly was assembled and departed the gatehouse, Richard and Edgar sharing the lead with Dan.

Fortunately the journey was swift and uneventful. In no long time the horsemen came in view of the riven oak that marked the western limits of Northeave — that place, deserted now, where in days of yore the swells of

Ridingham, ardently attached to their sport with all its attendant dangers and fatigues, had met to hunt venison and flat-head boar in Marley Wood.

The riders, espying the chimneys of Mackery End rising from amongst the tree-tops, drew their horses in to a slower gait as they made their careful approach to the lodge. Richard and Edgar meanwhile were feeling a trifle on edge, their adventures of the preceding day only too fresh in their memory.

The party reined their trusty steeds to a halt, and from its periphery of yard and outbuildings they made a survey of the old manse, studying it and the grounds with a cautious scrutiny before proceeding. A spotted lion is not a thing to be taken lightly, heaven knows, and with their keen awareness of vision the men kept a wary watch of the premises for a time, ere it was judged safe to move in closer.

Their examination was attended only by the whistle of the wind in the pine boughs. No stealthy movement in the shadows did they glimpse, nor did anything suspicious come within range of their horses' senses. It seemed they were in luck, with no savage carnivore afoot in the neighborhood this morning. And so in a body the riders pricked forward to the stables. There all looked to be secure; no evidence was there that the spotted lion of yesterday, or any other predator, had attempted to breach the shut door.

Richard and Edgar too examined the portal, and the ground before it. Would Owen's footprints in the snow be visible to Dan and the others? Would they recognize the imprint of his sea-boots — the same mysterious, round-toed marks that had been discovered in the courtyard of the Hall? For the mariner had agreed to look in on the horses today. Fortunately the tramping of Edgar and Richard and their mounts had churned up the snow to such an extent, that the incursion of Owen was near-impossible to detect — particularly if one were not looking for it.

Without further ceremony the riders dismounted, and Richard himself strode ahead to open the door. Their trusty steeds were unable to contain their delight as Gray Gilbert and Ramble were led forth from their dreary prison. So too were the captives in every way pleased with the reception accorded them by their stable-fellows. Inquisitive and full of spirits, they tossed up their ears and flirted their tails, and nosed one another with their muzzles of velvet, their playful nips and eager whinnies expressive of their mutual joy at the reunion.

Having accomplished their errand the party started off for home, Ramble and Gray Gilbert following on leads, and after a hasty tramp through the snow returned without incident to the Hall.

After luncheon Richard and Edgar by chance learned the cause of Mrs. Flitch's indisposition, and from no less an individual than little Elzie Peek. They happened to be passing the drawing-room where the maid was at her dusting, and where they were fortunate enough to have the tale from her own lips as she blushed and dimpled it out to them.

At a late hour on the night preceding, while the Hall had been wrapped in slumber, had come a faint jingle of keys and a heavy tread in the passage leading to the kitchen. Mrs. Flitch, concerned over the identity of the thief who had been raiding her larder, from her quarters adjacent thought that she had heard a noise, and had gotten up her candle and her courage to investigate. For Lady Martindale had impressed upon her the need for strict economies in these times of ours, and Mrs. Flitch was determined that the thief, whoever it was, should be brought to account for the eel, capon legs, grilled mackerel, and other fare that had gone missing.

She halted at the door, which stood ajar, and listened awhile. It was unmistakable, the faint noise that had put her on her guard — a muffled sobbing, which seemed to resonate like a ghostly lament through the kitchen.

Her light cast a pale luminescence over the dresser, with its carvings of odd figures and gothic grotesques, and its glowing, moon-faced plates, that stood just inside the room. With some slight hesitation the cook pushed open the door, the rays of her taper pouring themselves over the stone flagging, and the long, long table that stretched before her. Still the noise persisted, although its source was not yet visible. It seemed to arise from the far end of the kitchen, where an antique, high-backed settle held sway in the chimney-corner.

The eyes of the cook narrowed slightly, as she guided her considerable bulk over the flags towards the darkened hearth. As she proceeded the sobbing rose in volume, and it became clear that the anguished individual was resting on the settle. Now who could it be, Mrs. Flitch asked herself, who would be weeping in her kitchen in the night-time? And what relation had this to the midnight thievery?

No such cat thieves in my kitchen had been her retort to Constable Pettiplace's absurd suggestion. Mrs. Flitch was a servant of long experience, and never before had she heard of a cat caught sobbing over a cream-pot.

With searching eyes she scanned the chimney-corner, and as she drew near it she raised her light and demanded — "Here, now! Who are you and what d'you think you're at?"

Came a final, choking sob, as though from a start of surprise, and then — nothing.

For no reason that the cook could divine, a feeling as of some looming evil took hold of her. Perhaps it was the sudden quiet — one minute there had been the pitiful whimpering of one stricken with grief, the next there was no sound at all. Warily she eased her eyes round the arm of the settle, to see who was there. What she found acted only to magnify her dread.

There was nobody.

Mrs. Flitch fell back a step, certain that there had been a presence there only seconds before, that now was gone. Her free hand crept towards her throat, as she recalled some of the alarming disturbances that had been reported over the years, concerning the legend — the Martindale family story — that her ladyship maintained was no legend at all, was not a curse, was nothing, because foolish folk always would be talking.

All in a moment the looming evil closed about her like a shroud. On the alert, the cook glanced to her right, to her left, again to her right, and all around her.

"Hallo! Who's in my kitchen?" she demanded.

Afraid that some specter was readying itself to leap upon her unawares, she flashed her light round the chimney-corner, the open hearth, the brick walling, the rush-bottomed chairs. Where was George Pettiplace when he was needed, she wondered? Safely asleep in his bed in Ridingham no doubt.

Then a faint exclamation escaped her lips, as her eyes began to perceive the outline of something dark which had started to form itself on the brick walling. It was a shadow, one given life by no light of hers, nor by that of anyone else's, but which appeared to be taking shape of its own accord on the brickwork in the chimney-corner.

Steadily, stealthily, like a misshapen giant, it rose up before her, bigger and blacker than any shadow had any cause to be, flowing upwards and outwards as it spread itself over the bricks and mortar from sanded floor to beamed ceiling. Mrs. Flitch, so much frightened by it she could feel her hair curling on her head, shrank back in alarm. Then, detaching itself from the wall, the phantom swung round to face her, more like an angry cloud than a solid substance.

A qualm of panic set the cook's heart to racing, and the hand that gripped her candle to trembling. Her free hand, that which had stolen towards her throat, had taken hold of the collar of her nightgown and was shaking it with palsied fingers.

"By the powers," she managed to gasp out, "by the powers, what devil is this . . .?"

Ordinarily as steady and solid of nerve as of flesh, she thrust a clenched fist to her teeth in the realization it was the creeping shadow of Haigh Hall that confronted her there. Shapeless though it was, it had about it so horrid an air of menace that its identity was scarce in doubt. For was it not in this same chimney-corner, centuries ago, that the cobbler, Crispin Nightshade himself, had fallen dead at the sight of a shadow?

The cook, overcome with horror, stood transfixed by the phantom that had crept forth from the wall, and from which an eerie, unearthly growling now proceeded. At the same time a portion of the dark malignity had thrust itself towards her like a claw, and was making groping motions in the air . . .

Mrs. Flitch had seen quite enough. Wrenching herself free of its spell, she uttered a shriek and retired in haste to her quarters, locking and bolting the door behind her. Then she flung herself onto her cot and drew the blankets over her head, and for several minutes could be heard reciting the prayers of her childhood with wonderful fidelity under the bedclothes.

"And that's the lot of it, sir," the gossipy Elzie testified in conclusion, "as it were told me by Mrs. Flitch from her pillow this morning."

"That's rather a curious tale," Richard remarked.

"It's the truth, sir, to the best of her knowledge, so said Mrs. Flitch," stated Elzie.

It seemed plausible — even likely — that the shadow that had brushed the stovepipe hat from Sir Padrig's head in the library was the same that had frightened Mrs. Flitch in the chimney-corner. But what cause had it to be sobbing in the kitchen in the dead of night? Whoever had heard of the "weeping shadow" of Haigh Hall?

This new mystery would require a deal of thinking out, Richard decided, so suiting the action to the word he filled a fresh pipe and sat himself down to it. All thought of Sir Pharnaby was tossed out of window. Later he and Edgar spoke to Gwenda Goodwick, and when questioned about it she shook her head bright with tumbled curls. She had indeed visited the kitchen on the previous evening, she told them, although at an earlier hour than Mrs. Flitch had done, to secure a capon leg for Melon-head. However she vigorously denied having shed so much as a single tear in the endeavor.

Shadows of the Past — and Future

W H E N word of Mrs. Flitch's indisposition, and the cause of it, reached Owen's mother in the gatehouse, it produced in her a cold shiver of recognition, and certain misgivings as regards the future, arising as they did from her acquaintance with a terrible incident from the past.

That incident was the death under mysterious circumstances of his lordship, Sir Pedr Martindale, at the Hall some ten years earlier.

Though of course one could not speak of it publicly, Lady Martindale having decreed that there was no legend connected with the Hall, no gruesome family story, no curse upon the Martindale male line dating back to Sir Padrig, for her late husband the baronet had died a natural death. So had Dr. Bussey concluded, and his verdict had been widely accepted, for Dr. Bussey was a distinguished physician. Mysterious circumstances did not enter into it; the notion that anything sinister might have occurred in connection with his lordship's passing had been summarily dismissed.

Still the legend of Haigh Hall — the gruesome family story — remained fresh in the minds of the common folk of Ridingham, and in particular of that regrettable class of people who always would be talking.

The nerves of Mrs. Flitch were in a disordered state, as was the kitchen in her absence, so much so that Mrs. Aberdovey had been prevailed upon to assume command of the cook's minions, so that less disorder might be on show at the family meal-table. As a result the widow had ample opportunity to hear of Mrs. Flitch's adventure, in its every riveting detail, from those who had had it from the woman's own lips as she languished in her sick-bed. For Mrs. Flitch had narrowly escaped destruction at the hand, as it were, of the creeping shadow — the family legend that did not exist.

Or was it now the weeping shadow? For try as they might, the inmates of the Hall could fathom no cause for the shadow to have been sobbing in the chimney-corner, nor for its having selected Mrs. Flitch for its victim.

The coroner ruled that the baronet had perished of a heart seizure. But this was wrong, and Mrs. Aberdovey knew it to be wrong; but not so her ladyship, who, all these years on, still had but an imperfect understanding of the facts. It was Morgan Aberdovey who had discovered his lordship that day — that awful day — and it was to his wife and only to her that he had communicated the particulars of the horrid scene. But he too now was dead, leaving only his widow to relay the circumstances of the baronet's passing. But in the interim she had told no one.

Mrs. Flitch's indisposition had produced an uneasiness of the soul in another as well — Mr. Edgar Harbottle. Hearing of the shadow that had sent the cook flying to her bed, the youth's late fears had been rekindled. Again his thoughts were harassed by a suspicion that he himself, although not a Martindale *per se*, might be next in line for the attentions of the family tormentor. These worries he had communicated to Richard, who in his turn had consulted Mrs. Aberdovey — he and Edgar being now members of that select circle who knew of Owen and the skimmer — the result being that the two had been invited to call on the widow at the gatehouse that evening, as she had something of importance to disclose to the future lord of the manor.

Some talk of her son passed first, and how the villain Amos Teech had done him a cruel injustice, and how Owen by day was keeping his lonely vigil at Northeave while awaiting word from Jolly Jumper Yard. It was evident from her conversation that Mrs. Aberdovey was in the dark as regards the delightful Henriette, and of the fact that while keeping his vigil her son had been consorting with an acknowledged murderess.

This, of course, was not the reason she had invited the two to the gatehouse, but, prompted by Mrs. Flitch's experience, it was to give young Edgar a truthful account of his uncle's death, the particulars of which had remained a close secret for years.

"My Morgan," she began, in wistful voice — "my Morgan, having come home at last to the marshes, always was full of yarns of the sea, which he often shared with his lordship. However a quiet, stay-at-home, regular life has its compensations, as he soon discovered . . ."

She hesitated briefly and bit her lip, as one does who finds herself entering upon a difficult task. But she had too much inner strength of character to falter once she had resolved upon a course of action.

Sir Pedr and her husband had been as near friends as the relationship of lord to servant gives leave, not only from a correspondence of temperament and interests, but from their common heritage. For both had been descended from those most ancient of Britons, the Welsh, a restless and fiery people, yet for all that a poetic race of bards and harpists who reveled in their lilting speech and soaring Cymric traditions.

"You must cast your mind back some ten years," she began. "It was in the hind-end of the year, and the solstice was near upon us. It was at a late hour of the afternoon — it already had gone dark — when his lordship betook himself to the farm office."

Edgar fingered his collar uneasily. It was in the farm office that his uncle had suffered his fatal attack. But why had his lordship gone there? What business had called him to the office? For in the confusion of his death it had never been explained.

"It was on account of the bones," Mrs. Aberdovey said.

She let her eyes rest on Edgar's, then, blinking back sudden tears, hastily averted her glance. She fumbled for a dainty square of lace with which to pat the moisture from her cheeks.

"If not for the bones," she resumed after a minute, "his lordship might still be alive today. If not for the bones . . . if not for my husband, who had unearthed them . . ."

"Bones?" said a concerned Edgar. "Which bones are those?"

"A piece of jaw-bone," the widow answered, slowly, "with a few teeth in it, and some bits of skull, that had eroded from a patch of turf aside the causeway. It was my husband who found them, and who brought 'em to the farm office for Sir Pedr's inspection."

"And this is why my uncle went to the office that afternoon?"

"Yes, sir."

"'Pon my word, I've never heard of any bones."

"No, Mr. Edgar, you haven't — nor has her ladyship — nor has anyone but my husband and myself, as he pledged me to secrecy in the affair."

"And why was that?"

"His lordship believed that dire results might follow, and wanted none to know of the discovery."

"I shouldn't wonder he thought the creeping shadow might have a bearing on the case," Richard suggested.

The widow agreed. "I gathered as much, sir — but my Morgan never did say for a certainty. His lordship had wished for silence in the matter."

"Creeping shadow — I was afraid of that," Edgar groaned.

"Where might the bones be now?" Richard asked.

"Nowhere, sir," said Mrs. Aberdovey, "for after his lordship's death my husband, fearing there was something evil about them, did pitch 'em into the waters aside the causeway, not far from where he found them. And he cursed himself and the day he first had seen 'em."

"And Lady Martindale knows nothing of these bones?"

"No, sir. His lordship had not cared to worry her. He told my husband so."

Richard threw himself back in his chair, in an attitude of reflection. Of course his lordship had so done, he reasoned, in view of all that Mr. Gecks had related concerning the Martindale male line after Sir Padrig — concerning Sir Price Martindale, who had been thrown from his horse at a bullfinch, and Sir John Llewellyn, who had taken a tumble in the library, and Sir Dafydd, the baronet's grandfather, who had fallen into a stream in the dark and been carried away. Naturally Sir Pedr would not have told his wife of the bones, for clearly he had believed they had some relation to the shadow, whose appearance often preceded the demise of the reigning head of the family.

Nor could he help but be reminded of the grisly relic that had been discovered by Toddy outside the curtain-wall, and which was kept in a closet in the very office where his lordship had perished.

"And there was something more, sir," said Mrs. Aberdovey, dabbing at her cheeks again — "something more as pertained to his lordship the baronet that day, that her ladyship never was to be told of."

"Oh, yes?" said Edgar, not sure he cared to hear it.

"This something more is a thing your husband witnessed?" Richard asked.

The widow nodded grimly. "A thing too horrible, sir — too odious — to be disclosed to her ladyship at the time, or indeed at any time. For my Morgan, he didn't wish to distress her mind as already was grieving for her loss."

"Nevertheless he told you of it?"

"Yes, sir. Days afterwards it was though, when he could bring himself to speak of it."

"It is something that he saw there in the farm office?"

"Yes, sir."

"And what was it, Mrs. Aberdovey, that your husband saw?"

Again she hesitated and glanced aside, worrying her under lip with her teeth and drying her eyes.

"At first my husband thought it a prank — the bones, I mean," she explained after a moment, "but his lordship was of quite another mind. He believed them to be a token of the curse. My husband had left them in the office, by his lordship's instruction, and gone about his business. When he returned he found his lordship there, examining the bones one by one — and then — and then — "

She paused again to collect herself before describing for them, in hushed tones, the details of the horror to which Lady Martindale never was to be made privy. No sooner had her husband entered the office, she related, than a crouching figure draped all in black had appeared on a wall.

"Who goes there?" Morgan Aberdovey had demanded, thinking it the shadow of an intruder, and drew his cutlass. But of what use is bladed steel against an enemy having neither form nor substance?

The figure had risen to a standing posture before him, when a piece of it had reached out from the wall like a vengeful hand and, seizing the baronet by the throat, lifted him several feet clear of the floor. And there his lordship had remained, struggling mightily the whiles to free himself and thrashing about, his lungs a-gasp for air, a hideous choking in his gullet — the very picture of a condemned man writhing and twisting on the scaffold.

Just as the cobbler's poor drudge of a cousin had writhed and twisted in her hempen halter on that festive day when she had been launched into eternity.

Then of a sudden the body — distorted of countenance, discolored, eyeballs starting from its head — had yielded up its ghost, and gone limp; at which point the shadow withdrew again into the wall, and the corpse with an awful thud fell to the floor.

"True as gospel, sir," whispered Mrs. Aberdovey with a shudder. "My husband, so terrified, he never afterwards could forget the sound of it. Of his lordship's — his lordship's — "

And there had he lain, Sir Pedr Martindale, reduced to a crumpled heap on his farm-office floor, while the shadow — the family curse that never was — had crept stealthily away along a wall and was gone.

Edgar, scarcely able himself to breathe, felt a crying need to loosen his collar or he must faint. For this appalling scene — the grisly nature of his uncle's death, the sheer vileness of it — had both sickened and terrified him.

Out upon the thought! Out upon it!

Of course there was no legend, no family story, no curse. So Lady Martindale had decreed, and so she believed — *because the truth had been kept from her.*

Dr. Bussey had been sent for, but his lordship already had been an hour gone and beyond the reach of mortal physician, distinguished or otherwise. The doctor's verdict? *Cor suffocans,* a suffocating seizure of the heart, or as it is more commonly reckoned — death by the visitation of God.

"But it was no Holy God of mine nor yours that did visit his lordship in the farm office that day," Mrs. Aberdovey observed.

The doctor had been perfectly satisfied with his verdict, she recalled, as had been the local constabulary, and Dr. Grubble the coroner, and most of the notables of Ridingham, all of whom had accepted it on the strength of the physician's sober authority.

"But he was wrong," Richard noted.

"He was, sir," said Mrs. Aberdovey, "and only my Morgan to tell him different. But my husband felt he had been sworn to silence, so as to spare her ladyship."

"I expect the bones were nowhere to be found when the doctor arrived?"

"Yes, sir, my husband had taken them away."

No bones, and nothing remaining of Sir Pedr Martindale, Bart., but the tablet to his memory, in a prime position beside the chancel in the Church of St. Mary-in-the-Mews, and his coffin in the family vault beneath.

A clock in the room chimed the hour. They were sitting round the fire now with no light but the blaze, my brother in frowning concentration as he thought over the widow's recollection of events. But after some further talk he and the others were unable to arrive at a solution to the important problem that remained.

Edgar, likely heir to the Martindale estates, appeared to be next in line for the attention of the shadow. Yet why had it not revealed itself to him? In the library, in the presence of Richard, a stranger, it had tumbled the stovepipe from Sir Padrig's head — Sir Padrig Martindale, a Justice of the Court, who had pronounced judgment on Nightingale's cousin. And why had it appeared in the kitchen? What possible advantage was there to be gained in scaring Mrs. Flitch? And above all, what had brought the vengeful murderer of so many Martindales to tears?

The likely heir to the Martindale estates — who by his own admission had little more than tuppence to his name *in banco* — was hardly cheered by this discussion, convinced as he was that his youthful existence already was in eclipse. Because the shadow had yet to reveal itself to him did not imply that it never would. As Richard pointed out, however, there was no shame in fearing an omen so perilous, the which Edgar more or less had resigned himself to face, with as much of the vaunted courage of his ancestors as he could muster.

As for my brother, he had been gripped by a sudden inspiration, and shortly afterwards he and Edgar took their leave and tramped round to the farm office. Fascinated by the revelations concerning Sir Pedr's death, my brother was curious to examine the spot where it had occurred. He had no idea what he might find there, but the place seemed worthy of his and Edgar's closer attention.

The snug little chamber was untenanted at that hour, Dan Hedges having retired. They prepared a couple of wax-lights, and for their comfort lit a small fire in the chimney. As their eyes roved about the empty office and its inventory of rustic appointments, it seemed to them as if every shadow lurking there had assumed the appearance of something alive. Passing the closet where the boot was kept, they resisted the temptation to open it; instead they moved on to the stretch of oak walling where, by Mrs. Aberdovey's account, the phantom had risen up to throttle the baronet.

"I should say it was about here," Richard estimated.

Edgar nodded glumly, the thought having sent his fingers again to his collar.

Richard studied the length of wall carefully, exploring every facet of its textured surface, before halting a moment to fill his pipe that it might aid his concentration. For some minutes then he paced up and down, absorbed in thought. Now and again his eyes swung round and he would examine the wall again, as if to clarify something in his mind. At present he had no tenable theory that might explain the shadow's appearances to himself and the cook and its seeming indifference to Edgar. But as he well knew, theory and fact often are far removed.

These were deep waters. Indifference to Edgar . . . Edgar strictly speaking not really a Martindale . . . no connection to Edgar . . . indifference to Edgar . . .

In the next instant he took the pipe from his mouth and rose a little on his toes, his thinking brought to a sudden stand. Dash it all, how could he have been so thick? How had he missed the connection? For hadn't the facetious placement of the stovepipe hat on the bust of Sir Padrig *been Edgar's doing*? And wasn't it the shadow that in passing had struck it from the Justice's head?

He glanced at Edgar, thinking that perhaps he ought to communicate his discovery to the youth. At that moment, however, his eyes detected a seeming reflection in the mirror over the fireplace. Something he thought had moved in the glass. Was it a shadow that had fallen across it? Then he and Edgar heard a sudden step behind them, as a frightful image — ghastly and awful with its unkempt hair, flapping ears, and scar athwart its jaw — loomed up in the mirror.

Alarmed, Edgar gave a gasp and blurted out — "Yoicks, what a sight!"

They wheeled round to confront the specter, which proved to be nothing more than the rough-hewn fellow of a cheeky groom — whose name, by the by, was Diggory — staring at them in surprise. He had thrust off his cap and with his huge, sticky-out ears, scarred cheek, and hair that proclaimed at best only hearsay evidence of combing, he did indeed look a sight, or a fright, or something to that effect. He told them that while passing the farm office he had observed a light in the window, and was curious to know who it might be at such an hour.

"Thought we'd seen a goblin," Edgar explained, as he and Richard hurriedly put out the fire and departed.

The groom, not a little concerned, stood awhile scratching his chin and looking after them.

"Smite me dumb! Goblins in the joint? Goblins won't do — rum things — no fit end for a poor jack, that's sure," he muttered.

Then he returned his greasy cap to his head and ambled off.

THE FOURTH CHAPTER

Remembered on Waking

R U M things goblins may be, but it's just such a night as this as might have drawn them forth on their revels. The air is dank and raw; again a thick fog has settled down upon the marshes. At the Hall no one is abroad, or so it appears, as the mist comes stealing over the battlements, and creeping round the corners, slowly, stealthily gathering into one single, dense mass that fills the courtyard.

Then from out of the fog a man steps, taking his solitary way through the snow. His wizened form is buttoned tight in an old watch-coat, there is a slouch hat on his head, a cutlass at his belt, and in his hand he carries a small lantern that shines dimly amber in the dark. It is bracing weather, the sort of which Sam Gander is so fond, though his crinkly little eyes can see nothing that is more than a few feet in front of them.

It is an ill night to be wall-walking, Mr. Gander has regretfully concluded, and so, having no cause to be abroad this evening, he has bent his steps again towards the Hall.

As he is passing the servants' door, however, that which lies across the yard from the gatehouse, his progress is arrested by an unknown something that smites him on the cheek and bars his way, as effectively as if a curtain had been drawn across his path.

"'Ere — what's this, then?" he demands of no one in particular, for no one is there. He turns sharply on his heel and peers upwards, where the rungs of the cord-ladder upon which he has stumbled can be seen rising into the night.

Then he looks down again, and notes there a trail of footprints in the snow — prints made by a man's round-toed boots — running from the ladder to the gatehouse lane. These marks he recognizes, for it is not the first time he has seen them.

"Ooh, this is better," he chuckles to himself, and turns again to the ladder gently swaying from its collision with his cheek. "So where does this go, then, eh? Me Lizzie won't like it, but what she don't know won't hurt her. I'm seventy-seven come St. Odo's Day, and I'll do as I please. A fig for nosy Parkers, I say — daughters or no. Hee, hee!"

So saying he puts by his light — for he has no means of carrying it, save with a third set of fingers — and taking hold of the ladder commences his sure and steady ascent into the fog. The erstwhile publican who had re-formed himself is an avid climber, as his wall-walking has demonstrated, and in no little time finds himself at the level of the battlements, three stories above the yard. There, against the softest of cloud-light, the shadowy form of a ship's hull can be seen looming at the top of the ladder.

"Ooh, even better! I've seen yer more than once afore, me beauty," he cackles as he mounts to her deck, and smiling pats her rail with a satisfied hand.

The vessel is riding on the Hall roof, as if afloat on a ghostly sea of fog. Her stern, from which the ladder depends, juts out slightly over the roof's edge, where a mooring-rope has been fastened to one of the merlons. The deck itself appears deserted, with no evidence of either officer or crew.

To Sam's eyes it looks a fine place of escape — a hidey-hole, a *sanctum sanctorum*, a haven amongst the battlements — to which he might retreat and be quit of the annoyance of meddling doctors and relations.

"Getting still better," he nods, rubbing his palms and chuckling.

There before him is the cockpit with its lashed wheel, its crank-handles and deck-pedals. Above the wheel hangs a lantern not unlike that he had abandoned below; and by the simple expedient of a match he makes practical use of the instrument to guide his explorations.

Beside the cockpit is an open hatch that descends steeply into darkness. He calls down it but receives no answer. There appears to be no one about. This, too, Mr. Gander finds is better, and further relieving of annoyance. And so down the companionway he trots to the snug cabin below.

The cabin is a small space, exceedingly trim and orderly — for the vessel itself is not large — and so arranged and furnished as to afford the most comfort to its occupants. Scratching his chin in thought, he swings his light round in this and that direction. Its beam discloses a range of lockers on either side, a table midway with a silver lamp above it, a small cook-stove, and shut doors fore and aft. The adjoining compartments he finds are un-occupied — ("Even better!") — the one containing sleeping berths, the other being a store-room with an odd mix of appointments, among them a cage-like apparatus with a central screw-shaft running vertically from deck to overhead. The purpose of this structure is a mystery to him, and likely to remain such; so he closes the door and resumes his inspection of the cabin, musing to himself as he goes.

"None of 'em would believe it, what I've seen from the walk . . . why, the sight of it would blow a hole in their hats . . . yet 'ere it is in the flesh . . . what might they think of it now, me Lizzie, and me neffy . . . and that great booby of a quack . . . well, a figo for what *he* thinks . . . bother him and his gammon . . . what right's he got to be pshawing and poohing a body over bogberries and fen lentils and eel oil . . . a great stuffed head he is, as don't know enough to pour water out of his shoe . . ."

He continues in like vein concerning his physician's ceaseless scolding and disapproval of his entire mode of life. Worse still was his own daughter's joining in the refrain — ganging up on him, so he views it. But none of it mattered a penny-weight, for Mr. Gander had reformed himself.

"Well, get yer gone with yer, the pair o' yer — shoo!" he derides them, *in absentia*. "I'll show yer — I've me own place now, where none o' yers can find me — they'll think I've gone — cut me lucky — vanished — quit o' the lot of 'em — and let it be their own lookout!"

Even as his tongue is at its work his eye is yielding to curiosity, as regards the lockers ranged on either side of him. In the first two he finds nothing of interest to any but seamen, but on opening the third he is startled by a huge black cat who springs forth from its interior.

"Bandog and bedlam — who are yer, then?" chuckles Sam, crinkling in surprise. "This ain't yer boat, is it? Well, that's grand! For methinks yer've a sailorly look to yer. A ship's cat yer must be, and a lively feller yer are, and a handsome too."

It happens that Mr. Gander has long had a fondness for cats — those of the domestic variety, at any rate — and that, strangely perhaps, the sentiment was returned by most members of the tribe. In short, Sam Gander liked cats, and most cats appeared to like Sam. For cats are willful, independent, solitary beings who won't take no guff, as Sam has been heard to remark — words that, coincidentally, might have described his own character to a T.

Already the big tomcat is lolling on a cushion, submitting to his attentions and purring like a house afire.

"Ooh, a bold, dashing feller yer looks . . . like meself was in me youth time . . . well, it's a daft dog that don't admire a cat's finer qualities," observes Sam, nodding and chuckling.

All at once the cat makes a quick thrust with his paw, the which Sam counters with a feint, and then a playful tug at his tail, all of it in the name of fun. Fun it is, he understands, as does the tomcat himself. For cats, you know, are intuitive animals and great readers of human nature, and can be very trusting of those whom they sense do love and admire them. And those whom cats trust they trust entirely, with their whole heart and soul.

Says Sam, fishing in another locker — "Ooh, what's this 'ere, then?" — and removes a pewter mug, its surface stamped in high relief with the visage of a wicked-looking crone. He grimaces at the sight, shaking his head in disapproval. "That's 'orrible! I don't like that face — like three days o' bad weather. What's a gaud like yer a-doin' 'ere?"

In the next locker he finds a couple of pint-bottles, one of Willoughby gray, the other of seamen's rum, and a half-filled tin of biscuits. "Decent grub," he concludes, sampling a biscuit, "and more besides," as he runs his eye over the bottles and their contents — the sort of contents from which he, Samuel Gander, has nobly abstained on account of his having reformed himself. No bogberry juice these!

"What's this one, eh?" From the rum-bottle he plucks the stopper and takes a sniff of the liquor. Straightway he is reminded again of that booby of a quack, Bussey, and his endless preaching. "Ruin me constitution, eh? With bogberry? With oatmeal porridge? Fen lentils? Ruin *him!* He thinks I'm a geezer — a crank — a nutter. Well, *he's* anutter — hee, hee! Why, a feller may snack and sip as he pleases on his own boat."

The mood is on him tonight to be contrary, in light of his newfound discovery that lies aground on the battlements of the Hall. Truth be told it is not his first view of the mysterious craft, of which he has had glimpses on more than one occasion, at odd hours of the night, while pacing his rounds. But never had he broached the subject to anyone, as it would have served only to fortify his reputation as a geezer, a crank, and a nutter.

And so he is resolved this night to be contrary — if only for this night alone — and by this simple act of defiance put both his daughter and his doctor in their right places, if only in his mind.

"I'll show 'em," he vows, as he pours out a dram. "I'll show 'em Sam Gander still can guzzle with the best of 'em, same as he always did. I might even chew tobaccy tonight, if there's any to be found — or smoke me a fresh pipe — "

It is in such a frame of mind then that he touches the pewter to his lip, throws back his head, and downs his measure in several gulps.

I think that's about the right dose. So he fancies might have been the remark of Dr. Bussey, had the learned physician beheld his patient's draining of the mug. He chuckles softly at the notion, only to start as though from

a dream, as he finds his laugh echoed by that of another which breaks upon his ears. His eyes snap open and he blinks confusedly round, to see who
it is has joined his private party. He glances first at the cat, but of course
it was not he who had laughed, although his yawning has been prodigious.
Then his attention is drawn to the shut door in the aft bulkhead, and to
the trim, small figure that stands before it.

"'Ere, then — who's this now? Who are yer?" blurts out Sam. "I'll have
yer up for trespass. Whose boat is this, yers or mine?"

He rises from his seat and advances a step or two nearer, and stares the
stranger up and down in strange sort, from the tip-top of her flaxen head
to her neatly-soled feet. For the trim, small figure is that of a young woman, of undeniable attraction, whose dress however is something less than
modish. Winsome and smiling, the pretty stranger turns a face pale as chalk
to him.

"Wat you say? *Your* boat, you theenk?" are the first words that tumble
from her lips — lips that are like double rosebuds, accentuating the deathly
pallor of her countenance. Then she stops short and cocks her head to one
side, as if she is seeing him for the first time. "Ah, *oui* — it is *le petit père*
— the leetle papa of hair ladysheep — I know the face on you now. Wat
'ave you done, papa? You 'ave dreenk from gammer's cup. Wat for you do
that, eh? Now Henriette she moste speak to you her *pénitence,* and the so
lucky papa he be quaite and leesten. Is agreeable? You leesten?"

Having been taken a good deal aback, the lucky papa regards her in silence for several long seconds, which threaten to stretch towards a minute.

"Dreadful pale, ain't she?" he thinks, his mind racing, if already a trifle
slowed by the liquor he has consumed. Mystified, he resumes his seat and
pours himself another dram. Meanwhile the pretty stranger awaits his reply
with folded arms, and her soft-soled foot impatiently tapping — although,
curiously, without any sound of it reaching his ears.

"Is agreeable, papa?" she inquires at length.

"'Ere — why d'yer call me that? I ain't yer papa," sniffs Sam.

She throws up a careless shrug. "As you weesh."

"It's dead white yer are. What's the trouble with yer, then? You got the
consumptive? Who are yer, exactly, and what's yer business 'ere?"

"I am Henriette, and am shock to see the papa of hair ladysheep dreenk
soche theeng. Wat does signify?"

"Says yer? Well, I like a bit o' rum same as the rest — what d'yer think
o' that, now? Didn't know it, did yer? 'Ere, ye're not sent by me daughter
and that quack to be tellin' me what to do?"

"I tale a you only wat you moste *not* do. You weel leesten to me now, so you do not suffer same fate as Henriette, by making promise not to keel a your wife. It was vary bad of poor Henriette to keel a hair 'usband — soche villain man, I did not like him so moche, after while, and it make him vary cross. But *pénitence* I moste do. Weel you make promise then not to keel a your wife? Weel you do thees for Henriette?"

In answer Sam, feeling the warmth of the liquor, pours himself another drink and downs it with a flourish.

"'Ere," says he, passing a hand over his lips, a trifle unsteadily, "are yer daft? Kill me wife? Go on! Me wife ain't in a position for it. She's a-lyin' in the tomb aside her mother these three-and-twenty year now."

"Ah — so moche like Henriette are you! I am poor widow woman, you are poor widow man. Weel, late a me see. You make promise then not to keel a your *next* wife — wat you say? Is rasonable, papa?" she conjures him sweetly.

"Pertickler, ain't yer? But I'll have no female looking after me," returns Sam, "nor even a young one and a pretty. For Sam Gander can look after himself well enough. Did yer know I'm seventy-seven come St. Odo's Day — "

"*Un moment*, papa. Is it day of St. Odo, do you mean?" says Henriette, interrupting him. "The day of the so holy abbot — he of the monastery of Cluny, in France?"

"What's that? O' course it is — the eighteenth o' November, as be ain't too far off neither. And what other Odo would I be meaning? Bodo o' the marshways, d'yer think?" snorts Sam.

"Ah, soche 'appy *coïncidence!* For it is same day Henriette was born. Are we not overjoy? Who could 'ave imagine?"

"D'yer mean yer own birthday is same as mine?"

"*Oui.*"

"Odo's Day, as ain't too far off?"

"*Eendeed.*"

"Though o' course," smiles Sam, who has begun to warm not only to the rum but to the charms of the pretty stranger, "not in the same year, as ye're no more'n a younker compared to an old dog like meself."

It is another sort of smile that touches the lips of Henriette, one whose meaning is quite impossible for him to grasp.

"*Naturellement*, papa! For Henriette is leetle more than cheaile compare to soche deestinguish fallow — is not so?"

"And I'm another!" crinkles Sam. Sipping his rum, he is starting to enjoy himself rather a lot.

"And so we two be soche good friends together, no?"

Being good friends with so delightful a young person, resolves Mr. Gander, calls for another drink. Accordingly he takes up the bottle again, then pauses and holding it close to his face stares at it in some surprise.

"'Ere, now," he exclaims, "'ere's a twist — why, this is some o' me own rum."

By his own he means a sample of that liquor which was retailed at the family establishment, the Goose and Gander, by old Cuffley. His companion meanwhile has seated herself at the table, chin in hand, and is observing his activities with a gleam of impudence in her eye.

"D'yer fancy a dram?" he asks her. But she declines his generous offer, and in compensation he avails himself of a double portion.

"Bote you moste not 'ave a too moche now, papa," she reminds him, charmingly but firmly, "for wat would hair ladysheep theenk?"

"Shoo!" retorts Sam, his face reddening with his potations. "Me Lizzie won't say boo, if she don't know. At such an hour she's getting her winks o' sleep. But as for yerself, now — where are yer makin' for, and what for d'yer come here?"

She answers with a smiling roll of her head, nothing more.

"It's pale and stiff she is — a regular churchyard beauty," Sam muses in his cup. "Never seen her afore. But she's got spirit — spunk — dash — and a spice o' the devil about her, I'll be bound. She ain't one o' yer simple Susans, that's sure — that's grand! 'Ere," he tells himself, the liquor acting as oil to his thoughts, "this one's a pip, she is, but white as a ghost."

Then he straightens his collar, to make himself more presentable, and brushes down his shiny head, and grinning shows her his tooth through the gap in his lips. Her glance meanwhile retains its expression of droll humor.

To Sam she seems a delightful lass and a comely, that is until he is reminded of the fact that she is a widow of her own making, who has confessed to the murder of her husband.

But no matter. "Ye're a flirty, foreign little thing, ain't yer?" says Sam, in a tone of rosy *empressement* engendered by the rum.

"Foreign?" protests Henriette, in some surprise. "Who is foreign? I am as Fenshire as you or me."

"Well, where were yer born, then?"

"Born? In Ridingham, but of course."

"From Ridingham, says yer? With yer queer way o' gabbin'? Where did yer get that accent? Where were yer folks born, then?"

"In Blois."

Returns Sam with a puzzled stare, amplified by the rum — "Blah, says yer? Never 'eard o' Blah, not round 'ere. Ain't it on the Swale, by Newmarsh?"

"Not 'Blah', papa," she corrects him, gently, "it is *Blois*. Is pronounce B-L-W-A."

"Blawah? Blawah. Blah!"

"As you weesh. Is on the Loire, or was, before thees — 'ow you call — thees sundering of yours."

Sam scratches his head in confusion. Even in his present state the arithmetical faculties of the erstwhile publican now retired tell him that one and one certainly do not seven make. Almost two hundred years had rolled by since the sundering. How then can this young woman's parents have been born in Blois-on-Loire, in France? For had it not been struck from the face of the earth some two centuries ago?

"Ah, the time it does flee from us. Bote wat is matter, papa? Wat does signify whether is two hundred year, or bote two, precisally?"

"As plain as eye can see yer," answers Sam, "ye're not near so near two hunderd yerself."

"Thank a you kindly, papa," smiles Henriette, "bote you are teepsy, is true, and I am not so moche the chicken — is how you say? — bote already am poor widow long time."

"Ooh, same as me!" nods Sam. Unable to resolve the dilemma, he casts it from his thoughts — putting it down to overwork from a surfeit of wall-walking — in favor of the delightful creature who shares his table. Flush with drink, he is heard sighing like a swain in his admiration of her.

"Yer may be foreign, or yer may not be," he cajoles her with a nod and a wink, "but ye're a pretty chicken, that's for damn sure. For seven-and-seventy or no, I've still got an eye in me head."

"Ah, soche weeckedness! You are rascal. Eye in head? Bote is not two?"

"'Ere, now — what's that — two heads?" puzzles Sam, not following.

"No, no — two eye, papa. Bote," suggests his pretty friend, coyly, "if the caps fit, eh, papa?"

Recognizing in Henriette a kindred spirit — as it were — he bursts into a chuckle, which finds its echo in the little stream of silvery laughter that flows from her lips.

"You are funny fallow," she tells him, "like my papa. My papa, he was big sausage-stuffer in Ridingham. Oh, *oui!* First he learn from his papa and *oncle* in Blois, then he and mama take sheep for long coast. Come first to Nantle, then to Ridingham. Work vary hard."

In his turn Sam regales her with an account of his own ascent from the bottom, of the pre-eminence of the Goose and Gander amongst all the inns of Ridingham, in those bygone days when he had presided over a jolly company in the tap-room.

"It's a step like a Highland piper I had then," says he, the shine of past glories illuminating his countenance. "Free and easy Sam Gander was, the friend of every man — a knowing card — a 'fast goer' — as could warble a ditty with the best of 'em. How the lasses o' the town did hang about him, like flies on a honeycomb! Now it's me daughter's got the lolly, since she got the Hall. She's loaded, so it's old Cuffley now as works the tap, and it's meself as works the Hall. Hee, hee . . ."

The rum, as is its wont, in time insinuated itself into his brain, stirring memories of old to the fore of his consciousness and causing him to wax sentimental. Among them is an image of his late wife, her ladyship's mother, about whom Mr. Gander rarely if ever spoke, and whose loss had been the great tragedy of his life. An angel she had been, taken from him all too soon. An angel, who in her looks and temperament had been as unlike his Lizzie as a dock is to a daisy; for it was his Lizzie indeed who was her father's own daughter. It was the rum which had brought this latent sorrow of his to the surface, and given it voice. One could not be sure, but were those tears glistening in the eyes of Sam under his bushy brows?

Henriette, hearing his confessional, had been plaiting little folds in her dress with the tips of her fingers, her eyes downcast and thoughtful, as if absorbed in a similar meditation of her own.

"'Ow true, papa," says she, in sober reflection. "Wat great ogly wound it is, puts hole in heart that nayver heals. 'Ow the years they do run from us! And 'ow weak 'ave I grow in those years. Soche desire 'ave I to see — to see — " In a sudden, swift motion she clamps a hand to her brow and whispers, "'Ow I am shame," as if telling herself a secret; then she glances at her companion, and entreats him to remember his vow not to keel a his next wife, so that some day she, Henriette, may be forgiven perhaps, and her *pénitence* find its end.

This last about being forgiven passes him entirely by. It seems to him she must have made a rash marriage; it was this that had brought about its unamiable conclusion. He resolves not to duplicate her mistake.

Rallying, Henriette draws herself up and with an effort recovers something of her old manner, speaking as she does so of "the man who save me", of whose identity Sam has an inkling, if no certain knowledge. He takes another swallow of his rum and, eyeing her with a dewy glance, inquires if it might not be the master of this vessel whom she means? For it has trickled through to him that she herself is in no state or position to be captaining her.

"Young feller, is he?" suggests Sam. "Young — but not so handsome as meself? But me own youthful follies I've put behind me . . ."

"*Le capitaine?* Ah, *hélas!* he is not master," she confesses, "bote is *mon cher* — " Then she very nearly mentions him by name, but checks herself in time.

"Happy dog, he must be," muses her companion, his glance unsteady and straying. "Happy dog, yer young scamp . . . to have it all afore him, and not behind him . . . happy dog . . . not like some poor geezer . . ."

Slowly, surely, the level of rum in his pint-bottle has diminished, in inverse proportion to the extent of his intoxication. For an hour now he and his delightful acquaintance have been chatting and gossiping together, and chuckling over this or that point of amusement, each one magnified in his mind by the rum. He had been in high glee, but now the liquor had set in train the inevitable dulling of the senses that follows. For all good things, as we know, must have their end — even the contrariness of Mr. Samuel Gander this night.

So he pours the remainder of the rum into his cup, for good fellowship's sake, and drinks it down; wonders again at the manifold charms of Henriette; contrives to scrape up a grin to match her, one that stretches his face from ear to ear; and so sinks slowly into a kind of half-faint. Already his friend the tomcat has been dozing for some while, and presently Sam follows his example.

In such wise did the little party aboard the skimmer break up, or break down, and the jolly evening — as do all good things — pass to its close, and melt into an aery nothing; or so afterwards it seemed to Mr. Gander.

When he awoke, at the first gray peep of dawn — for he was ever an early riser — it was to find himself in his own bed, with a throbbing pain in his sconce. How he managed to clamber down from the battlements in his inebriated state he had no notion; instead the entire affair of the previous evening had assumed the aspect of a dream.

He groaned, and cautiously eased himself into a sitting posture. His recollection of events was all muddled up. There had been no vessel moored at the Hall, and no winsome widow adorning its cabin — how can there have been? Consequently it followed he never had blundered onto a cord-ladder by the servants' door, and scaled it three flights to the waiting craft above — how can he have done?

He rubbed his head in confusion, as if the massaging of it might drive the ache from his brain; but having no other explanation on offer he put it all down to the rum. It was this that finally roused him from his stupor. *The rum!* How can the rum have been the cause, he asked himself, when the rum itself had been a part of the dream? And not any rum either, but his family's own from the tap-room of the Goose and Gander?

"'Ere, what's happening 'ere?" he exclaimed, with a mystified frown. "What's the score? A pox on it! But I've reformed meself — not another swig — not a dram — not a swallow. Ooh, the pain is 'orrible. I'll have that quack struck off, see if I don't. From here on it's bogberry, and porridge, and marsh tea, and a plague on all pint-bottles . . ."

Needless to say his account of his alleged experience proved of interest to Edgar and Richard, to whom he related it in strictest confidence, after first obtaining from them their assurance that no syllable of it should find its way to the ears of his bothersome physician. Nor, as it turned out, was there any need for his auditors to be relaying its particulars to Owen, who, having discovered certain irregularities in the cabin — the cockpit lantern hung over the cook-stove, an old slouch hat skulking under the table, the biscuit-tin upset, an empty pint-bottle — had but to ask Henriette, when next she showed herself, what the trouble had been.

"Ah, *mon cher,*" answered that good lady, her eyes twinkling their innocence, "wat can but poor Henriette do? Was only young fallow — soche agreeable man — 'ave leetle *tête-à-tête* aboard sheep with older woman."

THE FIFTH CHAPTER

Maid's Day Out

WHEN Henriette showed herself proved to be the next day, after the skimmer had returned to Northeave.

A rich aroma of eggs, sizzling rashers of bacon, and fragrant hot coffee was in the air as Owen worked briskly at the cook-stove. Behind him in an alert posture on a cushion, nostrils sniffing that air and the enticing odors with which it was charged, was Melonhead. Moments later the cat's attention became focused on a dish of mackerel and saucer of milk which Owen placed before him. Needless to say the ship's cat did ample justice to this savory repast. Although it was his friend and shipmate who had served it up, it was in fact Gwenda Goodwick who had procured it for him, surreptitiously, and at some personal risk, from Mrs. Flitch's kitchen.

As for the mariner's own breakfast of eggs and bacon, bread and jam, and currant buns, it had been supplied by his mother ere the skimmer had left the Hall. In Owen's view it was better fare by half than the traditional lobscouse and sea pie — staples of the diet of merchant seamen all up and down the long coast — to which he was accustomed. Before departing he had cleared away the residuals he had found in the cabin — the biscuit-tin, pint-bottle *sans* rum, gammer's cup, slouch hat, etc. — left there by a certain party, and made an inspection of the lockers to ascertain whether anything had been taken. Truth be told he was not so worried about thievery, however, for a glance at the hat had left him in no doubt as to its owner.

The fact that the gammer's cup had been drained provided him with an additional clue. His chief concern was how and when the father of Lady Martindale had boarded the skimmer, what had transpired there in relation to the winsome widow, and just how much of his experience Mr. Gander might recall this morning. But what had happened to the old man's firm resolution against drink? For of course it cannot have been Henriette who had drained the pint-bottle. Like most everyone, Owen was under the impression that the erstwhile publican had reformed himself.

It was while he was absorbed in these meditations, at his work there at the cook-stove, that the widow made her appearance and laid his uncertainties to rest. But her arrival at this time seemed to stir within him another kind of uncertainty, manifested by nervousness, the source of which was not immediately clear. However his meaning, when at last he spoke, was plain enough.

"Crave pardon, madam," he said, his glance straying uneasily from the breakfast sizzling in the pan to the shut door of the forward compartment, and back again, "you're welcome aboard the skimmer, certain sure, but might you perhaps return at a later hour?"

Such words were not the usual from Owen Aberdovey. Straightway the curiosity of Henriette was aroused.

"Wat is matter, *mon cher?* 'Deed you seem moste — wat you call? — er, discomfortable, is not so?"

"It is not so," returned Owen. "If you please, madam — if you might heave anchor this morning, if only for a spell — not that it signifies — "

The widow frowned her lack of understanding. "'Eave anchor? Wat is 'eave anchor, *pardon?*"

"If only you might go away . . ." he hinted, darting his eyes again towards the forward compartment.

"Henriette go 'way?" she exclaimed in some amazement.

"Pray, madam, keep your voice down — "

"For why should Henriette go 'way? Wat 'ave you done, Owen? You talk a so strange. You want Henriette should — wat is word — hop it, as you say?"

His repeated, wary glances towards the shut door had not gone unnoticed, and had piqued the widow's interest. She averted her eyes, so as not to reveal the gleam of mischief that shone in them. A smile crept over her lips, and affecting disinterest she inquired —

"And for why did Owen sleep in hammock last night? For 'tis not the usual case. You are not weel, eh? Owen feel tire?"

The mariner replied that he was perfectly well, thank you, that he did not feel in the least tired, and that the cause for his having slung his hammock in the store-room was an eminently reasonable one. Beyond this he was not disposed to offer an explanation. In the end however there proved to be no need of one, for at that moment a bolt clicked, the door to the compartment swung open, and into the cabin stepped Gwenda.

Owen felt his heart give a thump. "Scorch me," he muttered, for the fat surely was in the fire now.

The eyes of Gwenda, like twin drops of dew on a May morning — my brother's words — shot from Owen to Henriette. Dismay flooded the features of Lady Martindale's handmaid and confidante.

"Owen, who is this woman?" she asked, a sharp rush of color staining her cheek.

He hastened to intercept her. She had been having a lie-in and, hearing the voice of Henriette through the door, had been in some confusion with whom Owen was speaking.

The mariner had hard work to conceal his chagrin. He blushed up to the roots of his orange hair, a response he in vain endeavored to conceal by pressing a handkerchief to his face.

"Owen, who is this woman?" the maid said again.

Henriette, regarding her with sly amusement, scarce could help herself. "And who is *thees* woman, Owen?" she demanded crisply. But ere he could answer a light registered, or so Henriette made it appear. "Ah, ha! I know the face on her now, sure. Is it not the Geeblets — the leetle minion of hair ladysheep? Ah," she sighed, with a woeful turn of her head, "so shy, the leetle meess, like partridge. Wat surprise."

Gwenda, hearing herself so described, was at first speechless, and could do nothing but stare aghast at Owen. The mariner thought of making some pleasant jocular remark, then thought better of it and returned to the cookstove, having found the breakfast in sudden need of his attention. He let a minute elapse while he busied himself there, leaving poor Giblets to simmer in a stricken silence of indignation and annoyance.

The maid in the night had stowed herself aboard — it was quite the literal truth. After returning to the skimmer, Owen had eased his craft down from the battlements and swung in alongside the gatehouse, where he had remained a few moments to take on the stores his mother had prepared for him. It was during this operation that Gwenda had crept aboard and concealed herself in the forward compartment. The mariner had been unaware of her presence until he had arrived at Northeave. Her explanation, when given, had been a simple one — she had wished to spend her day out with him, knowing the whiles that neither Owen himself nor his mother would have approved of her tactic. But as it was her own day out, to do with as she pleased, she had availed herself of her opportunity. Once resigned to the situation, the mariner had fixed up a berth for her in the compartment, and then had slung his hammock in the store-room.

At length he felt he ought to say something, but Gwenda got the start of him by asking again — "Owen, who is she?"

"This lady," he answered, breaking it to her gently, "is Henriette."

"And what does she mean," the maid demanded, "by Giblets?"

This unfortunate designation of course was that applied by the lady to Gwenda herself.

"Oh, yes?" said the maid, her voice rising a pitch on being so informed, and turned dagger-eyes upon the widow, whose expression bespoke her entire ignorance of any wrongdoing.

Owen, observing the direction in which the conversation was tending, invited Gwenda to be seated, as their breakfast was nearly ready. But she declined his offer. She preferred to stand, thank you, having found her circumstances that morning very disappointing. Here was her beloved Owen, a man deemed as honest as the day, and so much admired at the Hall, consorting in secret with a strange woman of questionable provenance — and aboard the same vessel on which she, Gwenda, had stowed herself away in the night!

What was she to make of it? Was this what her Owen had been getting up to every day at Northeave? Small wonder he had spent so little time at the Hall.

Gwenda of course very conveniently was overlooking the fact that the skimmer could be moved from Northeave only during the hours of darkness. Glaring at her rival (for such she believed Henriette to be) the maid demanded —

"And who is Henriette? For I never heard the name in my life. Who is she, Owen, and where did you find her? How did she come here? And what is she to you?"

Giving a fine imitation of a deaf-mute, the mariner made no answer but kept to his cook-stove, thinking himself a fool the whiles for the pains he had taken in befriending Henriette. As for the widow she seemed to take a mischievous delight in his predicament, regarding him with folded arms and an arch expression, as though it amused her to see how this rencounter between himself and his Geeblets might turn out.

Owen mopped his brow, hiding his frustration, then scraped the eggs and bacon into platters and set them on the table. The coffee he poured into pannikins. He already had cleared away Melon-head's breakfast, the tomcat having finished it off right sailorly and retired to his cushion to groom himself into an early doze. In his every action the mariner endeavored to maintain the even tenor of his ways, refusing to be disturbed by the turn events had taken.

But still Gwenda would not be seated.

"You have attached yourself to this — to this — this person," she said.

"Beg pardon, but she has attached herself to me," Owen corrected her.

"'Deed 'ave I," affirmed the widow — "for *mon cher* is best of friend to poor Henriette. It was vary great good fortune the day villain man drink from gammer's cup, late a me tale a you."

Not understanding, the maid responded — "What is she gabbling about, Owen? She chatters like a magpie."

The widow snapped her a swift look. *"Quelle insulte!* Wat is thees magpie? Is an eempudence, I theenk."

"It is thieving bird who steal from other bird's nest," said the maid, in mimicry of her rival's accents.

"Owen," Henriette warned, unfolding her arms and threatening to tuck up her sleeves — "you weel tale a her kindly to be not soche impertinent leetle Geeblets, or cheaile had better hop it queeck."

"What is this woman to you, Owen? What is she doing here?" Gwenda persisted. "Where has she come from? Does she live at Northeave?"

"She is naught to me," Owen replied, "for she cannot be else. And no one abides at Northeave."

It was urgent that he find a way to explain it to her, and after thinking over it a moment he concluded there was nothing to be lost by telling her all.

"She means naught to me," he said patiently, "and never can. It may be heresy to believe it, but sink me sure this lady is a ghost, and has been a ghost since long years agone."

For a minute total silence filled the cabin. Gwenda, slow to comprehend, looked at Owen; Henriette, batting her eyelids and smiling, too was looking at Owen. Even Melon-head, having noticed the lull in the conversation, opened his eyes and stared sleepily at his shipmate.

"Owen, you've got a cheek to tell me a thing like that. Whatever has happened to you?" lamented Gwenda.

The mariner, scarcely surprised, appealed to the widow for aid. She answered his plea with an airy lift of her brows and said —

"She vary cross with you. You like Henriette to give cheaile the treatment, how you say?"

"By your leave, madam," he nodded wearily — "and with all possible speed, afore the breakfast is many hours colder."

"Ravie! You shall 'ave it, *mon cher."*

So agreeing, Henriette raised her arms and promptly ascended into the overhead and was gone. Moments later she reappeared, descending again into the cabin and then sinking into the deck and vanishing with a smile and a parting wave of her hand. After another lapse of seconds she came gliding in through one side of the vessel — ("'allo!") — and went gliding out at the other — ("*adieu!*") — not unlike a specter flitting through a churchyard. Finally — as if this were not sufficient — she stuck her head in at a porthole and made a pouty fish-face, with much goggling and gulping, for the entertainment of her ladyship's minion.

"Avast, madam — you do exert yourself overmuch. Stint your foolery now," Owen advised her.

"Soche impossible fallow! Wat bore," chided Henriette; then again she was gone, only to reappear seconds later at Owen's side.

Gwenda, staring in frightened amaze, shrank back and pressing a hand to her head murmured, her voice quavering — "I must be out of my senses . . ."

"Perish the thought," Owen told her gently, "for this lady is as real as you or I."

"Geeblets tremble like aspen," Henriette observed.

"Pray, no more of that now," said the mariner.

"Ah, Henriette is *désolée* — "

"Belay your chatter, madam," he warned her, with a significant glance.

"*Voilà!* Now I am magpie 'gain," she sighed.

As inconceivable a thing as the legendary wild man of Slopshire, or the clock-giant of Ridingham, or other such wonders deemed more imagined than real, was the figure of Henriette in the eyes of Gwenda.

"Not to worry. You needn't be frightened," Owen assured her.

"But where — where did you find her? Did you meet her at Nantle?" the maid asked at length, screwing her courage up. By degrees her terror at the very idea of Henriette had begun to yield to a natural curiosity and her feelings for Owen.

"Nantle?" the mariner exclaimed, in some puzzlement.

"Did she not travel with you? For how long has this gone on? How long have you known this — this — ?" Her eyes searched his face for a moment, then turned hastily away.

"Weel you tale a her, *mon cher,* or moste I?" the widow said lightly.

"Bless my guts," Owen replied, "but you'll *not* tell her, madam. It was my own doing, Gwenda — my own, and the loathly dog Teech's. We came across her just yonder, in the old lodge over the road. Teech and I were to bide there awhile, but she affrighted him when she appeared and he sheered right off. I've had no peep of him since."

Briefly he related the circumstances to her. He did not take long over it, nor did he make mention of the widow's having got rid of a husband, or of her manner of so doing. Not that he was untruthful; he simply did not mention it.

"But why must she call you by that name?" the girl asked, her chin rising. "For my aunt taught me some few words of French, and *mon cher,* I'm sure, is not proper address."

"Is not proper address?" echoed Henriette, in some wonder. "'Ow can she talk a like that? Soche *sottise!* Moste we leesten to thees leetle fool, *mon cher?* And wat business 'ave she here? If hair ladysheep should find it out, your Geeblets could be for the chop, I theenk."

"Hearkee, madam, I am not your *mon cher,*" returned Owen, "and she is not my Giblets. You've attached yourself to me, smite me dumb if you haven't, for a cause known only to yourself. True, it was Teech and I as brought you aboard the skimmer, all unknowing, and to our mutual woe. Now kindly stint your gab."

"She's a rattle, I think," nodded the maid, glaring at Henriette.

The widow let her eyes grow wide and hurt. "Now there is good joke," said she. "Joste because we 'ave a leetle conversating, we are rattling. Bote wat of" — here her glance suddenly narrowed, as it bore in on the maid's — "wat of hair own conversating in the *boudoir* of hair ladysheep, eh? Hair leetle *tête-à-tête* 'bout thees an' that? Moche *embarras* for Henriette to 'ave 'eard soche theengs — "

The shocked expression on the face of the maid well served her in place of words.

"*Doucement, doucement,*" the widow consoled her, "is not so horror. Is not only cheaile and hair ladysheep that I 'ave visit, bote others too — his Gravysheep" — (meaning Treadwell) — "and Wheeskers" — (meaning Dr. Bussey) — "and the leetle papa of hair ladysheep — "

The maid turned horrified eyes on Owen, who had been anticipating her response. It was his unenviable task to inform her that yes, the widow, in her garb of invisibility, on occasion had gone a-visiting at the Hall, and had made herself familiar with some of the inmates there, all unbeknownst to the inmates themselves.

Henriette seemed to take a wry pleasure in the maid's distress. "Wat is the so trouble?" she said with a shrug. "Wat for should a you be surprise? 'Appen all the time, *partout* — averywhere — bote a the living peoples, they know no ting of it. They blind, they cannot see the Henriettes that be averywhere 'bout them."

This disturbing notion took several minutes to work its way through the minds of Gwenda and Owen. Once it had so done, it left little else to be said: for which of them was prepared to challenge the word of a dead woman on the topic?

"Well, what are you going to do about her, Owen?" Gwenda asked.

"*Oui* — wat *are* you to do?" said the widow.

Each stood awaiting his answer with lips pursed and arms crossed, the way a woman does when endeavoring to extract a concession from the gentleman of her heart.

Poor Owen! Managing the two of them would be no light work. So he got out his pipe and, stoking it into flame, comforted himself with a few whiffs. But there still remained the matter of breakfast. At length he responded, his words directed to the maid in particular —

"I think I should act very scurvily if I were to delay your bit o' breakfast much longer. For there is naught I can do about her, Gwenda — the lady is beyond the reach o' such as you or I. Lookee now, what would you have me do? Cast her overside? So come along and eat."

The maid gave an exclamation of annoyance, but in the end she had little choice. What indeed was there to do in answer to such a being as Henriette? And what else could Gwenda say? It was she who had stolen aboard the skimmer to spend her day out with Owen. How then could she censure Henriette for spoiling her game?

She made a show of eating, but finding that Mrs. Aberdovey's supplies were choice indeed, overcame her initial reluctance and fell to with an appetite. Now and then as they ate, some few words passed between herself and Owen, casually, quietly, as often they do between a man and a woman of long acquaintance. The mariner for one had decided to let good enough alone, feeling that he and Gwenda had scored a silent victory over the widow — the distaff and spindle in triumph over the broomstick and talons.

Henriette herself could not partake of the feast, for of course she could not eat. However she spent some minutes endeavoring to recall the taste of bacon and eggs, and bread and jam, and currant buns, and steaming-hot coffee — the coffee at least still was hot — but so very many years had passed in the interval, that after a while she gave it up.

After the meal was done, Owen announced his intention of taking his morning's watch on the stern deck, to scan the area and to keep an eye out for Teech. There still had been no word from Jolly Jumper Yard, and the mariner's hopes were beginning to dim. He in whom Captain Barnaby had reposed his trust was guilty of naught else than having reposed *his* trust in a loathly dog. Perhaps his letter of explanation had fallen into the hands of Mrs. Barnaby while her husband was from home, had been deemed a hoax perpetrated by a crank, and been thrown into the fire? Perhaps the captain himself never had seen it, and never would?

Or perhaps the constabulary in Ridingham had been informed of the theft, and even now were on the alert and preparing to cast their nets over him?

His sole gleam of comfort arose from his faith in the captain himself, under whom he had served these two years. Surely this was a sufficing reason to be of good cheer? Surely Jack Barnaby of all persons had understood the character of Owen, and deemed him to be incapable of treachery?

Taking in hand his spyglass he instructed Gwenda to "Bide you here till I make sure of the lookout." To Henriette he made no remark, the look in his eye substituting for speech.

It was a dismal, cloudy day, something threatening in its aspect, as he gained the deck and assumed his post at the rail. The skimmer lay hid in the snowy cover of a clumber pine, well back of the wood road. Alongside her the spiral chimney of ornamental brick to which she was moored rose above a cluttered patch of roof. Some score of yards away, out of sight and across the road, was Mackery End.

All round him the towering pines stood up stark and dark against the sky, like the spires of a living forest of cathedrals there at the edge of the marshes. For Owen and others like him who sought refuge from the world it was a delightful prospect. The air was filled with the tangy scents of pine and fir, and from his lofty post he could keep watch of his surroundings from behind a screen of shaggy timbers, without exposing the skimmer to the notice of strangers below.

For weeks now he had practiced this same ritual, always on the lookout for Teech, or for anyone else for that matter who might stumble upon his hideaway. Thus far he had discovered no trace of the loathly dog, and of others there had been only Edgar and Richard, whom he had rescued from the spotted lion. Having surveyed the area for some minutes with his glass, he concluded it was unlikely that he should be disturbed today, in the forenoon at least. Northeave had not acquired its reputation as a ghost village without cause.

Better to live alone and watch the world pass by and the year go round in peace — so of late had the thoughts of Owen been tending. It was better he had never heard of skimmers or flying luggers or gammer's cups. Better he had never gone to sea. Better he had never left the lonely but comforting seclusion of the marshes. Things had come to a pretty pass when, but for a turn of luck, he should have been accounted a hero, perhaps, for having aided in saving those aboard the packet-boat — not a thief and a traitor. Significantly, however, he had of late decided no more to bother his head about it; there was no point. There was nothing for it but to keep on, and to accept whatever was meted out to him by the captain, in whom he himself now must repose his trust.

Putting by his glass, he closed his eyes and drew deeply into his lungs the fragrant atmosphere of the woodland, which gave such pleasure to the senses. His mind the whiles was freed to reflect upon a curious event that had transpired, late on the previous evening, as he was about to depart the Hall. He had eased the skimmer down from the roof and moored her beside the gatehouse, as was his custom, for the several minutes necessary to plenish stores. As the hour was late, he reckoned there was little chance of his being observed. And yet — and yet — a troubling conviction had stolen upon him, as he climbed aboard, that his actions were being scrutinized by someone in the yard.

Then as he mounted to the helm to take the skimmer aloft, his eye had caught a subtle movement in the shadows under the curtain-wall, as though someone lurking there had stirred for but an instant. There had been no light but cloud-light, and the soft glimmer from the gatehouse window. After pausing for a time but observing no further activity, he had disregarded it as an illusion and sent the skimmer up and away over the wall.

Who could the watcher have been, if indeed there had been such a person and not simply a figment of a nervous imagination? It could not have been Gwenda, for she already was aboard the skimmer and had concealed herself there. Nor had it been Edgar, or Richard, or Sam Gander, he didn't believe. Had someone else discovered the existence of the craft, and hence that of Owen himself?

Ere he could continue in this vein he heard a shy step behind him, and the next thing he knew Gwenda, wrapped in a cloak and muffler against the chill, had placed herself beside him at the rail. At first she spoke no word, nor did he; they merely shared the view and the tangy scents of the pine forest.

We are not the formers of our own destiny — it was a conviction that had been growing upon Owen of late these past weeks. It was the randomness of life that daunted him. Wherever your lot casts you, there you be — now you must learn to make the best of it. For was this not the message delivered to mankind by the sundering?

Owen had filled his pipe again and stood smoking it in quiet reflection, having determined to abide his destiny, be what it might. *Aye, for we all must muddle through* . . .

Presently, to his surprise and Gwenda's, another member of the party arrived to join them — it was Melon-head. Having ascended from the cabin he came yawning and stretching towards them, before settling himself beside a scupper, there to keep a wary watch against the dangers of the world without.

Minutes elapsed, but there was no sign of Henriette — visible or otherwise.

To his further surprise, Owen of a sudden felt a single, soft press of lips against his cheek. They were the pretty lips of Gwenda, who had risen up a little on her toes to reach him, before resuming her contemplation of the woodland.

After a brief blush, Owen, calmly smoking, his eyes on the trees, remarked to nobody in particular, "So you've no feelings for Dan Hedges, then? For sink and burn me, the scuttle is abroad — "

He hesitated a moment. Strangely, the name Dan Hedges had put him in mind again of the figure he may or may not have seen lurking under the curtain-wall . . .

"Upon my word not. I have no more feeling for Dan Hedges than have you for that woman in there," said the maid.

Meaning Mischief

T HE fog had settled down thicker as the hours advanced. In the courtyard, only a dim square of light in the gatehouse window was showing to relieve the darkness. Already the skimmer had been removed from the battlements to the gatehouse lane, where for the moment she stood unguarded, as Owen busied himself with a final errand. He had asked if he might examine the mysterious boot which Toddy had unearthed outside the curtain-wall, on the chance that he might have some knowledge of its origin; for a thought had occurred to him on that score. So he had gone to meet with Richard and Edgar, secretly, in the farm office. Meanwhile a hamper of fresh supplies had been taken aboard the skimmer, and but for his errand all was in readiness for his departure.

As I've mentioned, the fog — or the marsh mist, as some call it — was very heavy tonight. Now and again Mrs. Aberdovey could be seen peering out at it from her window in anticipation of her son's return. For some time now had elapsed, and she was becoming concerned that something had happened to delay him. Of course it was discovery that she feared, and its inevitable result.

Imagine her surprise then, when a soft crunch of footfalls was heard on the snow outside, tending not in the direction of her doorstep but in that of the skimmer, which lay at her moorings under the curtain-wall. Watching from her window Mrs. Aberdovey had a partial view of the cord-ladder, and of the man's figure she saw was scaling it hurriedly to the deck.

How odd, she thought, and how unlike her son, to be departing with no word to his mother, in light particularly of his errand; for Mrs. Aberdovey too had been curious about the ancient boot with the bones in it. What knowledge Owen might possess of the relic she scarce could fathom. And why should he be setting off now in such haste?

She strained her eyes at the lattice but could make nothing of the figure, which seconds afterwards vanished inboard. It well might have been her son — or it might not have been. Fearing that all was not right, Mrs. Aberdovey drew on her coat, settled her cap-strings at her chin, and stepped forth to investigate.

As she approached the foot of the ladder she called her son's name, but received no answer. Yet she sensed activity of a kind on the deck aloft, and then in the next instant the mooring-rope was loosed and drawn aboard.

It was clear now that something was amiss. Fearful of arousing the inmates of the Hall, she took hold of the cord-ladder and mounted upwards. It was not the first time she had ascended to the skimmer's deck, and as she arrived there she observed a faint glow illumining the cockpit. It was the ship's lantern, which hung at the helm, and in its rays a man could be seen unlashing the wheel in preparation for departure. He had a boat-cloak about his shoulders, but he was not Owen, of that Mrs. Aberdovey was certain; and so she challenged him in a low voice —

"Who is it? Who are you?"

The stranger, starting, whirled to confront her.

"Who the devil's there?" he hissed.

His face was in shadow, but as Mrs. Aberdovey stepped towards him, and he towards her, the lantern-light spilled across it.

"You! What business have you here? Where is my son?" she demanded, as she beheld a familiar visage.

The eyes of the man narrowed themselves into wily slits.

"Scuttle me," he muttered, half to himself, "if it ain't his mother, come to fetch her puppy — and a lubberly old girl she is, too!"

"This is my son's vessel," returned Mrs. Aberdovey, sparks flashing, "and you've no business here."

A sneer gathered on the other's features. His manner towards her was coldly contemptuous. "Aye, a vessel which the rogue did commandeer, as I've heard tell, and remains in traitorous possession of, your lodgekeepership." And with an ugly laugh he resumed his activities at the wheel.

Meanwhile the indignation of Mrs. Aberdovey had swelled so far as to overwhelm her natural reserve. "What are you doing there? Why are you casting off?" she demanded.

"Get home with you," growled the man, waving her off with a gesture.

"My son will arrive at any minute," she informed him, undaunted, "and he'll soon sort you out."

He glowered at her over his shoulder. "Nary a chance." He was a hard-looking sort with a scar across his cheek, and huge, outthrusting ears like the handles of a slop-jug. He appeared confident she would not raise a cry for fear of alerting the Hall.

"What do you mean to do?" said Mrs. Aberdovey.

"Sink me, but what do it look like now, your lodgekeepership? For it's over the wall I'm bound — let slip moorings and stand away drackly-min-ute — that's clear enough, ain't it? Now sheer off, old girl, or I'll pound you a good one."

Mrs. Aberdovey scarce could believe it. How was it possible that he in-tended to make off with the skimmer, for what did a rude stable-boy know of piloting such a vessel? And what in heaven's name was keeping Owen?

Having loosed the wheel, the man rose in the cockpit and glared at her with a surly superiority.

"Well? Will you stand down, or take the consequences?" she persisted.

"Belay your jaw-tackle," he gruffed, "for it's damned tiresome it is, and a bore. Ship your oars and begone, d'you hear? There's no help for it. I'll be taking her aloft drackly-minute."

"I shall do no such thing — nor shall you," returned Mrs. Aberdovey, hands to hips and a pugnacious set to her chin. For she was of that same sturdy fiber as had been her husband Morgan before her.

The groom knotted his kerchief at his throat and clapped on his mari-ner's bonnet. "Won't do," he told her, shaking his head, "won't do at all," and took a threatening step towards her. "Get you overside now," he com-manded, with a jerk of his thumb towards the ladder.

But her tidy small figure stood firm, refusing to stir so much as an inch from her position.

"My son — " she began.

"Your son, sink me," said Diggory, cutting her short, "is impossible — the goodiest damned two-shoes as ever helmed a sky-boat — bleed me if he ain't. Now is it overside peaceably, or must I be casting you over?"

"If you are set on taking this vessel I'll not aid you in any way. I'll not be a party to any such thing," declared Mrs. Aberdovey, the immovable.

"Well, who asked you to be a party? Did I ask you to be a party?"

"When my Owen — "

"He don't know a damned thing about it. Your Loveydovey's a right pigeon, that's clear enough — got himself in a devil of a mess — "

"All on account of a traitorous shipmate called Teech."

"Well, that's his lookout, now, ain't it? But I'll be waiting no longer — it's heave hook and stand away now. I did near make off with the boat yesternight, and but for a meddling maid I should have been plying the sky-ways these four-and-twenty hours. So begone, and good luck t'you — "

"When my son — "

The ears of Mrs. Aberdovey had been straining themselves for any hint of Owen's return, but without success. All at once the cheeky groom made a swoop at her, but tripped on the skirt of his boat-cloak and nearly went down, affording Mrs. Aberdovey an opportunity to slip past him along the rail. He could have pursued her farther but he was not so nimble in his cloak, and moreover the minutes were at a premium. He scarce doubted but that Owen would appear shortly, so he gave it up and, turning on his heel, resumed his preparations at the steerage.

"Be it on your head, then," he called to Mrs. Aberdovey, "but she sails drackly. Why don't you push off?"

He adjusted the slide of the lantern, and studied his ship's helm — the compass or bittacle, the wheel, the crank-handles at his side, the pedals at his feet — as he made ready to take the vessel aloft. Mrs. Aberdovey look-ed helplessly about her. There was naught below in the courtyard but the marsh mist — not a trace of Owen. She dared not cry out, nor could she keep the groom from making good his threat.

But how came a stable-boy at Haigh Hall to be an able pilot of such a vessel as the skimmer? And how was it that he knew Owen?

It seemed but seconds now until the craft should depart, when sudden-ly the attention of Diggory — and that of Mrs. Aberdovey as well — was arrested by a shimmering figure that neither before had noticed, who had been observing them from the stern deck. It was that of a young woman dressed in white, her image strangely illumined as if by some weird, inner glow, which owed nothing to the feeble rays of the lantern.

The groom clapped a hand to his head and stared at her, open-mouthed, as if his very worst nightmare had risen up to thwart him in his hour of triumph.

"Who the devil — is it you again? Roast me — split me crosswise else — if it ain't *her* again!" he protested with a groan.

The stable-boy, whose astonishment appeared equal to his horror, was temporarily unnerved by the sight of the woman, she of the streaming yel-low tresses and countenance as pale as death.

"Where did she fall from? Come to that, who is she?" Mrs. Aberdovey asked.

"I am so good friend of Owen. I watch skeemer for him," Henriette explained. "And you are the leetle mama of him — you are the widow too, no? Ah, we both are sad widows together."

The leetle mama was a trifle confused. "I know of no such friend of my son's," she answered.

"Bote of course, he tale a you no ting about Henriette. It vary difficult for him, certally. It draive his Geeblets to distraition when she 'ear of it."

Mrs. Aberdovey shook her head doubtfully. "I fail to understand your meaning. But if you know my son, then you know that this vessel is in trust to him, and that the stable-boy in the cockpit is intending to make off with it."

"Stable-boy?" echoed Henriette, and as she trained her gaze on him her eyes widened and an angry look came into them. "Ah! I see the face of him now. Stable-boy? *Parbleu!* he villain man — the so-loathly dog — cause of all the troubles for Owen — "

"That's a blinkin' lie!" snapped Diggory.

A light suddenly flashed upon Mrs. Aberdovey. She drew her breath in a gasp, her hand shot to her throat and she blurted out —

"Amos Teech!"

"Never heard of him," sneered the groom.

"You are the man. You're Teech — the thief and traitor!"

"No, I ain't — won't do — no go — "

Groom indeed! Why, the villain fairly reeked of the sea. Why had she not tumbled to it earlier? He was the new man, who had assumed his post only a few weeks before. By this means had he insinuated himself into the Hall, and there had lain concealed, mole-like, awaiting his opportunity. What need had he to be braving the haunted wilds in his bid to steal the skimmer, when Owen would deliver the vessel to him?

The news had shocked Mrs. Aberdovey, but for Henriette the revelation was particularly distressing. *I watch skeemer for him* — and yet she had failed in her duty. Her little "visits" to the Hall had been concerned with Owen and his circle, not with grooms and outside men. "Henriette, she 'ave no truck — is 'ow you say? — with stable fallows." And so the presence of the thief and traitor amongst them had gone unnoticed.

As for Teech himself, in the weeks since he had "sheered off" he had labored to master his fear of the ghost from the gammer's cup, on the assumption there was little she could do to injure him. Still he regarded her warily, for there was every indication she could alert his former shipmate to his purpose. Again time was pressing.

"You have done my son a grave injustice," Mrs. Aberdovey told him. "You are the one who struck him down and made off with the skimmer. On account of your treachery the blame for its loss will be laid at his feet. You're the cause of all his trouble, as this woman says. When he finds you here — "

"Hoity-toity!" scoffed the groom. "But you've no atom o' proof against Teech."

"Then you confess to being the man?"

"No go — won't do — name's Diggory — word o' two-shoes a damnable humbug, sink me — "

The eyes of Mrs. Aberdovey were glittering points of indignation in the lantern-light. Stabbing her words with an angry finger, she retorted —

"That's no way to be speaking of my Owen, you — you — you mangy tod — you miserable object! You're a nice rascal, aren't you, to do my son so ill a turn? You're a white-livered hound and a traitor to be making him out a criminal."

"Put villain man under pump — eempudent fallow," exhorted Henriette in like spirit. "Soche eempertinence I never before 'ave seen. 'Ow I should like to 'ave rap at his smeller, I tale a you — "

The hound and traitor broke into a hoarse guffaw.

"She's a rum 'un, that one is — fine talk — but what's the good of it? What can she do about it? Aye, she's a rum 'un — and a dead 'un — cram me with rope yarn if she ain't. Aye, a dead 'un, I say — a goblin woman! But what harm can such as she do a body, eh?"

"And what is that supposed to mean?" demanded Mrs. Aberdovey, not comprehending.

"You think she's real, but she ain't — nary a jot of her — nary an atom of her, perish an' plague me — 'cause she ain't got any atoms. Look at her — white as any ghost. Clap your eye on *this* now — "

And so saying he tore the bonnet from his head and flung it at Henriette. Mrs. Aberdovey was astonished to see the bonnet pass directly through her gossamy figure and drop to the stern deck aft of it.

"What think you o' that, now?" said the loathly dog, in a tone meant to discourage further conversation.

Mrs. Aberdovey did not know what to think. The shock of it had sent a chill through her. Instinctively she recoiled — in fear, in terror — at what she had witnessed, the very same as Gwenda had done.

In the name of heaven, what *was* one to think?

The next moment wheels were heard turning in the bowels of the ship, chain belts began to roll, as the thief and traitor revolved a crank-handle at his side. With a rush the skimmer shot into the air. Mrs. Aberdovey was thrown to the deck. Upon regaining her feet, she saw dimly that the yard and gatehouse had fallen away below. The loathly dog, as he had threatened, had taken his departure.

She stared in mute anguish as the mist went spilling past them, blotting out the view — that is until an immense shadow loomed up dead ahead. In the same instant she felt the deck heave violently beneath her as the skimmer rolled to starboard, her pilot swinging the wheel over hard to avert a splintering of his ship's bows against one of the squat and very solid towers of the Hall. As they hurtled past it — missing it by mere feet — the tower rapidly was consumed in the swirl of their backwash.

"Get you below!" the traitor commanded his passengers, while laboring to steady his sky-helm. He was having difficulty navigating in the fog and dark — unlike Owen he was unused to the practice — and bent arduously to the wheel, his face rigid with concentrated attention.

His indecision and unease were evident to Mrs. Aberdovey, as were the erratic motions of the skimmer, and she recalled her son's remarking upon the villain's inexperience at the steerage. Next moment a sudden inspiration struck her. Now was the time to have a go at the dog, to prevent a second theft of the vessel.

To her surprise — and frankly, her shock — she discovered Henriette standing at her side. Or was she floating there? Her luminous form seemed to be hovering an inch or two above the deck, her hair, a portion of which hung loosely about her shoulders, and her gown untouched by the breeze that was whipping round them. Mrs. Aberdovey momentarily was thrown off her guard, but Henriette flashed her a winning smile and eased her fears by telling her —

"I 'ave plan for conquassating villain man. We moste save skeemer for Owen, *oui*, bote we moste 'urry. Wat you say? For you, the leetle mama, moste act for Henriette."

Mrs. Aberdovey found herself moved by these words, and rallied quickly, dismissing from her thoughts the notion that the figure hovering beside her was that of a dead woman. Dead woman or no, it was enough that she was a friend of Owen's; although why her son had not seen fit to confide in his mother on this point was a mystery. It was sufficient now that the woman had a plan of action for returning the skimmer to Owen's care.

"We moste give villain man the what for, no?" said Henriette.

"We must give it him, yes." The lips of Mrs. Aberdovey compressed themselves into a single, firm line of determination. "I'll — I'll broom out the cockpit with him," she vowed, in a tone so suddenly fierce that even Henriette was startled. "The man's an unmitigated liar, a thief, and a traitor. He has done my son an outrageous injury, and I shall see that he has his due."

The more thought Mrs. Aberdovey gave to the injustice done her son and to what he had been made to endure, the greater flamed her passion for dismantling the miserable object known as Teech. Now indeed was the time to act; but she must contain her ire if she were to act wisely and effectively.

"What must I do?" she asked.

"Vary good, mama. We moste jockey — is 'ow you say? — this so ogly and eempudent fallow, for Owen's sake. *Vite, vite!* Now then you leesten . . ."

Her plan she then poured into the attentive ear of her confederate, who deemed it a good plan, and a simple one. In accord with it Mrs. Aberdovey absented herself for a moment, groping her way down the companion-ladder to the cabin, and returning shortly with the needed item.

"This is the weapon you meant?"

"Precisally," nodded Henriette.

Mrs. Aberdovey weighed it critically in her hand. "A proper little dickens — easy in the gripping if not on the eye. It'll serve, I think."

"It is joste the ting, *oui*. Now you watch, mama, and Henriette show you 'ow is done. Bote you moste be ready."

"I'll knock the hound into next week," vowed her confederate.

At the moment Mr. Amos Teech — for there could be little doubt but that he and the cheeky groom were one and the same — was bent over the wheel, shaping his vessel's uncertain course through the fog. He had little reckoned on the fog, having been so consumed by his desire to recover the skimmer, which he believed to be his by right, that it had trumped every other consideration. His posture was tense and strained, his eyes fastened ahead, as he struggled with his task. His least concern now was the actions of his passengers aboard ship. Indeed they had entirely slipped his mind; that is, until a ghostly figure drifted into his line of sight in the forward window and, leering at him, called out —

"I see you, villain man."

"Sheer off, you devil!" was the kindly reply of Amos.

The widow obliged, only to reappear moments later sporting a fish-face.

"You are so vary pale. Are you not tire, villain man?"

Her concern for his well-being was met with a scowl and a disdainful swipe of his hand.

"Blast your deadlights — you hag o' Satan!"

Again Henriette obliged him, by causing her eyeballs to pop as she goggled at him through the glass.

It was the crucial moment. So absorbed was Teech in the piloting of his craft, while distracted by the antics of Henriette, that he failed to note the small slip of a woman who had crept up behind him. Her hot Welsh blood surging, Mrs. Aberdovey paused behind his bonnetless figure, raised her weapon and with a glint of triumph thumped it against the villain man's naked sconce. Like a stalk of corn wilting in place he sank quietly to the deck, and lay still in the folds of his boat-cloak.

Mrs. Aberdovey stood over him, smiling. "What a good idea that was," she said. The gammer's cup, which she had employed to such excellent effect, she stowed inside her coat. Moments later a luminous figure settled at her elbow.

"Flat as flounder — are we not rejoice? Now villain man 'ave his dessert." Henriette peered at the inert form more closely. "Ah, you brain him good, mama. Is he harm, do you theenk?"

"No brains to rattle — no harm done," observed the mother of Owen. Her rage gratified, she was reminded on a sudden of their predicament and glanced in quick alarm at Henriette. "Oh, my," she worried, "what do we do now?"

It had put an entirely different aspect on their situation, now that there was no helmsman in the cockpit. Meanwhile they were racing through the night with no particular destination in view, and no one to guide them to safety.

"Circumstances, they 'ave altercated, *oui*," nodded Henriette.

Peering ahead Mrs. Aberdovey could discern little beyond the tumbling masses of fog which were gusting over the rail and, passing by, went roiling and broiling astern. At the helm she was protected from the elements, unlike Henriette, who had remained on deck in utter disregard of them. Mrs. Aberdovey marveled again at the sight of her streaming tresses undisturbed by the shiversome wind that was flowing through them — for, as Teech had said, she had no atoms to be so disturbed. Instead it sent a disturbing shiver through the soul of Mrs. Aberdovey.

How had this mysterious being become a friend of her son's, she wondered — and why? Only then did it occur to her, after some little thinking on it, that if Owen himself were not affrighted of such a creature then neither should his mother be. But there was another, more serious matter to occupy her at the moment. For with every minute that passed they were getting farther and farther from the Hall, as the skimmer sped on, relentlessly, through the night.

Clearly Henriette could not pilot the vessel, though she had some slight knowledge of the helm; so the steerage must become Mrs. Aberdovey's responsibility. But first the insensible form of the villain man had to be removed from the cockpit. This she managed to accomplish, although being only a small slip of a woman she had rather a hard job of it, and was relieved when at last her burden had been deposited on the stern-deck.

Through the fathomy dark the skimmer sped, riding the fog-billows as once she had cleaved her course through riotous seas. To be sure it was an eerie feeling. Passing beneath them, Mrs. Aberdovey knew, was the vast expanse of the marshes; and yet no landmark of any kind was demonstrable to her eye. In the lantern-light she checked her compass heading — it was southwestwards — and shot a look of concern at Henriette.

"Where was he going, do you think?" she asked.

"Into the providences, vary like. Certally we be many mile from Hall. Bote no more than thees do I know."

Their situation was quite beyond anything in Mrs. Aberdovey's experience, needless to say. The first order of business, it seemed to her, was to slacken their speed. But how to go about it? Henriette, having some familiarity with Owen's actions at the helm, suggested that Mrs. Aberdovey depress one of the deck pedals, which she believed to be governing of the ship's velocity. Directly a reduction in their rate of speed was noted, and the more the pedal was depressed the more their forward motion eased.

That was better. Gaining confidence, Mrs. Aberdovey yielded to Henriette's further instruction.

"Now we moste take skeemer down, mama."

"Ah. And how do we do that?"

"Late a me see. I theenk it crank-handle there."

But a slow revolving of the handle produced an undesirable effect — the ship began to ascend.

"Moste be other crank-handle," Henriette suggested.

It was. This too was better. With a little conscious pride Mrs. Aberdovey remarked upon the smooth operation of the vessel, that which had been designed and piloted by her own son and whose helm she now had the command of. Forgetting for an instant their plight in her admiration of her son's achievement, she suddenly was reminded of the fact that somewhere below, who knew how far, the ground even now was rushing upwards to meet them. Or perhaps it was a stream towards which they were descending — one of many marshways that crisscrossed the landscape — and into which at any second they might be plunged at speed? For however was one to judge one's altitude when navigating in the fog and dark?

The answer, if it be one, was supplied by her ghostly confederate.

"Henriette go overside — see wat she can see, no?"

Alarmed, Mrs. Aberdovey had no chance to respond ere Henriette had slipped over the rail and vanished. Keeping a fast grip on the helm, while at the same time slowing her craft's descent, she anxiously awaited the woman's return. Although the skimmer's forward motion had been reduced considerably, its precise magnitude was difficult to judge given the darkness and the absence of landmarks — the absence indeed of anything save for the rush of fog past her bows.

Where were they? How far beneath them lay the snow-mantled earth? Indeed was it earth — solid ground — or was it a wilderness of black pools, miry bogs, and foul-running streams towards which the skimmer was descending?

Minutes had passed since Henriette had gone, when unexpectedly she came floating up through the boards and settled herself again at Mrs. Aberdovey's elbow. The tidy small woman, a trifle unnerved by the manner of her confederate's comings and goings, asked anxiously —

"Well, what did you find?"

"Vary dark — vary fog — allamost we 'ave lost our way, I theenk."

Then she urged Mrs. Aberdovey to action straightaway, because, in her words, they "moste draw up the ropes — *vite, vite!* — or we run *risque* of rueen."

Gracious heavens! The villain Teech, in his haste to depart, had left the cord-ladder dangling overside. If its rungs now should catch in a thicket, or on the limbs of a tree, or upon some derelict outbuilding, while the ship was in rapid motion, she might be knocked to splinters —

Apprehending the danger, Mrs. Aberdovey hurried from the cockpit to bring the cordage safely aboard. Scarcely had she started, however, than a rending crash was heard, followed by a massive creaking and straining of timbers. The ropes were torn from her hands as a violent shudder convulsed the craft.

The ground fog was so thick that seeing more than a few yards in any direction was all but impossible. And therein lay the key term — ground.

For it was ground fog that had enveloped the skimmer, so far had she descended in her flight.

Mrs. Aberdovey meanwhile had been hurled to the rail, and but for her firm grip upon it she might well have tumbled overside to her destruction. Clinging there, she beheld an indistinct form against the night, something like the yard of a masted vessel, but unkempt and shaggy, go raking across the deck, followed by another, then by a third, and by others beneath the bows, as the skimmer after a final, forward surge, amidst a shower of snow and pine-needles, came at last to rest.

Thereafter all was silent, and the vessel steady, save for a long, sleepy roll now and again, that proved her shorebound in the arms of a clumber pine.

Mrs. Aberdovey regained her feet and stared dazedly about her. Moments later the quiet was broken by a familiar voice.

"*Hélas!* now we are macaroon," said Henriette.

THE SEVENTH CHAPTER

Sabers Drawn

MRS. ABERDOVEY, wiping the sleep from her eyes, sat up in her berth and said — "Who is it?"

For some seconds she remained thus, listening for what it was had awakened her. In the night she had fallen into a deep slumber, from which she had not stirred until this minute. Somewhere, a new dawn was rising in the east; but in which direction east lay was a mystery, if the view in her cabin port was any judge. For a dense fog like a white sea had congregated there, a mist that sat like wool against the porthole of the forward compartment.

Before retiring she had secured the skimmer by shuttering the helm, and then had bolted herself in the compartment, glad to find that the vessel had *not* been reduced to a mangled wreck in the crash. Upon awakening her first thought had been of Owen, that it had been his voice she had heard calling to her. As well there had been the dull *plunk-plunk* that had sounded in her ear, the vibration of it having been communicated to her through the ship's timbers. A voice calling out was a thing she could fathom, but she was at a loss to explain the *plunk-plunk*.

Again she heard the man calling. He was somewhere outside, but of the words spoken she could distinguish little save for a rustic *hulloo*. There followed then another *plunk-plunk,* as of wood upon wood, accompanied by a hoarse whistle. It appeared that someone was endeavoring to gain her attention.

"Who is it? Who's there?" she returned.

Not yet fully awake, she lowered herself to the deck and groped about for her shoes. Her coat she had worn to bed, to keep off the chill, and as well her cap, which remained fastened at her chin.

Again a cry arose from without, followed by another *hulloo!* and a further *plunk-plunk* upon the hull.

"Who is it? I'm coming, I'm coming . . ." Then a different voice, that of a woman there in the compartment with her, answered —

"Two old fallows with leetle boats, mama, they 'ave desire to speak a with you," said Henriette.

"Boats?" echoed Mrs. Aberdovey, as she laced up her shoes.

"They 'ave just arrive. They find skeemer in tree — they vary surprise. They looking for skeeper. Thees a way now."

Drawing her coat tightly about her Mrs. Aberdovey went to the door, slid back the bolt, and looked out into the cabin. She heard the voice calling again, so up the companionway she stepped, flung open the hatch, and ventured forth on deck.

There she found the day struggling to assert itself, the marsh mist filling the air with a somber light. The skimmer lay at her ease in the boughs of a clumber pine, which were thickly loaded with snow, some of which had fallen off in wet heaps and lay scattered about the deck. The clumber was but one in a row of pines which bordered a noisy stream, and through whose shaggy draperies the skimmer had traveled successively to her resting-place.

The marsh mist, the bracing effect of the chilly air, combined to revive the spirits of Mrs. Aberdovey and shake off the final vestiges of sleep. Together she and Henriette approached the rail and glanced overside. Deep drifts covered the ground in every direction. Mrs. Aberdovey was disturbed to see how near the skimmer had come to the stream, whose waters could be heard rumbling along below. It was early in the season, and the marshways had not yet frozen over. The tree in which the ship had come to rest was situated at the very brink of the stream. The cord-ladder in part had been torn away, as Mrs. Aberdovey had only too late feared, and its entanglement in the pines had brought their excursion to a jarring close.

At the foot of the tree, drawn up onto the snow, lay a couple of small boats. They were oval-shaped and flat-bottomed, and had wicker frames covered with pitched canvas, in the style of the ancient Welsh. They were coracles, the so-called "basket" boats of those hardy Fenshiremen who plied the marshways. As I've said the boats were of small dimensions, like the two Fenshiremen themselves, who stepped now into Mrs. Aberdovey's line of sight. Their upturned faces were weathered and grizzled in the extreme, with stubbly beards, and eyes shining blue as cornflower under their hat-brims.

One of the men, who held a paddle, evidently had been thumping it on the skimmer's keel, which lay some few feet above his head, in an attempt to rouse her captain. His companion's thin voice it was that had sung out the rustic *hulloo*. The two stood gazing at the skimmer in some fascination, wondering no doubt how such a thing had come to be lounging in the arms of a clumber pine.

As she surveyed them from the rail, something about the pair struck Mrs. Aberdovey as familiar.

"I know these boys," she told Henriette. "They're Dud and Bodo of the marshways — coracle men, and former acquaintances of my husband's."

"Boys? Wat you mean boys, mama? They old men."

"Oh, seventy at least, perhaps eighty. But I was never more glad to see 'em in all my life."

The "boys", having recognized the tidy small woman at the rail, doffed their hats in greeting.

"If it bean't dame Gillian now — Morgan Aberdovey's widder — as be lodgekeeper at the Hall," said the one called Dud.

"Aye, so it be," nodded his brother, leaning on his paddle. "And what be she doing here, then? And whaur be the skipper, d'ye suppose?"

Though advanced in years, the two in their rough-and-ready garb were no churlish marshland farmers but skilled fishermen, whose talents were widely acknowledged. Plain and homely of speech, the brothers were much respected in the neighborhood and throughout the marshland.

The two gallants, bachelors both, returned their hats to their heads, and Bodo, indicating the skimmer with a flourish of his paddle, inquired —

"This 'ere boat — how do she get here, then? For never have I see'd the like of her."

"Nay, nor I, never have," said Dud, "never a boat in a clumber pine. But whaur be her mast and canvas?"

"Beat overboard in the wreck, most like."

"Aye, most like. Otherwise she do seem sturdy enough."

The brothers stood stroking their jaws and musing. They were tremendously interested to know how the boat had gotten from the stream into the tree, and how it was that dame Gillian Aberdovey of Haigh Hall had come to be aboard her.

"Where are we, boys?" she called down to them.

"Whaur be? Well, by Fitful Farm, good dame — some few miles to the southwest, but within easy journey o' the Hall, by the marshways," said Bodo. "We did pass the night with our cousin Minch, him as ye'll recollect be woodman and gamekeeper at the farm."

Untraversed by any road in most directions, the seemingly boundless expanse of marsh lying to the westwards and southwards of Ridingham was accessible only by way of the many streams — the marshways — that laced the countryside, and which afforded the sole means of travel in these more remote districts.

"We axes yer pardon, dame Gillian, but be this *yer* boat?" the brothers inquired.

Mrs. Aberdovey assured them that it was not her vessel, but rather that it had been in trust to her late son Owen. Observing the straits she was in, with her son's craft lodged in a tree, the brothers were sympathetic.

"Can you boys help us?" she asked them.

This last prompted an exchange of glances by the pair, and a few words of low-voiced conversation. At length Bodo, he with the paddle, answered —

"Aye, that we can, and wull. But be there others aboard, dame Gillian? Be ye not her skipper?"

"They be fonny leetle fallows, no?" Henriette chuckled.

Looking her way, Mrs. Aberdovey was visited by a sudden revelation. "The boys can't see you, can they?" she said.

Henriette, with a vague shrug, returned her glance apologetically.

"Bote why for should they see Henriette? Boys they 'ave not drink from gammer's cup. Henriette 'ave no need to be seen."

"Whatever does that mean?"

Another shrug from Henriette, eyes averted and a smile hovering round her lips; but in this instance she kept her own counsel.

Insensible of the presence of Mrs. Aberdovey's confederate, the brothers awaited an answer from the good dame at the rail.

"I did misspeak. There is no one else aboard," she called down to them, before communicating her eager assent to their offer of aid. Although they would be of little help as regards the skimmer, they were more than capable of returning her to the Hall, and were traveling that way in any case.

"Bote wat of villain man?" Henriette reminded her.

On the instant Mrs. Aberdovey's memory was refreshed concerning the unconscious Teech, whom she had dragged to the stern-deck and left there.

"Mebbe he freeze," Henriette suggested.

It thus became necessary to explain to the brothers that indeed there was another person aboard — a merchant seaman, who had absconded with the vessel, and whose dirty underfoot scheming had been to blame for all her son's troubles.

More questioning glances from the coracle men.

"And what troubles be those, dame Gillian? For Owen, he were his father's true son, and as fine a lad as ever rowed a boat," noted Dud.

"Why, it's good of you to say — "

Mrs. Aberdovey hesitated, for it had crossed her mind that the brothers knew nothing of Owen's troubles; that they, like most everyone else, believed he had been lost at sea in the channel off Nantle harbor while engaged upon a rescue. They knew nothing of his being alleged a thief and a traitor.

"This man aboard be friend o' yern?" Bodo asked.

"He most certainly is not," Mrs. Aberdovey retorted warmly.

Choosing her words with care — and omitting any reference to either Owen or Henriette — she described the situation for them. They lent wondering ears to her tale of perilous adventure, and at its conclusion took another admiring turn round the skimmer, rubbing their chins and gazing at the ship's flowing lines in a wholly different light.

For even here in these remote precincts folks had heard tell of the *Salty Sue*, the marvelous flying lugger that roamed the skies of the long coast. To know that the vessel lodged in the tree was of that same ship, and possessed of the same magical power of flight, to them was a stunner.

"Aye, but what keeps her in air?" they asked.

Although seemingly at rest in the clumber's boughs, the skimmer in actuality remained buoyantly aloft. She was not being held up by the tree, but was being held *by* it — gripped fast in its shaggy embrace. Had there been no clumber she still would be hovering there some few feet above the brothers' heads. As it was, however, more skill and strength than was possessed by the both of them would be needed to free her from the tree's entangling grasp.

It was then the brothers disclosed to Mrs. Aberdovey that of late some rather curious reports had been abroad on the marshes — reports of a mysterious flying ship in the dead of night as some folk had had sight of, when now and again a stray moonbeam had come peeping through the overcast. So in spite of her son's many precautions, the skimmer had not escaped detection by the canny marshlanders!

"Ever so grateful for your help. Now I must see about the villain man — er, that is — this man Teech — " said Mrs. Aberdovey.

With Henriette she crossed the deck to the spot where she had left him, but the loathly dog, he of the bruised sconce, was nowhere to be found. Mystified, they searched the area thoroughly. They looked in the cockpit, but he was not there. Nor was he in the cabin. He was not anywhere.

It was a complete puzzle. Where had the villain man disappeared to? Even Henriette had no notion, that is until she and Mrs. Aberdovey while searching the deck again discovered there a faint trail of crimson drops that led overside.

"What do you suppose has happened to him? For this blood — I expect it is blood — is worrying," said Mrs. Aberdovey.

"You swat him good, mama. Mebbe he bleed," Henriette suggested.

"Bruised he was, but I saw no blood on him."

Her companion gave a shrug. *"C'est dommage.* Bote now we 'ave more to theenk about other than villain man."

Repeatedly Mrs. Aberdovey called his name to the trees, but no answer was received. Meanwhile the coracle men had identified a set of footprints in the snow. Some time in the night or early morning, evidently, the loathly dog had clambered down from the ship and beaten a hasty retreat.

Ominously, the men found other tracks there as well — huge, several-toed prints, decidedly not of human making.

"Marsh devil!" Mrs. Aberdovey heard the brothers exclaim.

The news left her a trifle queasy. Nothing would be better now, she decided, than that the brothers should take her home, and swiftly too.

How then was she to proceed once she returned to the Hall? How was Owen to find his way to the skimmer here in this lonely and unfrequented spot? Only Dud and Bodo could aid him there. And it would require all her son's skill at the helm to dislodge his vessel from the clumber's grip.

For how much longer could Owen's secret be kept? How much longer before it was discovered he had not been lost in the channel, as had been reported, but for these several weeks had been in hiding at Northeave — and that both his mother and her ladyship's maid had been privy to the lie?

Came a sudden shout from below. Glancing overside, Mrs. Aberdovey saw the brothers standing motionless, their attention riveted by something on the farther bank of the stream. She traced their gaze to a line of dwarf-wood from which, at a point not far from the water, a bestial countenance could be seen glaring. The eyes of the creature were a brilliant yellow, and menacing in their fixed gaze. Two curved, saber-like fangs projected downwards from its upper jaw, a syrupy drool oozed from its lips.

Instinctively Mrs. Aberdovey recoiled on seeing the cat. Grim and terrible is the marsh devil — a dirk-tooth saber-cat, one of the most fearsome and feared of all marshland predators. Only the spotted lion is more to be dreaded than is the devil she-cat of the marshes.

A hint of panic showed in the face of Mrs. Aberdovey. To her surprise, however, it was Henriette through whom a shudder was observed to pass, like a rippling of the sea when disturbed by the course of a mighty zeug holding sway beneath its surface.

All at once Henriette clamped a hand to her brow and shut her eyes, as though she were about to swoon.

"I am f-feel unwell," she quavered. "Wat strange sensation is thees! Henriette feel not so good, mama. 'Ow weak am I grow — I am nauseous, allamost. There is — there is death here — "

Across the stream the dwarf-wood parted as the saber-cat, a gigantic female, crept forth onto the snowy bank. Over the murmuring of the water a horrid growl could be heard rumbling in her throat. Her muscles rolled beneath her tawny hide, her fangs glistened.

"What a giant she be!" marveled Dud.

His brother's tone was grim. "I'd as lief we be putting off now," he recommended, moving towards the boats.

Not once had the devil she-cat taken her eyes from the intruders on the opposite shore. Worse still, behind her now appeared a second female, one larger even than she, with sabers bared and fiery eyes blazing.

It was a hunting party. For amongst marsh devils — as it is with saber-cats generally — it is the females in pairs who do the shopping.

"We must step lively now," Bodo called. "Be you coming with us, dame Gillian?"

Mr. Aberdovey turned to Henriette, but of her companion now there was no trace. Like the villain man she too had disappeared. In a twinkling, it seemed, she had returned to those unknown shades from which she had sprung.

✿

PART FOUR

❧

THE FIRST CHAPTER

Breaking Covert

A N D what of Amos Teech? Alive — or dead? For the blood trail communicated only that he had sustained an injury. Where had he gone, and where was his corpse — if corpse there was? For once a spotted lion or marsh devil had had its way with a man . . .

It would have been an especially nasty end. And so perhaps the villain man was no more? Perhaps a period had been put to his earthly rascality? But what sort of creature might have scaled the clumber pine and found its way aboard to assault him and send him fleeing? Mrs. Aberdovey shuddered to realize how near she herself had come to destruction while asleep below. For had she been awakened and ventured on deck she almost certainly would have suffered a like fate.

It occurred to her that now there should be no chance of Teech's being made to testify in the matter of the theft, by confessing it was he who had stolen the skimmer. How then was her son to clear himself in the eyes of the world?

She regarded the vessel lodged amongst the pine branches with thought-troubled eyes. What else was there to be done now? Nothing. And so with a resolute air, and having almost forgotten about the predators glaring at them from across the stream, she stepped gingerly into the coracle of her friend Dud. There behind the thwart she arranged herself as comfortably as she was able, amongst the nets and other gear that occupied the bottom of the boat, and from the employment of which the brothers scraped their frugal living.

"Ever so grateful for your help," she said again.

The boys grinned cordially and saluted her with a touch of their hats, then dipping their paddles into the stream they applied themselves to their task. It was a precarious moment, the saber-cats eyeing them from the bank not many yards distant. Having put off from shore the brothers with calm, steady strokes sent their tiny basket boats ahead, in an easterly direction, the flow of the stream bearing them along smoothly and strongly. Their off-hand, free-and-easy sort of way belied the iron nerves that lay beneath, their seventy or eighty years notwithstanding, for in those years the brothers had seen and experienced much upon the marshways. So they exercised the utmost caution going forward, with only the slightest stir of their paddles in the water as they glided nearer the giants that awaited on the opposite shore. As the boats drifted slowly by, the creatures paced and snarled, the brothers and their passenger undergoing the scrutiny of cruel eyes that gleamed from whiskered faces, fiery orbs that shone wickedly from over the way.

One of the beasts ventured to dip a paw in the icy-running stream, only to withdraw it quickly, glaring and roaring at the boats passing by and displaying to them her grinning jaws of death. Despite their name these devil-cats of the marshes do not much care for water, and a plunge into a frigid stream is a thing they well can do without. And if these two already had breakfasted — on Teech, for example — they should be even less inclined to be daring the marshway. Perhaps they were not so hungry as it had at first appeared.

To Mrs. Aberdovey's surprise, the brothers suddenly shifted their paddles and with powerful strokes propelled the boats into a hidden tributary of the stream, which had appeared round a thicket on their right hand. This ancillary channel, they explained, would carry them away from the opposing bank, making it impossible for the saber-cats to follow, as there existed no crossing of the stream for some miles in either direction.

"For we bean't a-going their way," noted Dud, "but we be a-going our-a-way."

The many obscure and winding reaches of the marshland were as familiar to the canny boatmen as the dew is to the daisy. These haunted wilds the brothers had plied nearly every day of their long lives; there was not an island, thicket, hidden pool, or rivulet upon the flats that was a stranger to them. As a result they were able to pursue their course safely and rapidly, out of sight and scent of the carnivores.

As they swept round the thicket into the lesser channel, and the skimmer and its pine tree were lost to view, a terrible thought reared itself in the head of Mrs. Aberdovey. Had the villain Teech survived and purposely hidden himself until she and the brothers should depart, at which time he could make off with the skimmer unopposed?

Perhaps he had the means to free the helm? Perhaps there would be no skimmer in the clumber pine when Owen arrived? What terrible result might then follow, when Owen was unable to return the skimmer to the captain?

It was but another concern that weighed upon her mind, as the brothers paddled their way swiftly along towards the Hall.

Some miles and hours later found them nearing a plank-bridge over the stream, within eyeshot of a bleak stone parsonage that Mrs. Aberdovey recognized as that of Vicar Saltmarsh, in the domain of her ladyship's friend and neighbor Mr. MacWallop. As luck would have it, a gillie happened to be striding across the bridge at the time. From the cut of his plaid and the stoutness of his walking-stick, she identified him as being in the service of, and likely on some errand for, the aforesaid neighbor.

The gillie, having spied the coracles sweeping towards him, halted on the bridge and, peering at them with a fierce, unfriendly gaze not unlike that of a marsh devil, addressed the boatmen sternly and sharply.

"Get hame wi' ye," he warned, brandishing his stick — "for ken ye no this be MacWallop land? Awa' wi' ye!"

The brothers stilled their paddles and raised their hats to the servant in greeting.

"Good day t'ye, Mr. Lash," smiled Dud, tolerantly, "but the marshways bean't the property exclusive o' the MacWallop, don't ye know, but do belong to all the marsh folk."

The gillie squinted at the boatmen gliding towards him on the water. This Lash was that same fellow who had been driving the sleigh the morning Dan Hedges and his party had encountered Mr. MacWallop and Lawyer Wormwrath in the road.

"Is it yersell, Dud Llandudno?" the gillie called, after a moment's scrutiny.

"Aye."

"And Bodo?"

"And Bodo."

"And frae whaur wad ye be comin'?"

"Fitful Farm."

"And for whaur wad ye be makin'?"

"Haigh Hall."

"By this d'ye mean the hame o' that spiteful auld busybody? The auld corbie hersell?" demanded Lash. "For she's a fearful bad woman and a daft, that one is."

Mrs. Aberdovey, hearing this, controlled herself with an effort. The presumption of this flunky to be speaking of her ladyship in such terms!

"And who else would I be meaning, Mr. Lash," returned Dud, calmly, "but the good dowager lady and widder o' Sir Pedr? Though I bean't one to be crackin' about her in such bold terms as yerself."

"And wha' then should I be ca'ing her? A sonsy lass? A braw fine girl? Fie for shame, Dud Llandudno! For sic wad be lying, and lying be evil, and ye yersell ken right weel 'tis a' evil comes out o' thereaway — Haigh Hall that I mean. For is't no this same hell-cat and her law-writer Gecks as be angling tae cheat the Laird of his right o' way at Petty Sessions?"

Mrs. Aberdovey had heard enough. The flunky's words went ill down with her. Glaring at him, but hesitant to rise for fear of upsetting the boat, she fixed the gillie with a level finger and, as the coracle went sliding under the bridge, blurted out —

"May you blank choke on your blank-blank right of way and kick it!"

This outburst from their tidy small passenger came as rather a surprise to the coracle men — so much so, indeed, that for a space no words were exchanged, to allow Mrs. Aberdovey sufficient time for cooling. Instead the brothers gave their attention to the scene of rural quiet through which they were passing, and dipping their paddles in the stream sent the boats gliding along towards their destination.

Presently the causeway came in sight, then the towers of the Hall and the long sweep of battlements, at which point the brothers were hailed by a figure seen tramping along the shore with a lively little terrier-dog at his heels.

The day already was more than half spent as the men drew their boats in. Substantial was the perplexity of Dan Hedges to find Mrs. Aberdovey a passenger, nor did she immediately relieve him of his confusion. Instead she asked him to remain with the boys for a moment, out of view of the gatehouse, until he should be sent for.

More mystery! But the outside man dutifully obliged.

In the panes of the tiny latticed window beside the gate a shadowy face appeared, and then a second, and a third, their eyes having caught sight of the woman who was trudging towards them. Moments later the door was opened and several persons rushed out. One of them — it was Owen — undid the gate and swung it wide, to receive his mother into his arms. Behind him, watching from the step, were Edgar and Richard. Then they all withdrew inside, that no chance observation of Owen might be made by anyone in the courtyard.

The mariner in an agony of apprehension had passed a sleepless night, after returning from the farm office to find that the skimmer had been taken. Marks on the snow, discovered by lantern-light, had told a part of the story. It appeared that a man had made his way along the curtain-wall from the stables to the ship, and there had scaled the ladder to the deck. A jumble of footprints in the area of the gatehouse door had been more difficult of interpretation, but it seemed that Mrs. Aberdovey might have followed the man aboard, and there likely had encountered some trouble.

Owen had been much worried and the strain had told upon him. His face was drawn and he had been smoking continuously. But never once had he abandoned hope.

His mother assured him and the others that the trouble had not been nearly so grave as they had feared, as she described for them the events of the previous evening. Certain particulars related to those events she saw fit to exclude from her narration, however, at least for the present — you may guess which are those I mean. Then, after a brief talk with Owen, she asked Richard if he would call in Dan Hedges.

A few minutes passed ere the outside man came striding into the room. As his gaze lighted on Owen his eyes widened and he stared at the mariner in speechless surprise. The blood seemed to drain from his face as a ghastly chill stole over him. His mouth, although his lips were seen to move, gave forth no sound, and he stood looking at his lost friend as though he were an apparition in a dream.

Owen, observing his distress, flashed him a smile and took his hand in a cordial grip.

"Lord bless me — can it be — ?" stumbled Dan.

"As any eye can see," nodded the mariner. "Love my limbs, if it isn't pure joy to see you again, Dan."

Meanwhile Toddy, unable to contain his delight, gave a rapturous yelp and launched himself at Owen, whom his sensitive nostrils had that moment identified.

Dan Hedges having recovered from his shock, he and the mariner stood awhile exchanging gleeful words. Some explanation was in order — rather a lot of it, actually — and that portion that concerned Amos Teech, who had been masquerading as a groom, quite staggered Dan, as indeed it had done the others. Owen had suspected that Teech was alive and in hiding in the neighborhood. But it was the neighborhood of Northeave he had meant, not the stables at the Hall!

"Bold as brass — I'll give the scurvy rogue credit for that much," Owen said grudgingly, "for certain sure the dog thinks no end o' strong beer of himself."

Mrs. Aberdovey meanwhile had arranged for "the boys" to return the next day, that they might take Owen to the skimmer. Indeed the brothers had volunteered for the job, insisting it was the least service they could render to the son of their late friend Morgan Aberdovey. And as a bonus they would pass another enjoyable evening at Fitful Farm with their cousin Minch.

Owen for his part was confident that he could loose the skimmer from the tree. But how then should he proceed once that had been accomplished? Should he return to Northeave, or should he give it up and bring the skimmer in to the Hall? Should the truth at last be made known to Lady Martindale and the others?

After some discussion, a plan was formulated and agreed upon. Early the next morning the coracle men arrived to find Owen and Richard awaiting them on the bank. It had been thought wise for another to accompany Owen and the brothers, in the event that greater assistance were needed in freeing the skimmer, or for any other eventuality that might arise. So the passengers took their seats and the brothers resumed their paddles. Seventy years, eighty — it mattered little to these hardy boatmen of the marshways. More than once Richard found himself marveling at the dexterity and endurance they exhibited as their clumsy small boats went skimming — as it were — down the stream.

They traversed MacWallop land without incident — no sighting of Lash today — and pursued their journey swiftly and smoothly. Great was the relief of all concerned when, drawing near the place where the brothers had found Mrs. Aberdovey, they descried the clumbers silhouetted against a ground of mist, and locked securely in the embrace of one was the marvelous sky-boat of Captain Barnaby.

There looked to be no sign of Teech in the area, nor of marsh devils. And so the coracles rapidly were hauled ashore, the travelers gathering on the snow under the skimmer's graceful bows that rode above their heads. Some slight damage to her timbers was evident, here and there, caused by her passage through the trees; otherwise she looked to be in decent order. Truth be told the mariner was simply happy to have found her and in the same state in which his mother and the boys had left her.

Gingerly he climbed the ladder — it supported his weight with ease — and having scrambled aboard he urged Richard to "come along up." The two then made a hasty examination of the ship. The result — no Teech; no one, indeed, but a famished Melon-head, who sprang from his locker and greeted both of them warmly in anticipation of nourishment. Owen obliged him by fishing up some dainties from a tin, with a promise of more to come.

There had been no evidence of Teech, nor was Henriette anywhere to be found. Had the two widow women encountered one another last evening, Owen wondered? And if they had done, what had been the outcome? He made a note to inquire further into it when he should speak again with his mother.

From his pocket he drew a key with which he unchained the helm. A repair, albeit temporary, of the damaged cord-ladder was the work of several minutes. His next task then was to free the skimmer from the clumber pine.

"Dud — Bodo — crave pardon, but you must stand clear now," he instructed the brothers.

"Be ye puttin' off, Owen?" inquired Bodo.

"Aye, that I am."

"Well, ye may 'ave the pleasure of it then, for never have we see'd the like of it. Never see'd a flying boat in Fenshire."

"Nay, never," agreed Dud, "nor in Slopshire neither."

"Then you'd best keep an eye open, gentlemen, for I reckon you'll see one today," Richard assured them.

"Two eyes," corrected Dud.

"Four," said Bodo, "for we dursn't miss a thing as was never afore see'd in Fenshire."

"Nor in Slopshire neither," added Dud.

So remarking, the brothers withdrew until they were well clear of the stand of pines. There they halted and with hands at their backs turned admiring eyes on the skimmer, awaiting with interest the magic of the hover-stone that dwelt at her heart.

In the cockpit Owen applied himself at once to the helm. A slight turn of the wheel, another of a crank-handle, and Richard felt the skimmer stir beneath him. Her bows lifted slightly upwards and away from the clumber, but the resistance to this effort was substantial. Glancing round him for the cause, Owen identified an overhanging limb amidships, one shaggy with encumbrances, which by virtue of their entanglement with the deck-house and rail was impeding the skimmer's release.

"Mark the bough for'ard, sir. Pray if you would take this boat-hook," he instructed my brother, "and give press against it — grapple it just there — and there — to ease her clear, as I work her safe at the steerage . . ."

Richard followed his direction, as the mariner with a practiced hand made a small adjustment to the wheel, another to a deck-pedal, and spun a crank-handle. The ship tugged at her moorings, as my brother wrestled with the shaggy encumbrances that stubbornly refused to yield. Although her stern was unhindered, still her waist and bows held tight.

"Stay a bit, sir — for I've another thought," Owen called out. "I'll work her easy aft . . . now easy a-larboard . . . if you'll give another push against lubberly limbs there . . ."

His maneuver sent the ship's stern swinging out over the snowy earth. Richard could feel the groaning of her timbers underfoot as the skimmer struggled to free herself. Crouched at the helm Owen worked a deck-pedal, then the wheel, then a crank-handle, while Richard, snow and pine-needles raining down about him, fought with his boat-hook to thrust the trailing foliage overside. But still she was not clear.

Then a sudden inspiration struck Owen, and calling to Richard to grapple fast the rail he angled the skimmer to earthwards, until she hung stern-high; then using his singular skill he eased her gently aft. Miraculously the shaggy mass was lifted from the deck, as the skimmer backed herself away, freed at last of the clumber's covetous grip.

Another turn of the wheel swung her round again, where she hove to and leveled herself in the air as sweet and steady as ever did any marvelous flying cutter of the long coast.

"She should bear us home well enough now," Owen announced, after thanking the coracle men for their assistance. "What think you of the skimmer, sirs?"

The brothers, enthusiasts both, exclaimed over her beauty as she floated above them. "But what holds her up, Owen?"

"Bless and burn me if it isn't a small white stone, no bigger than your two hands," answered the mariner.

As one the brothers took off their hats and scratched their heads, while exchanging mystified glances.

"We axes yer pardon, Owen — but might any o' these stones be found 'ereabouts?" asked Bodo. "For after so many a long year it do be a struggle still to be carrying our boats along on our backs."

Sadly, no such magical stones ever had been unearthed in Fenshire, nor in Slopshire neither. And so the brothers bade their farewells to the skimmer and her crew aloft. Her pilot then returned to the helm, and with a press of his foot and a twist of his hand he sent the vessel racing upwards and outwards over the marshes. The boys and their coracles dwindled rapidly away astern and vanished in the mist.

Meanwhile an air of anticipation prevailed at the Hall, now that the news had got out. That is, now that Mrs. Aberdovey and Edgar in the interval had gone to Lady Martindale and revealed to her the true facts of the case concerning Owen, the incident on the reef, and the identity of Amos Teech. Gwenda too was present at the confessional, and acknowledged her guilt for having known of Owen and Northeave at the outset and not troubled to inform her mistress.

To the very great surprise of the conspirators, her ladyship, far from reproaching them for their secret confidences, expressed joy at the knowledge that her lodgekeeper-woman's son — that "excellent young man" as she always called him, whose father had gone to sea with Wulf Clipperton, through the good offices of her husband — still lived. Though disappointed they had chosen not to confide in her ("for we have no secrets at the Hall") she understood their concerns, and that prudence had been their watchword. For the fewer who knew of his presence amongst them, the better it was for Owen.

Word spread quickly as a result and soon the Hall was in a tremendous bustle. Numerous and varied were the expressions of astonishment; already on the wall-walk the figure of Sam Gander could be seen stalking along, his eyes scanning the clouds. By midday a throng of persons had begun to assemble in and near the courtyard. Almost the entire populace of the Hall was represented, chief amongst them Lady Martindale herself. Soon an expectant hush fell over the company, who in their small groups stood nervously shifting their feet and whispering to one another. But mostly they were observing the example of Mr. Gander — they were watching the sky.

It was Dan Hedges who first caught sight of the thing they were watching for. He was followed almost at once by Sam, who drew his cutlass and aiming it at a point to the southwestwards exclaimed —

"Whoopee! There — there — what d'yer think o' that, then? Don't that just blow a hole in yer hat? Hee, hee!"

Emerging from the mist was a wonder such as most of them never before had looked upon. A small ship's cutter — *sans* mast, *sans* rigging, *sans* canvas, *sans* most everything — came gliding in over the curtain-wall and, heaving to, was brought to a stand in air over the courtyard. In the cockpit, like a ghost new-risen from the locker of Davy Jones, was Owen Aberdovey, and at the rail was my brother Richard.

The company watched in fascination as the skimmer descended towards them, and settled herself in an angle of the curtain-wall not far from the gatehouse. There she was made fast by her pilot, the cord-ladder was rolled out, and the spectators gathered excitedly about her.

The matter having been brought to a head, the decision had been made that there no longer was any need to be concealing Owen's presence, and so no longer any need of Northeave. And so it was good-bye to the ghost village, as it had been deemed a jolly sight safer for Owen to be securing the skimmer inside the curtain-wall than without it.

The mariner's seeming return from the dead had caused a tremendous sensation, and everybody was talking about it. The company formed a welcoming circle at the foot of the ladder, as first Richard and then Owen descended from the deck. For Owen's part he had had misgivings what might be the reception accorded him, in view of his having deceived them all, as it were, for these several weeks. But as it turned out there was not a one amongst them who had a wrong word to say against the young man, who, as they always maintained, was as honest as the day, and as good a fellow as had ever rowed a boat — or flown one.

It was in the rustic drawing-room of the Hall, with his audience assembled round him, that the mariner gave an account of all that had befallen him since the rescue on the reef. Calmly he laid the facts before them, as he had done for Richard and Edgar. In such fashion was his audience made aware of the scale of Teech's villainy and of his masquerade amongst them. A buzz of conversation followed, a dozen questions crowding their tongues in contention with the many murmurs of admiration for Owen and his actions. The thought of this impostor Diggory, or Teech, or whatever he called himself, endeavoring to make Owen Aberdovey out a rogue was ludicrous, to any who knew Owen. For an honester man never stood in his own sea-boots.

"I laugh them to scorn," sniffed her ladyship, "who dare to say otherwise. What an atrocious fellow — and in my service! The black ingratitude of the wretch! Does no one know what has become of this dangerous person?"

Unfortunately, no one did know — not yet at any rate. Perhaps they never would know.

"Nonetheless this is an injustice that must be rectified. I shall have Mr. Gecks look into it," her ladyship vowed. "My lawyer is a man of some influence in his profession, and not without means of furthering a cause in which he is interested."

Yet this celebration of Owen's return was of necessity tempered by thoughts of the consequences that inevitably must ensue, once Captain Barnaby had reclaimed the skimmer.

"Then let this captain come hither," challenged her ladyship, "for as I understand it, he served with your husband under Clipperton, and Clipperton was a friend of the baronet's."

"He did so indeed, my lady," said Mrs. Aberdovey, who hastened to explain to her the circumstances of Owen's letter, which had been posted to Jolly Jumper Yard but to which there had as yet been no reply.

The pursuit of the law was only a matter of time, certainly. Owen was sure that once his note had reached the captain that the authorities in Ridingham would be alerted. But as yet no one had heard so much as a whisper, nor had the constable come calling; whereupon Lady Martindale decreed that should George Pettiplace dare show his tunic at the Hall in connection with Owen, that he should be prepared for a set-to with the legal lights of Ridingham, Mr. Everson Gecks in the van.

"For we are no poor, weak, timid creatures here, to be bullied into submission by some witless limb of the law, " she declared, "but we are fighters. 'Be courageous, and be fortunate' — for thus it is inscribed on the armorial bearings of the Martindales."

No sooner had she so spoken than the room resounded with the approbation of everybody in it. With one accord they communicated their readiness to stand behind Owen should the bailiffs, or the constable, or even the Lord High Sheriff himself, presume to take steps.

"Let a guard be posted," her ladyship directed, "that no lackwits from town may approach the Hall to catch us unawares."

Naturally it was her father who volunteered to stand first watch.

"But you are not a well man," his daughter reminded him.

"Damned impertinence! Who's not a well man? Somebody other, that's who," rejoined Sam, with a crinkly stare. "None o' yer gammon now, Lizzie, and a figo for yer doctor's. I told yer, it's to the wall-walk, says I, and I'll 'ave no females tellin' me different. Nor even the flirty, foreign little minx of a pretty chicken as the young feller's smuggled aboardship neither. What d'yer think o' that, then, eh?"

And so having said he promptly stalked from the chamber.

Her ladyship, something at a loss to understand him, inquired what little minx of a pretty chicken her father might be meaning?

"Well? Somebody speak up," she commanded.

However, because no one — not Owen, nor his mother, nor Edgar, nor Gwenda, nor Richard — professed to have the slightest knowledge to convey on the topic, her ladyship snorted and instead requested they "pay no attention to my father". She then ordered Dan Hedges to post a watch of his own upon Mr. Gander, that no harm should befall the former publican and landlord of the Goose and Gander now retired.

Owen meanwhile was greatly relieved and appreciative of the welcome given him by Lady Martindale and the others, and of their vows of solidarity. Still all kinds of rumors abounded, and a few who were quick to pessimism wondered what might happen to the young man if, like a fly in a paper cage, he should find himself ensnared in the toils of the law.

"For once the lawyer-folk have done with him," they whispered darkly, "he'll be nowt but a peeled grape."

Would Owen be tried as a thief and traitor? Such remained to be seen. But would anyone beyond the present company believe his story?

And where was the loathly dog? Had his voice been forever silenced? It would seem Fate had baffled Owen's last chance at escape — the chance that Teech himself might have been persuaded to confess. And yet perhaps it was better he had kicked it, for there should be no danger now of his testifying *against* Owen. For how was anyone, even a clever counsel, to refute him should he swear an oath that Owen had been his compatriot in the theft?

"I pray we are fairly rid of him," was the view, and the devout wish, of Mrs. Aberdovey.

The mariner had not the slightest shadow of proof on his side. All this it might be supposed should have disturbed him a little, but Owen had resolved to worry over it no more. Admittedly it was long odds against. But perhaps Mr. Gecks might prove of assistance; perhaps some clever barrister might tear the opposing counsel to rags. Perhaps there would be no peeled grape.

It was a long road that stretched ahead of him, yet Owen was resigned to his destiny, be what it might. Formulate plans for the future he could not do, but settle down with his cutty for a quiet smoke he could, and did. Now that he had recovered the skimmer, his charge of great trust from the captain, he had but to await that word from Jolly Jumper Yard for which he already had waited long. But now it was to be here, in the safety of the Hall, that he would do his waiting. Northeave and the beast-haunted wood and his stealthy visits to the gatehouse were naught but a memory.

Undaunted by the prospect of further waiting — although it left him with a painful sense of his own helplessness — he explained to his mother that he would bide awhile at the Hall, but that unless word arrived shortly from the captain he would take it upon himself to return the skimmer to Nantle, and stand the consequences.

"For God does give and God takes away, in the brief interval permitted us on this earth. Who are we to question that? She was entrusted to me by the captain, and to the captain she must be restored. It is my duty, Mother, and a man must not shirk his duty, or he is not a man. Certain sure my father would have regarded it in no way differently?"

And so saying he excused himself, that he might attend to matters in connection with the skimmer and her refurbishing.

As for his mother she remained yet awhile, rubbing her chin and musing. For so indeed — and in just so many words — would her Morgan have said it, had he been alive. Whereupon she stopped short, suddenly recollecting that she had not asked her son what had delayed him that night in the farm office, for in the present excitement it had quite slipped her mind.

Then in the next moment, as if in a dream, a picture of the villain man in his bloodied boat-cloak loomed up before her — for good and evil, death and life, are strangely mingled in this world — and seemed to speak to her, the beads of crimson dribbling from his lips.

Won't do. Have your fun now. My time will come.

A Merry Go-rounder

P O O R Elzie Peek! With most everyone assembled in the drawing-room to hear Owen's story, the dimpled little red-cheeked milkmaid of a housemaid had been detailed to the gatehouse, in Mrs. Aberdovey's absence, to stand vigil over its chief and commanding portal to the Hall.

Ever eager for bits of gossip, Elzie found none in the gatehouse, having no one there with whom to converse but herself. So instead she found employment in the cultivation of her fingernails, and the primping of her hair and apron in the mirror, and other like feminine concerns, with which she busied herself while awaiting Mrs. Aberdovey's return.

She was so occupied when of a suddenty there came a crunching on the snow outside, followed by a sharp *rat-tat-tat* on the latticed window beside the gate. A face loomed large in its leaded panes. Glancing a look from her countenance in the mirror to that in the window, Elzie's expression froze. Unable to move — unable to gasp, to swallow, unable to utter so much as a syllable — she stood gazing in horror at what she saw there.

A head had been thrust in between the bars, and twisted round to peer at her through the glass. Its flesh was stained a ghastly shade of blue, and underneath its mariner's bonnet a bloodied kerchief had been wound about its head and chin. Its features were roughhewn and sharply etched, its staring eyes fixed upon her.

It was a face fit to make the very dead cry out. The bloodstains and cadaverous hue afforded it a likeness to that bugbear of her childhood, Rawhead and Bloody-bones, stories of whom a fiendish elder sister had been wont to terrify her into the wee hours of the night.

For some seconds she stood motionless, her voice stilled in her throat (the which, for the gossipy Elzie, was no small accomplishment). Then a mouth opened in the head peering in, and with trembling lips inquired if, like a good girl, she might see her way clear to admit a poor jack to the bowels of the castle, ere he should freeze afore its portcullis?

Gaping mutely, the maid shrank back and nearly fainted. She searched the apparition's horrid visage, the bound and bloodied face, the bonnet screwed down on the disheveled head — a malignant demon in a boat-cloak is how it appeared to Elzie. But it was the sticky-out ears under the bonnet that stuck out, as it were, and caught her eye. A spark of recognition glimmered; she knew such a pair of flappers never had graced the Rawhead and Bloody-bones of her nursery days.

His lips a-quiver from the chill — and his flesh blued from same — the caller demanded that he be let in, for "there be a shiversome wind," gruffed Diggory, his jaws chattering like a pair of castanets, "that may make a stiff 'un of a jack where he stands, split me if it won't."

The maid understood his complaint and hurried round to admit him. The groom was ushered inside and made his way quickly to the small fire that was burning there, to warm his hands and his outward person and in general to recover himself.

Naturally the inquisitive Elzie was keen to know where he had been and what had befallen him, that he should have returned in such a state.

As he unchilled himself there at the fire, the eyes of the thief and traitor gradually hardened, his lips steadied, and he began to assume his usual bullying aspect. He explained to her that it had been a close-run thing, his having only just escaped a mauling by a marsh devil while returning from his day out in Ridingham. The fen-slodger who had been giving him a lift home would have bolted, said Teech, had he not been shamed into defending himself against the dirk-tooth by the groom's courageous example. Although he had lost the weapon with which he had hewn at the cat's tawny hide, and whose impalement in it had sent the monster fleeing, the groom had acquired a greater appreciation of his own resources as a result. He had passed the night, he said, as a guest of the slodger and his family, but the fare at their board had been unrefreshful — "not fond o' spitchcock — no go — nor o' milk stout neither" — and he was anticipating with relish a platter of grub from the Hall kitchen.

Elzie lent an attentive ear to his narrative, with mingled astonishment and sympathy, and advised him that there likely was no one in the kitchen at present, as most had gathered in the drawing-room to hear from Owen Aberdovey who had just returned to the Hall.

"Aberdovey? Weren't he lost at sea? Davy Jones?" returned the groom, with feigned surprise.

"So folk say. But I never did believe it myself."

"Never did, eh?"

"Never," declared Elzie.

"Sink me if it ain't a shabby low place, this world of ours, where folks be calling a man dead as lives and breathes — won't do — not a whit. You say he's yonder? And none now in the galley?"

Feeling the pinch of cold and hunger, he had listened with secret joy, while struggling to smother the half-grin that had tugged at his lips. It was a lucky chance, he reflected, his arriving at this moment. From remarks dropped by the maid, he calculated that at the very least he could satisfy his appetite, then have leisure to conceal himself, before the inmates emerged from the drawing-room. After a confusing and toilsome maze of a journey on the marshways — the only slodger had been he whose punt Teech had commandeered — he was in sore need of rest and refreshment, before hatching his next scheme of action, inklings of which already were stirring in his brain. He would triumph yet, and again at Owen Aberdovey's expense.

"Ain't it just like the puppy to go home to his mother," he murmured, with a scornful chuckle.

"And what might you be a-needing of Owen?" the maid asked him.

The traitor stopped short at the unexpected query, and had to fumble for an answer.

"'Tis true, his welfare is a close concern o' mine."

"And how might you be a-knowing of him?" persisted Elzie.

Another stumper. How indeed should Diggory the groom, a new man at the Hall, be acquainted with Owen Aberdovey?

"Look 'ee now — 'tis that I know *of* him is the meaning I meant," he said, fumbling again.

The maid hesitated. She never had liked the man particularly, and there had been some gossip abroad not to his credit. But in the end she shrugged her indifference and led him forth into the yard.

"And there be his ship," she announced, nodding towards the skimmer. "Be you a-knowing of her? For she's a wondrous fine craft as can sail the skies. Heard you now of the flying lugger of the long coast?"

"Aye, I've heard tell of her — scuttle-butt, belike."

"Owen's ship be of that lugger," the maid said proudly.

"The devil you say."

"I do say," returned Elzie, "nor be I a devil to be saying it, Diggory Incognito."

"Damme," the traitor swore under his breath, "ifn't here be another meddlesome maid to perish and plague me."

Nonetheless he was well pleased to find that his scheme of action was taking shape so easily. His face under his bloodied kerchief grew hard with concentrated attention, as he ran his eye over the skimmer's bows. He was resolved to grasp his opportunity whilst he may. The scheme that he had devised was ridiculously, ludicrously simple, and occasioned a harsh guffaw on his part, which the maid returned with a mystified glance.

"Look 'ee here — you must belay your gab for a spell, and serve me by telling none as you've clapped an eye on me," he enjoined her, his voice quick with impatience, "not till peep o' dawn at least. For these Hall folk are apt to be a bit lubberly in the ways o' the world, and matters might well go foul and a-wrack for Diggory."

"And why for should I be a-doing it? And why for not till the dawn?" Elzie inquired.

The groom, smiling mysteriously, placed a warning finger to his lips and said no more; the which, in concert with his shocking appearance, was sufficient to so bewilder the maid that she undertook his commission without protest.

As she had returned to the gatehouse she did not see him pause in the loom of the skimmer and, glancing up, clench his fists vindictively. It was at this precise moment that the face and jowls of Melon-head appeared at the top of the cord-ladder. The cat's emerald eyes meeting Teech's glance, a growl of considerable ferocity stirred the animal's whiskers. The traitor fell back a step, absently patting his bloodied countenance, in recollection perhaps of the painful event that had occasioned his injury.

"By the by," said he, speaking to the cat — "nary another drop o' blood will you draw from *me*, shipmate — won't do — or 'twill be your own hide as pays the price for it. So avaunt, pal, and be warned! Bide you here awhile and put a seal to your ruin."

Then drawing his cloak tightly about him, and his bonnet down almost onto his nose, he hurried off, after first ascertaining that no observer beyond the tomcat was present in the yard.

Melon-head, watching from the deck, flattened his ears, hissed and spat, as if he too had been reminded of the unpleasant incident. Then raising his head he sniffed the air in the direction of the Hall; and in keeping with his adventuresome nature he scampered nimbly down the ladder, to follow wheresoever his curiosity led him.

A short time later a delegation of visitors arrived at the Hall and made their presence known to Elzie. Upon hearing their request, she opened the gate and pointed them in the direction of the tradesmen's entrance round the side. After a few minutes, when no one had come in answer to their summons there, the visitors took the considerable liberty — being familiar with the Hall and its environs — of admitting themselves.

A murmur of low-voiced conversation could be heard in the drawing-room, the which they surmised to be evidence of the assembly the maid had told them of. To await its adjournment they conducted themselves not to the little back-parlor but to the kitchen, having been attracted by sounds of activity there. You may imagine their surprise at what they found.

"And who or what have we here, then?" they demanded.

"As honest a man as breathes," said Amos Teech.

The table before him was spread with an array of victuals he had mined from the larder, and to which he had been applying himself with considerable gusto. The arrival of the newcomers caused him a moment's concern, having interrupted him at his feeding and his ease, and he regarded them with wary eyes.

"Honest tells us nowt," replied a short, broadish fellow whose chin ran down into his neck.

"Scorch me, 'tis no go — won't do — strangers in the galley — queer customers these. Who the devil are you? Identify yourselves, or be drowned in a puddle," the honest man blurted out.

"We're no strangers," said another of the callers, "we're tradesmen from Ridingham, here to collect on our accounts."

Having ascertained their purpose, the groom relaxed his manner. His air of easy assurance returned, as did his appetite. "Aye, not surprised — joint is skint" — this spoken with his mouth full of food — "lubberly outfit — old frump not up to snuff — "

"It isn't her ladyship with whom we have our business, if that is whom you mean," interposed an elderly little man with pensive eyes and a kindly, cultured face — it was Mr. Pinchbeck — "but with her nephew, Mr. Harbottle. I'm afraid he's months overdue."

His fellow tradesmen grumbled and nodded their concurrence.

Teech swept them with a shrewd look. "Harbottle? 'Tis matters o' coin be weighing on him again, eh? So-ho! Good luck t'you in that quarter — no blood to be got out of a turnip. Sink me, that's plain enough."

"You're a saucy one," said Dousterweed the tobacconist, he of the chin and neck. "Come to that, who are you, and what's happened to you? For speaking of blood, man, you look a fright."

"Like the very devil," nodded the tailor, Woolsack.

"Must have talked back to the wife," suggested Casken, the vintner.

"Or the other woman, eh?" chuckled the hatter, Derby, through his black mustache.

Teech, his mouth stuffed with a pasty, offered no comment. Rather he made a sweeping gesture over the board, inviting the newcomers to partake of the good things fortune had placed at their disposal.

"A square meal," he announced, once he was able — "with the compliments of Harbottle."

The shopkeepers hesitated. They glanced doubtfully at one another, and then again at Teech.

"We're here to collect what's owing us," Woolsack explained.

"And what of that?" shrugged the groom. "Collect it in part here. Being the gentlemen you are, sure you'll not refuse the chance to replenish yourselves? And at Harbottle's expense?"

More doubtful glances. But their resolve was fast ebbing away, after surveying the good things before them.

"He claims to be an honest man," the tailor noted.

"Honest as the day is long," said Teech between mouthfuls of pie and swallows of ale.

"But the days are shorter this time of year," Casken observed.

"All the more cause to lay in whilst we may," the tailor dittoed.

A brief colloquy apart from Teech ensued, in which the shopkeepers discussed again the object of their visit.

"Unless Mr. Harbottle settles today, we must send for the constable," reminded Dousterweed. "It's to be cash, or cash — Mr. Harbottle may take his choice."

"If we don't get our money, at least we shall have a meal," said Derby. "He took from us, we may take from him. Why shouldn't we partake, as this mannerless rogue suggests?"

"But then we should be taking from her ladyship, and not from Mr. Harbottle," Mr. Pinchbeck observed.

"It may be all a humbug, but I consider we shall have either satisfaction today, or some of this excellent lamb," was the view of Woolsack.

"Or some of this fine-looking ale," said the vintner.

"For if we've been trimmed — "

"It's a daft dog that won't lick a dish," noted Sweeting, the confectioner.

It did not take much longer. As one they drew their chairs up to the table and fell to with an appetite.

"Beautiful — beautiful," murmured Teech, munching and leering. "For men must do as they've been done by, messmates, or so the Scripture says, split me if it don't."

The example of Holy Writ, it appeared, was sufficient to temper most of their scruples.

"And is not Mr. Harbottle going in for the Church?" said Dousterweed.

The remark prompted an explosion of mirth amongst his fellows, Mr. Pinchbeck excepted.

"That's it — that's it — eat hearty, messmates," applauded the groom. "To your health, and to the victors the spoils," he said, toasting them with a stoup of Willoughby gray.

The shopkeepers joined in with much heartiness, again except for Mr. Pinchbeck, who felt himself somehow to be trespassing.

"I drink to the speedy conclusion of your errand," said Teech, toasting again. Many pleasant jocular remarks followed the seconding of his pledge. It did not escape his notice, however, that the time was swiftly passing, and that soon the kitchen would be alive with hurrying domestics, once the assembly in the drawing-room had adjourned. And if he himself should be found on the premises . . .

Accordingly he rose from his seat and with a flourish announced his entire readiness to enter again upon his day's labors, ceding the disposition of the victuals to the care of his messmates —

"To the shopkeepers of Ridingham!"

And so having said he left the room. Finding the coast clear, he pulled his bonnet low and slouched off in the direction of the stables, where he intended to pass the balance of the afternoon asleep in the loft.

" — in case matters be driven to extremity."

Such were the first distinguishable words to be heard as the drawing-room door was opened and the members of the assembly began filing out, some ten minutes after the loathly dog had sidled away.

"And a desperate character he must be," nodded Dan Hedges, being one of a group who had exited together.

"Called himself Diggory Incog — Incog — " struggled Rolf, one of the stable-boys.

"Incognito?" Richard suggested.

"That's it, sir. Sailorly sort o' cove, sir. Said it were Zingaro gypsies as raised him, but it were all a flam, that's certain. I'd a suspect he might be yarnin' us."

"Zingaro gypsies? There's a whopper," snorted Edgar.

"He was hired after we lost Tim Waghorn, as went home to Locksley to care for his sick father," Dan explained. "This Diggory happened along, looking for work."

"Work!" scoffed the stable-boy. "A do-nothing monkey. Bone-idle most all the day — the jug-eared pirate!"

"And the falsest that ever drew breath," averred Owen, who with his mother had joined the party.

"And nothing certain is known of his fate?" Richard asked.

"Disappeared he did, sir, bruised and bloodied," said Mrs. Aberdovey, "but not at my hand. A thing on the marshes accosted him in the night. I shudder at the thought of it."

"It's likely then he's passed out of the picture for good."

In the kitchen meanwhile the shopkeepers had become talkative, loud, even clamorous in their festivities. Now that the assembly had adjourned, it was to the kitchen that Mrs. Flitch and her minions had bent their steps, and there were witnesses to an appalling scene.

Grouped round the table like a pack of stray hounds on their haunches were the shopkeepers, their jaws and tongues making a sufficient clatter to shield their ears from the approach of the domestics and their chief. All of them, that is, save for Mr. Pinchbeck, who glanced round apprehensively as the door was filled by the ample presence of Mrs. Flitch, and her minions crowding up behind her, all gazing on the spectacle in blank astonishment.

Astonishment, to find a horde of tradesmen in the kitchen, the contents of the larder spread before them, the which grub they had been shoveling into their gullets with an eager dispatch. To be feasting on pasties and lamb and downing porter and Willoughby gray, was an entertaining and appetizing occupation of an afternoon. But Mrs. Flitch, whose nerves had been in disorder of late, did not find it so.

Glancing up from their festivities, the shopkeepers encountered the hostile stare of the cook, who demanded to know what was the meaning of this affront to her ladyship's house? For although tradesmen had been received in the Hall kitchen on many a prior occasion, never before had any seen fit to make themselves at home there without the courtesy of informing the staff.

Flushed of cheek, the tobacconist, Dousterweed, rose and proceeded to explain that he and his fellows had come to see Mr. Harbottle on particular business, and that it was this same young gentleman who, he testified, had given countenance to their feasting.

The eyes of the cook flashed their indignation.

"It bean't like Mr. Edgar to be so generous with her ladyship's edibles, and it bean't Mr. Edgar as gave leave for shopkeepers to be making merry in my kitchen. And I should swallow down my grin, Caleb Dousterweed, afore I should be taking one gulp more of her ladyship's ale. What then be your particular business with Mr. Edgar?"

"It is soon told," answered the tobacconist. "We are here to collect the just debts that are owed us by the young gentleman. He has had his week's grace; now we shall have our money."

"Belike you've eaten it," suggested Mrs. Flitch, eyeing the remains that littered the board, of which only a single item — a jug containing an inky, dark nectar, which was found to be bogberry juice — appeared untouched.

Another of the tradesmen produced a receipted account as proof of his claim upon Edgar. To his surprise the cook made a swoop at it, tore the receipt across and across, dropped the pieces to the stone flagging, and for good measure trod on them.

Retorted Derby, whose receipt it had been — "My brother-in-law, Mr. Jeremiah Slaw, who is landlord of the Lizard's Head at Dragonthorpe, shall hear of this."

"And what's the good of that?" inquired Mrs. Flitch, regarding him severely with arms folded upon her bosom.

"Never again shall he recommend the Goose and Gander to travelers bound for Ridingham," threatened Derby.

The cook laid her palms against her substantial hips and smiled. "Belike landlord Cuffley then, of the Goose and Gander, the finest posting-house in the city of Ridingham, no more should be recommending the Lizard's Head to travelers bound for Dragonthorpe to westwards?"

"Aye, she's got you there, Fred," Woolsack admitted.

"The which," said the cook, with an ominous crossing of her arms, "is not to say you bean't welcome at the Hall. But you bean't welcome in her ladyship's kitchen without her ladyship's leave."

The shopkeepers, their hunger appeased, took the hint — indeed they barely could scrape back their chairs fast enough. The cook was directing them to the little back-parlor hard by the tradesmen's entrance, when Edgar and my brother came striding along in the cross-passage.

"There he is," said Derby, pointing.

"Mr. Harbottle, sir," Dousterweed called out.

"If you would, Mr. Harbottle, please sir," said Mr. Pinchbeck, "a little bill — amounting to a mere eight-and-twenty — "

The youth shot them a startled glance.

"Assyrians — confound the luck! Can it be a week already?" he asked.

In a body the shopkeepers came rushing towards him. "Mr. Harbottle, sir — please, if you would pay us now, sir, or we must send for the constable . . ."

The youth had but one means of escape available to him. Needing no urging he thrust aside the vaunted courage of his Welsh forebears and, setting his chubby frame in motion, took to his heels.

"And there he goes!" the tradesmen exclaimed, taking up the chase.

"She is an excellent good girl, and much attached to him," Lady Martindale was saying as she stood in close conference with Treadwell in the next passage. "Although despite my assurances he remains in some doubt as regards his future. Perhaps we must shape out a little conspiracy of our own to bring them together, eh? What think you, Treadwell? Is it not a perfect match, my Gwenda and that excellent young man, Owen Aberdovey?"

"Very much so, my lady."

They glanced up in surprise to see Edgar hastening towards them. The youth, breathing hard, for he was easily winded, paused only to nod his respects to his aunt, before resuming his career. Throwing over his shoulder the words "my aunt will do the civil", he vanished round a corner.

"Whatever did my nephew mean by that, Treadwell?" her ladyship asked. "And why is he fleeing as though from a house afire? Can the Hall be alight?"

"I'm sure I don't know, my lady," answered Treadwell, "but I should think it unlikely."

At a furious pace the shopkeepers, one by one, then came charging up, each stopping to smile and lift his hat in deference to her ladyship, before scurrying on.

Lady Martindale cinched up her eyes and snorted. "Who are these people, Treadwell? And why are they pursuing my nephew?"

"Tradesmen from Ridingham, my lady. Mr. Dousterweed, tobacconist. Mr. Sweeting, confectioner. Mr. Pinchbeck, bootmaker. Mr. Derby, hatter. Mr. Woolsack, tailor. Mr. Casken, vintner," explained Treadwell the imperturbable.

"Yes, but why are they after my nephew? From the sound of it they have no very charitable designs on him."

Treadwell cleared his voice and was about to explain, when the noise of a dog's energetic yelping broke out in the corridor. Seconds later a small dark-colored animal went flying past their feet, followed by a gaily-barking Toddy.

"Lay on the terriers," the plucky fellow exclaimed. "Loose the hounds. Intruder on the premises! You may race like the wind, sable-coat, but it's all up with you. I'll buff your jerkin, my lad — see if I don't."

"Powers above, Treadwell, whatever was that?" said her ladyship, staring after them.

"Unidentified tomcat, m'lady, domestic species — *Felis domesticus.*"

"And what is he doing here?"

"Frisking with Toddy, so it would appear, my lady," said Treadwell, neatly disposing of the matter. "And now as you were remarking, my lady, about Miss Goodwick and Mr. Aberdovey . . ."

It was later that night, as the Hall was settling in to sleep, that a creaking of boards was heard in another passage, that leading to the kitchen. Its source was Mrs. Flitch, who was making her final tour of inspection before retiring. To all appearances she had quite recovered from her nightmarish experience of the shadow. No sooner had she arrived at the kitchen door, however, than the dread she had felt on that prior occasion returned in full measure — for her ears had detected a sound of some kind from within.

For an instant she paled, and looked as if she were wishing herself elsewhere. Drawing on all her resources of nerve, she considered what her response ought to be. Must she face the thing alone, as she had done before, or ought she to raise the alarm? But sure it could not be the shadow again! For this sound was not like that of the earlier night; this was no sobbing from the chimney-corner. Pushing in the door, she listened attentively. The interpretation was clear — someone was enjoying a nocturnal feast in the Hall kitchen.

The sound was of the greedy chewing, munching, gobbling, swallowing kind, as of someone bolting down a meal. As she pushed the door in farther, she noticed there was a light burning on the table. Certainly no creeping shadow would have need of that.

Somewhat eased of her fears, she pressed ahead, believing she was about to collar the miscreant who of late had been pilfering small items from the kitchen. He was a sloppy eater, whoever he was. But why remain in the kitchen and run the risk of discovery? Why not take the edibles and consume them elsewhere? Sheer laziness, concluded the cook.

Having regained full charge of her senses, she brushed back her sleeves and crept silently towards the table. As she drew near it her nostrils detected a familiar odor, one which brought a gleam to her eye and a smile to her lips.

No shadow she ever had heard of that was fond of alcoholic spirits!

The lone figure of a man, in a state of considerable dishevelment, sat hunched over the table. His back was to the cook, and before him lay a number of dishes which he was eagerly sampling, one after the other, and washing down with liberal quantities of grog.

"I'll teach you," vowed Mrs. Flitch, drawing herself up.

A faint rustling alerted the miscreant. Instantly he jerked round in his seat, a half-eaten cutlet in hand, and thrust his bloodied countenance into the glare of her taper.

"Aye — *Teech* it is, old girl," said the hardened traitor, grinning ferociously.

The eyeballs of Mrs. Flitch started from their sockets. Her jaw sagged, the gory spectacle of the groom throwing all the hairs up under her mobcap. But it was not "Diggory" whom she saw before her, for Mrs. Flitch too, in her childhood, had known the horror of Rawhead and Bloody-bones . . .

Of a sudden her nerve ebbed and, uttering a shriek, down she went in a swoon on the stone flags.

Alow and Aloft

A T last the fatal day had arrived. After spending rather more money than his aunt had allowed him, Edgar had been faced with a circumstance only too familiar to college men — the necessity of *cashing up*. And he without so much as tuppence to his name.

Everybody knew what these shopkeepers were, trying to bully it over a poor, struggling trog, by pursuing him to the literal steps of his family seat. And these were merely his Ridingham creditors; for he owed money besides yet to numbers more in Salthead. The idea of it, that a gentleman scholar should be expected to settle these little accounts before he had even taken his degree!

At first he sought concealment in the lumber rooms at the top of the Hall. But the loopholes piercing the walls there afforded him only a slim view of the courtyard, and none whatever of the gatehouse and gatehouse lane; thus he should have no means of ascertaining whether the tradesmen had departed. And as he had separated himself rather abruptly from Richard, he had no one who might communicate to him that information and thereby relieve him of his vigil.

And so the time wore on, Edgar waiting the issue with no little impatience. At length he could wait no longer. His watch, and the appearance of the sky, told him that the day was waning. Almost certainly the shopkeepers must have gone by now. Stealthily he crept forth from his retreat, a disused staircase serving as his avenue to freedom. About halfway down its treads, on the final flight of stairs, he paused to listen. The quiet was encouraging. At the foot of the staircase he opened a door and peered out into the corridor, one not far from the drawing-room.

Then straightway he shut the door again, for gathered in a knot at the end of the passage were the Assyrians, holding an animated discussion with Richard.

More waiting! What to do now? Nothing, he decided — save for easing the door open a crack and thrusting forth an eye, to keep watch of the situation.

In time the conference adjourned and the Assyrians, preceded by Richard, departed the corridor. Could it be the shopkeepers were retreating at last? Had Richard persuaded them perhaps of the folly of their enterprise? In the light of recent events, Edgar had come to regard his fellow college man not only as a friend, but as something of a trump. He meant to see that this good deed of Richard's should not go unrewarded.

It would not be much longer, he expected, ere the tradesmen should be on the causeway pursuing their journey home. So reasoning he strode boldly into the passage, and directed his steps towards the kitchen — for he was rather hungry after all the fleeing and concealing — when he heard voices ahead. Stealing up to the corner, he peered around it. Instantly his heart leaped into his throat, for there were the Assyrians in front of the drawing-room door, and to whom should they be speaking but to Lady Martindale and Richard!

Ominously the party, led by his aunt, then entered the drawing-room and shut the door behind them.

That tore it. Alarmed by this development, the youth made a volte-face — a right-about — and set off in the opposite direction.

"Asking your pardon, Mr. Edgar — " came a voice from behind him.

It was Treadwell — drat the luck! Edgar was forced to slacken his pace. "Oh, yes?" he called over his shoulder, not troubling to turn around.

"Her ladyship, I'm afraid, Mr. Edgar, requires your attendance in the drawing-room. Mr. Hathaway and the tradesmen from Ridingham — "

"Tell my aunt I'll join them presently," relayed the youth, edging away from him along the wall.

"You'll excuse me, sir, but her ladyship would have you know it's most urgent," Treadwell persisted — "otherwise very grave results may follow."

Jiminy, there'll be a murder now. Already Edgar could feel the concentrated essence of cowardice oozing out upon his forehead.

"Er — the deuce you say — fancy that — I suppose I'll have to see what my aunt wants — I seem to have lost track of the time," Edgar muttered in frowning reproof to his watch.

"May I conduct you, sir? It's just along here . . ."

"Not to worry," Edgar assured him, still edging along, and still not turning round, "for I know the way . . ."

"As you wish, sir."

The moment he was out of view the youth erupted in a burst of energy as if his very life were at risk, and flinging himself round the next corner was gone.

All thoughts of the kitchen and his appetite had vanished in an instant. Now he cast about him for another haven of safety, and emerging onto the courtyard he spied it at a glance. There was no scrap of cover between Hall and haven; he could but pray that no one was watching.

Dusk had begun to settle over the yard as he mounted the cord-ladder to the skimmer's deck. Breathing heavily, he paused at the head of the companionway and called down it to Owen. The answer he received was favorable, and without further ceremony he descended the steps.

The mariner invited him to have a seat at the cabin table. Grateful, Edgar sank down onto a cushion. He suddenly was feeling very tired. Exertion of any kind always made him tired, and some minutes elapsed before he recovered his breath. Then, as succinctly as he was able, he described his predicament to Owen. The mariner, nodding his understanding, suggested that he bide awhile in the cabin before chancing a return to the Hall. He was sure, given the hour, that the shopkeepers would soon be gone, and from the cabin ports Edgar would have a clear view of their going.

Owen, as it turned out, was preparing to nip ashore, where his mother was making supper for himself and Gwenda in the gatehouse.

Having thanked his friend for his kindness, Edgar wished him a merry evening. Once Owen had gone he closed the lantern — he wanted no light showing in the ports — and stretched himself out across several cushions alongside the table, intending to rest for only a moment, but instead was instantly asleep.

As in darkness had he slept, so in darkness did he awake. At first there was complete silence, and he wondered what o'clock it was. Certainly the Assyrians by this time were home and dry in Nineveh, for no one with an ounce of sense would be traversing the causeway at night. Then, as he was about to rise, there came a mechanical purring in his ear.

Startled, he heaved himself upright and struck a match, to find Melonhead sniffing curiously at his face. Truth be told he felt a trifle uneasy in the cat's presence, given what Henriette had related of the animal's history. When the cat yawned and stretched, however, Edgar found himself involuntarily following its example.

Through a port he descried a light in the gatehouse window; otherwise the yard was in darkness. Feeling assured that he was in the clear — until morning, that is, when he should have to face his aunt — he lighted the silver lamp over the table. He had begun searching the lockers for a bit of refreshment when he stopped short and abruptly put his head to one side, listening.

What was that odd sound?

It seemed to be coming from behind the door of the forward compartment. Tiptoeing closer, Edgar put his ear to the panel. What he heard there was a low, plaintive whimpering, as of someone suffering inexpressible anguish.

Edgar recollected the experience of Mrs. Flitch in the kitchen, and the sobbing that had attended her encounter with the creeping shadow. Or was it now the weeping shadow?

The notion that it might be the shadow — the Martindale family nemesis — on the other side of the door froze him to the spot. But what possible business can have led the shadow to the forward compartment of the skimmer?

Listening closely, he found he was able to distinguish a few despairing words amidst the sobbing — "Oh, my cheaile! My cheaile!" The voice of the speaker struck him as familiar, and not at all like that of an avenging family curse. At length he took courage and gingerly opened the door.

A thin shaft of light from the lamp streamed into the compartment and poured itself over the figure of the young woman who stood there. She had just dropped her hands from her face, upon her sudden exposure, and was regarding Edgar with mute and pained surprise. Tears stained her cheeks. Her brow was ruffled, her countenance as white as death.

"'Ow you 'appen 'ere?" she whimpered, in some confusion.

Instinctively she averted her eyes, so that Edgar might not observe her distress, and her embarrassment perhaps at having been so discovered.

Edgar too had to fight back his surprise. For this was not the delightful Henriette, the winsome widow with the dazzling smile, the ghostly peach to whom he and Richard had been introduced. This was another person entirely. Once so amiable, she gazed at him unsmilingly through her tears.

"Well, wat you want 'ere? Where is Owen?" she asked.

"I — I — I fell asleep," stammered Edgar. "I — I — "

Then a shudder convulsed his ample girth as a new thought struck him. All in an instant had it struck; already he could feel the blood ebbing from his face as the full horror of it dawned.

"'Pon my word," he quavered, sick with fear at the notion — "'pon my word, it couldn't be — it simply couldn't — "

Was it possible, he asked himself, that Henriette and the creeping shadow were one and the same? Could Henriette be the malevolent phantom

— for phantom she clearly was — who for centuries had dogged the male line of the Martindales?

Could Henriette be the one on whom Crispin Nightshade, the cobbler of Ridingam, had laid all the drudgery of his household? His poor relation, whom he had caused to rise from her coffin by means of the haunted leather that she might perform her labors even after death? His cousin and poor relation, who subsequently had escaped from him and who later had been hanged as a murderess?

Had not Henriette confessed to having murdered someone — her own husband — with the gammer's cup? And was this not the basis of the *pénitence* she had been condemned to render?

Edgar bit his lip, silently digesting this bit of speculation — or was it information? *Was it the truth?* All at once a shiver engulfed him, and he slumped back on the cushion.

It did not seem possible it was Henriette who had laid the curse on her cousin Nightshade, and on Sir Padrig Martindale, the Judge at her trial, and on the Judge's male heirs of succeeding generations.

It did not seem possible that it was she who had murdered Edgar's uncle in the farm office — had lifted him up and strangled him, while Owen's father watched. It did not seem possible it was Henriette who had murdered his brave train of ancestors — Sir Price, Sir John Llewellyn, Sir Dafydd — wreaking destruction upon the family.

Could Henriette be a murderess many times over? Was it for this reason that the gammer's cup had been cast into the flames? Had someone in years past discovered her secret, and banished her to Northeave? And now, importantly, was he, Edgar, destined to be her next victim? Had his time grown so short? Was he to be wiped from the face of the world, so young, so full of promise — and under the very towers of his ancestors?

If it all were true, then Henriette was a most excellent dissembler, who had fooled even Owen. For Edgar and Richard both felt that the mariner knew rather more about the widow than he had hitherto disclosed, that she had told him things about herself that remained a secret between them. What then to make of her ready devotion to him, the tender regard that shone in her eyes whenever she looked at him? Was this too a subterfuge?

And here she now was in the skimmer, laboring under some great burden of emotion, some hopeless and overpowering sorrow — Edgar could not believe it to be a sham. It all seemed so strange and unreal. But was not Henriette herself in a sense unreal? And what of her spying, her secret visits to the Hall? What explanation for it other than to gather intelligence, and thereby attain her end more easily — the ruin and extinction of the Martindales? Edgar simply could not believe it — he could not believe any of it. Still he began to be very afraid of her . . .

And so why frighten the cook?

Such was the chilly tenor of Edgar's reflections, when a clattering step was heard on companionway and a voice called down to him —

"'Ere, now — what's a-goin' on 'ere? Who's in there? Yer best not be bailiff's men, or constable's men, stickin' yer noses round 'ere, or it's h'out yer goes!"

Edgar shot to his feet as a grizzled figure in an old watch-coat hobble-dy-clanged his way down the treads and stood regarding him with a crinkly gaze. Having recognized the lad, however, the newcomer's bushy brows went up and a grin stretched his face from ear to ear.

"Ooh, so it's yerself then, neffy — and the flirty, foreign little thing — me pretty chicken. I did think there might be a scrap — interlopers and strangers and such — but so long as it's yerselves, then, I'll be keeping me steel scabbarded, and me alarum at the quiet," said Samuel Gander.

He had completed his tour of the wall-walk, he explained, and had been trotting home to the Hall when his keen eye had discerned a light in the skimmer's ports. Knowing Owen to be in the gatehouse, he had taken it upon himself to investigate the matter.

"For I ain't so old," he reminded them, "that I can't mix it up with the best of 'em — hee, hee! — though mostly me scrappin' days I've put behind me. The fisticuffs I leave to me Lizzie now."

Having seated himself at the cabin table, he invited Edgar and Henriette to join him. The youth quickly accepted, but the widow, having recovered a deal of her composure, advanced but slightly — her mode of motion being more akin to gliding than to walking — and indicated that her preference was to stand.

"Wat surprise. You are on the guard, papa? You watch for the enemies of my Owen?" she inquired.

"Yer Owen, says yer?" returned Sam, chuckling. "That's grand. But suit yerself. Why yer should be partial to a young feller not near so handsome as meself, nor so much the charmer, is a pertickler bafflement."

"You are rascal, papa. Wat shame you are so moche the younger of Henriette."

"What's that? So much the younger, she says? I'll need to pinch meself. Ooh, she's a good one, neffy, she's a good one! She's a pip," enthused Sam.

"Peep? Wat means thees peep?" queried Henriette.

"It means he thinks you're a trump," Edgar explained.

The murderess gave Edgar a pretty look, which he appeared to sustain with difficulty, for it had sent another chill through him. Hesitating what he ought to do, he cast about for a solution, and found it in a locker — a pint-bottle of rum.

"A little Dutch courage might be just the ticket," he reasoned. After the late revelation, which he believed to portend a fatal consequence to himself, something had to be done. He had to forget all that he had learned about Henriette and the shadow. Drowning his fears in a pint-bottle was indeed the ticket.

"It's a bit o' me own rum," Sam confided to him.

Edgar glanced at the bottle. "'Pon my word — so it is. From the Goose and Gander. Fancy that."

As it turned out Edgar did fancy it, and rather a lot too, as he swiftly drained a dram. "Oh, dear," he said, stopping short, "I trust Owen won't object, for it's his private stock." Then he tossed up his shoulders, as if throwing away dull care, and poured himself another. "Owen's a regular feller — the best that ever lived. He'll get the picture. Say, what's this, then? Jiminy, ain't it a wonder!"

To his shock he discovered that his grizzled relation — devotee of bog-berry juice, marsh tea, and cow's milk — had joined him in his carouse by dispatching a measure of rum at a swallow.

"What's the trouble, neffy?" returned Sam. "Didn't I tell yer o' me late evening with the pretty chicken, she as did give 'er husband the boot? For I've had me a think on't since then, and it ain't such a plague arter all, this rum. It's the family's own, the same as was served when I was meself Mine Host o' the Goose and Gander."

Meanwhile the drowning of his fears had commenced for Edgar, as he plied the pint-bottle stanchly. Thoughts of a rather gloomy cast filled his brain as he waited for the liquor to take effect. Mr. Gander too had drunk unto himself a goodly allowance, while reminiscing over his publican days, so that a second bottle had to be procured from a locker. It was the last of Owen's stock, and its contents would have to suffice.

Time passed. Edgar, his head reclining on his hand, soon was sunk in a deep reverie. Although he had been concerned for his personal safety, thanks to the rum it no longer signified. *Vita brevis* — was that not what he had learned in college? Mortality, and life's brief span — there was no contending against it; to do so was but a fool's errand. Presently he shifted his head's resting-place to the cabin table; a loud snoring ensued. In a like state, but sitting upright with his noggin thrown back and his mouth ajar, was Sam Gander.

Henriette meantime had been absorbed in her own reflections. So forcefully had they come over her again, that she scarcely heeded the presence of Edgar and the leetle papa of hair ladysheep. But eventually the state of their carouse — the hush, the snoring — caught her interest and, drying her eyes, she glided up to the table. She had not failed to note the altered manner Edgar had assumed towards her — she had sensed something of his discomposure and fear — and she wondered what its cause could be.

As she hovered there she stretched a pretty hand towards Edgar and, closing her eyes, bent her whole concentration on his dreaming mind. It did not take long. Startled, she opened her eyes again and glanced at him in surprise.

"Wat is thees? *Ma foi* — the cheaile — he theenk I am shadow?"

This set her to pondering for some minutes; then, still deep in thought, she began to move away when abruptly she checked herself. Glancing at the two asleep at the table, she reached a hand to the silver lamp. Instantly the light went out, plunging the cabin into darkness. Then she glided from the room and was gone.

Not long afterwards, under cover of the dark, a man came silently stealing through the courtyard towards the skimmer. He had tiptoed down from the stable-loft, where he had enjoyed a restful nap, and drawing near the ship was prepared now to execute the ridiculously, ludicrously simple plan he had concocted.

He observed a light in the gatehouse, but none in the skimmer's ports. Nevertheless, for certainty's sake he crept forward and peered in at the lattice, to confirm that Owen was ashore and not aboard his vessel. Satisfied, he returned to the skimmer and quickly scrambled aboard, drawing the ladder up after him.

On stealthy feet he crossed the deck to the cockpit and unlashed the helm. The ship now was ready-primed for departure. He drew his bonnet down tight, and his boat-cloak more snugly about him, and was about to lay hold of the wheel when a menacing growl pulled him up short. Glaring at the thief and traitor from the companionway, with fire in his eyes, was Melon-head.

The tomcat's warning brought an answering snarl from the loathly dog.

"Won't do, shipmate," said Teech, blackening — "won't do. 'Tis no go tonight. You'll not catch me peering in again at the hatch, as you did afore, and be savaging me with your claws. It's over the wall I'm going, and for the last time. I'll get quit o' this lubberly outfit — split me if I don't — and if you move to stop me it's overside you'll go."

And so saying he took hold of the helm and sent the vessel aloft. Gently, up and over the battlements, she floated, then out and across the home fields and on to the marshes fast a-slumber under the snow.

Ere he knew it a dark mass of forest rose up before him — the eaves of Marley Wood. With a turn of the wheel the black mass swung to larboard, as the ship assumed a southwesterly course that skirted the trees. Peering ahead the dog made some further, slight adjustment to his helm, so as to gather altitude, for his craft still was but low over the flats. His objective was to keep the wood in view to larboard for as long as possible, then hold to his compass heading thereafter.

While studying the way forward — what could be seen of it — his concentration was of necessity directed therewards; so that it came as something of a shock when Melon-head, growling and spitting, leaped into the cockpit and sprang with considerable animation to the wheel, to which he clung with a fierce tenacity.

"Damme! Stint your foolery now — begone — sheer off, you fiend o' hell!" Teech exclaimed, endeavoring to peel the cat from the steerage. But his efforts were thwarted by bared fangs and raking claws. He had no alternative but to relinquish the wheel, or risk further injury to his person like that suffered by his face. And so over went the helm, under the tomcat's weight, and the skimmer with it.

Glancing round, the traitor scarce could believe it. The mass of forest with its towering spires, which only seconds earlier had been riding off his larboard beam, now lay athwart his bows and was approaching at a rapid clip.

"Scorch me," gritted Teech at the looming disaster, "if this blasted devil ain't to be the ruin o' me — wood's a-comin' and plenty on it — "

Peering outside the cockpit for a better view, one not obstructed by the holy terror clinging to the wheel, he failed to notice the outjutting limb of a clumber pine that had come swiftly up on the skimmer. A rude *ka-thump* signaled a meeting of the tree-limb with the forehead of the loathly dog. A numbing blow, it sent him reeling, the bonnet flying from his head, and laid him out cold upon the stern-deck.

Moments later came the second collision — the meeting of a stand of Scotch firs with the bows of the skimmer.

In the cabin Edgar sat up in the dark, the force of the crash jolting him from his dreams.

"By gad — that rum's got a kick in it," he murmured, shaking his head. He passed his fingers through his hair and gazed about him. It was unavailing — there was nothing to be seen but the dark. To remedy the deficiency, he searched in his pockets for a light and struck it.

He discovered he was seated on the deck underneath the cabin table, his back slumped against a locker. Overhead a creaking noise betokened the rhythmic swaying of the silver lamp.

Dazedly he struggled to his feet. What had happened? He managed to steady the lamp, even to light it, then heard a groan somewhere in the cabin. From the shadows rose up Sam Gander, massaging his shiny head and wincing.

"Ooh, she hit me," he complained.

"Who hit you?"

"She did — the pretty chicken."

"She didn't hit you."

"Sure she did. Look there! Ooh, a tapper to me geranium. What d'yer think o' that, then?"

"She didn't hit you," repeated Edgar, yawning.

"Yes, she did — yes, she did — she hit me."

"She can't hit you. She's a ghost."

"She's what?" crinkled Sam, as if he had not heard aright.

"She's a ghost. Haven't you tumbled to it yet? She can't hit you. And besides, she ain't even here."

"Well, some feller hit me, and I'll know who it was . . . mix it up with Sam Gander, will yer . . . h'out yer goes . . . mix it up . . . "

Then his voice faltered, and wound slowly down like a watch; his expression assumed an appearance of porridge, and dropping onto a cushion he was quickly asleep again. Edgar as well, although jarred to brief sensibility, found the lure of Morpheus too potent for resisting, and soon followed Sam's example.

Another gloomy morn, of a dead pale cast through lack of sunlight, had risen over the marshes when consciousness returned to the traitor lying on the stern-deck. Shivering inside the folds of his cloak, he opened his eyes and grimaced at the pain that was beating like a hammer inside his head. Slowly his mind drew the scattered shards of his recollection together. The shaggy limb of a clumber pine had collided with his brow and rendered him senseless. It was the second time in as many days he had been knocked as flat as a flounder, the first being his crowning at the hands of Mrs. Aberdovey and the gammer's cup. It was no enviable record.

"Ahoy there!" he heard someone call.

Now who could that be? Without attempting to rise, he swiveled his eyes round in his head but saw no one.

"Ahoy!"

There it was again. Gradually he became sensible of a confused murmur of voices, arising from under the bows of the skimmer.

"Halloo! Is ony body yon? Come doun an ye will."

"Wha be the joker?"

"Frae whaur do she come?"

"Wha kens? Wha' shall we do?"

"Oot wi' yer tows and grapple 'er, gillies, and be canny."

"Aye, that we will."

"And dinna fash — for yon comes the Laird."

The next Teech knew a stout length of cordage had been flung over the ship, spanning it from rail to rail, and tightened down. Moments later a second rope was secured in the bows. Meanwhile the sound of horses' hooves plodding through the drifts had arisen, and of greetings exchanged between the men below and the newcomer in the sleigh that had come up.

"How came it yon?"

"We dinna ken muckle aboot it, Laird. Belike 'tis a fule joke."

"Never in a' ma days hae I seen sic a spectacle."

"But wha's can it be, Laird? And why for put it there? And how?"

"Never ye mind. Naebody kens, but methinks she's in bonny fine trim, an' ma ain sell's tae the boot of it. For 'tis upon ma ain land, indeedy, an' 'tis lodged in ma ain bit o' timber she is. And as 'tis trespass forbye, and abandonment, 'tis but juist an' lawfu' tae claim possession an' right o' salvage."

"Salvage?" Teech muttered. "Salvage won't do. Salvage is no go!"

"Sae we'll tak' charge of her the noo," resolved the Laird, "an' deil a nay-say will I hear, or ma name isna Phergus Ivor MacAllester MacWallop."

Chiefly, the Law

"SALVAGE!"

The word had stuck in the throat of Teech, and while he was coughing to get it up his jug-ears detected a noise on the companionway, that of heavy feet mounting to the deck.

He glanced round in quick alarm. He had thought the vessel to be his alone; plainly he had been wrong. But who could be aboard her? Not the puppy Aberdovey, certainly, as he had been in the gatehouse when the ship had left the Hall. No matter — an answer would not be long in coming.

Stiffly the thief and traitor heaved himself to his knees, and on all fours crawled round to the starboard side of the cockpit, from where he might observe without risk of being seen. With a sleeve he mopped his bloodied brow, victim of its collision with the tree-limb. His brain, too, was smarting, and his teeth were chattering from the cold, as he waited to discover who was ascending from below.

At last the final steps were heard, and a chubby figure on uncertain legs issued forth on deck. Yawning, stretching, and blinking at the gray dawn, Edgar lumbered across the boards to the rail and glanced overside. A combination of daylight and the sound of voices had roused him, and somehow he had managed to drag himself from the cabin to see what the matter was.

How foreign to him was the scene, which did not in the least resemble the courtyard at Haigh Hall. Where was the curtain-wall? Where was the gatehouse? Where indeed was the Hall itself and the towers of his ancestors?

Gone — vanished — nowhere in sight.

The instant he appeared a dozen pointing hands singled him out. They were the hands of the gillies who were milling round below, all of them in some wonder how and by whom the spectacle of a ship's cutter sitting in the Scotch firs had been manufactured in the night.

"Wha's yon?"

"I ken the lad, by ma certie. 'Tis young Mr. Harbottle."

"He o' the Hall? The nevoy?"

"Aye, the vera same."

From the seat of his sleigh the little rusty screw of a Laird, closely mantled in his Inverness cape, leveled his gaze and his weighty cosh of a walking-stick at Edgar.

"The auld corbie's nevoy!" he exclaimed, as if it were an accusation and not a statement of fact. His eye was hard and unswerving, and the lines of his face were grim. "Aweel, I'm no surprised — young Harbottle o' the Hall, is it? An' 'tis mony thanks t'ye, young gentleman, for the gift o' the boat."

Edgar's glance surveyed the upturned faces below, before recoiling at that of the little rusty screw with the hangdog mustaches who was shaking his stick at him from the sleigh.

"Jiminy! If it ain't MacWallop," he gulped.

With energy, but with some difficulty too, his aunt's odious wretch of a neighbor clambered down from his seat. Moving with his familiar stride — really more of a hobble, accomplished with the aid of his stick — he lurched through the snow right up to the skimmer's keel, which hung over his head, and pounded his cosh against her timbers.

"Be this her boat? The auld fiddle-face?" he demanded.

"Whose boat?" returned Edgar.

"Fie an' shame on ye, sir, fie an' shame! 'Tis the auld corbie's boat, I'm thinkin' — the warrior frae the Hall."

"Oh, dear. Is it possible you mean my aunt?"

"An' wha else wad I be meanin'?"

Edgar shook his head. "It ain't her boat."

"'Tis yer boat, then, belike, young gentleman?"

"Not at all."

"Aye, ye do seem ower young for't. Then wha's boat is she? An' how came she here? An' wha' business hae ye in ma trees forbye?"

Edgar shrugged. He had not the slightest notion how the skimmer had gotten here, or even where "here" was. He recognized Marley Wood, but aside from that . . .

"This be MacWallop land," the Laird informed him.

That certainly boded no good. What a mess he had gotten himself into, Edgar reflected — but simply the latest of many.

"Be her master aboard?" queried the Laird.

"No, he ain't here."

"Whaur bides he?"

"Well, that's rather hard to say . . . it might be at the Hall . . . or it might be on the quay at Nantle . . ."

The rusty screw threw back his ears. He whipped the fur hat from his head and leveled it at Edgar.

"Then I'll hae a judgment — I'll prosecute for trespass," he said, raising his voice for the benefit of his followers.

"You can't do that."

The youth's response was received with the scorn that it merited.

"The wreck is on ma ain land, and as Laird I do claim right o' salvage, for wrecks be salvage," stated MacWallop.

"The deuce you say. What wreck?" Edgar inquired, glancing about him at the skimmer riding easily on her bed of firs.

"Ye yersell. Ye're fair stranded! All wrecks in the domain o' the MacWallop do belong tae the MacWallop. I an' ma gillies hae seized ye. That's the law."

"Say, what is this? I never heard of such a law."

Smilingly the Laird glanced at his followers and shrugged, as much as to say — "Isna this mad work, ma gillies?"

Edgar for his part only could conclude that the man was laboring under a grievous misapprehension. Before he could respond, however, a clatter of feet was heard on the companionway. Moments later Sam Gander appeared and came trotting over the boards to join him.

"'Ere — what's all this, then, neffy? What's the fuss?"

It seemed that he too had been roused by the murmur of voices on the chilly air.

"You won't like it," Edgar warned him.

"Eh? Won't like what?"

Simultaneously there arose a howl from below, from the throat of the rusty screw, one that stirred his mustaches and breathed new fire into his gaze, and that sent his hat once more flying from his head to be leveled at the newcomer.

"Ha! 'Tis the deil's ain imp himsell — the gude God save us!" he cried.

The eyes of Sam narrowed to carroty slits under their bushy brows. "Ooh — it's the wretch, is it? Devil's imp, says yer? Well, that's grand," he exclaimed and, drawing his cutlass, announced his readiness to "mix it up" with any and all comers, first among them the odious enemy of his daughter's house and person.

"D'ye ken yon daft fule body, ma gillies?" the Laird called to his men.

"'Tis the Gander himsell — the fiddle-face's ain sire — and though a littlish man, natheless a muckle great bletherer. Up wi' yer blade, auld fule — for ye'll no be bringin' yer warlike ways tae MacWallop land."

His speech served only to inflame further the emotions of the bletherer.

"A figo for yer littlish man! What d'yer think o' that now?" retorted Sam, brandishing his cutlass. "A pox on yer and yers. I'll have yer up for trespass. Who let yer come in? What's yer business at the Hall? For if me Lizzie finds it out — "

A chorus of guffaws erupted from below.

"Yon be the bletherer, ma gillies. The doited fule," chuckled the Laird, "tak's MacWallop land for his ain manse an' mains. But dinna wonder at it, for 'tis this same fule as disna ken his ain right o' way in the Close. But come Sessions day himsell an' the auld corbie weel may be surprised, I'm thinkin'."

From the rail Sam glowered his crinkly indignation.

"Bother yer Sessions day! I'll soon sort yer out. 'Ere, whose land is this — yers or ma Lizzie's?"

Another burst of laughter. Mystified, Sam turned to Edgar for an explanation.

"What's the score, neffy? Is he hard up for a brain in's nob? H'out he goes, an' he can take his face with him. Ooh, it's 'orrible."

"This ain't the Hall," Edgar told him.

"Shoo! Not the Hall, says yer? O' course it's the Hall, neffy . . ."

Only then did Sam pause to glance round him at the Scotch firs, at the expanse of snowy marsh stretching off towards the wood, at the Laird and gillies assembled below — and above all at the utter absence of battlements, gatehouse, stables, courtyard, indeed of Haigh Hall itself.

"'Ere — what's happened?" he said, scratching his head. "Where's me wall-walk?"

"Whaur, indeedy?" the rusty screw hooted in derision.

"Eh?"

"Deaf, as weel as daft," the Laird confided to his followers.

Sam, snapping him a pert reply, was persuaded by Edgar to sheathe his blade. The memory of Mr. Gander ordinarily was very tenacious, but for the life of him — and the same went for Edgar — he found his recollection a blank so far as the skimmer and the bed of Scotch firs were concerned.

What had happened to the Hall? How had the skimmer come to be shorebound in a clump of trees on MacWallop land?

"We've been seized," Edgar explained.

"D'yer mean he's pinched the boat?"

"In a manner of speaking. It's to be trespass — and salvage."

"What's to be done about it, neffy?"

Edgar's face was glum. "No help for it now. This wretch of a MacWallop is a very low-lived party. Harbottle," he sighed to himself, "this really takes the prize. But deuce if I can remember *how* it was taken."

The odious neighbor meanwhile had no such thoughts to trouble him. "Dooms me," he congratulated himself, "'tis the auld corbie's sire — *and* her nevoy. 'Tis the baith of 'em I'll hae . . ."

Then he pounced, accusing the two of deceiving him. For if the vessel were not the property of the old corbie, he asked, what business then had her father and her nephew to be aboard her?

"By that does yer mean me Lizzie? Well, this ain't her boat; it's Aberdovey's. Bandog an' bedlam, ye're a fine one to be speakin' o' corbies, with a face like that on yer," retorted Sam. "Don't yer bother us now with yer gammon. Shoo!"

Again the Laird pounded the keel with his stick.

"Hout awa', auld carle, tae speak sic fulery tae the MacWallop! Dinna pit yersell intae a kippage, sir. Come doun the noo, an ye dare, as I'm juist minded tae acquaint ye wi' a thwack o' the pate. For 'tis a bit body an' a scaff-raff y'are."

"And ye're another," returned Sam.

It was at this juncture that Edgar, alarmed at the bellicose tone the discussion had assumed, made a last attempt at an explanation that might satisfy the Laird.

"The boat is Owen's — Owen Aberdovey's. Though in point of fact it ain't his own, exactly, but belongs to a Captain Barnaby, of Jolly Jumper Yard — that's in Nantle. He's master of a merchant lugger called the *Salty Sue*. The skimmer was in Owen's charge — "

"Was it, indeed? An' does this Barnaby make claim the noo?"

"Well, he — he ain't here."

"An' the mair's the pity. Tak' charge of her, Mr. Lash — ye ken wha' ye maun do. Secure yer tows there, gillies. Then ye maun send tae Ridingham for the constable."

The eyes of Amos Teech acquired a desperate cast, for what his jug-ears had heard had filled him with concern. Secure your tows, then send for the constable — all, it seemed, was lost today. The loathly dog should have no further chance to reclaim the skimmer. His ridiculously, ludicrously simple plan had been knocked to smash.

Hurriedly he swung round and crawled on his hands and knees to the forward deck. There, under cover of snowy branches, he contrived to slip overside and hide himself amongst the deeper boughs of the tree in which the skimmer lay. There, out of sight, his jug-ears now his sole means of following events, he resumed his vigil.

To Edgar and Sam the Laird made it clear that they should have to disembark — that is, be made to abandon ship — once the constable arrived.

"Then a' shall be decided at Petty Sessions," he assured them.

"Don't count yer curtains afore they're up," was the advice of Sam, the which was received with much laughter and a wealth of nodding and grinning.

Over the ensuing hour it seemed that nearly every man, woman, and child in MacWallop land — farm servants mostly, some tenant farmers, a few passing rustics, even a tinker — had been alerted to the news, and had come tramping through the drifts to form an audience of curious spectators round the skimmer and her guardian gillies. The murmurs of amazement were numerous as they milled about, staring round-eyed and open-mouthed at the vessel resting in her bed of Scotch firs. Had the like ever been seen in Fenshire, they wondered, goggling at the spectacle that overhung their heads? A subject of even greater interest, perhaps, was the mystery of how it had gotten there.

In the meantime, a little distance off, but within view of the firs, on the eastern edge of MacWallop land, a party of horsemen had ridden up. There they had been intercepted by a trio of gillies brandishing claymores, who were under strict orders "tae gie naebody but Constable Pettiplace leave tae venture nigh the firs." Foremost amongst the horsemen were Dan Hedges, Owen, and Richard. The party had been assembled that morning to hunt for the skimmer. They had found her, but for the present they could do little but remain observers from afar.

In a short while a carriage from town arrived, and the crowd of spectators round the firs gave place to permit the dignified passage of the constable. At his heels strutted a brother officer, of lesser rank — it was a cousin of his named Pontypool — and together they approached the tree in which the skimmer lay at her ease. Straightway the Laird came hobbling towards them, smiting the snow with his stick, and demanded "that the scaff-raff be hauled up for trespass", meaning Edgar and Sam, and by extension her ladyship, whose property he believed the skimmer to be.

"All in due course, sir — all in due course," the constable assured him with a benevolent air. "First I'll have to take the particulars, if you please."

From his tunic he drew his notebook, in which he proceeded to enter some few lines of notation, being those points he judged the most relevant to be gleaned from the excited and rather expansive testimony of the Laird.

"And I'll hae the caterans hauled up for't," MacWallop reiterated, with a flourish of his stick, "or I'll ken the reason why."

"I'll attend to it, sir," said the constable, nodding comfortably, "that is, if there's any hauling up to be done, as is laid down by law."

"An' hark ye tae this, sir. 'Tis salvage I hae in ma mind for the wreck, sae I maun hae a guard placed ower it — a braw, sturdy man, an' a sooth-fast, o' yer ain choosin', sae be it, till the matter be brought for'ard on the Sessions day."

The constable's pencil ceased its activity. His eyebrows rose.

"A guard, sir? Pending reference of the matter to the Bench?"

"'Tisna mony days hence the noo. I'll hae the boat watched."

The constable, brushing down his whiskers, gazed with a thoughtful air at the skimmer, then turned again to the Laird, his face a picture of suave assurance.

"Not to worry, sir. As I've said, it'll all be dealt with in due course. As for the vessel, sir, well — she won't fly away, sir, she won't fly away."

"She had better not."

"And how came she to be so situated in your Scotch firs, if you please? And equally important, sir, how is she to be got out of 'em again?"

"These, sir," said the Laird, glaring at the miscreants watching from the rail, "be matters I dinna ken mysell, though ye need nae fear, for I mean tae ken the ways o' the caterans afore lang. Aye, that I will, that I will. But list a wee, constable — why for d'ye no pit yer queries tae the fule bodies themsells?"

"I was just coming to that, sir, for I must take their particulars as well. It'll just be a moment, if you please."

The constable strutted up to the ship and rapped smartly on her keel with his knuckles. (The constable being unusually tall, her timbers were within easy reach.)

"Have you a ladder to hand, gentlemen?" he called to the pair aloft.

They did. Hitching up his belt he ascended to the deck, and approached the scaff-raff with a respectful attitude.

"Will you oblige me now with a brief summary of the events?" he said, opening his notebook.

It was Edgar who recounted for him the circumstances, what he knew of them, that had led to their present difficulty. At first the constable's responses were sympathetic. The discussion had not gone far, however, ere he arrested his pencil and turned a doubtful eye on the youth.

"Half a moment, if you please, sir. You report you have no clear recollection how this vessel became loosed from her moorings in the courtyard. And which moorings might those be, sir? And which courtyard?"

The answer he received was not very satisfactory.

"I dare say it might be so, sir. But as there is no marshway betwixt the courtyard and here, along which the vessel may have plied her course, it remains unclear to me, sir, how she came to be resting in some Scotch firs belonging to the gentleman below."

The next answer was even less satisfactory.

The officer permitted his glance to rove about the deck. It had not escaped his observation that neither ship's mast nor canvas was in evidence, and that the helm had been outfitted with gear of an unfamiliar design, and no discernible purpose.

The next answer the constable received was the least satisfactory of all.

"I dare say this puts a different aspect on it, sir," he said, his eyes opening wide.

"Don't it!" nodded Sam.

The officer eased the strap from his chin and rested his gaze on the witnesses awhile in silent appraisal. In the course of his career Constable Pettiplace had been treated to many a wonderful yarn, but none so wonderful, perhaps — or so much a whopper — as that related by Edgar, punctuated by the animated interjections of Mr. Gander.

Weighing the matter thoughtfully, the constable took several paces up and down the deck, as he digested the import of the testimony he had received.

"It's curious, right enough. Do you mean to say, Mr. Harbottle, that this vessel here is a kind of bird?" he asked.

"Er — well — not a bird exactly, but a flying ship. She's the property of a Captain Jack Barnaby, of Nantle. He has another ship as well that flies — "

"Ah, so there be two of them, eh?"

"Now you've got the picture. This first ship of his, a lugger called the *Salty Sue* — certainly you've heard of it? The marvelous flying lugger that sails the long coast?"

The constable shook his head. "Not a peep, sir — I've heard of no such object. Of course I ain't one as is much for the reading of newspapers, as such might interfere with the timely performance of my duties. I don't rightly know as whether you might not be pulling my leg, sir — begging your leave. But a bird — a flying ship — well, it stands to reason, don't it, sir, that a ship can't fly, any more than men do?"

"But men *do* fly," Edgar insisted. "You may ask Owen — Owen Aberdovey. For it's he who has charge of the skimmer, as she's called. Owen will show you how it's done, then you may see for yourself that men and a ship can fly. How else do you suppose she got here?"

"Aye, what d'yer say to that? A puzzle, now, ain't it?" crinkled Sam.

The officer deliberated long and hard on this point, before concluding that the matter was in need of considerably more thought, the which it was not in his purview to undertake.

"You see how it is, sir. My place is to take your particulars. What you tell me might well be so, but such is for the Justices to decide. That's the law. And the law, as we all know, sir," he declared, "is the law."

"Well, I like that," groaned an exasperated Edgar.

"Move along, move along — shoo!" chided Sam, whisking the officer away as if he were a troublesome fly.

The constable was unruffled. His tone remained unflaggingly respectful and composed, his expression unchanged. He proceeded —

"It's my duty, sir, to inform you, and you as well, Mr. Gander — and meaning no disrespect to her ladyship — that a charge of trespass is to be lodged against you. This being private property — MacWallop land — the landholder, Mr. MacWallop, intends to pursue the matter to the utmost of the law. As well he has seized this vessel, that which you term a skimmer, as be wrecked upon his property, and for which he intends to claim right of salvage. You'll have a chance to explain it all to the Justices, same as everybody else. If there's been a mistake, then it'll all be cleared up satisfactory, no doubt."

Edgar's countenance fell. It was plain that the officer did not believe his story. *Better the constable had kept himself abreast of the times,* he thought. What — not read newspapers? And what of the Llandudno brothers? As remote as they were from town, had they themselves not heard rumors of a flying craft that had been seen over the marshes? Was not most everyone within a circuit of thirty miles better informed than this string bean of a servant of the law?

Calmly the officer put away his notebook. "Now then, gentlemen, I'm afraid you'll have to come along with me. Nice and orderly, now. Not to worry — all will be settled by the Justices at Petty Sessions, as will be fast upon us."

Things had not gone well this morning, and there was nothing for it now but to yield. Edgar only wished he could recollect just how things had gone so awfully unwell. Before leaving, however, it was necessary that he shutter the vessel. First he relaxed the helm, as he had seen Owen do. As the cage-coil was released, he felt the deck stir briefly underfoot. (The constable, needless to say, remained unmoved.) Then he lashed the wheel.

"That's the lot," he nodded sadly, and with a final glance round he departed the cockpit.

The constable descended the ladder with the air of a man bringing a difficult task to a successful end. A murmur ran through the crowd as he was joined by Edgar and Sam. Conscious of their eyes, and even more of their voices, the pair were shepherded by a gillie to a saddled horse that awaited. Meanwhile their quarrelsome neighbor had resumed his seat of empire in the sleigh, arms folded and countenance triumphant, his bandaged foot riding on the dash-rail like a prize from some pharaoh's tomb.

"I'll have the watch posted directly," the constable announced. "You may proceed with the business, gentlemen, of securing the vessel."

The watch was to consist of the officer's cousin and subordinate, Pontypool. It was a lonely and most out-of-the-way spot, this stand of firs on the edge of the marshes, within a stone's throw of the darksome wood. It was no inviting prospect for a man of Pontypool's town-bred constitution, but he hardly dared tell his superior so. Meanwhile the tie-ropes, or tows, securing the vessel fore and aft had been fastened to stakes driven into the ground, for precaution's sake.

"Keep on your post till dusk," the constable instructed his cousin. "The vessel for the time being, pending reference of the matter to the Justices, is on no account whatever to be removed from its present position." Then to the Laird in his sleigh — "You may go along now, sir" — and to Edgar and Sam — "Gentlemen, you may return to the Hall."

And so they parted company. Edgar and Sam, upon their single steed, received a gillie's escort to the limits of MacWallop land, where they joined Dan Hedges and his party. Briefly, but omitting any mention of Henriette, Edgar related for them what had happened aboard the skimmer after Owen had left for the gatehouse. How had the ship become unmoored? It was a mystery upon which no one was able to shed any light. Although none of them had seen Amos Teech, Owen nonetheless suspected that the thief and traitor lay back of it.

As for Edgar, he made oath at least a score of times that he himself had had no role in the mishap. The last he knew they had been blissfully dock-ed at the Hall; upon awakening, he and Sam had found themselves shore-bound in a clump of firs on MacWallop land. Nevertheless, taking courage, and inspired perhaps by the example of his Welsh forebears, he valiantly accepted the blame for it.

"This stupid muddle is entirely my fault. 'Pon my word, I don't see how a feller could have made a more dreadful mess of things. Nice bit of work, Harbottle."

Guilt-ridden over Owen's predicament, which was even more hopeless than it had been before, Edgar cudgeled his brains trying to work out how the skimmer can have gotten into the Scotch firs. Was it at all possible that in his fuddled state he somehow had been the cause of it, and could not now remember? Regardless, the ship again had been lost — this time, to all appearances, for good and all — and to none other than their dirty skunk of a neighbor.

"This really takes the prize," he sighed, shaking his head.

Upon reaching the Hall, Edgar, Owen, and Richard deliberated further in the gatehouse, where Mrs. Aberdovey had prepared for them a nice collation and some warming drinks. It was here Edgar learned, to his great astonishment and relief, that one catastrophe at least had been averted, i.e., that his debts had been paid by his aunt, who had settled with the tradesmen and sent them on their way — minus a "larder fee", in respect of the edibles they had consumed in the kitchen. As it turned out it was Richard who had persuaded her to this action, by recounting for her certain experiences of his own — a trifle exaggerated perhaps in their particulars — while an undergraduate at Bearsnose, and by example implying that these little pecuniary excursions of her nephew's were simply a matter of course for a college man.

Edgar could scarcely contain his gratitude; and yet in the next moment it seemed hardly to signify, in consideration of the dreadful straits his other trump of a friend, Owen Aberdovey, now was in. See where the mariner's destiny had led him! It was enough to make any grown feller weep, Edgar complained — as if Henriette herself had not done enough weeping for the both of them.

"Bless me!" said Owen, catching his breath at Edgar's words.

Something in his tone stirred the youth's curiosity. Briefly he described for them what he had heard after he had boarded the skimmer — the sobbing in the forward compartment. While speaking he noted Owen's growing reserve, the averting of his eyes, and repression of the boyish grin that ordinarily marked his countenance.

"She talked of a child. I dare say there's more here than we're privy to," Edgar ventured. "Do you know anything of it, Owen? Is she — is she — ?"

At the reminder his brow darkened, as if a sudden cloud had gloomed it over.

"Is she what, Edgar?" Richard asked.

Is she the vengeful agent Owen's father had seen strangle Sir Pedr Martindale in the farm office? Is Henriette the creeping shadow, a monster bent on the destruction of the male line of the Martindales, and by extension of Edgar himself?

So much was in Edgar's mind, yet he could not give a word of it voice.

Was this the secret that Henriette had shared with Owen, and that the mariner, with understandable reluctance, to this point had kept from Edgar and the others? For it had seemed there was rather more in the relationship between himself and the widow than he had made known.

But he would have no opportunity to disclose it at present, now that Edgar had lapsed into silence. The youth simply could not bring himself to speak of his own impending destruction.

The next day the Hall received a visitor in the shape of Mr. Gecks. The attorney was ushered into the drawing-room, where my brother and Owen had been in conference with Lady Martindale. The business of the attorney bearing upon the substance of that conference, her companions were invited to remain. The business of Mr. Gecks, it turned out, was to report upon his interview with Mr. Wormwrath, counsel for the Laird, who, for the time being at least, had the whip hand of them in the matter of the skimmer.

Unfortunately the interview had gone rather badly, and straightway her ladyship's ire was expended upon her odious neighbor.

"The silly fool is a greater blockhead even than I took him for. His insolence and ingratitude are not to be endured. He is the most insufferable creature on the face of the earth. What that slippery little toad needs, Mr. Gecks, is a good poke in the chops."

"Sorry, chief," said the attorney, his eyes shining frankly and bluely on his client, "but Wormwrath I fear is immovable. I might as well have tried to snatch a pound of butter out of a black dog's throat."

"Well, the man is a black dog."

The lawyer's tone was grim — not at all like his usual manner. "We haven't so much as a leg to stand on, and well he knows it. MacWallop is entirely within his rights."

"Powers above," returned her ladyship, "and have we no rights left at all?"

"In this instance, in the eyes of the law — "

"The law? The law? Where is the law when the dirty skunk takes an axe to my fences and burns them?"

"I do sympathize with you, chief."

"Where is the law when that spiteful little man, with no vestige of decency in him, brings suit against me for trespass on my own ground?"

"It's a rank injustice, I grant."

"What, have we no longer starch in our spines? Have we become such feeble weaklings that we permit ourselves to be trodden on? That the law itself indeed, in these times of ours, *invites* us to be trodden on? Will you remind me again, Mr. Gecks — of what good to us is the law?"

The attorney straightened his shoulders, and in his rich Fenshire brogue had just commenced an explanation, when his client cut him short.

"Ridiculous, and a perfect flam," she sniffed. "I'll be brief. I don't care a whoop about precedents or legal subtleties. It was only the baronet who kept the imbecile in check. He was afraid of my husband, you know — the ungrateful piker!"

"Can they really bring it off?" Richard asked.

"I greatly fear so. Their chief obstacle is to explain how the vessel was placed in the trees," the lawyer replied. "However it does not rest with us, and as I can think of no pretext for reopening our discussion of the morning — "

"What, nothing to take the snap out of him today, Mr. Gecks?" her ladyship inquired.

The attorney, knowing his client as he did — she being a woman accustomed to minding nobody's opinion but her own — smiled tolerantly.

"Nothing at present, Lizzie. I fear the matter is closed for now. But it will play out before the Bench directly, for Petty Sessions are nigh upon us. And country Justices may do surprising things."

But her ladyship, being the woman she was, was equally confident on her own points.

"My neighbor is a man used to getting the best of any bargain. But he'll find we'll not shrink in the washing — won't he, Mr. Gecks?"

"Of a certainty, chief," he assured her.

And there the matter lay, leaving Owen Aberdovey to contemplate his prospects, which seemed very dim now indeed. As he departed the Hall he felt his cheek touched by a breeze as soft as a whispered secret.

THE FIFTH CHAPTER

Something Right Somewhere

A NEW day was rising in the east — Sessions day, marking the opening of Petty Sessions in Ridingham.

As if by a miracle a rare, sunny dawn had broken over the marshes, putting to flight the relentless gloom of Fenshire skies. Everywhere the snowy flats lay gleaming in the sun, the marshways that riddled and crossed them shimmered.

As the morning progressed, the citizens of Ridingham were treated to a sight as never before had been seen in the quaint old town. Not long past eight o'clock the town gates were opened and a shaggy red mastodon came plodding in from the causeway. Behind the beast, riding some twenty feet in the air, was the skimmer. The lengths of rope with which the gillies had seized her had been secured to the mastodon's harness, so that the animal's considerable strength could be employed in dislodging the vessel from the firs. Once free, she had been towed to Ridingham to provide evidence for the first case that was to come on at Petty Sessions.

For Mr. MacWallop, having a degree of influence in the law courts, had arranged that his case should be the first, holding pride of place before even his other action for trespass, that concerning the right of way in Hatter's Close. For once the skimmer had been loosed from her perch, the marvel that she was had become only too clear to the Laird, and as well to Constable Pettiplace, who had superintended the operation.

And so there was no doubt about it, that men and a ship could fly, as Edgar had maintained; although the question of what held her aloft was a puzzle. It had made the Laird doubly happy to be salvaging so valuable a wreck, and doubly fortunate that the skimmer had chosen his own Scotch firs upon which to cast herself. For it had eased his pain somewhat, that incurred by the expense of hiring a thunder-beast and driver to bring the vessel in.

It became almost like a holiday in Ridingham, as the mastodon and its burden came to a stand in the road before the courthouse. An air of excitement prevailed, and one might have been forgiven for believing that a circus had arrived in the town, for nobody ever had seen a flying ship before. By nine o'clock all was gaiety, bustle, and activity there in the road. Numbered amongst the throng were many of the distinguished worthies of Ridingham, lending luster to the occasion. Those of the graybeards in attendance had seen wonders in their day, but nothing to rival that of a ship's cutter floating in air. Even the Llandudno brothers had paddled their coracles to town to see it. Suddenly everybody was interested in the case that was to open Petty Sessions.

Lady Martindale and her party soon arrived, her ladyship being concerned in both actions for trespass that had been brought by her neighbor. A long, low, vaulted chamber, darkly paneled in oak, glowered upon them as they entered — this was the courtroom. Illumination was supplied by a few wax-lights, and by a single, high window, long and narrow, and crossed with iron bars, through which the sunbeams were filtering. There was comparatively little free space in the room, much of it reserved for persons concerned in the cases that were brought. Members of the public who could be admitted occupied benches behind those taken up by the interested parties. Those in excess had been banished to the road outside, where they passed the time gawking at the skimmer, or jawing with the mastodon man, while awaiting news of the case.

The back benches this morning were filled to capacity with a gabbling throng of spectators. There barely was room for a well-fed child to pass, so much enthusiasm was there for the case.

"See where the termite crouches," her ladyship remarked, glaring dark eyes at her accuser. Flanked by Lash and some other of the gillies, the said MacWallop was lounging on a bench across the way, his mummied foot elevated on the pew-back before him.

"He looks a confident gent, don't he?" Edgar worried.

"He looks more a nasty little toad to me. But pride goeth before a fall," his aunt reminded him. "Nor is that pest the sole exemplar of confidence in these chambers, as I have myself every confidence in our Mr. Gecks. But in the law I have none."

A man and his wife, as they were passing, smiled at Lady Martindale and nodded their compliments — "Good morning, your ladyship."

"What's good about it?" the widow demanded, and sent them scurrying.

"I wonder, where is Mr. Gecks?" Mrs. Aberdovey asked.

"There be no sign of him," said Dan Hedges.

"Ah — there he is now," Richard indicated.

They saw the attorney enter from a side-door and take his place in the well of the Court, at a table reserved for the use of counsel. There he disinterred a sheaf of documents from his blue bag and began arranging them in little piles before him. Mr. Wormwrath, who had been seated already for some while, regarded his adversary with smug satisfaction.

"There's the wretch's hireling, at his old tricks again," her ladyship remarked.

"He looks a rough customer," Richard said.

"Forever bringing suits in law for his unmitigated nuisance of a client. One would think he had no other business to occupy his hours. But our Mr. Gecks will soon sort him out."

The aim of Petty Sessions was to deal summarily, *sans* jury, with legal matters that did not warrant a hearing in the more formal setting of Quarter Sessions. Counsel, when present, served in an advisory capacity, in conjunction with the Sessions clerk, to illuminate and clarify applicable points of law, but did not as such argue cases before the Bench.

"Certain sure, Mr. Gecks will need his wits about him this morning," Owen said.

The others nodded their agreement. It was imperative that the case be brought to a favorable end, for the alternative simply was too hideous to contemplate — MacWallop triumphant, and the skimmer declared his property.

"'Ere, would yer look at that face — ooh, it's 'orrible," muttered Sam, grimacing.

The countenance so impugned was that of the termite as he lolled upon his seat, a face whose air of confidence fairly shouted — "I'll hae ma verdict — I'll hae ma judgment — the baith of 'em!"

Yes, my brother reflected, it was indeed too hideous to contemplate.

Her ladyship, casting her eyes round at the few paintings, dimmed by smoke, that hung upon the walls, remarked — "I'm not at all sure I care for the manner in which our public buildings nowadays are decored. My word, will you look there. What! Cherubs in a courtroom? It looks to be one of those funny, French things, by Boudoir. Is it by Boudoir?"

"I'm certain I don't know, my lady," said Mrs. Aberdovey.

"Well, it very likely is. However my sight is so short these days — "

"Silence, if you please," intoned the constable, as the Justices, three in number, entered, and ascended to their places at the top of the courtroom. These magistrates, none of whom possessed a legal degree — only the Sessions clerk had that distinction — all were gentlemen of consequence in the town, whose service on the Bench was undertaken in the spirit of *noblesse oblige* and an interest in the common weal.

The Chairman of the Justices, one Squire Goslow, flanked by his fellow magistrates, calmly surveyed his domain. The Chairman was a grave-featured, elderly man, with a heavy growth of white beard and whiskers ascending up to his brows on either side. The Sessions clerk, Mr. Phlax, in the interim had assumed his post at his desk in the well of the Court. He was an alert, active little man, with smiling black eyes that he was in the habit of blinking very rapidly.

The Chairman peered down from the Bench. In his turn Mr. Phlax, a rising young solicitor in the town, rose.

"What is the charge?" the Chairman asked.

"May it please the Court," said the clerk, "a case of trespass."

"Who brings it?"

The clerk read out the full text of the charge. He then nodded to Constable Pettiplace, a signal for the officer to usher the defendants in the case, Edgar and Sam, to the dock that stood beside the Bench. This dock was a kind of small, wooden pen, like that used to restrain farm animals, for the accommodation of the accused.

"Be courageous, and be fortunate," Edgar had been repeating to himself while waiting. *Rather better to be fortunate, and not to need the courage,* he reflected as he stepped into the pen.

"Not to worry, neffy," Sam assured him, "for so soon as our Mr. Lawyer spouts his mumbo-jumbo, his statues and his cognizances, it's h'out we goes."

"Is counsel present?" the Chairman asked.

Messrs. Gecks and Wormwrath respectfully made themselves known to the Court. The Chairman then turned his attention to the defendants.

"You have heard the charge. How do you plead? Guilty," he said, "or not guilty?"

At this precise instant the eyes of Richard caught something in motion in the high window. At almost the same time the beams of the sun were interrupted there as if by an encroaching cloud. But this was just the start. A further, profound darkening of the courtroom, as though by a hand that had swept down from heaven and blotted out the light, sent whispers racing round amongst the spectators.

"Silence, if you please," reminded the constable from his station at the door.

"How do you plead?" the Chairman said again.

Meanwhile a confusion of voices, as of people in a state of great excitement, had been rising on the air, as had other evidence of a commotion — sounds of children running and dancing about, and exclaiming with glee, of dogs barking and people clamoring, in the road before the courthouse.

The spectators shot questioning glances at one another. Whatever could the matter be? Already many had lost interest in the proceedings and were chatting excitedly amongst themselves.

The Chairman, having for a moment lent a wondering ear to the disturbance, endeavored to assert his authority.

"Order," he commanded, rapping on his desk. "Order."

In the dock the defendants glanced at one another in bewilderment.

"Jiminy, what's the fuss?" Edgar asked.

"Ooh, there might be a scrap any minute," said Sam, rubbing his hands and chuckling. "Mix it up, mix it up — bother their Petty Sessions — let's see what the score is, neffy," he suggested, moving to exit the dock.

"Order," droned the Chairman of the Justices. "Order."

Audible now through the high window were some of the individual voices being raised in the road outside.

"What in the name of wonder — look 'ee there!"

"Body o' me, what is it? That ain't a cloud."

"Saints and angels!"

"Ned, come away from there!"

Now that the curiosity of most everyone had been aroused, the people surged about like startled horses, their expressions of alarm awakening every echo in a vaulted chamber still dimmed by the hand that had erased the light.

Owen, his heart pounding, jumped to his feet. A light of another sort had dawned in his mind — a ray of hope, of deliverance, shining through the gloom.

Richard darted him a look, as it rushed upon him what the matter was. "Gracious, Owen," he said, "is it possible your luck has turned?"

In a body — and ignoring the Chairman's repeated calls for order — the spectators flung up their hands and made for the door. Ere anyone knew it they had thrust it open and were beating a path to the road outside, much to the dismay of the constable.

"Order," persisted the Chairman of the Justices, banging his gavel. "Order, order. This is a Court of law."

But the hubbub rather increased than diminished.

"Now then, now then — I'll have to take steps," the constable warned as the river of humanity, all unheeding, streamed past him into the corridor and was gone.

"Clear the courtroom," the Chairman ordered, a trifle belatedly.

Constable Pettiplace, finding the room vacant but for the Justices and Mr. Phlax, all of whom had stuck doggedly to their posts, begged his leave of them that he might discharge his duty, by seeing what the trouble was in the road. His petition granted, what met his glance there was a wonder and a marvel to behold.

Under a brilliant heaven an enormous shadow had come gliding to a stop on the ground before the courthouse. Shaggy red thunder-beast, mastodon man, the assembled crowd in the road — all lay prisoned in the spell of its umbra. The traffic had come to a stand, and everyone was gawking and pointing into the sky. The constable raised startled eyes to the object of their admiration — the source of the shadow, and a phenomenon such as never before had been glimpsed in Ridingham.

It was a thing of wild fancy, and yet there it was in plain view above him. Haloed by the sun, it was the underside of a mighty vessel which had stationed itself in the air over the courthouse. What a magnificent sight she was — as buoyant as a cork, and riding gracefully on the breeze. From his vantage point he saw that she bore three lofty masts, although her lug-sails at present were furled. Along her high-curving beam stretched a rail, and along it a line of faces could be seen peering down, those of merchant mariners in blues and jerseys, scarlet jackets, and seaman's bonnets.

She was a stout-built craft, to all appearances mighty staunch and skyworthy. Her hull, the constable noticed, had been wrapped crosswise with lengths of ship's-cable, doubtless to strengthen her timbers for flight. From her main on high fluttered a white ancient, and blazoned upon her prow were the words — SALTY SUE.

The officer's eyes roved briefly to the skimmer, which seemed dwarfed now by the giant looming above her. If the skimmer were like a baby boat, he reflected, then this other undoubtedly was the mother craft.

Richard, gazing spellbound at the sight, pushed back his hat and exclaimed — "Well, I'm jiggered."

The mastodon man had ascended to his cab, having encountered some difficulty in keeping his restive beast in check since the arrival of the lugger. Meanwhile Richard and others of her ladyship's party pressed forward into the road, where a cord-ladder of some length depended from the deck of the vessel.

"Ahoy!"

The call came from a stalwart-looking individual in a wide blue coat festooned with buttons, who stood amongst the ship's company at the rail. The lineaments of this skipperly salt were not unknown to Owen, nor was his voice, the tones of which struck very familiarly on his ear.

"Ahoy! Owen! Owen Aberdovey!" called the captain — for indeed it was he.

Owen, uncertain at first what to expect, stood a moment motionless. Then, having nerved himself sufficiently, he thought, he raised a hand in acknowledgment of the greeting.

"Smite me dumb and split me, 'tis good to see ye! Easy, lad, and stand by now," the captain instructed him from on high, "while we fetch her in safe and sweet and all a-tauto."

Owen nodded his understanding, and after a brief word with the constable the two of them commenced a gentle shepherding of the spectators to a safe distance, out from under the loom of the vessel. When this had been accomplished, the captain signaled his steersman standing aft at the helm. Directly the great ship swung majestically round and began her slow descent into the road. At last her long keel touched ground. All eyes then were bent upon the ladder as the members of her company scaled nimbly down it, as easily as if the distance were no more than a child's leap.

In advance of his men, Captain Barnaby, he of the wide blue coat, came clinking up to Owen with large, skipperly strides. He wore a cutlass at his hip, a pair of dreadnought trousers secured by a belt of many pockets, and sea-boots. A thickly-coiled mass of shawls and mufflers, like hawsers in a rope-yard, hung from his neck, and his great silvery head was crowned by a mariner's bonnet.

"Give me yer hand, shipmate," said he, Owen obliging, "for sarten sure I'd thought ye'd gone to bunk with Davy Jones these many weeks," and gave his lost mariner a joyous clap on the shoulder.

A gentleman stout in body, and valiant in heart — in such words had Owen described his superior to Lady Martindale and others at the Hall. All grins and salt and skipperly good cheer, the captain paid his compliments now to her ladyship by doffing his bonnet and making a respectful sea bow.

"My name is Barnaby," he announced in a booming voice of ready cordiality.

"I know who you are," said she. "Do you know who I am?"

"Cherish my guts, yer ladyship," he answered, bowing again, "I do. For douse me if ye bean't the barynet's widder."

"My husband was a friend of Captain Clipperton's. You knew Clipperton?"

"A name to conjure with, yer ladyship, or I'm a jack mackerel, for no finer skipper to serve under ever stood in sea-boots. And the lad Aberdovey — scorch me but his own father did serve with Clipperton too."

"It was the baronet who made it so."

"I bleeve I've heard tell o' that afore," the captain nodded.

Others of the party now were introduced to him.

"I'm happy to make your acquaintance, to be sure," Richard said with enthusiasm.

The captain was a large, hatchet-faced man, with piercing eyes, a bold beak of a nose, and a chin as narrow and pointed as the prow of his vessel. When he flung out his gloved hand it closed about my brother's fingers as if to swallow them in its iron grip.

The captain and his men had been overjoyed to hear that Owen Aberdovey still lived. They had thought that the skimmer had been lost in the rescue, a victim of the ice storm, and that Owen and Teech had drowned, as no trace either of them or of their vessel had been discovered. Early reports that the skimmer had plunged into the channel soon matured into common knowledge. Some of the passengers had observed the skimmer's uneven flight after she had deserted them on the reef, and amidst the chaos of raging hail and spindrift believed they had seen her drop into the murky waters.

And so the mournful news had been conveyed to Mrs. Aberdovey that her son was presumed lost at sea. The passengers and crew huddling on the rocks had been safely recovered; not a one of them had succumbed to the jaws of the waiting zeugs, the hugeous fierce dragons of the deep.

Importantly, Captain Barnaby had returned to Jolly Jumper Yard after a brief voyage to find Owen's letter awaiting him. And so they had fetched out at once, captain and company, and had sighted the skimmer in tow before the courthouse as they were passing over Ridingham.

"Aye, she did put on her best speed for ye, lad," said the captain, filling his cheek with a quid, "for ne'er was such duck of a craft as the *Sue,* and nary another so stout and true, and sweet to her sky-helm — 'less it be the skimmer herself, eh? Though sink me this do be remote country, benorth o' the woodlands here, and somewise out of our ordinary course. But once she sniffed her way there was no stopping her. Asides which the exercise of her cage-coils does keep her in trim."

"'Ere, what d'yer think o' that? There's a figo for Bossy and his facts. It's the exercise as keeps her in trim," chuckled Sam Gander.

"Look 'ee now, lad, here's Bob Sly," the captain went on, motioning to a lanky, straight-backed, soldierly member of his company to step forward. Nodding and smiling, the first mate of the *Salty Sue* advanced with a nautical, rolling gait, and clasped hands with Owen.

"Aye, the cappie's mighty glad to see all's right as a trivet and shipshape with ye," he announced, with a long wag of his head, "and 'tis no less goes for the lot of us, by gum."

"It's right good of you to say, Bob."

"And look 'ee here, now — here's Spider Joe, lad — and Nat Conger — Will Spatchett — Adam Windlass — " enthused the captain.

One by one the members of the company presented themselves, taking Owen's hand and welcoming him back like a modern Lazarus from the abode of Davy Jones.

"Ye've been hard tasked, shipmate," the skipper allowed, "and 'twould ha' been sure death and sarten there in the channel, sink me, and deserved too, for a scurvy knave of a traitor, or so it might have been writ; though I should have regretted the loss o' the skimmer. I bleeve I'd not have given a louse for yer fortune, lad, after the tempest, were it not for Mr. Sly."

"Bob? Why, what has Bob to do with it?" Owen asked.

"Nary a thing," returned the captain, assuming an air of mystery, albeit with a grin lurking at the corners of his mouth — "soak me and bleed me, save for the fact he did clap eye on all in his glass."

Not wholly comprehending, Owen glanced again at the first mate, who responded with a knowing nod, and who then broke into a cackle and slapping his thigh exclaimed —

"Aye, right enough. Nor louse nor flea, by gum!"

It required the captain to step in and explain. It turned out that Owen had Mr. Sly to thank, in large part, for his deliverance from infamy. It really was very simple. It seemed that the first mate had been observing the progress of the operation in his spyglass. Through the blizzard of salt-spray and hailstones he had kept a careful watch of the survivors on the reef, and of the zeugs snapping hungry jaws in the waters hard by. No sooner had the skimmer, with Owen and Teech aboard, settled into place alongside the rocks than Bob Sly had shifted his glass to her deck. He was watching, moments later, when the loathly dog rose up and, taking Owen by surprise, dealt him a vicious blow, stunning him. The last Bob had seen of the skimmer amidst the confusion, she had been charting an erratic course dangerously low over the tumbling waters. The next he knew she had vanished in the gloom. To the first mate it seemed impossible that she could have survived, given the weather and particularly with Amos Teech at the helm. And certain of the passengers afterwards had testified they thought she had gone down in the channel.

Hearing all this, Owen gave a rueful sigh. He shook his head in frustration, and not a little wry amusement, chiefly at his own expense. All of his and his mother's worrying, it appeared, had been for nothing. The dreadful crime he believed had been imputed to him had been the product solely of his imagination. Now it was clear why news of it had never reached Ridingham or had appeared in its daily papers.

As for Captain Barnaby, it had come as no shock to him that the thief and traitor had been Amos Teech. It seemed that Teech was a distant cousin of Mrs. Barnaby's — a sufficing reason for the skipper to have awarded him a post on shipboard. The captain had long suspected the man of being a scoundrel, however, and his doubts had been confirmed when Teech had been accused of cheating his messmates at cards. Amongst the company the man was universally disdained — even Melon-head detested him — and the captain had been preparing to sack the loathly dog, only to have Mrs. Barnaby intervene.

The captain had followed the sea his entire life, and ordinarily was not the sort of man to submit to female government. But in the matter of Mrs. Barnaby and her cousin, scoundrel though the man was, and in the interest of familial harmony in Jolly Jumper Yard, he had been persuaded to make an exception.

And where was Teech now? Nobody knew. A lot of people there were who would like to rattle his bones for him, and bring him to book. Some remarked he must bear a charmed life; yet the dog had had his countenance mauled by Melon-head, his sconce thumped by the gammer's cup, and his brow smacked by a clumber pine.

A just recompense, perhaps, for his leveling of Owen at the reef.

Ere the skimmer had been removed from the firs, Melon-head had been discovered on the stern deck, wreaking destruction on a mariner's bonnet. From this it had been deduced that Teech had indeed been aboard her, and that it was he who had been responsible for her straying over MacWallop land. But this was found to carry no weight with the Laird, who remained immovable.

The captain, until he had received Owen's note, had been mourning the loss of his ship's cat, whom he believed had gone down with the skimmer. For the animal had vanished from the *Salty Sue,* and it was conjectured he had sought the sanctuary of his locker during the gale. And so the captain had been doubly rejoiced to hear that Melon-head, too, still lived. The cat was a superb ratter — as indeed are most felines serving aboard ship — and for this had earned the admiration of the entire company.

But enough of this palaver, so decided Constable Pettiplace, who found himself torn now between the spectators frolicking outside the courtroom, and the Justices within, who had been demanding order, order. As an officer it was his duty to restore that order. The law was not a thing to be trifled with; Petty Sessions must go forward. However the constable had not reckoned with so potent or so stalwart and sturdy a force of nature as was Captain Jack Barnaby of Jolly Jumper Yard.

In the meantime the captain in booming voice had made it clear to one and all that he intended to pay the fine for trespass, for the skimmer was his, and his alone, which certain ship's papers aboard the *Salty Sue* quickly would establish. Moreover he could show that the vessel was not a wreck, by the simple exercise of her cage-coils; that she had not been abandoned, as Edgar and Sam had been found aboard her; thus any claim to right of salvage on the part of the complainant was not in order. It all was as clear as the sun that shone overhead.

Mr. MacWallop and his solicitor had been studying this new opponent closely. The Laird was not pleased. His indignation had been greatly roused, not only by the interruption in the steady beat of his march towards a judgment against Lady Martindale, but by the sudden prospect of losing the skimmer, now that he had come to understand what sort of a ship she was he had in his possession. Not only ought she to be worth a fabulous sum, but with such a craft in his coach-house what need had he any longer to be tussling over right of ways?

There was nothing for it but to close with his new opponent at once, with all the ambidexter ingenuity of the bar at his dispose, as embodied in his steely and formidable legal adviser.

Noting their approach, Owen drew his skipper aside and spoke to him briefly in low tones. The captain frowned, crunching his brows and stroking his long chin. His eyes, as keen as a goshawk's, regarded the Laird with a thoughtful interest. Then he nodded and, drawing himself up, transferred his quid from one cheek to the other in readiness for the task at hand.

Hardly had Mr. MacWallop stumped up to him than Captain Barnaby, all sailorly grins and sea salt, took his arm and guided him out of earshot of his legal adviser. The Laird was rather surprised by this, for usually the sight of Mr. Wormwrath bearing down was sufficient to give most any adversary pause. But of course the captain knew nothing of the lawyer's reputation. Instead he begged leave for a minute's private conversation with his client, then proceeded to drop a few whispered words into that gentleman's ear.

All at once the Laird stiffened. His head came up with a jerk, his lips behind his hangdog mustaches parted in amazement. He drew a startled breath and for a moment was shaken out of his composure. Then almost as quickly he recovered himself and, turning a livid glare upon the captain, challenged him to —

"Prove it, an ye can!"

The lawyer threatened to interpose himself between the two men, but his client stayed him with a gesture, brushing him back with a flick of his cosh.

The captain, closing one eye hard and shaking his head with a grave, mysterious air, as if he were about to impart some terrible secret, whispered again. MacWallop listened, disbelief writ large upon his countenance. He thought he had not heard correctly, and so the captain, with a slow, steady emphasis, whispered a third time. The Laird stood in a kind of frozen wonder, like a man in a trance. Something there was in the captain's words had chased all the blood from his face. A hint of panic showed in his eyes and he glanced furtively round, to ascertain whether anyone had been near enough to overhear. His stricken gaze he then returned to the captain, regarding the hatchet-faced old warrior of the sea as if he were some frightful specter in a dream.

"How the deil? How? How, man?" he demanded.

The captain's eyes bored steadily into those of his adversary.

"Soak me in bilge-water," he answered in an undertone, "afore sich ever should escape these lips. Howsomever, ye must look to yer own compass in the matter."

After a little reflection, the Laird nodded his understanding. He mumbled a kind of rebellious acquiescence, and like a sullen child lashed out at the snow with his stick. His face seemed drained of its former energy; his hangdog mustaches hung like dogs.

"'Tis neither beef nor broth o' mine," he retorted, in frowning disgust, and hobbled back to confer with his adviser. Not only his visage and voice, but his whole body, conveyed the impression of a punctured balloon.

Something — at long last — had taken the snap out of him.

Events now advanced with speed. The captain agreed to practice very strict reserve in the matter, if his adversary should do likewise, i.e., should refrain in future from bringing turbulent suits in law against Lady Martindale or her assigns on the subject of trespass, right of way, and other such bilge intended solely for his own self-aggrandizement. Both present charges of trespass were to be withdrawn. It was agreed as well that his attorney, Wormwrath, and her ladyship's representative, Mr. Gecks, should cast the agreement in proper legal form, to make it official in law.

"You are taking a wise stand," said Mr. Gecks.

"I fail to see what other stand one may take at present," returned Mr. Wormwrath, glaring snake-eyes at the captain, "when a client's lawful concerns have been so rudely, and might I say, so inexplicably, frustrated by a stranger."

The attorneys then conferred with the clerk, who in his turn conferred with the Justices, who in their turn ordered the parties in the case to come forward.

"The charge of trespass in the matter of the skimmer," the Chairman announced, "has been withdrawn."

From her ladyship's contingent a cheer went up.

"Silence, if you please," reminded the constable.

"In reference," proceeded the Chairman, "to the second charge of trespass, that concerning the disputed ground in Hatter's Close, it too has been withdrawn."

That moment the soft-toned, deep-voiced bells of St. Mary-in-the-Mews chose to proclaim the hour by chiming a pleasant little tune, as if in celebration of the victory. Some there were in her ladyship's contingent who expected the constable to call upon the bells for "silence, if you please."

The shattered wits of Mr. MacWallop had yet to recover themselves after his disastrous defeat, and the entirely unlooked-for manner in which it had been accomplished. Having failed in his purpose, the Laird said nothing but left hurriedly in the company of his adviser and the gillies. Hobbling past the victorious party, he glowered on them a moment in resentment of their triumph and good fortune, before retiring.

"Well done, Mr. Gecks," congratulated her ladyship. "The unmitigated nuisance has been mitigated. The skunk has finally gotten the worst of a bargain."

Mr. Gecks shrugged his shoulders and buckled down his blue bag. "Of a certainty," he said wryly, "I'm much obliged to you, chief, but in all fairness I confess that my ignorance of the matter is positively monumental.

I should very much like to know what it was our robust nautical friend there relayed to our nuisance that induced him to abandon the cause."

"He seems a cool feller," Edgar remarked. "Perhaps Owen — ?"

The mariner shook his head in swift denial; then abruptly he halted as his thoughts took an unexpected turn, his eyes widening in surprise.

"Bless me and burn me," he pondered aloud, "but mightn't it have had something to do with my father?"

Sun and Shadow

H ABIT, it's said, inures us to wonder; but my brother considers it unlikely that anyone could become accustomed to the spectacle of the *Salty Sue* holding sway in air over the courtyard at the Hall.

The afternoon was fading fast over the boundless extent of marsh. Richard, having neglected Sir Pharnaby of late owing to the press of other business, had shut himself up in the library to resume his study of the Crust letters. The casement lattice afforded a view of Captain Barnaby's ship riding at her ease beside the wall-walk, and it was this that had prompted his meditation on habit and wonder. Never, he reflected, could he himself become used to such a sight, not at the Hall, not at Mead Cottage, not anywhere.

All afternoon he had been assembling materials related to one of Sir Pharnaby's lesser-known compositions, the beautiful *Marsh Music for Oboe and Strings*. An acknowledged masterpiece, if little heard, it is a luminous work, the oboe's plangent outpouring tinged with a sadness redolent of the marshes, evoking that timeless atmosphere of long ago for which Sir Pharnaby Crust is justly celebrated.

By and by, after some few hours, his work was interrupted by Edgar, who entered munching on an apple and full of good tidings. Finding Richard hard at his employment, he could scarce refrain from a buoyant "Hey day!" in announcing himself and the news.

"What d'you think, sir? They've just done with a little chin-wag in the drawing-room — my aunt, Owen, and Captain Barnaby — and what d'you fancy is the upshot of it?"

"I don't suppose you'll be long in telling me," Richard smiled, easing himself back in his chair.

"Dare say I won't. The captain has offered Owen a free hand in piloting the skimmer. Well, he's given him the ship, just about — made Owen her captain. Although his owning it ain't in an official way, o' course, but still it's as good as. Here's the picture. Owen is to go out on his own, as it were, while expanding the Barnaby shipping empire. He's to be agent for the captain's dealings hereabouts — his long-distance hauls — but he's to have the local trade for himself. The captain feels there's much new opportunity for the both of them to be had in these remote parts. Well, Fenshire may seem remote to a gent from Nantle, and vice versa. And the skimmer, though her capacity is small, is so much the faster means of transport over land carriage and the marshways. She is to be moored at the Hall, for the captain understands that Owen has been looking to return. There's a chap in Nantle called Frobisher — Allan Frobisher — who's a sort of broker for the captain's cargoes, who is to be Owen's partner in the business. Owen knows him well, and he says the feller's a trump. So he'll make occasional visits to 'head office' there in Nantle, for the coastal trade, and here in the marshes he'll be his own man."

A new sun had risen to gild the destiny of Owen Aberdovey. Doubtless the captain, sensible of the young man's innate integrity and steadiness of purpose, and having known his father Morgan well, had marked him out as a seaman to be watched. And of course it was to Owen that he had entrusted the design of the skimmer. It was Owen who had taken the seventh hoverstone and fitted a mechanism round it in an old ship's cutter and made the vessel soar. The captain would be unhappy to lose so valuable a member of his company, yet he would not be lost to him *in toto,* but rather would be embarking upon a new venture for the Barnaby shipping enterprise. The seven hoverstones had been given to the captain by Mr. Threadneedle, the retired grocer from Truro; now it was the captain, in his turn, who was to be sharing the seventh stone with his *protégé* Owen.

"I dare say my aunt has taken a fancy to the 'robust nautical gent'," Edgar hinted.

"Perhaps she senses a connection to the baronet. For the captain and Owen's father had served on Clipperton's ship, and Wulf Clipperton was a friend of your uncle's."

"You may be spot-on, sir. She seems fascinated by him. I expect he's a delightful feller, in his way. And o' course a married feller, in his way. But you've heard his wife is something of a tartar. At any rate he's to stay for supper again to celebrate Owen's good fortune."

It was then that Owen himself, in excellent spirits and much lightened at heart, entered the room, in the company of Mr. Samuel Gander. There they all joined in the news, with Owen being congratulated on his turn of luck. How changed he was since those anxious days spent hiding at Northeave! The color had returned to his cheeks, his eyes had regained their sturdy hazel tint, even his hair seemed to shine with a crisper shade of orange.

But all was not yet pudding and pie. It had occurred to Owen that he must remain staunchly on his guard, in the event that Teech should surface for another go at the skimmer. But in this he was to be assisted by Mr. Gander, who had pledged to keep an alert watch for the dog from the wall-walk.

Came then a faint movement to interrupt their discussion, as of something stirring there in the room. An instant later the Welsh stovepipe hat tumbled from the head of Sir Padrig. Something that was like a chill wind went sweeping through the library; yet the casement was shut fast.

Alarmed, the four started up and glanced about them. The waning sun in the lattice, and the candles on the table combined to shed a dim light of a palish, brassy tint into the darker corners of the library.

"Where is it?" Richard asked, scanning the room.

They all felt it — the air of menace, and sense of approaching evil, with which the air had suddenly become charged.

"*There!*" said Owen.

His eyes had been attracted to the shapeless mass that had begun forming on a wall beside the head of Sir Padrig. The thing was perfectly black, and resembled nothing so much as a large ink blot. It was positioned a little above the skirting-board, and as they watched it began to move, stealthily, in a low, crouching fashion, along the wainscot towards them.

The hairs rose on the nape of Richard's neck. Instinctively he recoiled, the others following his example.

The phantom, as it drew nearer, began to detach itself from the wall to which it had seemed a part, and intrude its inky substance into the room. A weird, unearthly growling accompanied the transformation.

The fingers of Edgar sought his collar; already he thought he could feel a hand with a grip like a smith's vice closing on his windpipe. For he well recognized what the shadow emerging from the wainscot portended. It was the bugbear that of late had haunted his imagination, an evil spirit from the bottomless pit, and it had come for him.

Yet stay — was it not Henriette who was supposed to be the shadow, or so Edgar had led himself to believe?

A drop of moisture trickled down his brow and stung his eye. Blinking, he saw the phantom rise to an upright posture, then step out from the wall. A single, dark appendage resembling a claw stretched gropingly forth, in a way that made him shudder. A recollection of his uncle and how he had died flashed into his mind.

"Nothing else for it now," he groaned. It seemed that he had accepted his fate — his destiny, if you will. Indeed in the past few days he had become resigned to it. Now the critical moment had arrived. Would he be found wanting when put to the trial?

Nearer the specter came, odiously writhing its single claw with which it seemed poised to seize the throat of the nearest Harbottle to hand.

"Stand aside, neffy," Sam Gander interposed, "and let me have a go at 'er!" And unsheathing his cutlass he flourished it before the shadow, partly as a demonstration, partly as a warning, of his skill at arms. "Mix it up with me neffy, will yer? Come on, come on — yer miserable object — clear out — shoo! — go on, get off'n me Lizzie's property — clear out — shoo! H'out yer goes!"

With a despairing heave of his shoulders Edgar advised him to "put up your blade, for it's all on my account", when, to his considerable surprise, Owen stepped between them both and, kindly but firmly restraining them, explained —

"Crave pardon, Mr. Edgar, but it's not on your account that the shadow's come. Rather, it's on mine."

"Yours?" the lad exclaimed.

"Aye. Well, bless me and burn me, it's not on my account so much, you understand, sir," said the mariner, correcting himself — "but on hers."

And from a pocket of his coat he produced the gammer's cup.

"I have been keeping it close, sir, since the skimmer first was taken. Smite me dumb if any harm should come to it — if it should be lost — "

"But what has the shadow to do with you? Or with Henriette?" Richard asked.

The gammer's cup lying in plain view in Owen's hand, the shadow responded to it in a most unfriendly manner. A shapeless dark cloud of menacing evil, the specter crept towards them, growling. Nearer and nearer it came. How much the form and character of the shadow of their imagination it possessed! No doubt but that this was the feared avenger of Haigh Hall, the family legend that her ladyship maintained did not exist — only because others had kept the knowledge of its presence from her.

"Jiminy," Edgar gulped, loosening his collar again. There was no time now to dwell upon his fears, or on Owen's words, ere the phantom should catch one of them by the throat and under the pressure of its strangling grip —

"Why don't a you stop that? *Ma foi* — cheaile, wat fool are you! You go 'way now. You moste not interfair in wat does not concern you," spoke up Henriette, and gliding past him interposed herself squarely between Edgar and the bugbear of his imagination.

"She want Henriette," the widow explained. "She not want cheaile."

Edgar, only too happy to oblige, retreated, mopping his brow.

"Certain sure, this is all my doing, Mr. Edgar," Owen confessed.

"Yours?"

"Aye, for sink me it was I who took the cup from the ashes at Northeave. And it was I who gave Henriette leave to rove about the Hall on her little visits. It was this that alerted the shadow, which Henriette does tell me had been slumbering for some while — since the passing of his lordship the baronet. It is Henriette's presence here has set the creature to roaming again."

Owen started to move towards her; to his surprise she warned him off with a gesture.

"No — you leave," she told him.

Owen would not hear of it.

"You leave," she repeated, more firmly this time. "All moste leave. *Vite, vite!* Thees between shadow and Henriette."

Still he would not go — nor would Richard, nor Sam Gander, his cutlass at her dispose, nor even Edgar.

In answer her brow kindled, her strange eyes snapped fire.

"You leave now!" she commanded, pointing them to the door.

Startled, they fell back a step or two, so fierce was her outburst, and so unlike her. Astonished at her vehemence, Owen searched her face for clues. He was in some doubt whether she was entirely equal to the task, whether the phantom might not prove too much the match for her.

Out of temper, the widow stood her ground. "Do not be scrapulous with me. You will go."

Still they hesitated. The phantom, snarling, crept closer.

Addressing Owen, Henriette exclaimed in a fevered tone — "You weel leave now, *mon cher*. It is Henriette's affair, and she weel settle it. What for should a you weesh to interfair in hair business? She weel come for you when it is done. For now *adieu.*"

She paused a moment to let her emotions subside. Owen was about to respond but she silenced him with a look. Then, resuming her former bearing, she instructed Sam Gander — "Papa, kindly put sword down, *s'il vous plaît*. You go 'way now. It is for Henriette to feenish — only she. It is no ting to do with you. Nor with any Harbottles. Wat does shadow care for Harbottles, so long as they be not Martindales? It moste be settle now between us, after so many long year — woman," she vowed, tucking up her sleeves, "to woman."

To the door she glided, shepherding Owen and the others before her. Protesting, but not daring to oppose her, they retreated in spite of themselves.

"*Vite, vite* — hop it!" she flared.

In thrall to her ghostly influence, they stumbled backwards into the passage, and were amazed to see the door whisked shut behind them by a flick of the widow's hand in the air.

"Sink me and scuttle me," marveled Owen, "but I'd thought it impossible for her to — "

"Hallo! You had no inkling she could influence earthly matter?" Richard asked.

"None, sir — none at all. It's a right stunner, certain sure."

"Ain't it!" Edgar agreed.

"Ooh, she's a pip, she is, the pretty chicken," Sam exclaimed, rubbing his hands and smiling. "Now she'll mix it up something grand, like me Lizzie — hee, hee!"

Of all the many daughters of Eve, this Henriette certainly was amongst the most mysterious, and the most surprising, ever conceived.

Eagerly they listened, their ears pressed against the oaken panels of the door. To add further to the mystery, however, they heard nothing — all was as silent as a tomb in the library. Not a word, not a recrimination, not a blow struck, to the disappointment of Mr. Gander. After some minutes and no scuffle they gave it up, and occupied themselves instead in guarding the door so that no one should enter. But no one approached, and as the time passed their concern over the quiet in the library mounted.

At one point, while Sam was watching the door, my brother and Edgar drew Owen aside, and in low tones pleaded with him to tell them all he knew. The mariner, recognizing that the hour was at hand, and that their request was eminently reasonable — yielded at last.

"What relation has Henriette to the shadow, and what is this business she is settling between them? What is the trouble?" Richard asked.

"It's on account of her husband, sir," Owen explained, "her husband as she did murder with the gammer's cup."

"The feller she brained with a rap on the noggin?" said Edgar.

"Crave your pardon, Mr. Edgar, but it wasn't that way. Sink me, she didn't strike the man with the cup. She poisoned him with it."

"Poisoned!"

"It was the belladonna, as it's termed."

"Belladonna," Richard repeated. "Isn't that what they call the deadly nightshade — ?"

A look, appearing at once in the faces of Richard and Edgar, communicated to Owen that his words had had their due effect.

"Let me explain. Likely you'll recall — for I know, Mr. Hathaway, that Mr. Gecks has described for you certain circumstances of the legend — that the cobbler, Crispin Nightshade, had poisoned his master the shoemaker, not only because he resented him and coveted his shop and tools, but because he coveted his master's fancy little wife. Did Mr. Gecks tell you she was a fancy little *French* wife, and that her name was Henriette?"

"He did not," answered Richard.

"I never heard she was French," said Edgar.

"It is because no one knows of it. It was forgotten," Owen explained.

"But was the cobbler not the murderer of his master? And was that not the inspiration for the name Nightshade?" Richard asked.

"The unvarnished truth o' the matter, sirs," answered Owen, "is that it was she who murdered him — Henriette. It was she who mixed the belladonna with his broth and gave it to the shoemaker, her husband. For women, as you know, have ever been the betters of men at poisoning. It's the readiest means for 'em, certain sure, and hardest to trace. It was Henriette who killed her first husband, by way of poison, and it was she who killed her second husband, ditto."

"Jiminy, the peach a murderess — *twice over!*" Edgar breathed.

"She's that, and more. It was she who mixed the potion that put the stranger from the inn to sleep, so that her husband could remove the boots from his feet. But once he himself had come under the spell of the haunted leather, and began to beat her, she killed him too — by slow poison. He himself knew little of the practice; bless and burn me, it was all her doing. It was an art or something like it in her family, upon her mother's side, so she told me, going back to the old days in France — the mixing of potions to make a person sleep, for a time only, or for all time. And so both her husbands died at her hand, and no blame ever was attached to her."

"Beg pardon, Owen," Richard said, "but did Nightshade not perish here at the Hall, while returning a pair of boots to the Judge? For so I recollect

Mr. Gecks telling me. The shadow — the cobbler's poor relation, who had laid a curse upon him and the Martindales and had died a murderess herself on the gallows — rose up and frightened him to death. It was in the chimney-corner in the kitchen, that same where Mrs. Flitch heard it weeping."

"Smite me dumb, sir," Owen answered, "if she had no better success with husband number two than she had with number one. It was poison, sir, not the shadow, that killed him. She had mixed it with a favored liqueur he was wont to drink of an evening from the gammer's cup. Over several nights she mixed it; afore he knew it he had imbibed near a fatal dose. And the rum thing is, he scarce suspected her. So muddled had his thoughts grown, on account of the haunted leather in which he oft had been immersed, he believed it was the shadow had returned and was making him ill.

"The gammer's cup was the cobbler's own — a queer, odd relic he had discovered in a shop and found to his liking. Being not the sort to die in a hurry, he lingered on, growing worse and never conceiving it was Henriette. It was but by chance he succumbed the day he took the Judge's boots to the Hall. He was in the kitchen, the cook administering him a tonic for his ill health, when the end came."

Edgar recalled the weeping that had drawn Mrs. Flitch to the kitchen, and that which he himself had heard in the skimmer. In the latter instance it had been attributable to Henriette, but what of the former? Who was it Mrs. Flitch had heard?

"Doubtless the same, Mr. Edgar," Owen replied.

"Meaning Henriette?"

"Aye, sir. She had gone there in the night, on one of her visits, to the place where her husband died. As she confessed to me, it had moved her to reflect upon her sins, and to bemoan the path she now trod, which was of her own making, and to grieve again over the great loss she had suffered — her secret sorrow. It was her presence in the kitchen that drew the phantom out.

"Indeed they hate each other, Henriette and this shadow, which in life had been her husband's poor, mad cousin, who had come to despise him, and to despise his wife too. For they had cast upon her all the drudgery of their household, sentencing her to a life of ceaseless grind — *even after death*. What right had Henriette to have acted so haughty towards her? Although fancy in her taste and habits, she was no high-born lady but the daughter of a sausage-stuffer. And yet it was Henriette herself, burn me and bleed me, who incited her husband to put the haunted leather on the dead woman's feet, and raise her from her coffin, thus denying her her final rest."

"The deuce you say!" Edgar exclaimed.

"It seems Henriette is full of surprises," said Richard. "But what was she mourning over? What is this great loss you spoke of? Edgar said she mentioned a child — "

Owen was about to answer when the door to the library flew open and their startled eyes met Henriette's. Not only was she deathly white, as was usual for her, but she was trembling, too, as one does when recovering from the passionate exercise of emotion. There was in her appearance such a degree of weariness as Owen never before had seen in her. The disordered state of her hair and gown was evidence that the strain of contending with the phantom had told upon her.

She gestured for them to enter. Nervously their eyes searched the library, the tiers of shelved books, the window seat, the bust of Sir Padrig, the wealth of artifacts lining the walls, and particularly the stretch of wainscot from which the creeping shadow had arisen.

"No worry. She 'ave gone," Henriette told them.

Nevertheless they proceeded cautiously, glancing before and behind them as they went. Had they indeed seen the end of this hateful business of the shadow? Would Mr. Gander be free to sheathe his cutlass?

"No ting to worry 'bout more," the widow assured them.

They stood a minute silently observing. They noted that the stovepipe hat had been returned to its place on the Judge's head.

"Gone, then?" said Owen, watching her closely.

"*Oui.*"

"For good and all?"

"For good and all," she replied, avoiding his gaze; then added, in a lower register — "and now Henriette too moste go 'way."

"Perish the thought! You've won — carried the day," Owen said. Then, noting her response, which seemed constrained and joyless, he asked her — "Bless me, you're not serious?"

"Henriette nayver more serious, *mon cher.*"

"What do you mean you must go away?"

"I moste take my *adieu* of you. It is — 'ow you call? — part of the bargain. Bote I am fatigue now . . ."

It turned out that the price the shadow had exacted from Henriette, in exchange for its standing aside, was that she should depart and never see Owen more. As well the bargain guaranteed that in future nothing should entice the slumbering phantom to rouse itself in answer to any Harbottles who might be in residence at the Hall.

"She care leetle for Harbottles — only Martindales," Henriette explained, "and Martindales, they 'ave run their course pretty moche. Bote onless Henriette go 'way, hair mind she may change it. She may theenk deeferent. She draive hard bargain, as you say, bote I 'ave agree. So tomorrow I moste go 'way. I 'ave promise."

"Dash it all," said Richard, "this is no bargain."

Edgar for some moments was speechless. His existence, and that of his male heirs — in trade for Henriette's agreeing to depart and never again to see Owen. And the sun only just beginning to shine on Owen's bright future there at the Hall!

"'Pon my word, it ain't sporting," he complained.

"But Mr. Edgar, it will preserve your life," Owen reminded him.

"Well, I like that! I'd not give you tuppence for such a bargain. It's extortion, and extortion ain't sporting. I won't be the cause of it."

However it seemed that fate had willed otherwise, as Henriette already had agreed to terms. The shadow had withdrawn, and it was incumbent on her to follow its example.

She drew Owen a little apart. "Wat does signify, *mon cher?* You do not care for Henriette," she told him, affecting lightness, "and she does not care for you. Owen he moste be free to marry his Geeblets, no? He cannot 'ave Henriette, and Henriette does not want him."

Owen was fully conscious she did not mean what she said, but he understood her reason for saying it.

"Take a me back to Northeave, if a you plaise. This is the return I do make you for 'aving saved me," she said, in a voice of mingled tenderness and firmness.

"Saved you?" puzzled Owen.

She added something more but it was lost in a whisper. She lowered her eyes, on the lids of which something like tears could be seen glistening, and straightened her gown a little and brushed back her hair.

Owen, like the others, had recoiled at the proposal that she go away forever. This, he reflected, is what comes of bargaining with shadows! Agitated by a host of contending feelings, he took a step towards her, but she shook her head in tight-lipped objection.

To pursue her lonely way — to tread the solitary path her earthly deeds had marked out for her — to suffer through her *pénitence* until her spirit had been washed clean — such was her fate, before and after Northeave. It was not meant to be shared with Owen Aberdovey.

As we know it is the way of nature that the old should die and be forgotten, and the young should live and be happy. Henriette, although she appeared young, was but an illusion of youth — a shadow of a kind herself, of days long past and a life long done. Her time had come and gone. A disembodied spirit, she had been condemned a prisoner in this nebulous state between one world and the next. She herself — her mortal self, that which had walked upon the earth — survived only as a pile of moldering remains somewhere, in some nameless grave.

Owen shuddered when he thought of it — the vast and awful loneliness of time. It was he now who was young and whose fate was to be happy. It was Henriette who was to be forgotten.

He glanced at her again. "Henriette," he said.

For a moment she brightened, and lifted her eyes. "You nayver call me Henriette. It is allaways 'madam' thees and 'madam' that. Joste because I am poor widow woman twice remove, you need not call me so."

Flushing, Owen endeavored to collect his thoughts and was embarrassed to find he had difficulty doing so. Henriette for her part could not hide the quaver in her voice.

Owen's response came as a surprise to her, and indeed to him as well. He placed himself before her. She did not warn him off this time, but instead raised her chin and looked up into his face, unsure what to say or to do, what to expect. For a moment her glance faltered. Then her expression softened; her eyes, full of a wistful tenderness, lingered on his. For a brief interval the mask of her manner dropped from her. Her hair, untidy, and falling across her brow, her rumpled gown — tokens of her struggle with her ageless foe — her pretty countenance as pale as death — on these things Owen's own eyes lingered for a time. To him she had never seemed lovelier, this long-dead murderess and fancy little wife who had poisoned two husbands.

He searched her face, then reached shyly for her hand that he knew to be beyond his grasping. She regarded him with curiosity, then proceeded to entwine her fingers with his, so far as she was able, in her thoughts imagining that it was so.

Owen shook his head gently. "I won't hear of it," he told her. "Not Northeave. If go you must, there is a better way."

The Boot on Another Leg

"**D**ID you not tell me, Henriette," Owen went on, "that your name once was Roget?"

At the mention of it the widow's expression brightened considerably.

"'Twas the name of my papa — his family. That is, was my name. Henriette Anne Lise Roget. Was my — wat you call it — maid's name."

"There is an elderly man living in Ridingham. My father knew him of old, and I have known him since I was a boy. His name is Pinchbeck — Mr. Hiram Pinchbeck. By trade he is a bootmaker, and the name Roget figures far back in his family tree."

"It is common name," Henriette allowed.

"There is a tradition in Mr. Pinchbeck's family that they are somehow related to your husband. By that I mean your second husband."

"Bote his name not Roget. Nor Peenchbeck."

"Mr. Pinchbeck has in his keeping a relic which has been passed down in his family. It is a tiny lace band, such as might have circled the wrist of a child. It is blue in color — for I've seen it — and is embroidered with the name 'Lise'."

Henriette started, and the sudden change that came over her face was remarkable. She looked at Owen with her heart in her eyes, into which the tears were swiftly flowing.

"*Ma chérie* — my Lise — my cheaile — " she murmured.

She pressed her hands to her cheeks, down which the tears had traced long, glistening lines. No one spoke, not for a minute at least, while Henriette wept quietly. Then, struggling to recover herself, she said softly —

"No, is eempossible . . ."

"Might Mr. Pinchbeck be a relative of yours?"

"It cannot be," she said, "it cannot be, for my Lise — the shadow she did keel a her, I know. She curse a my husband, and she keel a my cheaile! Was in the winter Lise she catch fever — she sink, she shrivel 'way — "

In vain she endeavored to restrain her tears, which burst forth again in a fresh flood. For some minutes she was unable to speak. In time her grief abated, and her sorrow found words. It was in the hard winter, she said, following the death of her husband's cousin on the scaffold, that her child had been seized with the fever that had brought her to her end. Henriette had endured the special suffering that only a parent can feel, holding to her bosom a lifeless small one whom she had scarcely known, and never would know more.

When he saw she was able to converse again, Owen asked her — "Your own name Roget figures in Mr. Pinchbeck's family history, and the lace band has been preserved and passed down to him. How might this be?"

Sniffling, Henriette pondered a moment, her brow thrown into folds. Then she turned to him with a questioning look.

"Can it be Augustín?"

"Who is that?"

"Augustín Roget, my leetle brother. Bote 'ow? He not marry — 'ave no cheaildren — "

"Stay a bit. Can he not have married later? After — well, after?" Owen suggested.

Henriette, comprehending, smote her forehead in self-reproof. "Bote of course! Wat 'ave I theenk? 'Ow fatigue I 'ave grow. Augustín was bote cheaile himself when it 'appen. So Augustín, he 'ave cheaile himself — 'ave many, maybe — two, three, four . . ."

"One of them must have been Mr. Pinchbeck's ancestor. Certain sure, Henriette, Mr. Pinchbeck is a descendant o' your brother's, and so is a member of your own family."

"Thees most 'appy *coïncidence,*" the widow exclaimed.

"Yesterday I took the skimmer into Ridingham and yarned with him awhile. He is a bachelor and lives alone above his shop there in the town, with only a housekeeper to do for him. I've a notion he's a wee bit lonely. Howbeit he has a great many interests aside from his trade, and is a collector of antiquities. Indeed he has something of an antique air about him. He's a scholar as well, and bless me knows more of the history of Ridingham than can be found in any ten books. He has a special interest in his family's history, in particular its connection to the Rogets."

Henriette's eyes widened expressively.

"Do not a you see it? 'Ow moche I can tale a him of old Rogets — and 'ow moche he can tale a me of new."

"Perhaps you would like to visit him?" Owen suggested.

"Vary moche!"

"By my reckoning he is your great-grandnephew many times removed, and you are his great-grandaunt, ditto."

"Nayver before 'ave I been aunt — *tante Henriette*. So moche 'ave I in common now with hair ladysheep. We bote are aunts and widow womans together," said Henriette, drying her eyes with her pretty taper fingers and smiling.

"We shall see Mr. Pinchbeck tomorrow. But we must tread carefully. I must first sound him out; we can't spring you on him unawares. But given he is a collector, I've a notion he'll find the gammer's cup of interest."

Satisfied, Owen then explained to the others more fully the circumstances. They listened with interest and amazement. They were stunned to learn of the secret sorrow that Henriette had borne through the long years of her *pénitence* — the death of her only child, a daughter, who had taken ill and wasted away. Henriette was certain it had been the shadow's doing, in reprisal for her treatment at the hands of Henriette and her husband, in particular for the business of the haunted leather. Here then was the root cause of the hatred between them. Earthly centuries now had come and gone, and nothing had changed. Henriette's sorrow was the keen edge of her *pénitence*, sharper than any serpent's tooth. It was the cause of her sobbing in the chimney-corner, and in the skimmer — her anguished remorse over the child who was lost to her.

The next day found Owen, Richard, and Edgar in Shoe Lane, standing at the little wicket-gate before the house of the bootmaker. Ordinarily, calling on a creditor might have caused Edgar some distress, but in this instance he was less apprehensive. His debts of the one kind already had been settled. However his conscience in the interval had become sensible of another kind of debt, one arising from the mingling of his fortunes with those of Owen and Henriette, and he had felt the need to attend.

They rang the bell, and Mr. Pinchbeck himself in his shop-clothes appeared at the gate. It was his housekeeper's day out, he said, and he asked their indulgence. They in their turn begged his leave for the intrusion of chance visitors in the middle of his work day. But he good-naturedly waved them inside.

A warm smell of leather and tobacco, neat's-foot oil, and boot blacking filled the air as their host led them to a cozy inglenook, a little apart from his workshop. There he put a kettle to boil for the tea and unhitched some cups from a dresser. Gesturing towards the tobacco-jar on the mantel, he invited his guests to partake. Edgar thanked him but declined, preferring

the cigar he took from his coat. Richard and Owen however quickly loaded their pipes and soon had stoked them into smoke. Their host meantime
continued to potter around with the tea things until all was in readiness.

Once they had settled themselves, Owen presented Mr. Pinchbeck with
the gammer's cup, describing it as a curiosity he had acquired on his travels. It was the truth, of course — although he did not volunteer that those
travels included so near a place as Northeave. He hastened to add that it
was a special cup, a relic of some distinction and quaintness, that he believed Mr. Pinchbeck, a connoisseur of such things, might appreciate.

The bootmaker clapped on his spectacles and took the pewter in hand,
eyeing it curiously and turning it round this way and that, and examining
it in all its particulars. He scrutinized closely the features of the wicked old
lady whose toothless, grinning image projected in high relief from its surface. Far from being repelled by it, Mr. Pinchbeck considered the object
fascinating, and was much impressed by the workmanship of the anonymous craftsman who had fashioned it.

"I judge it to have been a local product," he concluded. "Fenshire without doubt, Ridingham most likely. This is local pewter, I believe, although
of considerable antiquity. These grotesques were once quite popular, in an
earlier, more superstitious age. But this one — I have scarce seen its like before."

"You're welcome to enter it in your collection, sir," Owen offered, "for
aye you've many a curio round this goodly shop o' yours, as I well remember."

The bootmaker, calmly smoking, regarded him with pensive eyes.

"Many were the times your father, Morgan Aberdovey, did call at my
door upon some errand or other for his lordship."

"And as often I was in his company as not since I was no higher than
a nutmeg grater," Owen recalled.

"Indeed, for his lordship often sought the services of this my humble
shop."

"It was the excellence of your work, sir. His lordship always praised it
highly."

"Yes," said Mr. Pinchbeck, nodding reflectively, "his lordship's ward-
robe was most extensive in the boot and shoe line." A curious glimmer had
come into his eyes as they rested on Owen. All at once he took his pipe
from his lips and, leaning forward in his chair, inquired "why it is so honest and upstanding a young man as yourself, Mr. Aberdovey, should resort
to prevarication with so old a friend of yours as I about this pewter here?"

The hush that followed was loud enough to be heard. To say that his visitors were surprised would be a gross understatement.

"Jiminy!" Edgar exhaled under his breath.

When Owen failed to offer an explanation, the bootmaker took it upon himself to supply one.

"You are interested, perhaps, in the haunted leather? I am disappointed in you, Mr. Aberdovey."

"Scorch me and burn me — hardly, sir — the gammer's cup — " Owen protested.

"Is that what you call it? You must tell me where you found it — the truth, now. And how did you know to bring it to me?"

Surprise succeeded surprise. Owen glanced at Richard, and Richard at Edgar, and Edgar at Owen, their faces registering confusion and disbelief.

"We — that is, Teech and I — Amos Teech, a messmate — we found it in an old lodge at Northeave. Someone had cast it into the fireplace. It lay half-buried in the ashes," Owen explained.

"Ah, so that's where it got to," nodded the bootmaker. He had picked it up again and was turning the cup round and round in his hand, admiring further the workmanship. "Do you see this tiny impressed mark here, at the bottom of the pewter? It is a tantagram — a Druidical symbol."

They peered inside the cup, and indeed there was a mark at the very bottom of it, one just as the bootmaker described.

"Sink me — I had no inkling — never noticed it ere this," Owen said, scratching his head.

"It's not likely you would have done, for it's not meant to be seen."

"You say it's a Druidical mark. But surely this cup is not as old as the ancient Druids?" Richard asked.

"Oh, no, no. Without question it is far more recent than that. Though it surely dates from before the sundering, for afterwards such grotesques no longer were made. No, the mark is a clue to its purpose. So you must tell me now, how did you know to bring the hag's pewter to me? For it's a bit of luck, you see — "

"Hag's pewter?" echoed Owen.

"Bit of luck?" dittoed Edgar.

"Oh, very much so. It has been a subject of the deepest interest to me. There is a tradition in my family that an ancestor of ours, the man known as Crispin Nightshade — a brother of our trade — possessed such a mug, and did drink from it nightly. I have searched for it for many years. Ridingham and Fenshire afford such a variety of legends, and tradition is as oft as not an inventor of fiction as a preserver of the truth. But in the case of the hag's pewter one is on more certain ground. It is no fiction."

Owen scratched his head again. "Bless me!" he exclaimed.

"You called the pewter a special cup. What did you mean by that, Mr. Aberdovey?" the bootmaker asked him. "For indeed it is special to me. I believe it might well be the one kept by my putative ancestor. He was a poisoner, and a resurrector of the dead, if one credits the stories. Well, certainly he did away with his master, an elderly shoemaker. And there is every reason to believe that the haunted leather is as real as the pewter. Black and secret arts surely lie behind the legend. And now to cap it all there is the Druidical mark."

"You say that it is a clue to the vessel's purpose. How so, Mr. Pinchbeck?" Richard asked.

"Simply that it tells me that this is no common drinking-vessel, but one fashioned by a gifted acolyte with another purpose in view, related to those black and secret arts. After the lapse of so many years, however, the nature of that purpose is, I fear, a topic only for speculation."

Observing his guests again to be trading glances, he repeated his call for information concerning the mysterious pewter, and how they had known the relic would be of interest to him. It was with a skeptical countenance that he heard Owen's tentative soundings on the subject of ghosts and the afterworld, and the rightness of penance, and the virtue of forgiveness. Mr. Pinchbeck, very reasonably, did not know quite what to make of this line, and in his kindly way told the mariner so. And then he asked again if his guests would please explain how they had known to bring him the hag's pewter?

There was nothing for it now, they recognized. The time had come.

"Ordinarily we would have hard work to explain it," Richard said, "but firstly let us tell you that you are not a descendant of the man known as Crispin Nightshade, the famed cobbler of Ridingham. Rather, more likely you are descended from his wife's brother, whose name was Augustín Roget."

The bootmaker removed his spectacles and stared. "And how do you know this, Mr. Hathaway?"

"From certain evidence we've gathered. It's dashed odd, I know — "

"And what is the evidence you have for it?"

"If you would be so kind, sir," Owen invited, handing him the gammer's cup, or hag's pewter, into which he had poured a measure of tea.

"And what am I to do with this?"

"Have a go, sir, and no heeltap," Edgar suggested.

"In celebration," Richard added quickly, "of Owen's finding the pewter for you at Northeave."

The bootmaker regarded his guests with a doubtful eye. He was unsure what their intent was in this toast of the tea leaves, but he was glad of their having uncovered a relic of such perceived importance to his family. He decided it would be harmless to humor them.

"You're madcaps," he said, and drank several swallows.

Seconds passed. Somewhere in the shop a clock ticked. His guests waited expectantly. Mr. Pinchbeck, who had shut his eyes while knocking back his tea, now opened them, and gave a start as they settled on a customer who had appeared as if from out of the air.

"My goodness," he exclaimed, hastily getting to his feet. He laid by the pewter and made a courteous bow. "And how may I serve you, my dear? How long have you been waiting? I did not see you there. And I heard no bell, and the wicket is — the wicket is — I do beg your leave, but how did you enter my shop?" he asked her, slightly bewildered.

"You are *Monsieur* Peenchbeck — the gentleman bootmaker of Riding-ham? He of whom Owen 'as spoke a so highly?" the lady answered, with a quaint politeness.

"My name is Pinchbeck, yes, and this is my shop. You are a friend of Mr. Aberdovey's, then? You have perhaps some mending to be done? A boot to be vamped? A pair of shoes to be made?" he said, presenting himself. The bootmaker was a slight little man, no higher than his pretty customer, who stood — or was it floated — but inches from him.

"Well, I tale a you, *monsieur*," said she, smiling, "I have no ting to be mended — aixcept pairhaps my soul — nor to be vamped, nor steetched, nor seamed, nor shoes to be made, for I 'ave nice leetle pair on my feet, do not a you theenk? But no 'urry, I find thees shop most agreeable. My fairst 'usband, you know, was *cordonnier* — a shoemaker."

"Indeed?"

"*Oui*. Big shoemaker in Ridingham. Averybody know him."

"So you are a friend of the gentle craft?"

"Oh, yes. My 'usband, he do vary well. Then he pass 'way."

"I grieve to hear that — may God rest him. You are a widow, then, my dear? And at so young an age," commiserated Mr. Pinchbeck.

"Was widow, then marry 'gain. My second 'usband too was shoemaker. He inherit shop, do vary nicely. Bote he too pass 'way."

"I see." A trace of doubt had crept into the kindly, cultured face. "It is much to be regretted. I am sorry for you, my dear — very sorry. So much sorrow in so few years! But if you'll pardon me, I can think of no such brothers of the trade in Ridingham who have — "

"Ah, bote you weel not know them. They before your time," Henriette assured him.

"Before my time? My word, how curious." Mr. Pinchbeck was silent for awhile as he pondered how such a thing could be. "And how came you to be acquainted with Mr. Aberdovey?" he asked at length.

"Ah," said Henriette, her eyes alight, her smile dazzling, "I know Owen from long time. He vary fine man. *Un marin par excellence.*"

Owen blushed as orange as his hair. "Mr. Pinchbeck — er, that is — er — bless and burn me, sir, but pray you must forgive us. This lady here — well, we have been rather less than candid with you — "

"So it would appear," the bootmaker agreed. "And what is your name, my dear, and how may I be of service?" he said, addressing Henriette, and as he did so he offered her his hand in his quaint, gentlemanly way. Henriette, not thinking at first, obliged him, in the execution of which the bootmaker's fingers passed clean through her own.

"My very word," he exclaimed, withdrawing his hand and gazing at it as though it were a complete stranger to his person. "My very word, how can this be? Who are you?"

"This lady, sir," Owen made haste to explain, "is Henriette. Afore her first marriage her name was Henriette Anne Lise Roget."

"Roget?"

"My brother, his name Augustín Roget," the widow volunteered.

Mr. Pinchbeck clapped a hand to his brow — that same hand that had passed through Henriette's — and looked at her in astonishment. A strange quaking had unsettled his heart. If you had mistaken it for a sign of fear, however, you might be forgiven for so doing. True, an element of fear was present, but only a small one, amongst the riot of emotions that went rushing through him. He glanced at the hag's pewter — the drinking-cup that purportedly had graced the lips of Crispin Nightshade, the cobbler of Ridingham — then again at Henriette.

Two husbands deceased, both of them practitioners of the gentle craft, both married to this same woman called Roget — and both of them *before your time.*

"What are you telling me?" he asked her in a voice not of dread, but of wonder and anticipation.

"Wat I tale a you," Henriette answered, commencing her ritual, "I tale a you truly, *monsieur*. Do not a you make the same mistake as poor Henri-ette. Was vary wrong of hair to keel a hair husband — bote of them — with the poison. Was vary bad ting, and for thees it is *pénitence* I moste do. So you had better leesten to me. Weel you make promise, you weel a not keel a your wife? Do not a you suffer same fate as Henriette. It is moche great punishment."

Mr. Pinchbeck's eyes were staring widely and roundly.

"But I — I have no wife," he said.

"Excellent! This is good start."

"However, there is my housekeeper — Mrs. Runcorn — "

"No matter," Henriette assured him with a shrug and a wave of a pret-ty hand, "'ousekeeper is not eemportant. You keel a her if a you like, eh? Wat for should a you weesh to do is no business of Henriette's, so long as 'ousekeeper not a your wife."

The bootmaker momentarily paled at this speech.

"I — I think I had better sit down . . ." Weakly he groped behind him for the arms of his chair. He fumbled for a handkerchief and patted his brow and cheeks with it, while endeavoring to recover himself.

"Belike I should explain, sir," Owen offered after a minute or two.

"Yes, Mr. Aberdovey — indeed — yes, you must," answered the boot-maker, having sought comfort in his pipe, and found it. "But I believe — indeed, I believe I already have divined much of the truth . . ."

"You have?"

"I understand now why you brought me the pewter. The name Roget — the Druidical mark — killed two husbands, both of them brothers of the trade. I understand as well why you inquired into certain of my beliefs, be-fore proceeding with your — shall we call it — demonstration."

It was as if a light had suddenly broken upon him — a mystical light. He appeared to have regained much of his strength, as alarm gave place to curiosity and — it cannot be denied — a certain excitement. Rising, he ap-proached Henriette and looked her gently and calmly in the eye.

"Henriette Anne Lise Roget! It's a pretty name. I dare say you are that ancestor of mine about whom I've conjectured for so many years. I'd not have believed it! You are the source of that tradition in my family — you are our link to the cobbler of Ridingham. So you were his wife, were you, my dear?"

"And you are my nephew, so many times remove. The descendant of my leetle brother."

"And you are my aunt — so many times removed. Well, well! What a funny world is this. Well, it changes everything. No — it *explains* every-thing."

"You are not frighten of Henriette?" she asked. "Many people, they are frighten after drinking from pewter cup. Like villain man, they run 'way."

"Frightened? Of you? My dear, I am delighted to know you. And as chair of our local historical society, I could not be more pleased. There is so much that you may be able to tell me about our family. For the Rogets, you see, all are gone from Ridingham. For instance, what was the name of your husband? The man to whom legend has ascribed the name Night-shade?"

"*Hélas! neveu*, it is so moche bore. His name Smeeth," she confessed.

"Smith? I should not have believed it."

"'Henriette Smeeth'. Wat you theenk of that now? Is great bore, no?"

"It is hardly boring to me. Quite the contrary. There is so very much to be learned. For my love of history and dear old things — "

"Bote *neveu*, I too am old theeng," Henriette reminded him lightly.

"I shall pledge not to inquire into your age," the bootmaker assured her in a like vein, "if you do not inquire into mine. For I am no chicken my-self."

"Papa say I am pretty chicken."

"Papa? Your father, do you mean?"

"No, no, not my papa. He was big sausage-stuffer in Ridingham. I mean the leetle papa of hair ladysheep."

"Do you mean Mr. Samuel Gander?"

"He the one. He funny leetle fallow. He make Henriette laugh."

And so it went. Ere long Mr. Pinchbeck had forgotten entirely that he was holding communication with a departed spirit, albeit one who happen-ed to be related to him, so easy and natural was their conversation togeth-er. With an air of pride he offered to show her round his workplace. Very gentlemanly and gallant, serving as both *conducteur* and cicerone, he guided her about the shop, enlarging upon all its various points of excellence. He was a craftsman of the first rank, and justifiably proud of the establishment where he plied his trade. He showed her his shop-board laden with work, and his tools — his iron stand and extra-heavy lasts, his awls, his hammers, skivers, or paring-knives, his rasps, leathers, his cobbler's wax, lingel, and laces — all of which Henriette remarked upon with interest and found reas-suringly familiar. As well he introduced her to the wealth of antique ob-jects that he had accumulated which were on display in the shop and above it, and which she studied with an eye as discerning as his own.

An easy rapport sprang up between them in the course of the tour, and soon they were talking and laughing together as comfortably as a pair of old shoes. Although separated by the centuries, it was plain they had much in common, not the least of it being their shared ancestry. A modest, elderly little man, of a generous and a courtly disposition, the bootmaker had been happy to find his relative so admiring of his workplace. There was a twinkle in his eye, and a lift in his step, his face and voice alike becoming more animated as he expatiated upon the glories of the gentle craft.

For her part Henriette had forgotten for awhile her grief in her admiration of his shop, and of the bootmaker himself, and was resolved that they should be good friends together. This was received as a favorable omen, for to do her justice the widow was an engaging personality, with much that was good and virtuous in her character. It was small wonder the ambitious Mr. Smith, otherwise Crispin Nightshade, had coveted his master's fancy little wife. Owen saw how happy she was now, and it greatly pleased him. Indeed this was a far better way, as he had promised — restoring her to her family — than relegating her once more to the ashes at Northeave.

She and the bootmaker were on such comfortable terms now, had become so absorbed in some happy other world of their own as they chatted together, and shared their knowledge of the Rogets and Pinchbecks of history, that the flight of time seemed as nothing. Already an hour had gone by, another was passing. Here was a unique mode of rendering her penance, Owen reflected, after the many years of secret suffering. Henceforth Henriette's thoughts and interests would lie elsewhere. Owen had been glad of her company for the period he had shared it, but the time allotted them, he saw, was nearly done. She was with her family now, and he must return to his.

As he and the others watched, the bootmaker withdrew from a pocket of his shop-clothes a small silver case. Inside it lay the ornamental wristband of pale blue upon which, in tiny, woven letters, was embroidered the name of Henriette's daughter. They saw him open the case and show her the band, saw Henriette's fingers leap to her lips, saw the yearning in her eyes, saw those eyes blink back sudden tears. Trembling, she stared at the relic in mute anguish, unable herself to touch it, to caress the delicate fabric, which once had caressed her daughter's wrist. Never in all her long life had she wanted so much to touch a thing, and hug it to her bosom, as to touch this single, surviving token of her dead child.

"When weel I see hair again? My Lise, my dear cheaile! So vary moche time alone. Wat horror it is when cheaile should die before hair mother — nayver meet again — ”

They saw her lips form the words, but no sound reached their ears, in so low a tone had she spoken them. They saw Mr. Pinchbeck, deeply moved, encourage her with words again too faint for hearing. But a while later Henriette was smiling wistfully at the old man through her tears.

Owen's gaze lingered upon her, until he felt a hand on his shoulder.

“I expect it's time we were going — dashed sorry,” Richard said.

With a final glance at the pair standing by the mantelpiece, Owen nodded his agreement — reluctantly — and turned aside.

“Aye, sir. It's for the best. Our business here is done.”

“Brayvo, Owen,” Edgar said quietly.

The mariner smiled. “Sink me, I'd look a right fool now, wouldn't I?”

And so they left Henriette and her nephew many times removed to themselves, and slipped away unnoticed.

We are not the shapers of our own destiny, as Owen had come to discover. A little while hence and he too might forget, and be forgotten. Like the many million spangles that deck the firmament, these things are in the stars. And the stars, as you know, are for the guidance of mariners, and it doesn't do to go against them.

       ぐ   ぐ   ぐ   ぐ   ぐ

The rest is soon told.

It was a few days after this that Richard, his study of the Crust letters complete, thanked Lady Martindale for her kindness during his brief visit that had stretched into weeks, and departed the Hall. He proceeded by train to Newmarsh, and spent some time in the reading room of the Municipal Library, continuing his examination of the materials in their Crust collection. At length, after an absence of more than a month, he returned home to Market Snailsby, bearing much new matter for his treatise. Many long hours of writing followed, and further visits to Newmarsh. As you may have heard, the Ridingham publisher, Mr. Van Ness, disappointed him by returning the manuscript (“too many words, Mr. Hathaway, too many words”). Ultimately it was brought out by the university press at Salthead, to general acclaim from a small circle of enthusiasts.

Owen Aberdovey and Gwenda Goodwick — when will their marriage come off, do you think? For at last report, as conveyed to us in a letter from Lady Martindale, no arrangements had yet been made. Nothing had been set in motion. As for Owen, he himself and the skimmer have been much in motion. Between his travels to and from the long coast for Captain Barnaby and his thriving business in the marshes, he has been little seen at the Hall. Even his mother is concerned. It might seem impossible to you that the memory of a spectral luminosity could outweigh the very live presence of Gwenda, and if he had had a mind to it my brother and I are certain that Owen would have married the woman on the spot. It is the identity of the woman — whether the lady's maid, or the luminosity — which remains a matter for conjecture.

As we later discovered, it happened that Owen's father, Morgan Aberdovey, had, early on, and utterly by accident, come into possession of certain intelligence concerning the private affairs of Mr. Phergus MacWallop. It was intelligence scarcely flattering to the Laird, the sort that, if revealed, would have put a severe period to the happy and very profitable course of his marriage. (Indeed there is, and for some while there has been, a Mrs. MacWallop. A substantial heiress, it is she who commands the purse-strings in MacWallop land.) Morgan Aberdovey had relayed the information to his master and friend, Sir Pedr Martindale, and in his turn the baronet had relayed it to the Laird's legal man of the period, Mr. MacFlam. Mr. MacFlam having been an accessory *ex post facto* in the business, retired from the field, and in his stead had appeared Mr. Wormwrath. Certain compromises were arrived at, and restitution made, the entire matter being kept strictly quiet as is the usual case between gentlemen. For as long as the baronet and Morgan Aberdovey lived, the arrangement had succeeded in keeping their rascally neighbor in check. But the death of Sir Pedr had left Morgan in a quandary. Should he tell Lady Martindale of the affair, or should he not? For the baronet had pledged him to secrecy; it was one of the gentlemanly compromises that had been reached. And so he never told her. And after Morgan Aberdovey himself died, there was naught to keep her ladyship's neighbor from frisking.

Fortunately, Morgan had broken his pledge — once, some years before, in Nantle, while enjoying a sup of rum one evening in the company of his old shipmate, Jack Barnaby. It happens that the captain has a prodigious memory, and the story Morgan had told him, the significance of which had been impressed upon him at the time, was something he remembered well. Owing to the strength of the rum, however, Morgan himself had no recollection of their conversation together. Neither his wife nor his son ever knew aught of the business, and after Morgan Aberdovey died the Laird seized his opportunity. And so had commenced her ladyship's years of legal wrangling with him in Petty Sessions.

As we hear reported, amongst some other correspondence from Lady Martindale, in the late spring of the year succeeding Richard's visit a mired boot was unearthed in a lonely stretch of country in MacWallop land. Dogs in the area set up a barking one could hear a mile off, attracting the interest of the gillies, and ultimately of Constable Pettiplace. It was more than a boot, actually, that was uncovered there — a boot, and a portion of a man's leg, with scraps of clothing still adhered, eroding out of a snow-bank. The leg had been severely crushed and mangled, as though by the action of mighty jaws. An investigation was carried out by the constable, and formalized by a coroner's inquest held at the Goose and Gander. The boot and clothing were judged indistinguishable from those known to have been favored by a stable-boy who had vanished from Haigh Hall, and who had called himself Diggory Incognito — otherwise Amos Teech.

In brief, the loathly dog had gotten his just deserts. The villain man and his bullying swagger were no more.

And what of the mysterious boot that Toddy had unearthed outside the curtain-wall, the one with the foot in it? To whom had it belonged?

Well, it was Henriette's, of course. Her moldering bones comprised the foot, and the boot had belonged to her husband, Mr. Smith. Its identification was the cause for Owen's having been delayed in the farm office, the night Teech had seized the skimmer with Mrs. Aberdovey aboard. Owen had tarried to make a thorough examination of the boot, so that he might question Henriette about it. For a suspicion had grown upon his mind that it was hers.

She had confided to him a deal more of her earthly history than he had hitherto acknowledged, amongst it the gruesome manner by which she had met her end. As she recollected it, a wintry sun had been struggling to assert itself, as she drove her husband's wagon along the causeway. She had been summoned to Haigh Hall that morning to claim his body. As she was bumping and jolting along, however, she and her horse were being stalked by a couple of marsh devils on the prowl. She had been within sight of the Hall when they had leaped upon her from cover, and torn her to ribbons. So had death come to her, in one of its most awful shapes. Those pieces of her that survived had been buried under the new snow that had fallen, a short distance from the causeway, where the cats had removed her while feeding. Gradually, over the years, the processes of nature had completed her burial, until such time, centuries on, when circumstances had brought her remains again to light.

"My poor leetle foot," Henriette murmured, after Owen had shown her the evidence on a secret visit to the farm office. She wrung her head sadly. It had been a pair of her husband's boots she had donned that day, because the weather had been bad and the journey promised to be a messy one, and the fancy little wife had had naught but pretty boots of her own to spare.

What disposition was made of the body of Mr. Smith, as we know, has not been recorded.

And what of those other remains, which Morgan Aberdovey had found years earlier and shown to Sir Pedr? Had they, too, been Henriette's? Or had they been those of Smith himself? The answer is unclear. In either case it would seem they had been sufficient to draw the creeping shadow forth, opportunely, to strike at the last male Martindale of the line. Then Morgan Aberdovey, thinking the remains bewitched, had cast them into the stream.

As we also have heard, searchers have yet to find the place where Toddy uncovered Henriette's foot. Likely it is for the best; there is no need to be disturbing the grave-sod over which none had mourned.

"'Pon my word," Edgar remarked to Richard, the day my brother left for Newmarsh, "I wonder how our Mr. Pinchbeck has explained her to his housekeeper? There could well have been a row in his timber-yard. You know how housekeepers are."

"How are they?" Richard asked.

"My gum, sir! Like as not it'll be all over town by now. For you know what my aunt says — foolish folk always will be talking."

THE END

ABOUT THE AUTHOR

Jeffrey E. Barlough was born in 1953, and holds a Doctor of Veterinary Medicine degree from the University of California, Davis, and a Ph.D. from Cornell. He has published some seventy research and review articles in scientific journals, and has edited several small-press publications of minor and archaic English works. His "Western Lights" series of fantasy-mysteries, begun in 2000 with the renowned *Dark Sleeper*, has been widely praised for its imaginative setting, eccentric characters, droll humor, and unconventional storylines. *The Cobbler of Ridingham* is his fifth book for Gresham & Doyle.

To learn more about Jeffrey E. Barlough and
the Western Lights series visit

www.westernlightsbooks.com

Imagine a world in which the last Ice Age never ended.

With much of her territory locked up with ice, medieval England was forced to seek a more habitable clime for her growing population. From every port, merchant-adventurers in their tall ships set sail to scour the earth for a new home. Amongst the places they came to was the land we know as North America. There they found a vast continent untouched by man — a wild, mysterious realm teeming with saber-cats and their kin, mastodons ("thunder-beasts"), short-faced bears, ground sloths ("megatheres" and "mylodons"), glyptodonts, flat-head boars, megalops, and other Pleistocene giants. Huge, vulture-like birds ("teratorns") roamed the skies, and predatory, toothed whales ("zeugs") the seas.

The shores of the continent were the most amenable to settlement, and there new cities were raised. On the long western coast, cities like Crow's-end and Saxbridge, Foghampton and Fishmouth, Goforth and Nantle quickly gained prominence, and there two great universities were founded, one at Salthead in the north and another at Penhaligon in the south.

Imagine a world where shaggy red mastodons in silver harness serve as proud beasts of transport, and where their southern cousins, the steel-gray shovel-tuskers, are employed in the building of roads for long-distance coach travel. Imagine a world where guns and gunpowder never were invented, where bow and blade alone are the measure of man's ferocity.

Then, in the year 1839, everything changed. It was the year of the "sundering", a cataclysmic event which some attributed to a comet or meteor strike, or a volcanic eruption of unprecedented violence — or was it perhaps something else? Irrespective of the cause, most life on earth was obliterated, and the world plunged into an even deeper Ice Age. In the words of Mr. Kibble in *Dark Sleeper* — "The sky was filled with clouds of smoke and grew very dark, and remained that way for months and months. Then the great ice sheets came down from the north and froze up the world."

By an accident of geography the cities in the west of the continent were spared, only to find themselves deprived of all contact with the outside — if, indeed, the outside still existed. For no one who had set out for England had returned, and no one had come from there ever since.

It has been some century and a half now since the sundering, and up and down the long coast life goes on. Victorian society, little changed since 1839, abides in her sundered realm with its array of fearsome monsters, marooned and alone, and a prey to powers even mightier than those of the wilderness that surrounds her — the powers of magic and the supernatural.

But why the "Western Lights" series? Author Barlough explains —

"The series title is derived from the sundering. For since that dread event the sole place on earth where lights still shine at night is in the west."

Dark Sleeper
(2000)

"Are you pleased with your station in life, man?"

So asks the dancing sailor, before unscrewing his own head and handing it over to a very startled Mr. John Rime, the cat's-meat man, one foggy night.

Mocking laughter pierces the dark sky. An enormous brindled mastiff is seen in the streets, walking upright like a human being. A little lame boy with red hair and a green face haunts the corridors of the Blue Pelican public house — eighty years after he died there. A sunken ship rises from the ocean bottom and comes sailing into the harbor. A manlike creature with great leathery wings is seen clinging to the spire of St. Skiffin's Church.

Such are a few of the mysterious apparitions afflicting the ancient city of Salthead. What do they mean? Who is responsible for them? And what of the marvelous glowing metal that looks like gold but isn't, and the exploded statue in a remote chapel crypt?

In a frigid world shattered by a cometary collision, where saber-cats prowl the mountain meadows and the old mastodon trains are fast disappearing from the land, something wicked has been released. Join Professor Tiggs and Dr. Dampe as they search for answers and uncover a 2,000-year-old menace threatening all that remains of earth.

The House in the High Wood
(2001)

It looked to have been once a very picturesque little market town, but had fallen into decay. Signs of neglect and disuse were everywhere evident, in the general disrepair of the houses, in the tattered casement-windows and tottering chimneys, the disarticulated doors, the extensive overgrowth in the churchyard and gardens and village green. Over everything lay a ghostly pall of silence.

"Driver," I called out, "what is this place? This hamlet below us?"

"Shilston Upcot," replied the coachman, then added, slowly and enigmatically — "or more rightly *was.*"

"Who lives there?"

"None what has a decent brain, sir," answered the guard. "Though there might be some — some folk as yet at the great hall, up there in the wood. But none takes to the village now, sir, unlessen they be off the latch. Crackers I mean, sir. Daft!"

What frightful secret lies hidden in the dismal ruined village high in the mountains of Talbotshire? Where have the inhabitants gone, and why have they gone there? Who — or what — lives now in the old mansion-house atop Skylingden point?

"There's deviltry here," said the guard. "The village, the mansion-house, the woods, the black waters — mischief — devil's work — "

"Aye," nodded the coachman. "The kind as don't bear thinking of!"

Discover for yourself the startling answer to the mystery of Shilston Upcot, in this second volume of the Western Lights series.

Strange Cargo
(2004)

She opened the case and from one of its compartments removed a lady's hand-mirror. The mirror itself was not of glass but of polished bronze, which reflected but poorly.

She turned the mirror over in her hands, examining every aspect of it with a mixture of fascination and dread. But nothing untoward happened, and so she returned the mirror to the dressing-case. She was about to close the lid when she heard it.

It was a noise like a hissing whisper, and it came from the mirror. A slithery, slippery thing it was, that whisper, dark and sinuous, like an evil vapor rising from a caldron.

"Djhana," it said.

A cold breath of fear raced up her spine, chilling her to the marrow.

"Djhana of Kaftor," said the mirror.

"I do not hear you," she answered, "no, no, I do not hear you — "

"Djhana of Kaftor," said the mirror again.

"No, no," she said, her head turning slowly from side to side and her eyes shut tight. "No, no, no!"

"Our mighty lord the earth-shaker commands you. Return — *or beware the Triametes!*"

Bertram of Butter Cross
(2007)

Something stirred back of the nearest tree. There was a rush of movement, and a face leaped into the gap between the branches. It was an ugly face, as faces go. It was a face with two angry, staring eyes in it, and a pair of lips drawn back in a hideous scowl, teeth bared and nostrils blown wide, the whole of it pasted onto a human head and framed by a tumbling mass of orange hair.

But there all resemblance to humanity ended, for the head was perched atop a grotesquely long, sinewy, and altogether unhuman kind of neck, round which the orange hair streamed down like a waterfall.

Jemma saw the head snake its way towards her through the branches, saw it push its face right up to hers; and stopping there, its eyes mere inches from her own, it glared at her and growled . . .

Return now to the Ice Age world of the sundering, and join Jemma Hathaway and her brother Richard, Ada Henslowe, Sir Hector MacHector and their friends in deepest Fenshire, as they struggle to solve the unsolvable — the mystery of Marley Wood.

Anchorwick
(2008)

It is hard to say just what sort of noise it was.

I swung the lamp round and scanned the darkened chamber. I saw no one, of course, and nothing. It was then that my ears caught hold of it — a faint, energetic whispering, as of a voice struggling to make itself heard.

My scalp tingled with a sudden sense of impending danger.

"Who is it?" I demanded. "Who is there?"

All in an instant I spied a glimmer of movement, and was struck cold to see a strange, ghostly shape swimming in the air before me. The words it was whispering were but two, louder now, and repeated several times over in a desperate, pleading tone —

"Help me!"

In *Anchorwick* author Jeffrey E. Barlough returns to the scene of the first book in the Western Lights series, the renowned *Dark Sleeper*. The time, however, is some thirty years before the events recounted there, with certain of the characters from the earlier novel returning in the new work as their younger selves. But they are not the chief focus of the story — that belongs to the narrator, Eugene Stanley, who has come up to Salthead and its fabled university to help his uncle, Professor Christopher Greenshields, in the drafting of the professor's latest scholarly tome. Little hint has young Stanley of the mystery and danger that await him there . . .

A Tangle in Slops
(2011)

Round a corner of the house it came — a huge, ungainly form, shambling along on its four oddly-curved, paddle-like limbs. A deep-voiced growl could be heard rumbling in its throat.

The moon's silvered beams were shining full upon it, when of a suddenty the monster reared up onto its haunches and stood awhile observing us.

"We must have our revenge!" sang out Stroppy, who of the lads appeared the more inebriated. "For the Foud's sake, have a taste o' this, ye brute!"

In a fit of courage he drew an object from his pocket and hurled it at the beast — a large, well-aimed object, which sailed like a shot from his hand and struck the looming giant square in the face . . .

When *Bertram of Butter Cross's* Ada Henslowe found herself called to distant Plumley down in Slopshire to aid her little orphan cousin Mary Trefoil, she had no inkling of the strange adventures that were to follow. Why had the creature that had slain Mary's father returned? Was its goal, as many feared, to eliminate, one by one, the Trefoils of Orkney Farm? And what of the enigmatic green woman — the apparition in the mossy-green mantle — who had been frightening the citizens of Plumley? Was she indeed the ghost of Tronda Quickensbog, wise woman and soothsayer, on a mission to avenge the desecration of her relics at the farm? These and other mysteries will need to be resolved if Ada and her friends are to thwart a looming danger from centuries past.

Also included in this volume is *Ebenezer Crackernut* — the delightful tale of a very bad squirrel, and the author's first Western Lights story for children.

What I Found at Hoole
(2012)

To all appearances the room was unoccupied.

Moments later a feeling as of doom impending swept over me with a chill. Whose house was this, I wondered? And how had I come to be here?

Hanging from a peg was a tiny silver call, such as might be used to summon a domestic. It was a curious little thing, of a peculiar and antique workmanship. I saw at once that it was valuable. Much intrigued I was about to apply it to my lips, to test the sound, when I became aware of a stealthy movement in the room.

A figure — that of an elderly man with grave features, craggy and deep-seamed — sprang up from behind one of the wing-chairs on the hearthrug. He eyed me uneasily. "What do you mean to do?" he asked.

As I raised the call to my lips he flung a warning hand at me.

"No, sir, no! Do not sound the call!" he cried, in a tone of stifled horror. "Take heed, sir — *lest the devils be unchained!*"